Birds in the Black Water

A Dark, Paranormal Drama

KODIE VAN DUSEN

Published 2022

Hardcover ISBN: 978-1-7782271-2-7

Paperback ISBN: 978-1-7782271-0-3

E-ISBN: 978-1-7782271-1-0

For information, visit www.kodievandusen.com

To my husband, Mike, for being crazy enough to marry a writer.
And to Jordan, who called me 'strange and well-versed' not knowing
it would change my life. I hope there's a library where you are.

Foreword by the Author

Birds in the Black Water was simultaneously the easiest and the hardest story I've written. It was the hardest because it took losing someone I love to write it, and because at some point I had to find a meaningful end to this chapter of my life both on the page and off. However, it was also the easiest because it was necessary; the story counseled and consoled me during a difficult time in my life. I returned to it every day without hesitation because it was a lifeline, and if it could be that for me, I hoped it could be that for others.

In 2017, a dear friend of mine took his life. This story is a sort of love letter to him. To the person who believed in me and my crazy dreams the most. To the one who believed there was magic in my words. To the one person who can never read it. I've never been good at saying goodbye but putting this book into the world has felt like a good start.

My hope is that you will be able to take something from these pages. A lesson. Something to apply to your own life. Or even just a meaningful distraction from the craziness enveloping our world.

Music was another lifeline through this, like I know it is for so many other people, so for that reason, I've included a playlist of songs at the back of the book relevant to my protagonist, Neviah, and to me throughout this journey. There's also a link to my website where you can access a full interview about the events inspiring this story.

As a reminder, this book deals with subject matter that may be triggering to some readers. If you feel you are having a mental health emergency, please don't hesitate to call 9-1-1 or visit your nearest emergency department for support.

And if you enjoy this story, I humbly ask that you consider leaving a review to help it reach more people who might need it.

All my gratitude,

Birds in the Black Water

Prelude

She stared at me from the other side of the mirror, its surface cloudy with age. She lifted her hand as I lifted mine; touched a finger to her lips in tandem with me. And when I touched the surface of the glass, her hand reached out to clasp mine, holding it so bone-crushingly tight I thought it would shatter.

Her face transfigured into a wraith, a phantasm, a dark spirit so black she absorbed and crushed what little light trickled in through the bedroom window. Her fingers were suddenly long, black tendrils that wrapped around my wrist like a hot, metal bracelet, burning the skin and yet cold to touch as I tried to squirm away.

When I jolted upright in bed, the skin around my wrist felt raw like it had been chafed by rope where the creature touched me. A welt formed on the skin, still clammy and pale from the night terror. My pillow was wet, long hair matted and soaked with sweat.

"The dreams are back," I spoke to the man keeping careful watch of me from the corner. The vibrant yellow and red plaid of his button up was muted and grey in the dark as he rocked alone in the chair. My vision swam with fatigue, pulse quickening when a hand touched my back, jarring me fully awake.

"It's okay. I'm here," a man's voice, slurring with sleep, uttered from beside me in bed. In the time it took to register my husband's voice, the figure in the corner fled the room, replaced by shadows. I stared wide-eyed and trembling into the darkness.

The darkness stared back.

PART I
Chapter One

"You're sure you want to do this?" I asked my client.

Shadows played against Julie's face like claws reaching to suck her into the darkness as I turned—it was a hazard of my vocation, seeing monsters in the shadows where there were none. I counted to ten before my heart settled, though it never fully returned to normal, always marred by the stutters and trips of anxiety that struck me as often as blinking or breathing.

My focus centered on what I could see and hear and feel with certainty: birch trees groaning in the cold, critters scrambling through underbrush, a creek, twisting and bending through the nature preserve. Water encroached on its bank, widening into a minuscule river, heartier from thawing ice and snow; it weaved through eight thousand acres of forested trails backing onto the ranch Ezra and I had hammered and nailed and painted into submission.

"Really, Julie...we don't need to do this."

The river continued its path well beyond the reserve, cleaving through neighboring farms and fields. It snaked into the town where I was raised, then onto the nearest city nearly 150 miles away where problems proliferated like fruit flies on rotting apples

Our property, as the name on the sign outside the gate suggested, was a sanctuary. A place set apart for retreat, reflection, quiet. A place where parents and their children could reconnect and heal.

Or, at least, it was. Before the 'incident'.

"I want to keep going," Julie finally insisted.

I shook out my hair, a waterfall of fiery curls that fell squarely to the middle of my back, then drummed my fingers against my thigh. Her mouth hung open like she had more to say; knee bobbing up and down as her heel tapped down the wet foliage below her foot. She tried to steady her breaths, but the air quaked and wavered as it exited her lungs, puffing around her like a steam engine.

The thermos of passion tea offered to her hardly helped; it was sugary, not a relaxant, yet usually did the trick just fine. It steamed when confronted with the spring chill permeating the woods.

"What is it you're worried about?" I asked. Her hesitation felt like tiny, weighted fishhooks attached to each corner of my mouth, tugging at my smile.

"These shadows—"

"*Koels*," I corrected her. Natural shadows from the glade danced on the surface of the water as I wondered how I might explain the unexplainable to her. My mother had an arsenal of dark and deeply unoriginal explanations for the things I saw—demons, Satan, minions, Beelzebub.

My brother much preferred *interdimensional beings*, an attribution I might have gravitated toward myself, if it weren't for the misleading thoughts it conjured of UFOs and tiny green Martians and experiments regarding human anatomy. I breathed in the scent of pine and moss, counting to ten as I watched a squirrel wiggle from one tree branch to the next.

"Cowls? Like the scarf?" Julie asked, distracted from our session. She touched the scarf around her neck, still bundled against the lingering cold. The woods were still mostly dormant, as though the forest knew that the last snow of the season had yet to fall.

"It's *pronounced* cowl but spelled k-o-e-l. Like the bird. My brother named them." I picked at the skin around my thumbnail. My hands folded together when I noticed the nervous habit. A puddle of melting snow soaked my jeans as I sat beside her on the fallen tree trunk where she perched.

Julie wrinkled her face. "I've never heard of them."

"They're a type of cuckoo bird from Australia or Asia or something. Almost like a raven—jet black and about the same size, but with these beady red eyes and a really annoying call. My brother was really into biology."

I could almost hear the excitement in Jaak's voice the first time he explained to me: *They're parasites. They lay their eggs in other birds' nests, just like these shadows seem to find a host and cling to them. And they're known for being heard before they're seen.*

"Just a pain in the ass bird, really," I added quickly, not wanting to rattle her with the word 'parasite.'

"That makes sense. I just, I don't know..." Her breathing hastened as she shook her head. "I don't know," she repeated frantically. Julie removed her ballcap and ran her fingers through her hair, then stared at the hat. "I feel like you've—this wasn't what I was expecting. You keep talking about this *Other Side* like it's the realest thing in the world, but I can't picture it."

"I told you when you first started seeing me that this is about challenging beliefs. About yourself, others, the world," I said, wishing I could direct her back to the disclosure form she'd signed outlining the details of what was to come. It was a standard agreement, save for a single paragraph identifying me as a spiritual coach in equal measure to a licensed family therapist.

The oversimplified caveat was Ezra's idea, a legal safeguard against anyone questioning my eclectic blend of practices. It rarely mattered how concrete the things they experienced in their sessions were; the mind rejected the unthinkable like a bad transplant.

The longer a client stayed in treatment, the deeper I could go with them, the more I could reveal. Some stayed for a weekend while others eventually stayed as staff, but they all had to come to terms with things in their own way, some able to face the truth more readily than others.

"I just didn't expect it to be so *literal*." Her eyes were wide.

"Julie..." I sighed. "We don't—"

She interrupted me, "I don't want to end like this. Riley's been...How did you put it? Overstimulated?" She stared into the thermos as though contemplating the liquid was an act of divination on behalf of her son. "I don't know if it's because he's picking up on my stress or if he's due for a med change, but he gets unpredictable when he's like this. Yesterday I caught him hitting himself—"

"The *Other Side*'s not dangerous if you have someone who knows what they're doing—which, I do. But if you aren't ready, I can't guarantee where we're going to end up."

"End up?" She sucked in a breath.

"The beliefs, the thinking patterns we're going to challenge, they start somewhere. A traumatic moment. Or a significant one, at least. And if there's even a hint of trauma, there'll be Koels. That's why I keep bringing them up. It's not because they're something you need to be afraid of, but because when we start working through these memories—"

Her face went pale. "They still scare the hell out of me."

"When I was eleven, I think? I heard my brother laughing, like, full-bellied, *squealing* laughter." Thinking of him sent a throb of pain through my temple. "I went in and one of the Koels was sitting in front of him, smiling that awful smile—but it wasn't scary to him," I emphasized when her color drained further. "He was just a little boy, and he didn't even cry when he saw one for the first time. Hell, he didn't even realize it was unusual; he handed it a toy." A truck-trailer set used to haul around rubber farm animals.

"Brave kid." She gulped, and I saw the unspoken question of whether they could hurt us dancing in her eyes like the frantic twists of flame on a candle wick. I sighed, trying my best not to let my mind wander to thoughts of what was for dinner or Ezra waiting on the couch.

My energy was gone long before that final appointment.

I smiled anyway.

"Why don't we try something you've brought up during our meetings to get you used to the transition?" I postured myself in front of her, mimicking the openness of her legs as she sat, smiling warmly as I tucked my hair behind my ear on the opposite side that she did. Mirroring. The staple tactic of a good therapist. The client needed to see themselves reflected in their counsel.

It fostered trust.

"Think of that time you took Riley to the lake," I encouraged. Her skin was clammy with nerves as I pressed her hand into mine. "Just keep focusing on that memory. The details, the nuances..."

As the details came to life in her mind, the sound of beach water lapping at the shore filled the forest around us, though it was subtle against the noise from the creek. Seagulls cawed in the distance; mist pelted our faces, though our skin remained dry. The sensations disappeared abruptly when I took my hand off hers, her knee resuming the motions of a jackhammer.

"Why did you stop?" Julie asked, though she stood to leave as though her body was spring-loaded, waiting for release. "I want to be ready. It just gives me the creeps. It's like, I don't want to believe those things could be there, but part of me also feels like, why not? *There are more things in heaven and earth, Horatio...*" She laughed nervously, quoting Shakespeare's, *Hamlet.*

Julie disappeared behind a row of evergreens sheltering the small glade where I routinely conducted sessions knowing Ezra could find us if something went wrong. She untethered one of the horses grazing on the trail, then ducked below the foliage trying to spot me, eyes scanning the trees around us as though suspecting a Koel might materialize at any moment.

"You coming?" I remember her asking only because I remember how badly I wanted to be left alone, to let go of my smile and allow my features to become neither soft nor inviting the way they always had to be in the presence of a client. I urged her along, holding my breath.

When the sound of hooves finally receded, I was not alone.

I inhaled deeply and finally allowed my gaze to wander to the figures hiding in the shadows between the birches and evergreens, acknowledging them only in her absence. The Koels blended into the shadows; blacker than any dark place I had ever been misfortunate enough to find myself. Tall and slender, their sinewy figures were almost human. Tendrils at the end of each hand skimmed the trail, tips twitching as though communicating in Morse to an unknown receiver.

Permeating the cacophony of woodland noises was the familiar sound their forms made as they twisted and bent, as annoying and persistent as the call of their namesake bird, a clicking sound like a turn signal or the hands of a clock:

Tick, tock.

Chapter Two

"Julie caved," I called from the kitchen, shutting the door against the night. My hair hung loose and tangled from the ride home as I hung my coat to dry. My fingers tapped the arm of the couch as I joined Ezra in the living room, my wedding band glinting in the firelight as I tried my best to ignore whatever was unfolding on the six o'clock news leering at us from the wall.

"You still have work to do?" I asked, pushing aside the papers littering the couch until I could sit.

He slid his binder aside but didn't close it as he answered, "Was going over some notes for the staff meeting next week. Dinner's probably warm-ish if you're hungry?"

"Anything I can help with? For work, I mean?" I addressed him through the opening in the wall connected to our living room as the numbers on the microwave counted down, spinning the casserole he'd made until the cheese bubbled. I half-expected a reprisal for scheduling meetings so late again, and I was pleased when I didn't get one. He sighed and rubbed his face.

"Budget cuts. Need to figure out how to justify expenses for my department." Ezra leaned back, lacing his fingers behind his head, stretching his chest. The microwave hadn't signaled yet, but I plucked open the door and pulled out the half-warmed bowl, half-listening as I considered what show to binge for the remainder of the evening. I sank next to him on the couch.

"Can we put on something different?"

Faint traces of teakwood and mahogany echoed from his skin, remnants of his body wash. I wondered if I could sense the tiniest traces of leather still lingering from his jacket. Otherwise, the scent was entirely natural, one hundred percent Ezra, and more comforting to me than Valium as he wrapped an arm around my shoulders.

The tension that momentarily fled in his presence returned as an explosion erupted from the television a few decibels louder than whatever the news anchors were discussing when I arrived. My heart hammered in my chest, and I put the bowl down to hide my shaking hands, counting to ten once, twice, three times before—"Can we turn it off? Please?"

My eyes fixed to the screen only long enough to determine the sound came from a video, probably replayed for the thousandth time that day, of a transport accident somewhere too far away to concern me. My appetite vanished as the hood of the truck exploded into a swath of flames, but I continued eating with the expectation that carbs could fix anything.

And for what carbs couldn't fix, there was whiskey. Even thinking of it conjured the taste of it, the bite of it on my tongue, the warmth of it sliding down my throat and smoothing my nerves. Ezra frowned as I stood to retrieve the bottle, turning down the volume until the TV was silent, leaving only captions of what was being said running at the bottom of the screen.

"Better? It's almost done and then we can—" The sentiment was cut short by the involuntary sigh that escaped me. He maximized a second screen in the corner, replacing the news anchors with baseball. Anticipating my apology, he added, "It's fine."

"I didn't mean to interrupt." I frowned. "I just wanna watch—"

"Can I at least finish the game?"

I sighed, thumbing restlessly through the papers on the table, looking for a page to start my session notes—something I was not eager to admit I should have done before turning in for the evening. One of the pages was a calendar, filled with color-coded appointments telling Ezra where he needed to be and when, juggling his role as department head for his school district and part-time high school instructor. I frowned at a little blue note scribbled onto Tuesday.

"Did they move your meeting?"

"Shit." He drew in a deep breath, exhaled audibly. "I was planning to talk with you about it when you got home." He turned off the television entirely. "Yeah, they did."

"Why?" I slouched away from him when he tried to reach for me, crossing my arms against my chest and doing something horribly akin to pouting. "You said there wouldn't be any until after—" Ezra interrupted with slipshod excuses about the finance minister's schedule.

"What about your schedule?"

"I know, but unless you want me to lose my job..."

He shook his head when I straightened at the possibility, mind darting to our account books and the income hemorrhaged into maintaining the farm. One thought tumbled into the next: what a burden I am, that he wouldn't have taken a job so far away if I wasn't offering pro-bono work to people every time my heart bled, his life would be easier if we hadn't opened the farm, if he hadn't married *me*, how many clients have I been behind on collecting payments for—

"I won't." Ezra squeezed my knee, and it took me a few beats to remember what he was talking about. Inky darkness shifted in the driveway. "I just need to show up to the meeting and get the budget proposal done. Any ideas? They want to cut the speaker panel next year for my religion curriculum, but that's the best part."

"I'm not the right person to talk to. You know where I stand on teaching that stuff in school." I gave him a fading smile and scooted back to fix my hair, skin crawling at the unexpected change to our week. My pulse hammered in my wrist as I finger-combed my curls, trying to twist them into a braid, overwhelmed with the sudden urge to cut my hair down to its roots. A stream of muffled curse words slid under my breath as I resigned myself to an easy ponytail. It bulged in the band. I fought the urge to reconfigure it.

The skin prickled at the nape of my neck.

"Why don't you call my mom?" I breathed, rolling my eyes. "I'm sure her and the ladies from her church would have lots of suggestions. They'd probably be outside the school with picket signs if they found out those classes were on the chopping block—well, maybe not the *World Religion* courses. She'd be happy to see those ones go."

The room felt cold, suddenly, even with the fire blazing in the wall below the television. It blew out warm air that snaked across the floor directly in front of the hearth, then drifted up only to disappear before reaching us. I smiled, though his body sagged.

"You know it's not all bad, right?"

"I know," I sighed, considering my words carefully as I interlaced my fingers with his, weary of the disappointment in his voice. "It just feels like it's been a while since we've spent time together outside of work stuff though, you know?" Half-truths made for easy subject changes. "We're always doing it, or talking about it, or thinking about it. I don't know...been feeling for a little while now like maybe we're due for some changes, I just..."

Couldn't fathom it, if I was being honest with myself.

On most days, I wasn't.

"Well, there's talk of transferring my curriculum to the online school, since there's not a lot of demand for it these days. I've been fighting it, but..." He reached out and twirled a piece of my hair between his fingers, letting it drop back down against the front of my shoulder. I tried not to frown or look away as the elastic slipped from my ponytail. "It might be worth considering. It'll be a pay cut and less time in person with the students, but the position is entirely remote, and there'd be a little more freedom in what I teach, which is nice."

Ezra squeezed my knee and shook his head.

"If I have to go back early, let's do something fun this weekend. What do you say to skipping town after your meetings tomorrow? Unless—" He raised a brow with an exaggerated show of disapproval. "—you packed your weekend with meetings again?"

"It's just one in the morning."

Ezra shrugged when I asked him where we would go, but despite his uncertainty, a smile spread contagiously from his face to mine as we thought about it. I suggested dinner, my mind already fixated on pleasant thoughts of city food and fresh dumplings.

"Sure, dinner. What else?" He cupped a hand around the back of my neck, pulling me close and pressing his smile against mine. Ezra's fingers kneaded the tension at the back of my neck, replacing it with a new kind of tension. He nuzzled my neck, lips grazing only long enough to distract me; I laughed, limbs flailing in half-hearted protest as he scooped me from the couch.

"Ezra! Put me down!" A fist thumped weakly against his chest.

"I miss you."

"I miss you, too! But—what are you doing?" I squealed, laughing as he carried me down the hallway; my legs kicked weakly, playfully. The old wood floor creaked with every step toward the bedroom. "Ezra! Put me down! I have legs, you know?"

He grinned. "Mmm-hmm. I know you do."

"Are there any bands playing in town tomorrow?" I replied as he tossed me onto the bed, his body sinking down on top of me until his lips could nibble the side of my neck. He took a deep breath and dropped his forehead against mine, taking a few seconds to realize I'd spoken.

A groan rumbled in his throat, followed by laughter. "Dunno, but we can check. Seriously, that's what you're thinking of right now?"

"Dinner and music, then?" I beamed.

"It's a date."

Chapter Three

The room was glowing when I opened my eyes the next morning, and I couldn't be certain if it was the sign of a nice day—the sun streaming in brilliantly through the curtains—or if I was the source of the radiating light. I could feel it glowing from every pore as I slid out of bed next to Ezra, wrapping myself in a blanket to thwart the drafty windows and doors. Snowflakes fell lazily outside the window, though the ground was warm enough to ensure they wouldn't stick. I inhaled deeply, relishing the promise of spring.

My euphoria deepened at the scent of coffee beans grinding, tethering me to the pot like a spirit. My sigh came out as more of a purr, rumbled in my throat as my shoulders melted back, unable to carry tension if they wanted to, which they didn't. I could hear Ezra stirring in the bedroom, so I started the kettle for his tea and leaned back against the counter to wait.

When Ezra came out a few minutes later, he found me with my phone in hand, bouncing lightly like an excited schoolgirl. I held the phone out to him. "You'll never guess who's playing in town tonight. Guess," I urged, though he was already reading the marquis.

"Do you know if they're any good?"

"No clue." I shrugged, tinkering in the cupboard for mugs when the coffee pot slurped to a halt. "But they only do *Dark Water* covers,"

I said, referencing the popular though antiquated band Ezra and I were enamored with even before meeting each other; it was an oft-recited conversation piece for us as a couple that we had, at one point, attended the same concert alone because no one was as smitten with the group as we were. Ezra and I might have stood back-to-back, completely unaware, and the notion was so romantic that I was inclined to believe it.

The sentiment was cut short when I thought I glimpsed a shadow passing just outside the kitchen window, but when I looked out, warm mug cupped between my palms, there was nothing but light. I stared down into my mug, seeing myself reflected there, though my face rippled as the dark liquid trembled between my shaking hands. I blew on the liquid as Ezra slid my phone back.

"Dinner at that Japanese place on the corner of Thames then?" He smirked at the contented grunt that escaped me as I took my first sip of coffee for the day; it was black, bitter, and a little too hot, as my first, impatiently slurped cup often was.

"Literally, perfect. I might even dress up."

"Black dress?"

"Oh yeah." I set the mug down and draped my arms over Ezra's shoulders as he grabbed me by the waist, pulling me in for a quick kiss. "Or maybe that white one I like. We'll see."

"What about that grey one?"

"Don't like the way it fits," I dismissed, turning my attention to collecting a small mountain of breakfast ingredients in my arms. Frozen bananas, yogurt, chocolate, and peanut butter teetered precariously in my arms as I watched Ezra disappear down the hall.

Instead of putting everything down on the counter, I pushed the ingredients to one side of my body, hugging them against my torso with one arm while fumbling through the cupboard for protein powder with the other. I moved slowly toward the blender, the supplement canister stacked precariously on top of everything else, careful not to move too fast lest everything—

Knock. Knock. Knock.

I jolted, sending the groceries splaying forward, heaving out a quick sigh of relief when most of it landed on the counter anyway, save for the peanut butter jar. It rolled toward the edge of the counter, daring me to reach for it; when I obliged, I succeeded only in knocking my coffee mug from the counter with a clumsy punch of the arm. It shattered against the hardwood floor, steaming black liquid seeping between every crack and crevice in the boards.

Knock, knock.

"I'm coming!" I shouted, hopping over the puddle toward the kitchen door. I froze and turned back, picking up the peanut butter and putting it back where it belonged.

With a heavy sigh, I unlatched the deadbolt, twisted the rusty, bronze lock, and turned the handle, ready to tell whichever client it was that it—whatever 'it' was—would have to wait until I returned on Monday. Several acres of unmaintained woods stood between my house, the offices, and the guest cabins, to discourage exactly this sort of visit.

The door swung open, my lips dangling open with a polite, "What can I do for you?" loaded in the chamber, along with an empathetic, "That sounds like it's very difficult for you. I'd be happy to talk with you about it in more detail on Monday" ready to fire just as quickly.

And then I froze.

Standing outside of my door, shivering violently, dark hair wet with sweat and melted snow, cheeks flushed and rosy on either side of his quivering lips, was a little boy I had never seen before; a little boy that should not have been there—couldn't possibly be there, I thought, staring at the woods behind him, without an adult lingering somewhere nearby.

"Is your mom or dad around?" I asked.

The boy began to cry.

Chapter Four

"You're sure you don't want me to stay?" Ezra shrugged on his coat as he spoke, using his toes to prop up a boot that laid toppled. The furry liner was dark with melted snow as he jammed his foot in, and I winced vicariously. Gloves and a toque went on next with quick movements that indicated his question was merely a formality; my response would change nothing.

"Gabriel—you said *Gabriel*, right?" It was the only useful information the boy had provided after nearly twenty minutes of questioning. I smiled when he nodded, though the expression felt conjured and ingenuine as Ezra slipped outside to begin his search, our weekend plans slipping away with him. My toes tapped against the leg of the table, halting the moment I noticed the tick. "While Ezra's out looking for your parents, I need you to tell me anything else that you can remember. I know—"

I held up a hand when he protested, no doubt to tell me for the dozenth time that he didn't know where his parents were. "It's okay. I just want to know more about you. Is that okay?" He nodded after appraising me for several, spanning moments. "How old are you, Gabriel?"

He held up six thin fingers, chewing his lip.

"Six?" I responded to his quick succession of nods with another smile. "Six. Good. That's a good age to be. Do you know when your birthday is? What month it is, maybe?"

He thought about it, tongue pursed between his lips, then nodded. "Halloween. We, um, we had a birthday party, and my mom and Gary and Uncle Andy came, and some of the kids next door came over and we had cake," he said, hesitantly at first, then picking up speed as though even thinking of the sugary treat had energized him.

"It was chocolate with orange sprinkles and mom got ice cream and candles and there was pizza for supper."

When he lapsed back into silence, I asked, "What about home? Tell me about where you live. Is it a house, an apartment...?"

"We live by a park. In a 'partment."

"Okay..."

"It has a big slide that goes in a circle like this." Gabriel whirled his finger around in the air. "And a swing set and a wall to climb up." He mimed climbing motions, then shot to his feet, spreading his arms wide as he described every park within a 200-mile radius. "And a sand pit that was this big, and sometimes I get to have ice cream after."

I nodded eagerly, hoping for more. "Very cool."

"Gary didn't like taking me to the park, so I only got to go sometimes 'cause Mom doesn't have a license." Gabriel pouted, clamoring back into his chair. I picked up my phone to do a quick search but put it down when I realized his details hardly narrowed down the search criteria; the nearest town was hardly a metropolis, but still large enough to make the search futile. The phone gave a single, curt buzz to indicate a message was waiting.

"When is she coming? She said she's gonna come pick me up soon." Gabriel glanced worriedly at the door, the heel of his boot thumping against the chair leg with renewed momentum as he added, "Is it soon yet? She said I had to be good. Am I being good?"

"Really good," I praised. "Is Gary your dad?"

"No! He's my mom's booooyfriend," he said in a high-pitched voice, face wrinkling. "K-I-S-S-I-N-G—That spells kissing." Gabriel picked at a groove in the wooden tabletop with his fingernail. "He kisses mom and it's grooosssss. I don't know my dad," he added. "My mom says he's important and that's how come he doesn't have time for us, but I think if he's so important he should *make* time for us. Then he can buy us a big house with a pool and waterslide and—"

"You don't like where you live?" I cocked my head when Gabriel responded with an indifferent shrug, though the silence that followed said everything. "What about brothers and sisters? Do you have siblings?" He shook his head. "What about Gary, does he have other kids?"

"Gary doesn't like kids," Gabriel said, legs swinging in his seat.

"Why do you say that?"

"Because it's true!"

"Okay, okay." I held my hands up, then stroked my chin as I considered where to go next. "Listen, Gabriel, my husband's out right now trying to find whoever brought you here—"

"I walked by myself! I told you!"

"You ... walked."

"Yes, Uncle Andy let me ride in his truck and then told me I was 'posed to walk the rest of the way so I got out of the car and then he went back home, and I kept going on the road until I got to the sign that said 'Sanctuary'. S-A-N-C-T-U-A-R-Y. Mom made me learn how to spell it so that I wouldn't miss it and told me I was 'posed to find Neviah 'cause she would know what to do and then I had to give her the letter—oh." He frowned, jolting to his feet. "I forgot."

"What letter?"

Gabriel went to the door where his coat was heaped on the floor. He dug in his pocket until his hand emerged holding a crumpled ball of paper. It was nearly illegible when he unfolded it, ink smudged by the melted snow seeping through the cheap, fabric liner of his jacket. He handed it to me, and I read quickly, curiously, at first, then paling when I saw the unmistakable pen strokes of Martha's signature, signed after 'Yours Truly'.

My mind was sucked back to memories of the last time I'd seen her; she was still a minor then, coming to counseling under the thumb of her parents. For the last ten years, the image that lingered longest of her was that of a young girl, jet black hair glistening under the streetlights, nestled in an emergency blanket as police lingered in her parents' driveway. And her screams, mingling with my own.

"What does it say?" Gabriel wondered.

"Hey, there's a box of old books and toys Ezra hauled out of the closet." I nodded toward a sealed tote bin in the corner of the room, waiting for Gabriel to notice it. "Why don't you look through it and see if there's anything you like while I give Ezra a call and see if he's found anything?"

Gabriel shrugged, though he moved quickly, snapping off the lid with lively, practiced motions. A small molehill of toys formed on the kitchen floor by the time Ezra picked up on the third ring. "Hello?"

"Ezra, I—"

"Hello? Wait a—" More static, the sound of clumsy hands fumbling with the phone, branches crunching below heavy steps, and then, "Sorry, service is bad out here."

"Come home. Wait a second..." I pulled away to look at my phone when an incoming call came through, silencing it when I saw the large letters warning me DO. NOT. PICK. UP. "Sorry." I pinched the bridge of my nose, focus momentarily shattered. "He had a note."

"A note? Any contact info?"

"No. Apparently an uncle dropped him off up the road."

I smoothed the piece of paper against the table, some of the words corrupted by wrinkles. I stared at it like I might an artifact in a museum, studying the cursive like it was an ancient but familiar language—though in a museum, I thought, it would have been under heavy guard, captive under a glass dome with signs warning observers, 'DO NOT TOUCH'. But I couldn't stop touching it, couldn't stop tracing the intimate and familiar curves of Martha's signature.

Tick, tock.

Chapter Five

Ezra paced slowly beside the bed, holding his phone to his ear as he checked messages, his earbuds lying dead on the dresser. He mumbled curses, poked a few digits, listened again, all while sifting through the bedside drawer for a pen and paper. He scribbled down a few notes, grumbled something discontented under his breath.

My phone vibrated on the bed next to him.

"It's your mom. Do you—"

"Don't answer."

He lifted a brow and sent it to voicemail. "I missed a work call. They want me to go up a day earlier because I missed a meeting this morning." Ezra glanced back at my phone as it pinged, eyes scanning the screen, reading. "Your mom wants to know if you're still helping with her garden tomorrow. Did you forget? Do you want—"

"No, I'll cancel. She's called like five times."

"You should go." He motioned for me to follow him to the kitchen, unphased by the invisible shadows tucked into the corners of the hallway. "I'm gonna have to start packing tomorrow now. Might hit the road tomorrow night so I can avoid traffic in the morning. It's okay," he promised when I sat at the table and dropped my head into my hands. "We can still do something tonight. Do you want—"

"No, it's fine." I looked up, sighing. "It's not the same."

"I mean, we can't go to town, but—"

"It's fine." I picked up a stuffed black and white horse Gabriel left beside the chair leg. The other toys and books were jammed back into the tote, lid no longer able to close from his haphazard Tetris-work. I opened the bin thinking I might fit the toy in again, only to find myself staring at familiar images of dragons and knights—my handiwork—gracing the cover of a manuscript bound with thin, leather strings dyed burgundy like dried blood.

"What's that?" Ezra reached for it. I stared at his hand.

"Story," I said numbly, not relinquishing it.

"Is it one of your brother's?" he asked, motioning for it with his fingers. I reached to give it to him, earning a puzzled look when I failed to let go. I scolded my fingers and forced them open, stepping away from the book, then second guessed the distance and inched closer again. The unexpected intrusion from my brother sent hot acid rising up, scalding the back of my throat.

"Did you illustrate this one?" Ezra asked, flipping through the pages. "'*The knight, Sir Ivanguard, carried with him a terrible and lonely secret,*'" he recited from page one, not realizing the pages themselves held onto a lonely and horrible secret just the same. The pages had been locked away, out of sight and out of mind, for nearly ten years, and though I'd have preferred they stayed that way, it was a small comfort to have Jaak in the room with me.

"Yeah, was one of the last ones." *The* last one, actually.

"How come I've never seen it before?" Ezra frowned, turning it over in his hands. "I always liked his stories. A little dark, but still." He shrugged and closed the book, tucking it under his arm for later. "It's a shame nothing ever came of these—some of your best work."

"Yeah, well..."

The room stayed silent until Ezra suggested we make plans for the following weekend. Thai food, another band, maybe we could go to that bookstore I liked on the corner of—all I could think about was how the night was supposed to have gone: swaying into each other as our songs played, whispering fond memories over sweating pints while jealous onlookers wondered what we'd done right, stumbling into some hotel room to put a pretty ribbon onto the night.

A Koel peered in through the screen door.

Ezra followed my gaze, seeing nothing.

"Koel?" he asked.

"Koel*s*."

"Think Gabriel will nap for much longer?" Ezra rubbed a hand along my knee and gave a quick squeeze, drawing my attention away from the window. "What did child services say when you called? Are they gonna be any help finding Martha? Any history?" Ezra kneaded his fingers into the cemented muscles of my shoulders. I groaned, relaxing as much as I could.

It wasn't much. I eyed the whiskey on the fridge.

"They, uh..." My eyes widened as he targeted a knot. "...wouldn't tell me, but it didn't sound promising." Without intending it, my hand slid down to touch the letter in my pocket. "She's an adult now, so they can't do much about her. He obviously needs to stay out of her custody right now if she'd drop him at a stranger's house—"

"You're not a stranger. Martha knows—"

"*Knew*," I corrected, inching away from him when unravelling the knots became too painful. "And I'm a stranger to him. They asked if we'd keep him here, since we're on their foster list already. Apparently, their houses in town are full, or I think they'd try to get him back there, jog his memory. But technically, Martha left a note leaving him to us, so I told them he can stay until they figure something out. I hope that's okay?"

"I mean..." He hesitated. "We'll make it work."

"I wrote down the social worker's number on the calendar there if you need to talk with her. Inaya or something." I dropped my head into my hands, then tilted it up to stare at the ceiling. "Why me? Ten years and she came back to me. It means something, doesn't it?"

"She trusts you," he said, the easy answer doing nothing to assuage me. My mind wandered to images of the three Fates huddled over an infinite expanse of threads, the strings weaving in and out, touching where one person's life connected with another's. I imagined them taking Martha's thread between their fingers with my own, submerging them in a trough of glimmering, melted gold to make them inseparable.

I pulled a bottle of bourbon from the top of the fridge, taking out a shining, crystal tumbler from the cabinet and holding up a second to present to Ezra. Ice cubes plinked into each glass, cracking as the liquor poured over them. I took a sip, waiting for it to have an effect and doing quick math to guess that Martha must have been hardly more than twenty-five. Just barely an adult, yet still far too old, in my opinion, when my only memories of her were as a teenager.

"I tried to see her when I got word she was in that group home here in town, but they wouldn't let me in because I'm not family," I sneered, taking another sip of bourbon, letting the burn work its way down my throat. "Then she ran away just before she turned eighteen, so they stopped looking for her pretty quickly."

"How could they just—"

I shrugged. "She was an adult. That meant she was old enough to be responsible for her own decisions, in the eyes of the court."

"How bad are the Koels since he got here?" Ezra asked, following my gaze as it shifted to the natural shadows in the corners of the kitchen. I took a shaky breath and reached for the bourbon again. My hand was trembling as I refilled my glass.

"Bad." I took a slow sip. "Spades of 'em."

"So, I mean, if there are Koels, that means you can probably work with him eventually, right? Start getting him ready to go under, then when it's time, you might be able to find—"

"It'd be at least a year before he's ready." I motioned for him to follow me into the living room and sat, swirling the ice cubes in my glass, listening for signs of Gabriel stirring in the bedroom. "She wouldn't have given him up like this if she wasn't in trouble."

"But you don't know that for sure."

But I knew *her*. And I'd already lost her once. I stared down into my drink, the dark liquid revealing nothing. The clock on the wall seemed especially loud, and I frowned, wondering if its rhythm wasn't slightly off-kilter. "She wouldn't have ended up in foster care if it wasn't for me, so I owe her this. We could find her, bring her back here, give her a home. If we could just…"

Go back in time? Change the things I'd done? All of my 'if onlys' were cut short by the sight of Gabriel hovering in the doorway, a baggy sports hoodie hanging down to his knees. A bear logo growled ferociously from the center, circled by the name of a local high school.

"Gabriel." I gawked, jumping to my feet. My eyes darted to the clock, its syncopated tolling now steady, though the minute hand had jumped several steps ahead of where I thought it should be.

A trio of Koels snickered behind him. It sounded as if their joints cracked each time they twitched, which they did often and erratically, though they had no joints or bones or anything solid within them at all to give permanence to their structure. They began to click like a symphony of out of sync clocks, bodies shaking in a seizured frenzy.

Tick, tock.

Gabriel looked like a boyish ghost of Martha past. Same raven hair, shaggy and uncut, skimming along the shoulders of Martha's old sweater. He had the same ivory skin, though his eyes were a much lighter brown than Martha's, laced with hints of gold and honey.

I couldn't be sure if Martha gave the hoodie to Gabriel innocently—just another tattered hand-me-down—or as a message to me; a callback to the first day I'd met her.

A sentimental reminder of all the ways I'd failed her since.

"Deep breaths. We'll figure this out." Ezra gave my shoulders a quick squeeze. He leaned down to whisper in my ear, "We'll talk about it later, once he's in bed. I'll get Gabriel to help me with dinner, see if he remembers anything else. You should call your mom."

"I don't think that's a good idea. I can't deal with her in the middle of all this. My skin crawls just being there. I step into the house and feel like I'm about to bend over backwards and spider crawl up the stairs like I need an exorcism."

I took Ezra's hands in mine and kissed each of his knuckles when he failed to be impressed by the comment.

"Can we please just drop it?" I begged, throwing in that if I stayed, I could get some things done we'd been putting off. Installing new latches on the stall doors in the barn, washing the truck, helping with—

"Gabriel, buddy," Ezra spoke louder, stepping away from me, "why don't you go to the bathroom and wash your hands so you can help me cook supper? I was thinking we could make pizzas. How does that sound?" Gabriel hesitated, looking at me, then Ezra, then back to me.

"Go wash up, Gabriel." I nodded. "I'll just be—"

"Call her." Ezra tapped the table twice with his fingertips, then left, following behind Gabriel to the bathroom at the end of the hallway. I watched the parade of them—Ezra, Gabriel, the Koels—as they disappeared through the doorway, then stared at the phone.

Tick, tock.

Chapter Six

I liked overcast days. Some people might have found them unsettling, with my condition, but overcast days meant less sun, fewer shadows to play tricks on my mind. If there were Koels, they were either fully visible amid the grey landscape or kept their distance entirely. I was used to feeling watched; sometimes so used to it that I could make myself forget for a while.

The first Koel, however, greeted me in the driveway like a valet.

My parents' house looked idyllic, a modern cottage exterior with a dark, cobblestone driveway and path leading to the front door and garage. I did my best to ignore the out of place lawn ornaments that decorated the yard; Koels that had long ago chosen my mother's house as their preferred haunt. A few lingered in the grass or poked their heads from behind upstairs curtains, but I breezed past them with a practiced ignorance I'd been honing since fourth grade.

"Mom, I'm here! Heading 'round back."

Curtains swayed behind the windows as I called into the house, breeze wafting through and airing out the winter musk. Past the kitchen and down a step into the foyer, I glimpsed my mother's piano, the glistening black surface matte with dust. A Koel sat behind it, hammering the keys the way a child or an animal might; it bashed the notes with clumsy fingers.

Though the act was soundless, each mis-struck chord grated against my ears like screeching tires or grinding metal, made worse only by vacant memories of a time when the instrument filled the house with sweeping melodies I once danced to giddily as a child.

Through a white, wrought iron gate with curling ornaments atop the balusters, a long, narrow yard stretched out behind the house, every inch perfectly manicured. Grass and garden boxes lined the sides of the fence to frame the coupe de gras at the rear of the property—a pond with a grandiose cascading water feature that my parents seldom approached, choosing instead to observe it from the comfort of the climate-controlled sunroom off the back of the house.

"Give me a hand, would you?"

My mother emerged from the back door directly into the sunroom while I registered the elaborate spread set out on the iron luncheon table. A pitcher of water with fragrant chunks of lemon glistened with sweat, a testament to the manufactured conditions within the dome when everything outside the room still ached with cold.

An old, black cat sunned on the window ledge, blind, deaf, and lame in one paw for years, but seemingly immune to death. He hissed at me; I resisted the urge to hiss back.

"What's all this?" I asked.

"Well, your birthday's coming up in a couple weeks, and I know you're busy." The glib, self-assuredness of her smile made me wish she kept alcohol in the house. Dad would have something, but the fancy brandy wasn't meant for the kind of drinking I wanted to do when I was there. She set a tray of dumplings on the table, nudging aside a gift-wrapped box that was tied off with a shining, yellow ribbon.

I looked out at the yard, refusing to consider the gift.

It would be wrong.

It's not that I went out of my way to be ungrateful, only that my efforts to appreciate her gifts were usually met with low-grade punishment, a sentiment to which she would almost certainly retort, "Classic Neviah, always exaggerating, always making me the bad guy."

The Koels from the front yard trickled to the back of the house.

When she bought me a palette of colorful eyeshadow on my sixteenth birthday—never mind that eyeliner was the furthest my desire for makeup went—I gave it the good college try. I watched makeup tutorials and came to my birthday dinner with what I thought was a pretty accomplished red and black smoky eye. Still, I remember the words "caked on" and "three-dollar hooker" coming out of her mouth, though she's since assured me she would never have said as much. Memory, I've come to find, is such a fickle thing.

However, the incongruous gift giving was only the tip of a much deeper, much more damaging iceberg for us. In psychological terms, our *schemas* about the world never aligned. Though the sign of a mature mind lies in the ability to properly accommodate new information into existing ideas, my mother's ideas about life haven't changed much at all in the time I've known her. And when new information doesn't align, it causes deep, deep distress.

A Koel in the yard raised a finger in my direction.

My existence has always been the embodiment of her dissonance. In so many ways it was like we were two characters in the same story, but depending on whose vantage you took, the genre was drastically different. That's to say that she was living in a G-rated *PureFlix* film while I was in something out of Guillermo del Toro's nightmares.

The visions started early, for me.

She started by explaining it as night terrors, forcing me to pray with her until I calmed down and could fall back asleep. It worked for a little while. But when the intensity of the visions deepened, when they were no longer confined to sleep, she took me to the pastor.

He glamorized it, which I also liked, for a time. I remember being called on during service to come to the pulpit and be prayed over. He made a show of speaking in tongues and rubbing holy oil against my forehead that left a greasy streak and made me think of the *Lion King*. Mom's elbow jabbed into my ribs when I giggled at the idea of him calling me *Simba*. Instead, he said I had *eyes that see beyond the flesh*, which sounds pretty cool when you're ten.

I looked up from my plate of dumplings. Mom was holding her own in the one-sided conversation, something about the cottage and did I remember the Wilkins family from our old church, and—my attention shifted to the yard, looking for something more interesting than her or the gift on the table to give my attention to. As I scanned the barren patches of garden, I felt the creeping dread of something being slightly out of place, though I couldn't identify what it was.

Perhaps it was just Jaak's absence I felt.

When he started seeing the Koels too, that was too much for my mom. It was exhausting, hearing us both screaming at night, and when prayer no longer helped, she couldn't adjust her schemas to make room for the new information. Instead of her schema being wrong, *I* must have been wrong somehow—never her darling Jaak, who could do no wrong. The fault rested solely with me, either through what I did or what I failed to do about the shadows she couldn't see.

Jaak, witnessing the tension between mom and I, was left to form his own conclusions, which is when his theory of interdimensional energy sources was born into existence. He was at the cusp of puberty when he started seeing just how bad the rift in our family had become and took solace in holing up alone with his books when the tension was too palpable.

When she found his copy of Vonnegut's *Slaughterhouse-5*?

She blamed me for that too.

First, the cover image on the book was a skull, and mom never fared well when confronting reminders that the nature of her mortality was limited. Second, the name was aggressive. It was a book about war, after all, so why shouldn't it be? But beyond those things, Jaak loved it for its nuance; the story of a man who, in the face of trauma, became unstuck in time, bouncing through the events of his life in a non-linear manner as he tried to adapt to war trauma.

At its core, the book was about pain.

Something Jaak knew well.

The protagonist's post-traumatic stress manifested in his belief that he, at certain points in his life, was abducted by an alien race that perceived life in more dimensions than humans could. To them, everything happened at once; there was no past or present or future, only a smattering of moments that were always happening, dimensions beyond those that humans could perceive.

To the aliens, it was evident that our lack of knowing, our ignorance to these extra dimensions, was the source of most suffering, which was the bulk of Jaak's theories. He was certain that was the answer—mental suffering must come from somewhere else entirely, a different dimension, given that mental energy isn't something easily seen or categorized despite the valiant efforts of neuroscientists everywhere. The idea was that if we could see the invisible energy that laid behind our conscious mind, we'd crack the code on mental health.

Ignorance was not bliss, rather, quite the opposite.

This led to theories about a collective unconscious tying us together through morphic resonance, or the unseen transmission of mental, emotional, and intellectual energy between members of a species. And if that energy existed, in theory, then perhaps the Koels were tied to it somehow. Creating it, or perhaps consuming it, though Jaak was never able to test that theory.

He would still need to be alive to do that.

Which led to my interest in dark matter—because I needed more than literature to inform my theories about the shadows. Plenty of perfectly intelligent people in the scientific community were already studying it; invisible, passing through us constantly, leaving no trace of itself except through fleeting observations of it acting on the nucleus of the cells it touches.

Some scientists have speculated that dark matter might make up more than five times the amount of matter in the universe compared to the regular matter we can observe. In theory, it could mean an entire dark particle universe, perhaps one perfectly paralleled to our own.

"Can you come?" Mom's voice cut through my thoughts, reminding me that I hadn't touched my plate in awhile as I stared vacantly at the yard. I stuck a dumpling in my mouth for good measure, hardly registering the taste or texture of it as I tried to regain my footing in the conversation. She huffed out a breath and said, "To the church retreat? To lead the workshops?"

"Maybe." Fat chance in hell. "I'll have to check with Ez."

She frowned. "I'm sure you can make time."

"I mean, I have a business to run, right?" I stuffed another dumpling nervously in my mouth before I'd finished chewing the first. "And we have the horses to take care of, so if Ezra's out of town working that week, it won't work. What week is it?" I feigned interest and pretended to make a note of it in my phone, her eyes darting to the gift for the dozenth time.

I sighed and pulled it closer.

It amazed me how readily she changed topics if I mentioned the horses. She hated them. Hated that I owned them. They were the only creature on the planet I was certain got more of mom's blame displaced onto them than me. I ripped open the gift wrapping on the package and let it fall to the floor, not wanting her to mistake gentle unwrapping for sentiment, after quickly scanning a card proclaiming I was on the cusp of thirty-five—closer to forty than I cared for.

I blinked at the box of colored pencils.

"You don't like them," she said, smile dropping when I didn't immediately light up at the sight of them. Her arms crossed over her chest, right leg crossing over the left in the classic fighting pose of the passive aggressive. If she was a client, I would have intentionally opened my stance trying to make them follow my lead; for her, I crossed my arms right back.

"It's just unexpected, coming from you."

"First I don't support your art enough, and now I support it too much," she overstated, her hand flashing toward the expensive box of pencils as though she could wish them away with a flick of her wrist. The last time I remembered her taking interest in my art was in tenth grade when she decided that the things I painted were too dark; a conversation that ended, as I recalled, with the pastor being called for an intervention that, in my limited experience, felt a lot more like a dramatized exorcism than the conversation she insisted it was.

"Have you *seen* me draw since Jaak died?"

"I don't *see* you do anything," she snapped, rising in a huff. Her chair wobbled behind her as she pushed away from the table, aggressively clearing away the platters of food. "How can I when you can't be bothered to visit? Really, Neviah, the lack of gratitude is just—"

"Don't do that." Fuck. "If I wanted to be with clients today..."

She straightened at the implication, so I followed her lead, stacking my arms with plates and pitchers to take in. There was no middle ground with her, which meant that if she thought the conversation was over—which she did, evidenced by the tightness of her lips and manic efforts to clear the table as fast as humanly possible—it was over. It wasn't until I turned to go inside and saw the yard reflected in the patio doors that I understood why it looked different.

A Koel stood where Jaak's greenhouse should have been.

When I turned, Mom paled.

Chapter Seven

"Neviah, calm down," she hushed as she caught up with me. Her steps were shorter and heavier, right leg pulling behind her with a permanent limp. It was only when she tried to move fast that I noticed it; a souvenir from an incident we were forbidden to talk about, a subject always met with quick diversions, long periods of passive aggressive silence, and conjured busy work.

"He *made* that." I covered the lawn with long, quick strides and stood on the barren patch of dirt beside the pond, paying no mind to the gathering Koels. My hand gestured erratically at the grass where it was faded from years of being covered by the greenhouse.

"The boards inside were rotting—*rot-ting*," she justified.

Jaak's gardening interests were unusual, I could admit that readily enough. The begonias he planted in the makeshift greenhouse every year were his pride and glory; large troughs of them, vibrant and yellow, or otherwise fiery and red. I'd always wondered why he didn't just mix all the colors together, maybe add some orange to give it balance; the yellow and red patches competed too much for attention, but Jaak's vision was refined in ways mine was not.

I might have drawn the pictures for the stories he wrote.

But it was Jaak who had the vision.

"Why didn't you tell me?"

"When you react like this?" Mom stood next to me, clutching her cardigan shut. "Gee, I wonder why." She looked sideways and wrinkled her forehead. "It was falling apart, Nev. I get that it was a special place for him, but the whole garden was special to him. If you'd just—"

"Where are we getting dirt?" I sighed, ignoring her confusion at the sudden change.

My eyes darted to my phone, beginning the countdown in my head, subtracting every second with pleasure from the afternoon I'd spend in captivity, listening to her tell stories about Jaak, pretending like she knew what he'd have wanted. It was still *his* garden when I'd arrived; in seconds, the yard felt rootless and barren, and I knew I would never touch it again.

"What do you—"

"I went by his place on the way here, you know," I said coldly, glancing at her out of the corner of my eye.

While Jaak's apartment couldn't properly be called a slum, it was the best word I could find for it. It was the kind of place you'd expect for someone who'd moved out at seventeen. The seven-story complex was just down the road from Martha's old house, in an area where the nice suburban homes became smaller duplexes, bricks replaced by dingey siding, until reaching the main road where only apartments remained full of struggling and unsavory occupants.

Cigarette butts littered the floor outside his building. The halls smelled like unchanged kitty litter. An ugly green carpet covered in egregious dahlia prints as big as a woman's sunhat lined the hall floors; the carpet was a kind of green I had only ever seen where dogs had peed on the same spot of grass too many times, the lines of the dahlias thick and seeming to burst out of the greenery with a multi-dimensional effect.

"He picked that over you. Just remember that."

Her face turned red. "Neviah—"

"You know what? Forget the dirt," I cut in before a full-fledged fight could emerge. I backtracked when confronted by the horde of Koels blocking the front gate, detouring through the house instead without bothering to take my shoes off. My heart felt like it was getting higher in my chest, blocking my lungs as my dad peeked out of his office and motioned me in.

I flinched as dishes clattered into the sink behind me. Mom mumbled under her breath, no doubt reiterations of the things she'd already said, and began tending to the dishes with so much displaced aggression that I tensed, certain the platters would shatter under her touch.

"Dad, I really don't have time—"

"I have something for Ezra."

I carried too many memories of the long nights he spent holed up in his office grading theses, honing lectures, and buried under stacks of papers and books that wobbled precariously above his hunched body. His office, a dark den better suited to sipping brandy and smoking cigars, was more of a home to him than the several other rooms that made up the house.

The only pastime I remembered him enjoying outside of work was chess; his board was displayed prominently on the top of his bookshelf, the wooden pieces polished and oiled until they gleamed. It was the only game he ever wanted to play, and a rare occasion if I managed to win. Strategy and logic. Learned sequences played out with quick moves as the hands of the clock spun around their dial, play time winding down until a winner emerged victorious.

"*Posterior Analytics and Moral Antecedents.* The department is recommending it for my curriculum," my father said, pushing up his glasses to read the title in his hands, as though he couldn't be certain it was the right one. He nodded and waved at it. "I'm not sure what to make of it. Ezra will probably like it though, so I thought you could pass it along."

I shrugged, raising my chin. "Maybe I'll read it."

My dad made a throaty sound, shooing me with his hand. He sauntered back to the desk in the center of his office and took his glasses off, folding them. "You wouldn't like it. Very dense," he explained, shaking his head and reaching for the bourbon. "More Ezra's taste. I'm sure your mom has some books, if you're looking for something new to read."

He quirked a brow, but I saw no humor in the words.

"And another thing," Mom said, manifesting in the doorway.

I pushed past her into the foyer with mumbled goodbyes to my dad, cursing myself for not hearing when the passive-aggressive dishwashing ended. Her frustration was like a demon expelled from its host; it needed to occupy something at all times if it was going to survive. She tried to cut in front of me, but I focused on the front door as if she was Medusa and if I looked at her, I'd never escape.

"You didn't even notice right away. You promised you were gonna help with it and two years ago when I asked you to repaint it to seal out some of the water, I recall you suddenly were very, very busy that week and couldn't be bothered to come by, and last year you didn't even go inside; you just bought planters with me and stuck them on the back porch to—"

The Koel at the piano played on as I slammed the door.

She followed me, tossing the box of pencil crayons in the open window of the truck, speaking, though I could no longer hear her over the sound of my heart beating in my ears. I reversed and turned down the next street, away from her house, accelerating despite the signs warning me that children were playing nearby and that I should watch for pedestrians. I turned the radio up, drowning out the cacophony of Koels that chattered noisily in the backseat, casting worried glances over my shoulder every so often only to find that the seat was empty.

Dark Water screamed in my ear from the radio speakers.

The next street wasn't any better than the first: children played in the yards, garden enthusiasts got an early start tending their flower beds, bundled in heavy coats as they turned up dirt and planted crops that would tolerate the impending cold. Dogs sniffed at tree trunks and yapped at squirrels, and Koels lingered as a shadowy hoard in the middle of it all.

I turned the music up so loud that some of the older residents looked up from their spring chores, wondering at the noisy truck peeling through their neighborhood. For some reason, it made me even angrier to be seen by them, like a feral cat caught unaware, so I pressed harder on the gas pedal. The book on my front seat slid backwards, then forward as I slowed down.

I took so many turns down the winding, suburban streets, tears blurring my vision, I was no longer sure which way was out. I kept throwing hurried glances over my shoulders, trying to gain enough distance so that mother's Koels would vanish, tethered to her and unable to go far.

"You didn't even notice it." Mom's voice played on loop from deep in the recesses of my mind, even with the aggravated guitar strokes and crashing drums bellowing around me in the truck. I made another quick turn, exhaling sharply when the exit came into sight.

Two, tall brick pillars framed the exit; a left turn was all that was needed to set me onto the county road that cut straight through town and onward to home.

A Koel appeared between the two pillars.

My breath caught in my throat, heart hammering as I veered, avoiding the shadowy figure perched at the exit and nearly colliding with a van coming from the opposite direction. I pulled to the shoulder of the road as the driver faded behind me, his horn blaring, face no doubt contorting with inaudible profanities. My phone vibrated beside the pencils on the passenger seat.

My voice was thin as I answered: "Hello?"

"Hey...can you come home early?"

Hearing Ezra's voice on the other line brought no comfort, only shame that perched in my throat, forming a lump. I scanned the road for a place to grab food and coffee, feeling as though every ounce of energy fled my body. Straightening at the wheel, I wiped away the tears and took a deep breath to stop the trembling that shook my fingers.

Something shattered on the other end of the line.

Ezra cursed.

"Did something just break?" I asked, thankful I wouldn't have to explain why I was coming home three hours earlier than expected. "I can leave in a few minutes," I lied, spotting familiar, golden arches in the distance, deciding to take the long way home to curb any suspicion.

"It's Gabriel." Ezra took a rushed breath. "He won't calm down—just smashed his dinner plate because he said I didn't make the chicken fingers right. I'm getting too escalated to deal with him. He keeps asking for his mom and I'm not sure what else we can tell him. I need you to tap in so I can step back from this for a second."

I heaved out a sigh of relief, thankful to be needed.

"I'm on my way."

Chapter Eight

I jolted upright when the alarm tolled from the bedside table, reaching for Ezra only to remember he was already gone. The skin around my eyes felt dry and taut, the kind of hangover that came only after crying for too long—exactly what I'd done after Ezra left and Gabriel went to bed. The throbbing behind my temples intensified as I blinked, eyes acclimating to the sudden change of light as the sun pierced through the bedroom curtains.

Dad's book shifted and fell from the comforter as I sat up, legs swinging to the floor on the count of three before I could sink back under the covers. My efforts to read it had only added to my headache.

I didn't remember falling asleep.

If Ezra's run-down the night before was any indication, the best-case scenario involved Gabriel staying in his room for the day; still, I planned for compliance, filled the agenda with activities of general interest, created contingency plans for the original plans if Gabriel needed options, created sub-activities for areas I suspected he'd be most intrigued by—horseback riding, nature walks, board games. His mousy steps wandered into the kitchen twenty minutes later where he found me seated at the table, nursing a second cup of coffee.

I tried not to tense at his presence.

"I figured I'd make some eggs and hash browns," I announced, carefully assessing his face. "Or there's cereal and oatmeal in the cupboard if you're not into eggs. I know I didn't like them when I was your age, but my grandma had this great recipe for scrambled eggs that—"

"Where's my mom?"

Gabriel struggled to drag one of the heavy chairs from the table to the freezer, fumbling to climb it as he pulled the door open. I didn't correct him, instead merely paused and watched as I turned on a pan to heat my own breakfast. Perched on his tip toes, Gabriel pulled chunks of wrapped meat out of the icebox and dropped them onto the floor until he finally found what he'd been looking for. He tore open the red box of frozen waffles, not bothering to use the seam, but rather, punching straight through the center of the cardboard, ripping the plastic inner case.

"You want waffles?" I asked slowly, a smile spreading over my lips.

Gabriel didn't answer me. Instead, he opened cupboards and drawers, leaving them hanging agape when he didn't find what he was looking for next. Anticipating him, I nudged open the swinging door below the corner of the counter, revealing the toaster.

I fried myself eggs while he toasted his breakfast, then took down two plates from beside the sink, sliding one across to him so that he had it when the toaster popped. He juggled the hot waffles and dropped them on the plate, setting it on the table with a clatter.

"Oh," I said. "I don't think we have any—"

"Where's the syrup?"

"I don't think we have any." I frowned. "I don't really eat it, and Ezra likes peanut butter on his. There's a jar in the pantry." I nodded to it. "If you want to—"

"I want to go home!" Gabriel slammed a cupboard door, leaving some of the bobbles on the china cabinet teetering. He noticed them at the same moment I did and proceeded to drop them against the hardwood, one by one, leaving splintered glass strewn across the floor. I winced and moved in to stop him, but he darted to the living room, wailing like he'd been struck.

"Gabriel, I know this is hard for you."

"*Mom-ee-ee-ee!*" he sobbed.

"Gabriel." I sat on the other side of the couch, watching him bury his head into the cushions. "I know it's hard for you to understand, but I've known your mom a lot longer than you—since she was a teenager. Despite what you might think, I want her here as much as you do. So, if you'd sit down and eat some breakfast, we'll go for a walk and get you situated. You can tell me more about your mom and your apartment, and maybe we can—"

"I don't know anything! I told you that!"

Still, he rose and returned to the kitchen, sinking down at the table without grabbing anything else to eat. He draped his arms across his chest, skinny toothpicks folded against an equally pointed set of ribs. His face was blotchy and red with tears, and his lip trembled as he sucked in deep, shaking breaths through his mouth.

My silverware scraped my plate as I cut into my eggs, chewing slowly as the silence lingered, breaking periodically as he sniffed.

"You're sure you don't want anything?" I asked.

He shook his head adamantly. "No."

Gabriel fidgeted restlessly, bouncing in his seat with his arms hugged against his chest. I might have thought that the eggs on my plate had wronged him, judging by the way he glowered as I ate. I abandoned the half-consumed plate and slid my feet into my boots despite the emptiness still panging in my stomach. He snatched his coat as I tossed it to him from the rack beside the kitchen door. "Let's go for a ride. I'll show you around, and then we can eat."

"Whatever," he mumbled, fumbling to shove his arms through the coat sleeves. I ushered him outside, the gravel in the driveway swimming with puddles where snow had melted, ground still too cold to absorb the runoff. A few feet from the kitchen door, a private stable waited, just enough space for two stalls, two horses, and a loft for my office.

When we walked in, one of the stalls was flung open, nothing barring its contents from the outside world. I cursed, momentarily forgetting Gabriel as I listened to the stall door squeak back and forth on its hinges. I cursed myself for not installing a new latch like I should have, rushing to grab a saddle from the tack room, then shifting the blame to Ezra for insisting I visit mom instead of tending to the lock.

I didn't have to look to know my horse was gone.

A dark shadow stood in its place.

Tick, tock.

Chapter Nine

Gabriel nestled into the saddle ahead of me, flinching every time a branch or leaf brushed against him on the narrow path. The grey mare below us stopped abruptly, head turned as though she'd noticed something through the trees, which smelled unmistakably of pine and moss and black earth. I pulled the reins, steering her toward the sound, breathing deeply to calm myself.

"How do you know it's this way?" Gabriel fidgeted in the seat.

"Atalante stabled with my horse since they were foals. She knows her better than anyone," I said, stroking Ezra's horse along her neck. The mare's ears flicked back when I said her name. "After I bought Nidhya, Ata's owners called and said she wasn't eating or drinking since Nidhya left. They figured the two were bonded. Ezra ended up buying Ata for himself so they could be together, which is good, because contrary to how it probably seems, Nidhya gets loose a lot more without Ata around than when they're together. She's a good influence."

My breath hitched as the silhouette of a doe flinched in the darkness between the trees, much deeper into the woods than I dared take Gabriel.

I swallowed over the lump in my throat. "Technically, the ranch has about a dozen, but they're stabled on the other side of the property, since the guests use them and take care of them. Hold tight," I warned, waiting until Gabriel clasped the saddle horn before loping. Ata led us to the main road again, then started off to the left with the assurance of a bounty hunter.

As Ata guided us, I wondered how things were faring without me as other staff led guests through their daily chores—the essential manpower needed to keep the *Sanctuary* running. The ranch was a far cry from the write-off it was when we bought it, but still, the work that went into its upkeep was a constant weight. We scrounged money to purchase it from wherever we could in the beginning—Ezra's job, clients who could afford to pay top dollar for their experience, money from the wedding we sacrificed to make the ranch a reality.

"So, Gabriel...you go to school?" I pried, needing the distraction. If I thought too hard about our account books, it felt like molten lava cooling in my throat, leaving a giant lump that made swallowing or breathing impossible. Inevitably, Mom's voice permeated my thoughts, looping criticisms about why I'd wasted money going back to school when I was already in debt, already lined up for a job that might actually make us a decent living instead of pinching pennies.

"Mount Olive," he said with such certainty that I might have been hopeful had we not arrived at the edge of the creek to find Nidhya, an impressive black and white pinto horse not unlike the toy Gabriel found in the bin, grazing on the opposite bank. I flexed my fingers against Ata's reins as I stared at the water, my joints aching from the chill still in the air. Chunks of melting ice and driftwood flowed downstream; the water swirling where a log lodged against the bank and created a separate current.

"I went to kindergarten when Mom lived with her old boyfriend, but then we moved 'cause Mom had a fight with the teacher and said I didn't have to go 'cause she was nosy."

"Ezra's a teacher," I responded distractedly. "In a couple days when he's back, he'll take you down to the rec hall on the other side of the property, let you meet the other teacher and kids who go to school and live here with us."

Gabriel winced at the prospect of attending school again, or perhaps it was at the thought of being stuck there with the other children when he wanted so badly to go back home. I let it go for a moment as I contemplated how to cross the water to Nidhya.

Going the long way would disrupt our plans for the afternoon. Ata threw her head back in protest, but the nearest bridge to cross was a couple miles away and the sky already looked bloated with rain, so I nudged Ezra's horse forward, clicking when she hesitated. We stepped gingerly through the icy water, each lifted hoof leaving us unstable until it hit the ground again. The water beat against the front of the horse's chest, splashing up and soaking my shins as we crossed.

Ata stumbled forward, snagging a rock with her hoof, thrown by the speed of the current. The creek floor dipped low towards the middle of the stream, almost too deep for Ata to carry us, ascending again just as quickly a few inches later. She regained her footing, muscles rippling as she carried us up the opposite bank, hurrying more for her sake than for ours. Large pieces of driftwood were scooped from the shore and pulled downstream, lodging in narrow bends.

"Horses are intuitive," I said when Gabriel wondered how she found Nidhya so easily. "They sense things in ways we can't. Ata knows her better than anyone, and her senses are different; maybe she followed smells, or sounds, or knew Nidhya went this way before."

"Do you always let her decide where to go? How do we get her back?"

"I brought Nidhya's harness and a lead." I looped Ata's reins around a fallen tree, then slipped the harness over Nidhya's muzzle, forcing her head up from the weeds. My efforts elicited little more than a bored look from the mare before she resumed grazing, familiar with her role in the oft-repeated game of hide-and-seek. She tugged against me, trying to keep eating, finally conceding with the equine equivalent of a sigh as I clipped the rope below her chin.

"Can I ride her?"

I looked at Gabriel, then back to the mare, stroking the black and white patterns on her ribcage. "If you wanna ride, I can give you lessons. Right now, we're gonna walk her home behind us—the long way so we don't have to cross back over the river." I fought the urge to look back over my shoulder, to consider how reckless the crossing might have been. "Maybe later we'll head to the big barn if it doesn't rain and find a horse for you," I said, mounting Ata behind him. "And I've got board games at the house we can try later, if the rain doesn't hold out."

Dark clouds blanketed the treetops as we started toward a trail that looped around to the other side of the creek. The available crossings multiplied during the summer, when the river settled, but for now, most of the bridges were submerged and damaged. My mind shifted to thoughts of the summer programming, how many people we'd need to inspect the crossings once the rainy season ended, how much money would likely go into repairing the bridges this year.

We walked in near silence, the only sound the asynchronous clap of hooves against the trail, each horse occasionally letting out a quick snort, sensing something beyond the trees, and lingering to stare awhile before moving on.

My heart hammered, unable to see what they did.

Unsure if I wanted to.

Chapter Ten

When the sky let loose an hour later, I busied myself pulling board games from the closet. Dust hovered weightlessly in the air from the relics, and heavy drops of rain pelted the window, sliding down the glass in distended pearls glistening each time lightning struck. The expensive colored pencils from Mom laid scattered across the floor where Gabriel had been doodling as I cooked, much too nice for a child's clumsy art, but also far too nice to be left unused at all.

"I like this one." He handed me a box, abandoning the pencils to examine the games. I turned the box in my hands, frowning as I cautioned, "This one's tricky. I never really got it." I searched for an alternative, too mentally spent to learn a new game when thoughts of the surprise Mom stashed inside the pencil box still haunted me. I glanced at the cupboard door below the kitchen sink where the business card reading *Bell Haven Fertility Services* was shredded to as fine a pulp as my fingers could manage. "There's a lot of pieces to under—"

"I played it at home," he insisted, lifting the lid.

"I guess I prefer games where the rules don't change, and I can just—hey." I'd pulled out the rules from the box, but Gabriel snatched them, as well as the gameboard and ratty old game-pieces, away from me. He cleared a space on the coffee table and started the set-up process. I sat back on my heels, unable to hide my small, amused smile as I watched him take charge.

"It's easy," he declared. "I'll teach you."

"It takes…" I started to comment that it was a lengthy game, then looked out the window; the rain didn't look like it was going to let up anytime soon, and at least he was busy and calmed down. I nodded rather than disrupt the balance of the afternoon. "Okay."

"You set this one up," he said.

He gave me the game board to unfold on the table—a grid, not unlike a chessboard, adorned with pictures representing roads, hills, fields, and forests—as well as several dozen small pieces I didn't understand. There were plenty of tiny figures he placed that looked like people, though featureless, several others that resembled various livestock, a variety of farming tools and tiny weapons that looked like they fit perfectly into the hands of some of the larger character pieces. I started to lift a dragon, but Gabriel took it and shook his head.

"You don't have to worry about this one right now," he said, putting it out of reach beside the board. "All you have to worry about right now is this guy." He held up one of the larger pieces: a stallion head molded from cheap plastic, but ornately detailed, nonetheless. "This is your knight," Gabriel explained. "You gotta focus on your knight to win. And these are magic cards. They change the rules of the game sometimes and you don't know what they are until—"

"What about all these other pieces? Don't they—"

"Those ones I'll show you later."

"But what about when—"

"You've gotta learn this piece first." Gabriel took each of our knights from the board, one in each hand, and held them toward me, wanting to be certain I saw them. "Cause if your knight's not protected, the magic cards are only gonna take points. I'll teach you all the other pieces later, but if your knight dies, you lose the game, and if you don't understand how your knight plays and what he can do, then you won't play well, and all your villagers will die."

"Okay, but—"

"No *buts*. Mom says buts are stinky," Gabriel insisted, tiny hands balled on his hips with the sass and assuredness only a child could have.

I tensed at the mention of Martha, wondering if it might trigger him again, but he was too absorbed in the game to notice; we spent the next two hours engrossed in it, him proficient, me hardly getting by as I snuck glances out the window. It was hard to be in the moment with him as I wondered about Martha, wondered about his history, wondered when Ezra and I would find time to get away, worried about my other clients. And *Julie*, I thought, pinching the bridge of my nose.

I did my best not to be frustrated with how slowly she was progressing, ignoring that the faster a vehicle moved, the easier it was to lose control of the wheel; a bump in the road could be as fatal as a landmine with enough pressure on the gas pedal.

Chapter Eleven

Children's laughter erupted from the jungle gym, dozens of wriggling bodies climbing across its surface or otherwise chasing each other through the grass. The sky was a special kind of blue, a deep cerulean that seemed reserved for early spring when the promise of warmth and sunlight made it impossible to ignore. I hated every second of it, the sun too warm on my skin. A child plummeted down the twists of the slide; a little girl with raven hair following behind him.

Koels observed us from behind monkey bars, indiscrete in the sunlight.

"It's beautiful here," Julie beamed, mouth hung open with pleasure as she watched a trio of girls play hopscotch; the asphalt was covered in vibrant, pastel chalk in the shape of letters and numbers and what looked liked a child's clumsy attempt at a woman in a bathtub. The raven-haired girl plummeted down the slide and stuck her tongue out at me as she ran to hide, her face an uncanny reflection of Gabriel's. I blinked, attention turning reluctantly back to Julie.

What she had wasn't a memory in the formal sense of the word; not a memory of reality, at least. The place Julie anchored us on the *Other Side* was not situated in time; it was a patchwork of lived-in memories paired with expectations that were as real to her as anything else. It wasn't uncommon for dreams or wishes or even my own memories to seep into a client's experiences on the *Other Side*, but it was my job to wade through the mess.

"Not scary at all. It's perfect—everything is exactly how I thought it would be, you know, having kids? Riley!" she shouted.

I gripped her hand like a mother holding a toddler from traffic as she tried to bolt to the swing set where she spotted him, sucking in a sharp breath.

The *Other Side* was many things, but forgiving was not one of them.

"In and out, Julie," I reminded her. "We can't stay."

Exhaustion already clung to me like a second skin, my eyes circled with dark spots, souvenirs of sleepless nights tending to Gabriel, tending to the farm, tending to Ezra, tending to my clients, tending, tending, tending...

She ignored my warnings, grinning and stationing herself behind Riley at the swing set, readying herself to push him. Her chin lifted skyward, sunlight washing over her face as she listened to children singing nearby. A group of children no older than Gabriel skipped in excited circles as they played pattycake and recited nursery rhymes they'd all heard from their parents as infants.

"This park was by my condo," Julie explained, pushing Riley to the limits of the chain, waiting for gravity to bring him back to her. "Every day on my way home I would walk past it, and I always saw all the moms with their kids and thought, one day, I'm gonna do it."

As I looked around at the hordes of children, I realized there wasn't an adult in sight; no mothers gossiping while their kids played, no one reaching out when a child fell and scraped their knees. The children themselves acted peculiar; a little boy stared at the pebbles surrounding the base of the jungle gym, eyes wide and unblinking, smile too wide for his tiny jaw.

He looked like a wilting ragdoll forced to permanently hold his position.

"This is exactly how I pictured it, and there was an ice cream shop a couple blocks over that I figured we would walk to every weekend, and I was always gonna let him get two scoops because my mom *never* let me, and then in the summer, we would go down to the pier and—" She jerked when Riley jumped from the swing, landing in front of her, hugging her waist.

"Neviah, look!" She grinned. "He never lets—"

"Julie! Watch—" Riley reached behind his back and drew out a scalpel, the blade catching the sunlight and drawing Julie's attention as it sliced across her belly with dizzying speed. She staggered back a few steps, touching her stomach as a deep, dark smear of red soaked her blouse. Riley chuckled and clung to her hips as though nothing had happened.

"Hey, listen to me—you're good. It's not real, you're just remembering now," I urged, drawing her attention to the hospital gown that replaced her street clothes. Julie stood shaking in her flimsy hospital attire, stomach and hands soaked through with blood as she held them skyward, a cool, spring breeze whipping at the ends of her matted, sweat-soaked hair.

A wish held against reality was a delicacy for the Koels.

Their clicks echoed through the park.

Tick, tock.

"It wasn't supposed to be like this." Julie's eyes darted around the playground when she realized Riley was no longer beside her; hand returning to her belly to feel for the wound. Julie sobbed, every insecurity sliced open, every vulnerable part of her bared to the sun.

She gripped the lapels of my sweater, but I pulled her hands off, clutching them between my own.

"I had a plan," she wailed, blood transferring from her hands to mine. Women filled the field around the park, bodies robed in bohemian gowns that trailed the grass, hardly concealing their bare feet. Bodies arched and swayed, spines curling to the sky and then sinking down as they opened their chests, moaning in pain that could easily be mistaken for pleasure.

Others breathed in, hands stretching toward the sky in sun salutations before fanning out to the sides as they swan dove to the earth. They planted their feet, connecting their bodies to the earth as they rocked their hips, squatting. It felt like watching a coven of witches dancing around a fire at Beltane, overcome by hysteria.

"I'm a horrible mother," Julie concluded, though it was hard to focus on her as I watched Koels slip out of the shadows they were previously content to hide in. The women continued to sway and dance, moaning deep, guttural sounds as labor overtook their movements, unaware that the children had fallen silent.

The Koels delighted in the change.

"I just wanted him out of me," she said numbly, staring at the chaos as though it was hers alone to bear. The children began to scream, lunging for mothers who wailed for the little ones but refused to pick them up when they ran to them for comfort. Each time a Koel touched a child, the child's flesh bubbled and swelled as though they'd been burned. Julie touched her scar.

"I just wanted him out of me. I didn't care if he—"

Unlike the rehearsed, arching movements of the women in the grass, Julie looked as though someone was holding her head under water. Memories of contractions seized her body, warping her face with dread as she anticipated the pain she knew was coming.

"I didn't care if he lived or died." Her eyes went wide again, panicking as she remembered the day the doctors cut him out of her womb. "No one tells you how much blood there's going to be."

I held my breath as a Koel stalked quietly around the playground, following the raven-haired girl. Her hand clasped over her mouth as she bent around the structure, staying just ahead of its sight. Her fingers were soaked with snot and tears as she took cover under the slide.

"I don't know why I thought I could do it on my own," Julie said, words hitched on a sob. "After Mark left, I felt really confident I could get along without him. But I failed. I'm a bad mom," she reiterated.

"You need to listen to me," I snapped, turning her by the shoulders.

The sound of mothers wailing was like banshees howling in the night as the children were dragged away screaming by the shadows. The women continued to dance barefoot through the field, reaching for the children but never holding them. Julie's eyes widened, shocked by the sudden outrage in my voice. Many of the women in the grass tore at their clothes in agony, smearing wet soil over their bare chests.

"You are *not* a bad mom," I said through gritted teeth, giving her a small shake. "Bad moms don't make hard decisions for their babies. Bad moms don't move to new towns to give their kids a better life."

My breathing came out jagged as my mind wandered to thoughts of my own mother, of the business card she had left indiscreetly with the pencil crayons. A dull ache spread across my lower back.

I looked back to the raven-haired girl, but she was gone.

Some of the women dropped to their knees and cried with their faces in their hands, while others looked up and screamed curses at the sky. And still others continued their labor, ignoring the children at their feet as their bodies writhed in preparation for another. "You wouldn't have bothered getting to know Riley, learning to love him for who he is, taking him to the pool—"

"He loves the water," Julie interrupted, a half-smile lifting her face, eyes cast down as though she couldn't see what was going on around her, or perhaps, didn't want to. "I think that was the first time he ever really found himself, was in the water. He saw his reflection and he just...smiled." I blinked and a pool appeared in front of us, replacing the play structures. The sharp scent of chlorine filled the air.

"What do you see in the water, Julie?"

"Figures." Julie frowned. "Swimming in the pool—it's too dark to see the bottom, but I see my face. Or part of it, I think, and sunlight," she added, noting as it peeked out from behind a cloud. The wailing women collapsed in unison, panting as though they had prevailed through the final moves of a punishing performance. Julie leaned closer to her reflection, not noticing as the women, once young and beautiful, shriveled in the grass, skin tightening with wrinkles.

"But it doesn't change that I'm a bad mom." She sighed.

That was all it took.

Shadowy hands shot up from below the surface of the pool, tendrils tangling in Julie's hair as she let out a scream so cutting that the earth shook. The naked forms in the grass writhed and screamed with sympathy pains, their frail bodies crumbling into dust. The Koel pulled Julie's hair until her face submerged in the water.

It took three seconds for everything to go wrong, two seconds for me to untangle her hair and pull her loose, and only one for the Koel to wrap itself around my waist as I pulled us out of the illusion.

We surfaced on the floor of the clearing, gasping for air, my stomach burned and swollen where the Koel touched. I pressed my fingers to the growing welt, knowing I would have a scar nearly identical to Julie's. My next breath was a short wheeze, eyes unblinking as though it might somehow lessen the pain if I could keep from moving.

Julie's hair was soaked, dripping puddles around her feet as she bolted upright and scurried away from me. I reached for my bag in search of the first aid kit I kept handy. The world swerved uneasily, my eyes going wide as though they might center my balance somehow. I realized that my hand was groping dirt, nowhere near my pack.

My vision swam with stars.

The last thing I saw before pain shocked the world into blackness was the raven-haired girl standing over me, black hair falling across her face as she leaned down. She stroked her hand along my cheek, and though I couldn't feel it now, her fragile form trapped somewhere between realities, I could imagine it easily enough. Julie blinked, mystified as I reached for Martha, the little girl's form now hidden from Julie by whatever kept her blind to the *Other Side*.

"You said we couldn't get hurt," Julie stammered, backing away.

"No," I murmured. "I didn't."

Chapter Twelve

I woke slowly, as though coming out of a pleasant dream I could only remember vague bits and pieces of, like a paint by numbers with only a color or two in the proper place. The faintest scent of lemon hung in the air, and someone stroked their fingers through my hair before consciousness consumed the dream and my eyes fluttered open.

Hardly any light came through the bedroom windows, but I could see Ezra waiting for me at the end of the bed, arms crossed over his chest as he stared at the window, eyes tired and shadowed. I wanted to reach for him.

But my eyes closed again, too tired to stay open.

I could tell by the way his foot tapped against the floor that he was worried, though that worry would undoubtedly turn to anger the moment he realized I was fine. Only when I finally straightened myself on the pile of pillows did I notice the bandages wrapped around my abdomen; my hand went to them in the same instant that Ezra noticed me moving and looked up.

"Where's Julie?" It was a safe topic; reasonable information to request before moving on to the things he was right to be angry about. I tried to sit up further, wincing involuntarily.

"Back at her cabin," he conceded after a short staring contest. "You need to call and thank her; she had you bandaged and everything. What if she'd handled it worse? Or saw the blood and fainted or—" His face drained of color. "Geezus, what if it had been—"

"I wouldn't have let her get hurt."

"Do you even realize how bad this could have been?" Ezra darted to the bedside, pulling up the sleeve of my sweater to reveal the scars lining my arms; they were the watermarks and remnants of each time a Koel had almost bested me, but *almost* was the key word. I tugged my sleeves down, out of sight, out of mind, as blood rushed back to his face. "What happened?"

I looked away, focused on the wall beside the dresser as I tried with considerable difficulty not to throw up. Shaking my head was a mistake; the desire to vomit disoriented me, coating the room in swirling, silver stars as I insisted that he was overreacting.

"I lost focus. Won't happen again."

"You don't know that."

We stayed quiet for awhile, staring at each other so intensely that we blinked only if it became absolutely necessary. Eventually, he turned to the window, staring out at the night. I wrapped my arms around him from behind, staring into the darkness that cloaked the house and held us trapped inside, listening for any sign of disquiet lingering in the night.

"You could have been killed," Ezra said, softening.

"You know that's not—"

"I don't care how unlikely it is. You *could* have." He rubbed the space between his eyebrows, face pinched together as though a migraine was impending. I tried to touch his shoulder, but he stepped away, hands raised to caution me away from him. "You put too much stock in those things. What about Jaak? You used to think they were the reason—"

"But I *saw* her. There's always a chance of getting distracted, but it's an easy fix this time—we just have to find her." My smile felt manic, so I softened my brows and tried to relax my features. "And I know Gabriel isn't ready to go under, if that's what you think I'm thinking."

"Then what?" he pressed.

"And before you say it, I already tried calling that school he says he went to, but it didn't exist," I explained, trying to cover my bases. "I thought maybe it wasn't a kindergarten, so I searched daycares too but the closest is halfway across the country and—" He tilted his head, recognizing when I was about to say something he wouldn't like. "He has one of her old sweatshirts, right? From high school? So maybe I can use it to go under without—"

"Seriously?" Ezra ran his hands through his hair, gripping them behind his head as he leaned back and stared at the ceiling. He dismissed the idea as quickly as it came out of my mouth; going under with a token was like falling out of a plane and staking your life on the hope that you'd grabbed a parachute and not a regular backpack.

There would be no going back.

Usually, it wasn't intentional to go under without someone as an anchor; just a brief lapse of restraint, an unintended moment of connecting with someone or something too deeply, but even penicillin was an accident, wasn't it? And look how much good came from that happy little accident. I tried to say as much to Ezra, but it only made him pull away and curse.

"You're unbelievable. What about Gabriel?"

"What about him?" I sighed.

"We've got someone who needs our help. Suppose you're right and Martha is in a bad way. How much of an impact do you think that's already had on him? You know how messy it gets when kids come from bad homes, so maybe we should focus our energy on—"

"It'll be messy telling him she's not coming back."

He furrowed his brows. "But he'll adapt."

"Exactly," I said, catching an opening. "Gabriel is here and he's safe, so regardless of what happens, we can give him a good life. Martha, on the other hand..."

His foot tapped as he considered it. "I don't want you under without an anchor. I hear what you're saying; if something happens to Martha, he loses his mom forever and I can't make that into a positive thing. I just don't think we have enough of the picture to—"

"I understand there are risks." I tried to take his hands, forcing him to face me, but he snatched them away and turned to the other side of the room.

"Not to mention how intrusive it would be for both of them to start snooping around their history without their permission. Do you have any idea what her life's been like since—"

"Ezra..."

"Just one good reason." He stopped pacing to turn back to me. "If you can give me one good reason why you want to find her so badly that isn't based on your feelings, then by all means, you can go under without him right now—and don't tell me it's because she's in danger."

"She could be! She's out there," I insisted, resting my hands against the arms he held knotted across his chest. "Why would she leave him? Why would she leave him like this if she didn't have to? What kind of mother would do something like that?"

"I want to find her too, Nev."

"Then act like it! What's our plan?" I demanded, my cheeks turning red, though it was hard to see in the darkness that settled over the bedroom. Some shadows were darker than others. "We haven't talked about it at all since you got back, and I want to know what you're—"

"When were we gonna talk about it?"

"We're talking *now*. I'm not saying I wasn't busy too; I'm saying we need to talk about it sooner rather than later." My lip trembled, my eyes filling with unwelcomed tears. "I'm terrified for her. Not scared. Not nervous. I'm *terrified*. I know she wouldn't leave him like this."

I dropped onto the bed and sobbed.

"Why don't we wait and talk tomorrow?" Ezra sank beside me on the mattress. He draped an arm around my shoulder and pulled me into his chest, the whole bed shaking as I cried. He whispered gentle 'shushing' noises and ran a hand over my hair, promising me that everything was going to be alright. "It's been a long day, and we don't need to do this now. I just think if there's any chance the Koels are responsible for what happened to your brother, you need to be more cautious, that's all. I don't know Martha. I know *you*. I need you."

I wiped tears from my face. "I'm s-sorry."

"It's okay," he soothed, wrapping his other arm around me so that I was in the fetal position against his stomach, knees pulled to my chest.

"I'm sorry too. I'm not saying no, alright? I just...give me some time. I've been thinking about it too, Nev. I'm scared for her, too."

"I know you are."

"This has been a lot for us this last little bit," he said. I nodded against his leg, reaching up to wipe my eyes as he continued. "I have some news; I just don't know if it's good news or not. I was planning to tell you when I got back and then with everything else, I thought...I got an interview for that job with the online school. I don't know if I'm going to take it but—"

"You can't take it." I straightened. "You love being in the classroom. It's bad enough that you already gave up—"

"Why? I wouldn't have applied if I didn't think it was best for us. I'm thinking of us and of Gabriel. If we can't find her—I mean, he's in our care for now, at least, and I don't want to miss that. Whatever happens, we're doing it together, Nev."

Ezra kissed my forehead, and from the spot where his lips touched, an ache spread out, seeping into every inch of me like the slow rot of arthritis. Dull ripples of pain spread through each joint and fiber in my being, collectively becoming an immense and consuming sort of pain. It wasn't the kind of pain that touched my body, but something much deeper.

"You should get some sleep," he said, changing the subject.

"Yeah." I started to nod, but his lips found mine, a tender goodnight kiss that lasted another twenty minutes. He rolled over beneath the blankets, and I draped my arm across him, holding on until his breathing deepened and his snores came in regular intervals.

I acquainted myself with the darkness as I reached across him to dim the light. It nestled me inside of its arms, whispered sweet nothings against my ear, its breath cold on my skin. A Koel leered in from the window, reminding me that Martha was out there somewhere, hurting.

I lurched awake at the feeling that I was falling.

Tick. Tock.

Chapter Thirteen

"Neviah? Ezra?" A tiny voice called out in the dark as I tiptoed towards the kitchen, wincing at every groan of the floorboards. The silhouette of Gabriel's head poked out from his bedroom. A tiny hand gestured me to come closer, so I tiptoed a few steps in his direction.

"What's up, kiddo? Can't sleep?" I glanced toward the bedroom, wary of Ezra waking. Rather than continue whispering, I put a hand on Gabriel's shoulder urging him away from the door. "Me neither. I was gonna make myself a hot chocolate. How does that sound?"

"I don't have to go to bed?" His head perked up.

"Not yet," I decided.

"Why were you and Ezra fighting?" he asked, cozying up to the table after picking out a mug from the cupboard. I frowned, turning away to light the stove, and poured milk into a saucepan. Utensils rustled in the drawer as I searched for a measuring spoon.

"It was nothing," I said hesitantly, dumping the measured cocoa powder, sugar, and vanilla in with the warmed milk. I whisked until everything was blended and filled our cups, topping it off with a small dollop of whipped cream and a generous sprinkle of chocolate shavings.

"Was it about me?" Gabriel's nostrils flared, a precursor to tears.

"No." I frowned. "Sometimes grownups fight, that's all, and then they talk and get through it, which is exactly what Ezra and I did. It's all good. Why did you think that?"

"Mom and Gary fight," he said once he'd blown on his cocoa until it was cool enough to drink. It wasn't quite an answer to my question, but something he seemed to think I should know. Thoughts of Martha and Gary twisted through my head like mealworms as I wondered where she was, what he might be doing to her at that very moment.

"Oh, yeah?" I said, fingers drumming along my mug. My throat was suddenly dry, every swallow chalky. "You know what?" I pushed my mug aside, the taste of it suddenly bitter and uninteresting. I crossed my arms awkwardly so that they covered the bandages visible through my tank top. "How about I read you a story? Maybe that'll help us both fall asleep."

He nodded, slurping for any remaining cocoa.

"What book do—"

"I have one." Gabriel slid out of his seat and put his mug into the sink, taking my hand and tugging me along behind him to the bedroom. He went straight to the bed and laid on his belly in front of it, tugging the book from under the bed by the leather strings that bound it. The watercolor drawing of the dragon and the knight stared back at me for the second time in a month after years of being buried away. I frowned at Gabriel, then at the book.

"Where'd you get this? I thought—"

"I found it in the box of toys, and Ezra was reading it, but he left it in the kitchen after he was done, so I took it back even though he said I'm probably not old enough to read it even though I already saw scary things on the TV, and I already looked at all the pictures—they're not even scary. Dragons aren't even scary. Will you read it to me? Please, please, please?"

"If Ezra—"

"Please?" Gabriel begged, clasping his hands together in front of his body and bobbing up and down like he needed to go to the washroom. I stared down at *Sir Ivanguard*, wondering what I would do when I got to the final pages, too dark for an adult, even, let alone for a small child. Still, Gabriel pleaded with fervor, "Please, please, *pleeeaasssee?*"

"We'll read it quietly."

Gabriel hugged me around my leg, then scurried into his bed, scooting under the heavy comforter. He looked to me excitedly, forgetting for a moment that his mother was out there, somewhere, maybe alone, maybe hurt, maybe dead, for all we knew, and that was enough to urge me to slide in next to him and begin reading. For a moment he was happy, and that was enough.

Scanning the page was like hearing an old, familiar song.

I knew all the words.

My fingers licked the edge of the pages, flipping past an empty space at the front of the book where an old, handwritten page had long ago been torn out; the edges of it still left a jagged line along the inner seam of the manuscript. The old page disappeared into my parents' pond a long time ago, the pieces soaking up water, bloated and heavy until they sank down, dissolving until there was no longer a distinction between the words and the water that consumed them.

"Alright, *Sir Ivanguard...*"

The knight, Sir Ivanguard, carried with him a terrible and lonely secret; though he appeared hardly old enough to wield a sword, his soul was nearly 102 years old, reincarnated into the body of a young knight, barely older than his youngest son had been at the time of his passing.

Though people once fought to hear Sir Ivanguard speak, no one listened to him as a young man the way they had as an elder. Confined to the body of a child, Sir Ivanguard, stayed mute, a choice that awarded him special privileges in a kingdom cleaved in two for as long as he could remember.

"I like knights. And swords," Gabriel chimed in sleepily, yawning against my arm. I glanced down at him, then back at the book, deciding to draw out the conversation until I could hide the manuscript. He snuggled deeper into the blanket that was drawn up to his chin.

"Oh yeah?" I asked.

"My old bedroom was full of..." He paused to yawn again, eyes closing as he continued. "...knights and dragons, and there was a poster of a big castle, and I would use my Legos to build wagons, and there was a princess, and a knight, and he had a sword that fit in his hand."

"My brother was a big fan of knights," I replied, flipping the cover of the book shut, relieved when he didn't reopen his eyes. He made a quiet murmur that carried the inflection of a question, so I added, "We would always play pretend when we were kids, and I always got mad at him because I was the older sister, so I thought I should get to be the knight, but he insisted."

"Girls can be knights too," Gabriel said, his words slow and lazy and followed almost immediately by snoring.

I set the book aside, doing everything in my power not to think about it, not to look at it, wondering how I might hide it from Gabriel so that we'd never have to revisit it. I started to slip my arm out from under him, afraid the movements of my heart would wake him.

Then I paused.

My hesitation lasted only a moment as I relished the feeling of his warmth, his tiny breaths, his heartbeat, his hair tickling at my skin. I glanced around the small bedroom with its bright walls and shallow shelves; a room that was always meant for a child. Clients came and went from it sporadically over the years, but...but what? I wiped his hair away from his eyes, then carefully let his head fall to the pillow as I slid out, drawn to the far wall.

The dresser holding Gabriel's belongings leered at me through the darkness, tugging me closer until my hand rested on the handle, hesitating to tug it open. I should have kept moving, should have wandered to the bathroom cupboard, taken one of the prescription sleeping pills the clinic gave me after Jaak's death. I didn't want the pills, but the doctor insisted:

"Our brains need sleep, Miss Ross. That's when it does most of its processing. If it doesn't get a good, solid rest, it's going to be overwhelmed, and all sorts of problems will stem from it, both mental *and* physical, you understand? You need to take care of yourself; you need rest."

I pulled the drawer open anyways, holding my breath when Martha's sweater laid waiting on top of the pile of clothes as though it was placed there just for me, bear emblem rumpled but visible. It waited for me, waited for the moment I would inevitably reach in and grab it...

"Nev?" Ezra's voice was hoarse with sleep as he wandered into the hallway.

I pushed the drawer closed, jostling it against the hard wood. His steps creaked somewhere further down the hall, toward the bathroom. I tiptoed to the hall door with short, quick steps and pressed my ear against the opening, listening as he moved further away, then tiptoed to the living room.

My back faced him on the couch when he came looking, a throw blanket from the sofa draped lazily across my body, diaphragm rising and falling as I feigned the slow, steady rhythms of sleep. When he wandered back to the bedroom, I turned around, expecting to be alone.

Instead, my face was inches away from a smiling Koel.

I sensed for the first time that its smile wasn't void. It delighted in my solitude, seemed elevated by Ezra's unwillingness to help. The Koel leaned in until the air got colder around me, taunting me as it breathed against my face, forcing my eyes shut as it clicked against my ear.

Tick...

Chapter Fourteen

I went to a counselor once after Jaak died, and when I say once, I mean it quite literally. A single time. One shot for someone to prove they were capable of knowing me better than I knew myself. Their first move was trying to help me understand the feelings I was having about Jaak, which made sense to me—emotional validation, and all that.

However, execution is as important as intent in counseling, and they erred greatly in their technique. Instead of validating my grief, which was what brought me there, she wanted to talk about guilt, as though I was in any place to explore *that* particular feeling despite it being all I ever felt. So, she moved too fast, and I withdrew. Strike one.

Strike two was bringing up *parentification.*

Parentification, she explained, was when a child took on too much responsibility in their household, taking over the role of a parent who couldn't meet their needs. Maybe their mom was an alcoholic and they needed to take care of her when she couldn't function, or their dad got a bit handsy with their siblings after a few beers, forcing them to step in as a distraction, or there was never enough money and they had to work harder than the average child should to get by.

But she was dead wrong.

No one in my house drank or was on drugs. Mom was religious at putting meals on the table and keeping food in the fridge and paying the bills and praying for her kids. To be honest, I'd have preferred it if my mom was *less* involved in our lives.

I could have gone without the pretty house in the suburbs my parents moved us into after her accident, without the polished hardwood floors we were forbidden to track dirt onto, without the forced time at the kitchen table making conversation with a woman who never said anything substantiative. And on Sundays, I could have gone without sausaging myself into my Sunday best and shifting on rigid pews while mom deified herself with empty recitations.

I didn't bother waiting around for strike three.

Counseling, decidedly, was not for me.

When I opened my eyes, it took a moment to remember why I was on the couch. The morning felt unbearably cold despite the sun gleaming in too brightly through the living room window, and the sound of Gabriel and Ezra getting ready for their day was a little too loud from my cramped position on the sofa. Rather than rouse myself to join them, I dragged the blanket to the bedroom, closed the shades, and fell back to sleep for another two hours. I didn't want to wake up even then, but my phone buzzed noisily on the bedside table.

"Hello?" I neglected to look at the caller ID, wincing when mom's voice chimed from the other end with an enthusiastic birthday greeting that I didn't want. "Hi, Mom." The words rode on an exhale so deep I felt like I could move a sailboat with it. I rubbed the chalkiness of sleep from my eyes and threw my legs over the edge of the bed, dropping my elbows against my knees for a moment before pushing myself up. Mom quickly moved on to the real reason for her call.

"Are you coming to the retreat? Sign up was due yesterday."

"Yeah, I got the email." I switched the phone to my other ear, pressing it between my cheek and shoulder to hold it in place while I stretched, shoulders still stiff from sleeping on the sofa. I only half-listened to her babble, doing my best not to listen beyond what was needed to occasionally mumble a generic 'uh huh' or 'really, no way' or 'yes, I'm aware'.

"Why don't you just tell them to call *me* if they—" I blinked hard and fast to banish the sleep from my eyes as she launched into a lecture on etiquette, dragging myself into the hall. Gabriel's bed was already made when I peered in, and the dresser loomed in the corner; all at once, the night before collided with me, and everything that sleep had pushed away came careening back into the light—her sweater, the mono-syllabic warning of the Koel.

"Registration was due yesterday," she emphasized.

"I know," I huffed, pinching the bridge of my nose. "But I told you...Mom, would you listen? It's not good timing." I rummaged the medicine cabinet, popping a few pills from different containers; vitamins, anxiety medication—thanks, Mom—and an ibuprofen to quell the stiffness and pain in my joints and abdomen. The skin was red and swollen around the gash, in need of hasty rebandaging and cleaning, though I wished desperately I'd started the coffee pot before tending to it. I touched a hand the to the edge of the wound and winced.

"I'm not doing this right now," I repeated when mom's insistence became intolerable. "Just tell them I said 'no'...Yupp, whatever...It's first thing in the morning..." I groaned when she chastised the lethargy in my words. "I had a late night, okay? It's a Saturday. Get off my back about it. I told you I'm not helping if I have to do the adult retreat thing...Fine. No, I told you, I just need—"

Mom continued until it was clear I'd need more than a few pills to make my headache go away. I picked up a note tented by the coffee maker as I walked into the kitchen, elated to find the pot filled to a hearty twelve cups and piping hot on the burner, disheartened by the message.

> *HAPPY BIRTHDAY! Coffee is brewed. Taking Gabriel to run errands and pick up stuff for your birthday dinner. Love you. Don't wait up. (And try to get outside. It's nice out today).*

Another year Jaak would never see.

I pulled back the curtain to look out the window, checking that Ezra's truck was still gone. I couldn't be sure when they'd left, but looking at the clock, I wagered I had another couple of hours before they'd be home. I might have run a bath for myself or pulled out a book I'd been too busy to read as of late, brewed some sweet tea, enjoyed the afternoon having the house to myself. I could have gone back to bed, if I wanted, caught up on some much-needed sleep...

Instead, I listened to my mom whine for a few moments longer as I poured coffee into a thermos, shoving it into my backpack despite the anxiety already churning in my belly and scalding my throat with acid. I took a pair of tongs from the kitchen drawer and my bag into Gabriel's room, finding myself in front of the dresser once again.

"I really need to go now. Bye, Mom." I hung up, my heart quickening when she immediately called back, not once but twice before finally taking the hint and leaving me alone for the day. Heat rose to my cheeks with every vibration in my pocket, a fresh surge of adrenaline seeping through me, sending my body into high alert, sharpening my faculties.

Opening the drawer, I lifted the faded hoodie with the tongs, careful not to touch it as I shoved it into the bag, then tossed the tongs in with it. Throwing on some fresh clothes, I sped back to the kitchen, backpack slung over my shoulder before I could think too hard about what I was doing. I stopped on my way out, pouring three, fat fingers of bourbon into a glass.

I left my own note for Ezra:

Gone to my usual spot.
I'm sorry...

When I made it to the clearing, I pulled out the sweater with the tongs, careful not to touch it, and set it aside. The water was high from the spring rain, though it seemed to have reached its crescendo; soon it would calm, returning to usual for another season until spring came again, upsetting it, forcing it to fight for equilibrium. Until then, it thrashed wildly against the bank so that I wouldn't have recognized my own reflection looking into its agitated surface.

Tick, tock.

The first time I went under without an anchor—without anything to tie me to a specific memory that had been discussed and dissected at length with the person it belonged to—was when I was twelve. I didn't mean to, at the time. In fact, I hadn't even known it was possible. I was in the barn one afternoon, and the horse I was riding startled at a bird in the rafters; she bucked and sent me careening into the side boards, leaving a nasty welt on my shoulder that bruised on impact.

Someone was there suddenly with a cold-pack and an old rag from the barn to keep the ice from resting against my bare skin. The rag was nothing special; it was covered in oil, evidently last used while fixing a tractor or some other piece of machinery. But when it touched my skin, I had a momentary flash of the *Other Side*, of the old man who last used it wiping his sweaty palms against the cloth, stuffing it down into his shirt pocket, sweaty from the summer heat.

The memory disgusted me, but it could have been much worse.

In Martha's case, I couldn't be sure what I was walking into. She materialized from the earth, mass and shape filling the athletics sweater and lifting it from the ground so that it hung over her body as I touched it; the bear emblem snapping and snarling as the loose fabric twisted on her wiry frame. She was as I remembered, no more than fifteen, an innocent ring of yellow and red flowers twisted around her dark hair like a crown. Martha picked off Jaak's begonias one by one, each petal crumbling to dust between her fingers before drifting down the stream.

I watched the current take them, color fading around me.

Soon, there was only darkness.

Only black.

Chapter Fifteen

Time moved slowly on the *Other Side*, like watching a fruit fly pushing through an encasement of molasses. With no reference point, I fell slowly yet all at once found myself slammed against a cold, hard surface in the darkness.

There was no anchor, no one to guide me to a specific place in time. The world around me had reduced itself to an indiscernible void, but still, my back ached from connecting with something tangible, something real. My eyes struggled to readjust, and I wished for a lantern or a flashlight, though I feared what I might see, if I could see at all.

"Martha?"

The benefit of Ezra's religious education was that I'd been equipped with any number of theories about the *Other Side*, wanted or not. Ezra liked to speculate on what it meant, why I could see it, why others couldn't. Many cultures spoke in some form or other about some kind of spiritual plane, and many of them spoke of it as a place of duality: a place of either immense joy or immense pain, depending on the choices you made and the kind of person you were.

Whether you were born and committed to a religion that believed in the inevitability of heaven and hell, or simply a college student about to take shrooms for the first time, there was a common understanding that whatever happened before was going to determine the dichotomous fate of what happened after; what happened while you were alive would determine your ultimate fate once dead, while what happened sober would determine the trajectory of your trip.

In all my experiences of the *Other Side*, however, I hadn't encountered such divisiveness. There was pain, there was joy, but they existed together, mingling with one another, overlapping; the amount of each confined to what had been cached through each person's lifetime. Some moments were pleasant and flowery, ones that begged to be relived. Others were as consuming and difficult to handle as they'd been when first experienced.

"Gabriel?" I tried calling out instead, met again with silence.

I imagined that perhaps the *Other Side* I now wandered was like the thinnest edge of a coin, tiny canyons embossed throughout it, full of highs and lows. Ultimately, the coin was comprised mostly of just two sides, one side good, one side bad, but my work was done within the confines of that thin, nondescript bridge in between the two. A place that existed only as a way to connect one side to the other and form a singular whole.

Ezra once told me there were two different kinds of time: There was Chronos, linear, unstoppable time as we all know it, and then there was Kairos, those moments when time seems to stand still, that seem to transcend linear order. Like the seemingly infinite expanse of time when you realize you just hit a homerun at the bottom of the ninth, or that frozen moment occupied by the first kiss with a lover. Ezra described it as the time when God acts.

That's what I imagined this *Other Side* was.

That was where I did my work.

The dreamscape rippled, contracting around me. I sat back to watch as lightning struck repeatedly through the void. Light was separated from darkness as electrical currents pulsed through the dark. Along the horizon, cells divided within the orb that slowly formed around them, separating what was without and trapping what was within amidst an ocean of sound and vibration. From within that orb, a mass of flesh and bone slowly developed to form an island.

The island pulsed with life.

The contractions continued to ripple through what was once void. Pain came as I felt the orb begin to close around me on every side. It squeezed me, tighter and tighter, until blinding light gave way to a land full of shapes, forms, and creatures. All at once, the pain was forgotten, and new life stood at the center of all that had already been called to existence.

"It's a boy. Congratulations."

Martha cried when presented with her child and, alone in the hospital and absent a swaddling cloth, she pulled her sweater from the chair and wrapped it around her son. She rocked him, nuzzling his forehead and singing soft lullabies. She was older, and her hair was different, her dark bangs chopped off into a bob cut that tickled against the baby's brow.

Still, I'd have recognized her anywhere.

I rocked from within the comfort of her arms, feeling the love of a mother, encapsulated within the vantage of the wide-eyed baby boy. When baby Gabriel blinked, the cosmic arrangement shuffled and his heartbeat grew faster, enclosed in an unfamiliar darkness as the setting blurred in transition around us.

"I won't let him hurt you," Martha cried, rocking her child again. Gabriel's faced pressed against the bear insignia on the sweater she wore; the garment had pulled me towards a specific recollection of itself. "I won't let them take you from me. Here." She pressed a stuffed bear into his arms and instructed him, "Hold onto this and don't come out until I tell you."

The boy's pleas were indiscernible, as though I was separated from him by a layer of water. I watched Martha slip out of the closet and felt every animated throb of Gabriel's heart as muffled shouts shook the closet door. Finally, shaking with the gale force of a tornado blowing past it, the door collapsed to nothingness. Martha stood on the other side, stretching out her hand.

"Grab your bag, Gabriel!"

Gabriel tried to dart back to his bedroom, but Martha grabbed his wrist. I felt distant now, watching from somewhere outside of him, but I could still feel the sting of Martha's grip and the ache of bone as he tried to struggle away. It was dizzying. It was fast. The changes were hard to recall as one quick memory overlaid another before transitioning into another memory entirely.

"Hungry, Momma."

Martha and a man were visible through the kitchen doorway, and Gabriel's cries went unheard, or perhaps ignored. Gabriel pulled a chair up to the counter and teetered on one foot to reach the cookie jar against the wall. He looked over again at Martha. "Hungry, Momma." Each jump made me nauseous, and I fought to glean anything from the scenes as I rippled in and out of consciousness. Everything went black for a moment, and then my eyes opened to a tall man.

"The hell do you think you're doing?" he boomed.

I took the boy's vantage and tumbled. The room spun. My cheek stung. The chair toppled over next to me, and I could hardly see the kitchen through my sobs. Childish screams masked the sound of Martha's protests, but the thud of her body against the door frame quaked through the floor, leaving a chasm open in its path. Enmeshed within one consciousness, Gabriel and I fell through the pit as it opened and landed cross-legged in front of a TV.

"Welcome to your CVS News Report Tonight."

Gabriel focused on the screen and chomped on buttery noodles from the bowl in his lap. The sound of gratuitous grunts and moans from the couch behind him hardly registered, but I could hear it, the primitive mating grunts of a man that didn't seem to be on the winning side of brain development. Martha didn't seem entirely there; she stared at the ceiling and occasionally muttered some noncommittal response when the man asked, "You like that?"

"Mrhhmmm."

Gabriel fumbled for the remote to turn up the volume, but I was transfixed by the image of Martha and her partner reflected in the glass screen, the way I might gawk at a car accident. I wanted to scream, though my throat felt so swollen I was sure nothing would come of it if I tried.

"Today," the news anchor announced, "we have the latest updates in your community. Housewife takes her life at forty-two, prompts debate about efficacy of social service system." His face turned so that he was making eye contact with me through the screen. A smile erupted slowly across his face as he leaned forward, and I was wondering how much closer he could possibly get when it happened: His forehead pushed against the glass until it broke through the screen.

The little boy didn't so much as flinch, not missing a beat as he maneuvered the slippery butter noodles to his lips. They wiggled on the tip of the fork, all but a few falling off by time they reached his mouth. He fished in the bowl for more, a repeated process of taking what he could get, while I looked in horrified awe toward the scene unfolding in the TV.

"A horse trailer overturned on number 2 highway just outside of town earlier this afternoon. The driver, a thirty-three-year-old woman, taken to the hospital in critical condition." The TV host's voice rose to maddened squeals. He jumped on his desk, thumping his hands against the surface like an ape. Blood dripped down his forehead where the glass from the TV screen had punctured him. "Gabriel, stop watching—"

I blinked, and the TV screen was suddenly intact, the host safely back behind his desk, interviewing someone about something. Something about the political climate and who was responsible for the country's deficit, and where the government aught to be focusing their spending efforts. Something about something about somebody, pointing fingers between good and bad.

I shot to my feet, searching for an exit, jarred when the memory changed.

"Give her this."

Martha's sorrow was the only thing about her that seemed alive as she handed him the wrinkled paper. Her flesh was pale, her skin stretched thinly over pointed bones, eyes ringed by shadows as she bundled Gabriel into a familiar winter coat. I panicked at the sight of it, sweat seeping through every pore, wanting to absorb every detail, terrified I was only wasting time.

"Come on, we have to go." She zipped up his jacket.

Gabriel responded by opening his mouth so wide that his jaw began to pull away, allowing passage for dozens of Koels to emerge from his smile and begin circling above him. They moved so quickly around him that his form was barely visible through the black tornado that enrobed him. I cinched my palms to my ears to tolerate the piercing force of his screams, pushing forward into the mass of creatures as they chattered and clicked around him.

Tick, tock, tick, tock, tick, tock, tick—

"Gabriel!" I was screaming now, certain that the words sounded like gibberish as they left my mouth. Spit bubbled from my lips as I sobbed their names. "Martha?"

The air that churned around us pushed me to my knees more than once before I finally broke into the inner circle of Koels; they didn't try to grab for me since I was offering no resistance. I just wanted to get to the boy. Every muscle in my body strained as I fought to stay upright against the force of the whirlwind and reach for Gabriel. My knees throbbed where the bones had slammed against the ground, grinding the cartilage as I pressed forward.

The world had gone silent—save for the ringing in my ears, one of which had begun to pool blood down my neck. Even my own voice was inaudible as I screamed for Gabriel to take my hand, turning my head away to shield against the sting of the gyrating vortex.

I could hardly look up; the funnel was too strong.

"Gabriel, Martha, I—"

The Koels halted and turned at attention toward us. With the force of their movements suddenly gone, my body snapped forward, head hitting the floor with enough force to take the entire world with it, rendering everything back into complete, crippling darkness.

I tried to wiggle my fingers, but nothing happened. My eyes fluttered open, allowing light and vague forms to pierce through, only to fade to black again as my eyelids clamped back down. A small voice cut through the aches and pains that implored me to surrender myself back to the darkness. I willed my fingers to move until, finally, they twitched, but it was moving my lips that proved the bigger challenge. It felt like my mouth was sealed by thick, sticky honey.

"Murr-huh. Murrth-ah?" I managed, slurring the words.

"Mommy?"

When I was finally able to focus on my surroundings, it was Gabriel I saw, not Martha. He looked the same as he had when he'd arrived on my doorstep, bundled tightly in winter gear and soaked from the snow, cheeks pale and rosy; only, he looked older now, standing a little straighter and a little taller as he searched the woods alone in the dark.

"Mom?" he whispered, jolting at the sound of something moving in the bush. A rabbit scurried out of the underbrush and past his feet, nearly upending him. He held his hand against his heart, and I swore I could see each beat moving his fingers up and down.

"Gabriel!" I managed to stand, limping behind him at first as I grew accustomed to my legs, then faster as I caught up. I tried to grab his arm and turn him back to me, but my hand moved through him. He continued to hobble forward, calling out for his mother.

The temperature dropped.

He screamed.

A lone couch sat in the middle of the road, soaked through with rain or melted snow perhaps—it didn't matter. His mother was laying across it, her fingers a sickly shade of blue, her skin white and nearly translucent against her bones. She stared up at the wash of stars through the treetops. Gabriel screamed and nudged her repeatedly, begging for her to wake up, but the water bloated corpse only seemed to disintegrate under his touch.

I turned away to vomit, looking up to find myself standing toe to toe with a Koel. My shoulders heaved as I tried to draw in air that no longer seemed to exist, sucked into the dark void that had taken all light and warmth with it, sharing none. The shadow chittered violently, others coming to join into its symphony, whole body jerking with distorted movements. All at once, the Koels froze into contorted positions around each other, around me, except for the first.

"What do you want...?" My voice cracked.

The Koel leaned closer to my face, pulling me into its gravity so that stumbling back proved useless. I staggered back a few feet, only to blink and find that he was standing as close as he had been before. My breath clouded around me in wavering clouds as everything inside of me seized up; I felt like my blood was congealing into cement.

I repeated the question, screaming it this time, voice still cracking involuntarily as fear clenched my windpipe. In a final effort, I puffed my chest at it, only to have it jerk its head toward me, forcing my eyes shut from how close it had gotten to my face; I shrank away from its presence, tucking in my chin, pulling it against my chest so hard I thought I might snap my own neck trying to pull away from the awful creature. Its breath washed against me like a cold wind badgering a ship captain stranded at sea—the harbinger of a nasty storm yet to come.

I screamed louder yet, though my body continued to get smaller. Instead of answer, it reached out and ran its icy tendrils millimetres away from my cheek, so close I felt as though the hairs were being burned off from the cold, though it never actually touched my skin. My whole body shook pathetically, vibrating under its gaze, and I found myself still trying to clamor away from it even though it had already proven useless.

It never touched me, only raised a hand and pointed at Martha in the final moments before I lurched awake in the clearing. I tripped and fell as I tried to bolt to my feet, away from the sound of Gabriel's renewed screams, gripping my skull and falling back against the dirt, panicked and thrashing like a fish suddenly pulled from the water.

The deafening clicks and cackles of the Koels still echoed from the *Other Side*, and I would not soon forget that final glimpse at Martha; the Koel pointed a finger toward the corpse and opened its mouth, a familiar sound projecting from deep within its dark gash of a smile.

I paled and went completely still on the floor of the clearing, tears streaking my cheeks, realizing with full veracity the terrible danger that awaited Martha, or perhaps, had already found her.

The Koel had told me so:

Tick, tock.

Chapter Sixteen

"I don't have time for this. I told you I needed time to think about it and you—goddamnit." Ezra shoved aside odds and ends in the side table searching for his schoolboard ID. I turned my head to hear him, my right ear consumed by gentle ringing; a prelude to deafness that was surprisingly loud. My ear wasn't bleeding when I came back from the *Other Side*, which was no small relief, but I still felt like I'd stood too close to the speakers at a concert, and my skin was windburned.

"I *saw* it!" I insisted. "I was right. She needs—"

"You don't know what you saw!"

"I know not everything was *real*," I conceded, pausing until he turned to me. I stared at the ceiling, trying to take a deep breath that didn't want to come. "But I've never seen something like that before, something that wasn't in the past. It has to mean something, don't you—"

"Why do you think you can trust those...things?"

"I don't, but why would they—?"

Ezra raised his hands irately as we moved into the bathroom. He shaved the stubble from his chin, cursing as he nicked his jawline with the razor, preparing for the meetings that awaited him. I handed him a towel as he added, "I think you're reading too much into it."

"*This* was proof!"

"Forgive me for not trusting your feelings," Ezra retorted, rolling his eyes with a flourish. "It's Gabriel that's hurt by it if you're wrong. Do you understand how bright that kid's future is with the right help? Even with everything he's been through, the staff are still saying he's lightyears ahead of some of his peers. And that's *without* being nurtured. You really wanna take him under with the *assumption* that what you saw means something? Maybe this is your feelings—"

"Intuition," I corrected. "You've never doubted me before."

"You've never been so invested before." Ezra shook his head, frustrated by the semantic game. "You're making assumptions based on something that happened ten years ago! Even if you do find her, what then? Maybe she's too sick to take care of him, or worse, she's—"

"He can confirm if what I saw in the memories was true."

"Leading the witness, your honor."

I rolled my eyes in disgust. "Oh, stop it. You—"

"We can give him a new life." Ezra turned away, clutching the ID he finally found kicked under the bed. He gathered up his tablet and charger, taking one last look around the room before heading toward the hallway. He glanced at his watch and paused just outside the door.

The hall felt gaudy, still strung up with crisscrossed streamers Ezra and Gabriel decorated for my birthday dinner the night before. I'd held my tongue through pot stickers and a chocolate cake that Gabriel picked out so decadent it was hard to stomach more than a few bites.

"What if he doesn't *want* a new life?" I yelped, following him. "He doesn't want a new life; he wants it the way it was! He wants his mother back the way she was."

"He does, or you do?" We lingered, suspended in silence, my mouth dangling open dumbly until he raised a brow. "I've had a shit day, Nev. My interview's in fifteen minutes, and if I want to sleep tonight, I have a meeting first thing tomorrow I should have started prepping for three hours ago. I don't have time for this tonight. I don't—"

"Your meeting's not 'till ten. You can—"

"No." He shook his head, lifting a hand to stop me when I tried to go to him. His brow scrunched together as though he was staring at a puzzle he couldn't make sense of. "You went behind my back." Ezra frowned, my decision finally taking on its full weight, a splatter of black paint across our family portrait. "I said I needed time to think about it, and you—"

"I'm trying to make the right decision for everyone."

"Maybe there isn't one. Have you considered that?" His body wilted as though he had no energy left for basic functions, a robot about to power off. "It's not a special extension of what you can do, Nev; it's a sign that you've lost control. Do you not realize how insanely dangerous it is to be this emotionally invested in—?'

He sighed when I squared my shoulders.

"If you can't see it, I don't know how to help you," he said, the disappointment in his voice cutting.

He shook his head and pulled the office door shut a little too hard behind him so that it shook the walls, jostling the mirror in the hallway. I pulled away from my reflection, nearly bumping into Gabriel as I turned. My hand pressed against my chest, though my heart continued to pick up speed like a steam engine crossing a threshold, gathering momentum until it could no longer be stopped without time and a great amount of opposing effort.

"Gabriel, how long have you been—"

"What's 'going Under'?"

Chapter Seventeen

"I'm ready!" he insisted, kneeling on the bed, bouncing as though every inch of him was filled to bursting with his readiness. When I held a finger to my lips, Gabriel lowered his voice, allowing me to listen for Ezra's presence, hoping beyond hope I could sneak away to brush the horses or tend to the garden without having to interact with him again after his interview.

"You shouldn't have heard any of that." *Tick, tock.*

"I can *help*," he promised, pouting.

"You don't even know what I'd need help with. It's like…having a dream," I explained, pinching the skin between my brows, toes tapping nervously against the hardwood. "You can't always control whether you have a bad dream or a good dream, which can be scary if—"

"She's sick! I know she's sick!" My stomach rolled as he said it, proof of what I already knew. "I heard you say it! We have to bring her back! We have to," he said, tugging my sleeve.

"Why are you—*Stop!*" I gripped him by the shoulders and held him away from me, the sleeves of my shirt pulled over my palms to weaken the contact. My heart pounded emphatically in my chest; a vein throbbed in my neck. *Tick, tock.* "Gabriel, you need to calm down before—"

"Please, please, *please*," he wept.

"It's not—"

"She'll be all alone! Gary," Gabriel whimpered, stopping to wipe away snot as it bubbled under his nose, "he doesn't like when we're sick. My tummy hurt and I had to throw up, and he screamed, and I had to go to my room and stay there until I wasn't sick anymore and didn't—"

"Gabriel, it's not the same kind of sick as a tummy ache."

"I'll do whatever you need me to, I promise! And I won't let you have a bad dream, and we can keep it a secret just like when you let me read *Sir Ivanguard*. I didn't even tell anyone that you read it to me, not even Ezra, and I didn't even have bad dreams from the pictures."

"Ezra would find out..." I almost pointed out that we hadn't actually finished reading the story, had hardly begun, in fact, but stopped myself just shy of painting myself into a corner. For a moment, I felt like I could hear Jaak's voice goading me, urging me to act before it was too late, before Martha ended up dead just like him, and all because I'd done nothing.

"We could have a code," Gabriel whispered, wiping the tears from his eyes, hearing the office door open and Ezra's footsteps approaching from down the hall. "We could say that we're going out riding together and I'll say I want some time—"

Ezra opened the door, blinking at my presence.

"I was just going," I said, holding eye contact with Gabriel for a moment too long, just long enough that I was certain Ezra noticed the tension in the room stretching taut. "Gabriel was just asking if I wanted to go for a ride tomorrow. Begging me, practically."

"Oh?" Ezra raised an eyebrow.

"Yeah," Gabriel said, jumping to his feet and running to hug me around the legs. "I told her I want her to take me out into the woods and we could maybe have a picnic lunch and she could give me some more riding lessons 'cause I've been doing so good at it in the barn and the weather is so nice now and so we should go for a real trail ride with my own horse and—"

"Tomorrow morning," I decided, looking at Ezra earnestly.

"Maybe I'll move my schedule and come," he said.

Ezra examined us both a little too closely, and I wondered what he was seeing. I nodded, doing my best to smile as though it was the most welcomed thing he could have suggested, but finally, he shook his head.

"You guys go ahead without me," he decided. "I was just coming to let Gabriel know I'm gonna start making dinner before I prep for my meetings tomorrow, if he wants to help. You getting hungry, kiddo?"

Gabriel nodded, holding his breath until Ezra wandered out. Gabriel released a torrent of semi-whispered questions about our 'ride,' falling silent when I pointed a finger and gave a disapproving shake of the head. "We'll leave around nine thirty," I promised, ruffling his hair. "We can talk more on the way, but let's not mention it until then, okay?"

He nodded his head aggressively. "And make sure you get some sleep tonight. I don't want you half asleep tomorrow," I cautioned. Sanctimonious advice from someone who knew with certainty they would hardly close their own eyes, let alone get any sleep themself.

When Gabriel left to join Ezra in the kitchen, I sat on the edge of the twin-sized bed that never fully belonged to anyone, looked at the boxes stacked on the top shelf of the closet, covered in dust and cobwebs, and tried to draw in a breath that never fully came.

A draft snaked in through the old windows. The rays of sun beating through the glass fanned themselves across my cheek but brought no warmth. I squirmed under the light's touch, overcome by the feeling of being trapped under a magnifying glass as the orange glow of dusk fell over the room; a harbinger of the darkness to come.

Tick, tock.

Chapter Eighteen

"Have you picked a good memory from home? And thought about it until it's like a picture in your mind?" I fabricated my most convincing smile for Gabriel, trying not to distract him from steering the creature below him; the pony seemed massive, relative to his tiny figure. Sunlight streamed through the treetops but did little to light the way.

He nodded. "Mhm. When Mom invited—"

"Hold onto it 'til we get to the spot," I interrupted, shaking my head. I stroked Nidhya's neck to calm her. "I don't want to dilute it; you might start adding details if you tell me now."

The scent of the woods washed over us as we wandered away from my usual spot by the creek; I closed my eyes, letting the bath of light and sound and color and smell around us absorb me, though it did little to ease the tension steadily accruing between my shoulder blades. I tried to relax my jaw as I exhaled, shoving away my apprehension.

"Will Ezra be mad at me?" Gabriel frowned.

"No, just me," I assured, letting Nidhya guide us along the path forged by the creek, giving direction only when I pulled the reins to turn onto one of the bridges. Gabriel held his breath as we crossed the stream, relaxing just as quickly on the other side when the wooden beams no longer creaked below us. "You're sure you're ready to do this, kiddo? You feel relaxed and ready to go?"

I pinched the bridge of my nose to ward off the quiet warnings that hammered through my skull as the trees thinned out into an open field full of tall grass and wildflowers; some bloomed, others would remain dormant until spring passed away into summer.

Gabriel dismounted and pulled blankets out of our packs, spreading them on the ground as though he'd done it a thousand times.

"We don't have to do this, you know that, right?" I rested a hand on his shoulder, forcing him to halt his frenzy of preparations. He tried to jerk away, but I kept the pressure of my hand firm. "If you're not feeling up to it, we can go back, and Ezra and I can find a different—"

"We have to," Gabriel demanded, jabbing a finger against my thigh. "You don't understand! We have to find my mom! We have to! Ezra will never let us find her. It'll be too late," he insisted, though I struggled to focus as I watched the clearing around us fill with lanky shadows that watched with vested fascination as tears filled Gabriel's eyes.

He watched me take out my thermos. I took a deep drink from the passion tea, letting the sweet taste of it seep over my tongue, realizing that my hands were shaking as I pressed it against my lips. I offered it to Gabriel, who took one sip and grimaced.

"Not your taste, huh?"

Gabriel sank down onto the blanket as though I wasn't there, using the side of his hand to form a tiny pile in the dirt. I joined him on the ground, adding to his pile as I waited for him to work through whatever thoughts had his mouth opening and closing repeatedly like a garage door with a blocked sensor. Finally, he sighed and looked up, awaiting further instruction.

My hand swept out across the blanket, gesturing for him to lay down as I did the same. "We'll be right here on the blanket, but you won't feel it; your memory will just become very real, almost like a video game. But we'll be safe right here, like we're taking a nap. I'm going to count down from five and then it'll start," I explained, taking his hand in mine, shifting until I was comfortable.

"Five, four, three, two..."

In the final moment before the clearing went black, dread overtook me. It felt like being on the cusp of sleep only to have an insecurity weed itself into my head, hold me captive for the rest of the evening, and rob me of sleep. A lump formed in my throat that was so difficult to swallow I felt myself choking on it. I was unable to repress it as I teetered between one side and the next. I tried to pull back at the last second, sparing Gabriel, but I couldn't pull back fast enough.

Gabriel's hand went limp.

Chapter Nineteen

Gabriel waved a hand in front of his mom's face, frowning when she didn't respond. A man's arm wrapped around her on the couch, his dark hair pressed against the crown of her head. Pizza boxes laid flipped open, their contents half eaten, alongside game pieces scattered across a board on the table. Martha and the man seemed happy, bright smiles glued to their faces, though their eyes followed us like a living painting as we circled them, eyes wide with quiet warnings.

"This is Gary?" I asked cautiously, leaning in for a closer look.

"Nu uh. That's Uncle Andy. He, um...Uncle Andy came over and we...we had pizza. It was the good kind that I like," he explained as I examined the box on the table, trying to see the logo. My shoulders drooped at the generic franchise name, revealing nothing about the location.

I gave him a short nod, urging Gabriel to continue.

"What else?" I asked.

The room was unnaturally silent, and he turned white so quickly that there was no time to react; his bottom lip trembled so violently that he could do little more than whisper, "I'm sorry" as the apartment door burst open and the memory turned sour—he'd remembered only the positive bits and pieces of it, repressed the negatives that now overflowed like dirty laundry from a hamper. *Should have prepared him first.* Ezra's voice entered my head. *This is your fault.*

A man barrelled inside the apartment unit, his blond hair thinning at the edges, though his face seemed too young for him to be balding. I tried to look past him at the door number, but a barrage of Koels followed in behind him. Gabriel wailed at the sight of the man, delighting the Koels, their forms bumping into one another as they tried to reach Gabriel.

"Under the couch!" I shoved at him like he was an old suitcase that needed cramming into a closet, his tiny body frozen as he stared at the shadows. The bottom of the old couch was just high enough to squeeze him under, but there was no cover for me as the balding man seized Andy by the collar of his shirt, hoisting him away from Martha.

"You stay here. Don't come out until I tell you," I cautioned, only making Gabriel cry harder. Martha struggled as she tried to pry the two men apart, but her arms were too skinny and useless—not just compared to the men but compared to almost anyone. Uncle Andy stood out now against the balding man, who I presumed was Gary; Andy's lip was swollen and bloody where Gary's knuckles bit into him, his nose crooked and no doubt broken from the altercation.

"I told you to stay away from here!" Gary screamed.

"Martha doesn't seem to—" Andy was cut short as another fist collided against the side of his temple. He threw his forearm up at the last minute, blocking it only partially as it whizzed past and hit its mark. Gary's face turned dark red, his cheeks blotchy and hot with adrenaline.

"Gabe, sweetie, don't come out until I tell you," Martha cooed.

"*Mom-ee-ee-ee—*"

My head shot up as the words I'd spoken to Gabriel only moments before echoed from Martha's lips. She knelt beside the sofa where he hid, though she looked forward as she spoke to keep the attention of the two men away from Gabriel. She held a trembling finger against her lips to quiet him, eyes wide when he continued sobbing for her.

The room spun with dizzying speed; if she knew he was under the couch, then Gabriel had already been there. I hadn't protected him by hiding him, only fulfilled his role in a memory that was as fixed as concrete. *You're an idiot. Gabriel is going to get hurt because of you.*

A cramp tore through my stomach.

My breaths came faster as I searched the room.

Gary shoved Andy so that he rolled over the table, toppling the television onto the floor. Uncle Andy's face was busted badly enough that I hardly recognized him as the same man who was seated on the couch when we arrived; his skin seemed to swell and melt off his bones, a by-product of Gabriel's fear altering the memories.

Martha darted toward the men, screaming.

"Gabriel, I need more time," I urged when he begged to leave. I tried to explain that we couldn't just take her with us, but he didn't understand, screaming her name inconsolably as tears soaked his shirt.

I pushed aside his cries, hastening my search. Beside the front door, a key hook was fastened to the wall with old mail still tucked onto a shelf above it. I went to the hanger, tearing open each envelope only to find that the letters were all garbled, save for the vibrant image of a toy store advertisement that must have caught Gabriel's eye.

The hallway door shook as I frantically jerked the handle, but when it opened, led impossibly to the kitchen, the cupboard doors all open and empty as I clamored for something, anything, that would tell me where she was. Gabriel screamed, drawing not only my attention, but a Koel's; he was being dragged out from under the couch, clutching at his hair as though some invisible hand was pulling it, though there was nothing and no one there to move his body.

"Mom-ee-ee-*eee*," he choked.

"Gabriel!" I screamed, reaching out to him a moment too late; I moved fast enough to shield him from the Koel but too slowly to protect myself. A tendril pierced through my bicep, tearing muscle and skin in the same millisecond like a thick needle. The shadow wailed and clicked as I tried to pull Gabriel to the next room. There was no time to register my own pain before Gabriel's body contorted as if someone or something had struck him in the stomach.

My head spun at the loud, familiar thwack of skin against skin. I expected to see Uncle Andy on the floor again; instead, Martha was sprawled on the ground, cheek red between the fingers she had fanned against it. Gary reached out and picked her up by the fabric of her sweater, tossing her hard into the couch, her slender body giving him little resistance.

At the same instance, Gabriel yelped, neck snapping back.

"Mo-om-meeee!"

"Gabriel—"

Gary picked up Martha again and shook her. Her head snapped back on frail neck muscles before lolling forward, eyes drifting lazily open and closed as though trying to focus. I looked at Gabriel, who seemed to know more was coming, feeling everything his mother felt as it happened to her. He scooted backwards, eyes wide with terror as he stared at the Koels standing guard around the room. They turned to him as Martha's body went slack.

"Stay the hell away!" Gary tossed Andy, now matted with blood, out the door. The outside was faded, no doubt where an old 'no soliciting' sign had fallen off, followed by a fake, golden '62'. Its veneer had chipped away, revealing cheap, black plastic underneath. The door slammed shut just as I glimpsed the familiar, piss-yellow-green hallway carpet.

"Gabriel, open the hall door," I begged, watching Gary slam it shut too quickly for me to trust what I saw. Another cramp rippled through my belly as I thought of what waited beyond the door.

"W-why?"

"Just do it, please!" I begged, sidestepping an overly curious Koel as I urged Gabriel to the door of the unit. The pain in my arm radiated through the rest of my body; blood dripped down my arm, droplets raining from my fingertips. Koels jostled in a frenzy behind us, blockading the balcony, barring the view out the window.

"I need you to think about it really hard, okay? We're almost done," I urged when he hesitated to close his eyes, pressing my other palm against his cheek to turn his attention away from the shadows. "I think I know where she is. I don't need to know the address, I just need you to try to remember the carpet. What was on the carpet?"

He furrowed his brow and closed his eyes as he thought about it with the intensity of a law student studying for their BAR exam; the door swung open as he remembered, allowing us to step through onto a stained green carpet, adorned with massive, ugly dahlia patterns. There was only one other place I'd seen those flowers before, and the thought of going back made me dizzy; I grabbed Gabriel's hand and pulled us out before either of us could faint from the effort.

A man was watching from the trees when we surfaced.

He disappeared into the woods when we stirred, a blur of red and yellow flannel absorbing into the forest. Despite the nausea and vertigo brought on by standing too quickly, I bolted upright and ran to the treeline to follow, finding nothing but the horses waiting for us on the other side of the trail while songbirds flittered between branches.

I wanted to follow him, to go deeper into the shadows, but Gabriel was crying, not moving except for his shoulders heaving up and down each time he cried out for his mother.

I wondered how much harder he would have cried if he could see the shadow looming above him, its smile gaping, eyes wide as dessert plates and unblinking as it chittered.

Tick, tock.

Chapter Twenty

Pain shot up my arm as I pounded on the apartment door. The bandages wrapping my bicep had already soaked through twice since leaving home. I tried to breathe through the pain and hunger and fatigue that coursed through me, eyes fixated on the dahlias below my feet as I swayed. The hallway smelled pungently of mildew and smoke.

Someone in the unit called out: "I'm coming!"

Knock, knock, knock—The man with balding hair from Gabriel's memory was suddenly in front of me as the door swung open, his face contorting as he stared down at me, snapping, "The fuck you want?"

I blinked to sort out reality from the remnants of the vision still lingering from the *Other Side*. It cut in and out of my periphery like a scene spliced into an old movie reel. Each time it overlapped, I could see hoards of Koels waiting somewhere just beyond, revelling in the thousands of unsavory memories lingering in the building from those unfortunate enough to live there.

"My...um, I'm..."

I'd already seen two people buried before their time. Jaak's old apartment was only a floor up, and Martha's mom had lived only a few blocks away in a nicer part of the area. Both had taken their last breaths in that neighborhood, and now, there was Martha, back home again, though I wasn't sure for how much longer.

"You on drugs or something?" Gary relaxed as understanding washed over him, fear settling into annoyance. "Tommy don't live here no more. Go down to 23 if you're looking for—"

"I'm here for Martha," I interrupted.

"The fuck you want with her?"

"I'm a friend."

"Martha doesn't have friends." Gary crossed his arms, burlier than in the memory. I processed the gut protruding from under his sweat-strained t-shirt, the stubble on his face that was well-beyond that of a five o'clock shadow, yet still juvenile enough not to be confused for a beard. His jaw was heavy-set, squared toward me pompously despite the cheap, yellow-brown beer bottle in his hand. His thick fingers flexed around the neck of the bottle, opening, closing, opening...

"I'm a friend," I repeated, watching his fingers.

"Bullshit."

I shoved his chest, startling him enough to force him back a step into the doorway. As my hands connected with his shirt, I felt a burst of energy shoot up my arms, into my shoulders, sending my heartbeat into a galloping frenzy. I hit him again, calling out for Martha over his shoulder despite the late hour, straining for a better look inside.

My voice echoed down the hallway, drawing out some of the neighbors. I thought I recognized some of them from what felt like another life, a life where I had a brother, and my skin didn't crawl every night when I tried to close my eyes. An old man stepped out onto the vomit green dahlias and stared at us from afar, lighting a cigarette between his teeth. He took a long pull and ashed directly onto the carpet, eyes wrinkling as he tried to place me.

"Get out of my way, or—"

"Or what?" Gary's laugh was almost pleasant.

I thought of Ezra, laying at home in bed, unable to find me if he wanted to. He hadn't texted, hadn't called. Maybe he'd started to get up, then thought better of it, guessing he'd find me curled up on the living room couch where I'd slept every night since that first small lie. Or perhaps he'd known why I'd worn such a heavy sweater to bed and wasn't ready to talk about it.

"Hello?" Gary snapped his fingers in front of my face twice, my eyes glazed over again as I shifted between time and place. I blinked up at him, heart still thudding wildly, crazed energy still alighting every limb and extremity as adrenaline coursed through me.

"Who is it?" A woman's voice.

"Shut up—"

"Martha!" I screamed, resuming the steady thump of my fists against Gary's chest. I tried to wedge myself between him and the opening with my shoulder, yelling out for her until he grabbed my arms. "Let me go! Martha! It's me! Martha—let me go, you piece of shit!"

"Son of a..."

Gary shifted to grab me, and I could see her curled up on the couch. She was small and pale—hardly a lump beneath the throw blanket she was buried under. Her raven roots peaked out from below a bleach job that fried the rest of her hair. The black satin sheen of her hair from my memories was now matte and yellow, but still, it was undeniably her. She was still breathing.

"She's coming with me," I insisted, watching the neighbors slink back inside, no longer wanting to bear witness to whatever dispute had interrupted their slumber.

Gary spat at my feet.

I rushed him then, arm outstretched, hand reaching, fingers splayed out so that they could clip around his neck like a brace. His Adam's apple drove into my palm as my skin touched his. I didn't squeeze. I didn't push. I didn't strain my sore arm choking the air out of him.

All I needed was the touch.

"Gare-bear," I mumbled, gripping his neck as a thousand images flooded in and out around me. I shook my head, shifting through his memories as they came to me. His eyes widened and his muscles went limp. I hovered between this side and the *Other Side*, like I had while giving Julie her first, small glimpse of what was to come, only this time, the goal was not to heal old wounds or acclimate him to the process. The desire to hurt him consumed me.

"How did you..."

"Daddy wasn't in the picture at all, was he?" I guessed, focusing on the images that sifted in and out around us, taking guesses at what I saw. "He left—no, your mom never knew who he was, did she? There were lots of them, weren't there? Lots of men, in and out, all the time?"

"Please," he begged, hand reaching out as though he would gladly give me anything to make the pain stop. It was too late; he couldn't give what I already decided to take.

The Koels surrounded me, leaning in, reaching out; they could graze me, in that in-between place, but the damage was limited. Their tendrils licked at my skin, leaving what might have been mistaken for cat scratches or even paper cuts.

"She used to dance, and you would go and watch," I continued, diverting my attention from the Koels that snaked around me like the tendrils of Medusa's hair, swimming around me zealously as they wrapped around Gary. "There was someone there that took care of you, and then—and then what happened? What happened to the woman? The blonde?" I asked, watching her faded image lean down in front of a small child hovering behind Gary.

The man's face dripped with fresh tears.

"Let me...go..."

"I get it. She disappeared." I had to guess; the images were too disjointed without fully submerging myself in them. I followed patterns, his whole body vibrating each time I touched on something real. "Whoever she was, she disappeared. Didn't say goodbye. Didn't reach out. Didn't give two shits about her little Gare-bear. She gave you that name?"

"Please..."

"Martha is leaving. Like it or not," I promised as he thrashed, falling to the floor when I released him.

He gripped his head like an aneurism burst. Tears dripped from his eyes and snot bubbled under his nose. The Koels, unseen and untouched, descended on him like boorish scavengers; they couldn't touch him, couldn't mark his flesh with their cold touch, but still, they took something from him, something that even I couldn't see as he cried and cried and cried.

"Martha?" I ran to the couch, pulling back the blanket to prop her up. "It's me. Hey, Martha. Focus on me," I insisted, taking her hands. Bruises littered her arms; none of them seeming to heal the way they should. Her breaths were shallow, her pulse a whisper.

"What...?"

"I'll explain later," I promised, hoisting her feathery body over my shoulder when she refused to stand. Martha looked around the room in a daze, fighting against me when she saw Gary still laying fetal in the doorway. "He's okay. He's fine. We need to get out of here before he realizes that—stop." I took her hand, forcing her mind back to better memories, happier times, when she resisted me, the uncoordinated flailing of her weakened limbs more like ribbons tossing in the wind.

The Koels followed behind us in a procession.

Tick, tock.

Chapter Twenty-One

"There was no other way," I promised, arms crossed over my chest. Ezra nodded slowly, eyes glazing over as he stared at Martha. She laid nestled beneath a quilt in one of the guest cabins, blanket snug against her chin to ward off a chill that only she could feel.

"No other way," Ezra repeated numbly, as though the words held no meaning for him. He shook his head and turned away, unable to look at her as she trembled. Below the blanket, track marks lined her arms, dark scars on thin, milky skin. "Are we going to tell Gabriel?"

"We'll have to." I said, not expecting my voice to crack. I wandered to the window; the glass was old and fogged with grime, revealing nothing as I stared into it, the newer cabins too full to accommodate her. "He knows I was looking for her. I wouldn't have taken him under—"

"What the *hell* were you thinking?" he snapped through gritted teeth. I glanced at Martha, wondering if she'd make it through the night, if I shouldn't have taken her straight to the emergency room in town; there was a nurse on staff two days a week and I hadn't wanted to do Martha the disservice of airing her dirty laundry in front of the local hospital staff, knowing the town's penchant for gossip.

"She was in trouble." My voice was flat, and I didn't bother to look up as Ezra fussed with Martha's side table. He straightened the spoon, then lined up the containers of Jell-O and pudding sitting next to it, waiting for Martha to come to as I wondered what the town would say about me if her condition worsened through the night.

"Ez, she's fine now," I assured us both.

"She looks so damn sick."

"This is all we can do." I worried that if I took my eyes off Martha, the woman might simply dissolve and drift away with the slightest breeze; the draft coming from under the old windowsill might lift her and carry her away again, this time never to be found. I reached out to place a hand on Ezra's knee for reassurance but pulled away when he tensed. We sat in silence, watching the young woman's chest rise and fall in the flickering light of the bedside lamp.

"You said you'd never use what you do to manipulate people."

"What would you have done?"

"I don't know, but—"

"It was our shot!"

"*Our*," he scoffed. "Now there's a 'we?' This was you, Nev. You knew where I stood on things. What if you'd have gone all the way under? What if you'd touched Gary and couldn't hold yourself back enough? It's not just you that could have gotten hurt."

"Good. He—"

"You said there were neighbors who saw you, who could have recognized you from when your brother lived there. What if you both went under and he never came out? You know it's wrong, Nev." He paused, looking at me as though doubting it. "You know it's wrong, right? I get using your...your...thing...to help people. But to hurt them? To make them relive—"

"This is why I had to lie! Look at her, Ezra!" I flung a hand toward Martha. "She's alive, isn't she? I was right! If we'd done things your way, she'd be dead in an apartment somewhere. I told you she was sick. She looks like she's hardly eaten anything in weeks, maybe months."

"Her life wasn't worth yours—or Gabe's!" he boomed, gentling his tone with a forced breath as he scanned Martha to make sure he hadn't woken her. "You knew he wasn't ready to go under and you took him anyway," he continued, clenching his jaw, "and then you *kept* him there instead of pulling out the second you knew something was wrong. And I wasn't even around. If things had gone worse..." Ezra raised a hand to his mouth and leaned into it, as though stopping the words could stop him from thinking about all of the lingering *what if's*.

"Ez..."

I placed a hand on his shoulder, but he pulled away, taking a full step back and raising his hands to prevent me from stepping closer. "If we're not in this together, everything here is going to fall apart," he cautioned, motioning ambiguously around the cabin. "There are other people here that need you, Nev, including me."

I leaned my head back to stare at the ceiling.

Ezra watched, head shaking as though trying to wake himself up. "This wasn't your call to make."

"You'd have done the same, if you could have."

"You don't know that." He examined me as though he'd never seen me before. "But that's not the point." He gave me a final, sullen glance, shaking his head at the somber scene in the bedroom once more before turning to leave. The hinges on the bedroom door creaked, rust preventing the door from slamming as loudly as it might have as he escaped into the hall.

When he was gone, I finally acknowledged the Koels huddled in the corner like Fates. One of the three moved forward, its long, sinewy fingers dragging across the floorboards. Rather than face me, it stood behind me, moving so its chin hovered just above my right shoulder. I tensed and closed my eyes, turning my head away as he clicked against my ear: *Tick, tock. Tick, tock. Tick...*

With every click, the Koel's head turned sideways, rotating 360 degrees like the hands of a clock. I glanced at the ceiling to avoid making eye contact, heel tapping with increasing speed until Martha mumbled something indiscernible; the first true sign of life in hours. I moved to the bed as she twisted in the sheets, making small assurances, and stroking her hand. Her eyes fluttered open, chest heaving as she took in her new surroundings, unable to recognize anything.

"He'll come," she rasped. "I have to go..."

"He'll never find you," I promised, smiling as Martha dissolved into inexorable tears, no doubt at the overwhelming reality that Gary would never lay a hand on her or Gabriel again. I smiled down at her, patting the back of her hand and repeating the assurance until she was spent from crying. I tried not to let my smile falter when one of the shadows shimmied into bed behind Martha, curling around her spine.

I blew out a controlled breath. A shudder rocked my shoulders and I looked around to prove to myself that I was alone; that I had not drawn the focus of the Koels. I ran a hand along the gooseflesh of my arm, grateful to see what others could not. To learn of their existence but not see, to forever glance over one's shoulder knowing of the quiet violation that could be happening just beyond your awareness at any moment...if I didn't know better, I'd have sworn a finger traced my spine, a cool tickle caressing circles at the base of my neck.

When Martha finally rolled away, her breath settling into a rhythm of deep inhales and exhales, I let my eyelids succumb to their heaviness. My eyes drooped and my head sagged forward with fatigue as the hands of the old clock on the wall spun forward, one hour bleeding into the next. Martha was alive. Martha was safe. All was well.

And yet, in my dreams, the Koels persisted as though they knew something that I did not, as though my life was a play and they had already witnessed the second act and knew of tragedy yet to come:

Tick, tock.

PART II
Chapter One

For my clients, I've always been partial to the button-in-the-box analogy for grief, a concept I illustrate on paper, beginning with the simple drawing of a square. The idea is this: Imagine your life as an enclosed box. After losing someone, a button materializes inside the box that triggers pain every time it's pushed, and a ball forms made from all of the things that remind you of the loss (at which point I draw a button and a giant ball in the square, almost too big to fit inside).

The list of triggers starts off huge, and the ball takes up so much space in the box that it's almost inevitable that it's going to trigger the pain button. Then, over time, with even the smallest amount of effort, the ball shrinks (I draw my client another box of the same proportions with a button the same size as the first but make the ball inside smaller).

Now, when the ball bounces, it doesn't necessarily hit the pain button; there are still plenty of things in your life that could trigger it, only now, the triggers have more freedom of movement. You can go to a baseball game after losing your partner and not think of the last time you were there and fought. You can go to the park without thinking of the child you lost.

Until, of course, a day comes when suddenly, you can't.

The pain feels brand-new. The air leaves your lungs, and the world spins off its axis. The sound of whoever's voice told you the person you loved was gone sounds like it's amplified on studio-quality speakers in full surround sound, left on repeat inside your head.

Time and place mean nothing as past and present stack together, like you could cut through them with the single swoop of a knife. When the button is pressed, no matter how much time has passed or how small the ball of triggers has become, it hurts as badly as the first time. It drags you kicking and screaming through the process of mourning all over again; a path that is more of a labyrinth than a straight line. One memory careens into the next without warning like a car crossing into the next lane while the driver sleeps at the wheel.

After being at his apartment, thoughts of Jaak began circling like gnarly vines, as though the labyrinth was suddenly closing in. The ball might have been smaller than it was back then, but still, certain triggers always did it for me; I couldn't wear heels anymore, country music raised my blood pressure, cheap beer made me gag.

And suddenly, I'm somewhere else entirely.

I'm thinking of a dark hardwood floor covered in sticky beer stains that snag the bottom of my heels as I clop across it. My pantsuit—however cheap it was—looked out of place compared to the mechanical bull on the other side of the empty dance floor. I think I reached for my phone to call Jaak as his voice slurred from a booth behind the coat check window. A young waitress looked up wearily from the bar at him, then back to the bar lemons she was slicing.

"Geeze." I rushed forward as he slipped down the slight step leading to the booths. Before I got to him, he regained his footing, swooping forward to drape an arm across my shoulders for balance.

"How did you even get served?" I raised my brow, removing his arm from me but keeping a hand near his elbow to guide his swaying body.

His shirt was a yellow and red plaid that hurt the eyes to look at for too long. Though I imagined it might be considered fashionable with the college crowd, I wasn't sure that he was pulling it off. I smoothed down my short hair, smiling nervously at the waitress assessing us as we saddled up onto bar stools. He wiggled his eyebrows and slid a driver's license out of his pocket that marked him as thirty.

He had yet to breach nineteen, but even I might have been swayed by the well-crafted fake ID he'd presented and the scruffy beard trimming his jaw as he asked, "Shall I summon us another round?"

"I don't think you need another drink," I cautioned.

"You're not being fun, which means *you* need another one."

"I haven't had one in the first place."

"Well then, that's the problem now, isn't it?" Jaak raised his voice to be heard above the music pouring from the speakers; country tunes that had me inadvertently tapping my toes. "Oh, and Mom says 'hi' by the way and to give her a call when you can. I don't know what about," he added quickly, before I could ask.

I examined his ID one more time before handing it back. I don't remember if I thought it in the moment or only after the fact that the license was par for the course with him.

Jaak had been borrowing time since the day he was born.

"I don't have too long." I sighed and shook my head. My eyes darted to my watch, worn mostly for show. "I figured I'd pop by after exams to kill some time. It's too early to celebrate, though. Most of the questions were like, 'Which of the following answers is most correct?'. I hate those questions." I pouted. "Complicated for no reason. And wealth management is already so damn *boring*." I groaned, head thrown back. "Investments, insurance...blegh."

"On the contrary, I imagine they're trying to mirror the complexity of real-life decision-making, especially when you're going to manage peoples' entire financial lives." Jaak winked. I muttered complaints under my breath, unable to refute the easy wisdom of his observation. He nudged me with his elbow, asking, "Are you going to call Mom and tell her you passed?"

I exhaled sharply, eyes rolling with renewed vigor at her second intrusion into the conversation. "What do you think? I've gotta go back to my place right after to get ready for tonight so, seriously, I can't be too long." My way of asking not to linger on the topic of our mother for too long; I knew he shared the same opinions of her that I did, so there was no need to dwell on it when time was of the essence.

"Tonight? What's tonight?" Jaak motioned for the waitress. He held up a finger to me, pausing our conversation as he spoke to the young woman who was busily sliding coasters in front of us, trying not to make eye contact with my brother: "We'll have two menus and—"

"I already ate," I informed him, frowning.

"We'll have one menu," Jaak corrected, ogling the blonde waitress as she presented it to him and added, "And I will take your phone number, please and thank you." He waggled his brows. The waitress appeared torn between expressing her annoyance or continuing to tolerate the harassment that was an unwritten part of her job. She settled somewhere in between, huffing lazily.

"I'm sorry," I said, sliding a fifty across the bar to her. "For his bill."

"Awe, sis, always looking out for me," Jaak slurred.

"He, um, he's been here since eleven."

"Will that not cover it?"

"I tried to cut him off, but I wasn't sure if he was..." She appraised the unruly mess of hair he claimed made him look like a mad scientist, or Kurt Vonnegut. To anyone but Jaak, however, his hair only made him look untidy, bordering on homeless. "It's just me here today, and I didn't want to cause trouble. We don't usually have more than one or two of us on for lunch on weekdays, and I just...his tab's a hundred and thirty..."

My eyes widened. "Geezeus, okay. We'll take bar peanuts—"

"Awe, nuts." Jaak grinned. I slid my credit card, meant for emergencies only, out of a wallet matching the worn, leather messenger bag slung over the back of my chair. I frowned at Jaak. "I can't afford to pay for your drinks *and* dinner. We'll take some bar nuts so this one can sober up before I take him home," I addressed the waitress again, "and I'll—"

"I hear nachos are good for sobering up," Jaak chimed.

"I love you to death, but I need you to shut up for a sec, okay?" I patted Jaak's knee. "I can't afford to feed you. Did you bring any money? Hello?" I stretched out my neck as he stared vacantly ahead, thinking of something I'd never be able to fathom without being inside his head. He pulled out a twenty, so I nodded at the waitress. "Tip this poor lady," I insisted. "Eat some peanuts and let's get you home. Or—wait, do you guys still have the free popcorn?"

The waitress nodded, so I tilted my head. "Good. Popcorn, and keep it coming. I'll also have a pint. Any light beer you have on tap is fine with me. *Cheapest*," I corrected. "Cheapest light beer on tap."

The waitress came back a moment later with a large aluminum bowl of buttery popcorn. The scent of it brought back pleasant memories of trips to the movies with Mom when Jaak and I were young enough to enjoy it, but I pushed it closer to Jaak, resisting the urge to shove a handful in my mouth, not wanting to feel bloated. Jaak didn't turn to look until my drink was in front of me.

"You have a date tonight," he guessed happily.

I exhaled, shaking my head at his observation. "I just met him. I mean, I didn't *just* meet him," I revised. "We met online like a month ago and tonight we were gonna...Why were you here so early? You knew I was writing my exams. You could have waited—"

"I was lonely," he said matter-of-factly.

"Oh..."

"Hey, do you remember that time we camped out in the bush behind the house? The old house, before we moved to town, and before Mom and Dad got their new place?" Jaak changed the topic, and his mood perked up so fast I felt like I was suddenly ascending a drop-tower at an amusement park; up, up, up, then a sudden drop. That was always Jaak's nature: moments of profound insight and clarity, balanced by crippling dips in energy and focus.

"Those were good times, weren't they?" Jaak drew circles in a wet spot on the counter. "There was that shadow outside the tent, and we had no idea what it was so you were freaking out, and you took that two-litre and started hitting it through the tent yelling at me to run, and next thing I know, you're out the door and halfway to the house without looking back. Meanwhile, Mom's standing outside the tent with popcorn on the ground all around her cussing like I'd never heard before, let alone from her."

"I remember that. I mean, kind of," I amended, half of a smile pulling at my lips. What I remembered most from those years, however, was how heartbroken I was when Mom announced we were moving away from the country; away from the bushes and streams we'd grown up playing in, away from the horses. "You know you were too young to remember it, though, right? You remember what Mom and I told you."

He shrugged. "I remember how I felt when it happened."

"Amused?" I grinned encouragingly.

"...scared."

"I was looking out for you." I tried to laugh, but it sounded disingenuous. "Jaak, seriously, what's up with you today?" I struggled to board his train of thought; he shrugged, and the train changed tracks yet again as he probed for details about my date, immediately locking onto the one question I had been doing everything I could to avoid.

"How do you think he's going to handle...?"

"Probably the same as Mom did." *Denial.* Jaak didn't need to say 'Koels' for me to understand what he'd meant. I smoothed my napkin against the bar top, then glugged down the rest of my drink. I lifted my shoulders as though to say, 'What can you do about it, though?' "It's going to be what it's going to be."

"I'll drink to that," he decided. It was his way of asking for another pint. I shook my head, brows scrunching together a little too worriedly. To lighten the mood, I smiled glibly and motioned to the waitress for another round for myself. He looked artificially heartbroken the way only a younger sibling could be, then shook his head and gestured for me to carry on. "Maybe he'll surprise you. Are you lonely, sister?"

"Sometimes," I admitted, easily enough.

"Then you should fall in love," he decided.

I turned my head to look over at him as though he'd suggested I wear a banana suit to my job interview, ignoring the quick pang in my stomach at the thought of companionship. After staring at him a moment too long, I turned away and shook my head.

"I just want you happy," he insisted.

"I am happy," I declared, hand shooting up to steady him when he almost tumbled off the bar seat. He caught himself at the last moment. My heart sped up, pumping me with adrenaline, preparing me to intervene if there was another near miss. "Don't you worry about me," I said, shooing him with the hand I'd raised. Jaak stared down at the bar until I finally caved in and asked, "What's on your mind?"

He looked up, eyelids heavy.

"Oh, you know...just this and that. Oh!" Jaak bounced excitedly in his seat, searching for the backpack he'd arrived with. He dug through it, then thumped a stack of papers onto the stool beside me, choosing to sway on his feet rather than sit again. "I almost forgot to tell you."

I quirked a brow at him. "What's this?"

"I wrote a new story. I know, I know," he interrupted with a flourish of his hand when I opened my mouth to speak. "It's been a long time since I've written anything, and you've missed it terribly." Jaak held a hand to his heart, pretending to be faint. "But there you have it—the latest, greatest, and perhaps last installment in our storytelling chronicles. You'll do pictures?"

"Always do." I nodded, stuffing it in my bag and rising.

"Where are you going?"

"*We*," I emphasized, leaving the rest of the money for the tab on the bar with a generous tip, not bothering to finish my last beer, "are heading home. I'll drive you back to your place and then I need to go get ready. I don't want to go on a date looking like I sell insurance."

"You *do* sell insurance," he puzzled. "And stocks and—"

"Not yet, I don't."

"Ah, soon enough." He linked his arm around my shoulder as I led him stumbling to the parking lot. He hummed whimsically as he bobbed in and out against my side, every so often needing to be reined in lest he walk straight off the curb and into traffic. "In two weeks, you will ace your interview and they will adore you. I never realized how beautiful you are, sister."

"Make sure you take something when you get home." I frowned, pressing the button on my keys twice until I heard the locks slide open in the car. I opened the passenger door and gestured for Jaak to get in, but he only stood in place, grinning mischievously as my mind wandered, preoccupied with conjured thoughts of interview prep questions and what to wear and how painfully fast the two weeks was going to pass and whether I would be ready to—

"I mean it," he said, nodding sagely. "It's so easy, isn't it?"

"What is?"

"Not seeing? But I do see now." He grew somber, staring at the cracked asphalt of the parking lot, ignoring my hand as I motioned again for him to get into the car. I glanced at the parking meter, just past expiry, then looked at my watch as he claimed, "I see everything now. Promise me you'll never stop painting and drawing and living your life. Promise me."

"Okay, Dr. Manhattan, you see everything."

"Maybe one day, you'll see too."

"Maybe." I finally went to his side, bumping him with my hip to get him moving again. "Or maybe it's possible that you are very drunk and need to sleep it off. Here—" I held his head down so he didn't bang it off the door as he melted into the passenger seat. His head lolled against the headrest. Jaak closed his eyes, humming drunkenly to a song only he heard.

The turn signal clicked as we turned onto the street, leaving the Koels lingering in the dark bar corners behind. When we pulled up to his apartment, I offered to see him upstairs. Jaak shook his head vigorously, insisting I go get ready for my 'very important date'.

"I have a good feeling about it," he predicted.

"Eh, I have you. That's all I need."

"Take care, my beautiful sister," Jaak slurred, suddenly looking very tired, as though he might at any second burst into a spell of drunken tears, overwhelmed by the simple affair of standing upright. He wrapped me in a tight, swaying hug and kissed my forehead with a loud 'smack'. I wiped at it, making disgruntled noises as though he'd reverted back to giving me wet willies. At the door of his apartment, he paused and turned back, appraising me long enough that I shifted.

"I love you very much," he said, though he frowned.

It was a curious expression. Rather than dig at the meaning of it, I waved my hand as though I was trying to push him inside the lobby.

"Take care of yourself, drunkie. Sleep it off. And call me tomorrow to let me know how you're feeling, okay?" The last words were cut off as I slid into my car and closed the door. I pulled away, watching Jaak grow smaller behind me. His body was statuesque in its stillness as he watched me leave, frozen in place.

Forever trapped in the rear-view mirror.

Chapter Two

"I just don't get why you'd want that," my date said, quickly swallowing the mouthful of burger he was chewing. Glistening trickles of fat dripped from the back of the sandwich; Ezra sucked it away before wiping his fingers on a napkin. My stomach rumbled as I watched, the salad and fries I'd ordered no match for the meaty monstrosity in his hands. I tucked a short strand of hair behind my ear, the auburn bob cut beaten into submission by a flat iron. Lipstick stained my glass.

"It doesn't sound like something you'd enjoy," he added.

"Yeah, well...I'm not sure the point is to like it."

"Just a job?" he gathered.

"Exactly."

I shovelled a forkful of leaves in my mouth, chewing politely as I stared at the poster above our booth. The woman on it pressed a palm to each cheek, her mouth gaping open dramatically at the large, Frankenstein-esque monster glowering eternally above her.

The restaurant walls around us were filled with similar monochrome photographs of old, black and white horror films that all looked the same at first glance; they were blown up and printed on wood, glossed over to look new and antiquated all at once. The tables were a similarly aged wood, painted black; they formed a stark contrast with the faded, whitewashed wood panels lining the walls.

"It's all about telling a good story to the client," I said, pointing a French fry at him. "Everybody has something they want to believe is true, or that they're so afraid is true they'll believe it because they think it'll somehow suck less if they see it coming."

"So...you lie to your clients?" Ezra hesitated.

"No." I shook my head, swallowing the next fry. "There's no need for the story we tell to be a lie. It's about shifting focus within the narrative they've already constructed about the world. The insurance company I'm gunning for is a good one," I promised, having already had a similar conversation with my mother, surprised at her enthusiasm over the career choice. "I'll be selling the whole package. Investments and full protection, beginning to end coverage."

"Total protection is a fallacy, don't you think?"

"We give them something real," I insisted with a shrug. "Even if it's just peace of mind. Maybe their beliefs aren't 100% situated in reality, but we can always find things about their narrative that are in line with the truth of what we're selling. It's usually pretty easy," I said, taking a long pull from the glass of pinot noir in front of me. "Clients *want* to be convinced."

"How so?" He cocked his head back.

"Everyone wants to feel like the world is predictable, right? They want to feel like A leads to B; if I do this, then it will cause that to happen. If I buy the right protection, invest in the right policies, then I become invincible. Who doesn't want to be invincible?"

"Agency over the uncontrollable," he said, lifting a brow.

"I mean, it *is* agency, though." I shrugged away the sarcasm dripping from his words. "If I buy the right insurance policy, then it will protect me in the face of the unthinkable; maybe not entirely, but at least a little. They're making a decision that will keep the worst-case scenario from upending them. They might lose everything, but at least a good policy lets them know they're going to get some of it back, if not all of it. Or best case scenario, they don't lose anything at all," I concluded, shrugging definitively as I pushed my plate away.

"But some things can never be replaced."

"What I'm saying is—"

"Like parents."

I reached for a fry, despite the plate being further away, not fully understanding what he was getting at. He rested his elbows on the table and leaned toward me, a hint of anger tightening his jaw.

"*My* parents," Ezra clarified. I froze, letting the words sink in. "I was sixteen when they died. Car accident. Enough insurance money to pay for my degree and then some, but I won't lie, was a pretty dark patch in my life there for a while. I didn't want the money. Didn't want the car replaced. I wanted my dad back. I wanted family days at the ballpark." He shifted forward, urging me to challenge him. "Is there an insurance policy to cover that?"

"Ezra, I'm..." I couldn't speak for a moment, folding my napkin into as small a square as I could. I didn't look at him, couldn't. My body slumped in the booth as the pretenses that had held me up fled in a sweeping exodus. "My mom got into an accident too when I was around seven—maybe eight. I don't really remember " I took a deep glug from my wine glass, then another, waiting for him to say something. "I'm sorry about your parents...really...it's terrible."

He glanced at his watch, eyes darting to the waitress as though willing her to look our way and bring the check, freeing him. My heart hammered at the thought of him walking away, though I couldn't explain why. I'd used everything in my arsenal; the painted face, the flirtatious smiles, touching his arm as we spoke, keeping my shoulders back to extenuate my features.

"I didn't mean to open old wounds," I clamored in place of an apology. I could have stopped, but for some reason, didn't. Maybe it was the way he settled back in his seat as though he was ready to listen. Or the subtle understanding that he was the kind of person who, sooner or later, was going to ask hard questions. Either way, I took a deep breath, wanting him to stay.

"Mom was taking the horses back home one year after we went up to a cottage we share with my dad's friends—there're a lot of really nice, wooded trails there where you could take the horses out. I rode back with dad a day early that year because I wanted to get home in time for a friend's birthday party. Mom was driving back on her own and was pissed about us making her drive by herself.

"That'd been our tradition, I guess? Driving back together? I don't really remember," I said, blowing out a breath as though I could expel guilt through my lungs. "Dad told me Mom and I spent a lot of time together on the drives home. But anyway, my horse was finicky in the trailer...she didn't deal with changes well. She was already bugging out about being trailered, and then was on edge from Mom and I fighting.

"No one was there to say otherwise, but Mom claims that the accident was my horse's fault. She was throwing a fit and either she rocked the trailer or Mom panicked and hit the breaks too hard or a little bit of both, and the trailer went over sideways in the ditch. They were only fifteen minutes from home, so it was my dad and I that found them on our way to town. It was the morning after my friend's birthday, actually. I spent the night and he had just picked me up."

"I'm sorry," Ezra said, face softening. "That's hard."

"Yeah..." But it was the aftermath that sucked the most. Mom healed up fine, more or less. Hospital bills piled up, though—we sold the horses first, then the house. "We moved to the suburbs after. I *hate* the suburbs," I emphasized, shaking my head. Too many people. Too many Koels. "Mom was never the same when she came back. One of the nurses there gave her some scriptures when we weren't sure if she was going to make it. Her and Dad leaned in hard. She and I always had issues—I think that's normal for mothers and daughters—but after that..."

My shoulders jerked as a chill rippled up my spine, eyes involuntarily moving to the shadow seated in the empty booth behind us. I swallowed hard and forced myself to smile, picking up my glass without drinking. In those days, I courted normalcy with the fervor of a peasant girl seeking a prince; it was unlikely I would find it, even less likely I would keep it, but still, I ignored the oddities with vigor.

I worried Ezra would pursue the conversation further; instead, he stared at me for several, drawn out moments then shook his head, anticipating a change of topic was in order. "So what brought you back home? I don't get how someone graduates top of their class from Sterling and ends up back here, selling insurance, of all things."

"Family," I reiterated, frowning as I refolded the white napkin into a triangle, the long side of it lining up perfectly against the grain of the wooden tabletop. The contrast of black against white was stark and unyielding. The background chatter of other diners filled in the silence that lingered while he stared at me, waiting for elaboration. I diverged:

"Trust me—as soon as I have enough for a place anywhere else, I'm out of here."

"Why not leave now?"

I paused while the waitress came to ask if we wanted dessert, noting the way men at other tables tracked her with their gazes, watching the line where her black skirt skimmed the back of her milky thighs. Ezra hardly glanced at her as he asked for the bill and laid his money at the edge of the table; his eyes pierced through me, waiting for a response.

"Because I want to move to the middle of nowhere," I explained cautiously. "Or close to it. I have this vision of owning my own farm out in the middle of the country one day, about as far from people as I can get. I want to get horses again and have like, a big property with trails that I can take them through and stuff, and I'll finally be able to get my brother out of his apartment and introduce him to riding and..."

Realizing how excited I'd gotten just saying it out loud, however, I let my words trail off. I drowned my smile in a long sip of wine.

Acknowledging hope was a prerequisite for crushing it.

"My brother loves gardening." I smiled at my hands, the expression controlled. "He's had his own issues with my mom and moved out when he was seventeen, so he's in this shitty apartment on the other side of town. He still goes to Mom's all the time because she lets him keep a garden in her yard, but I want to get us our own place."

Ezra continued to stare at me, then asked, "What's *your* thing?"

"My thing?" I wrinkled my face as I asked.

"You said before everyone has something they want to believe is true or are afraid is true...You're part of everyone, right? So, you must have something." He finished off his beer and let the silence resume, forcing me to consider the question earnestly, though I still diverted.

"You don't like small talk, eh?" I leaned back, arms crossed.

"Wanna go get ice cream?" He grinned. "Ice cream," he repeated when I blinked at him confusedly. "You're not the only one who can change the topic, and besides, we still have things to talk about. Frozen cream, pumped with sugar, lots of flavors?" he said lightheartedly. "There's a place nearby. I've been wanting to go since I moved here."

"Okay, but—"

"C'mon then." He stood, smirking when I didn't move. "You had a salad and fries. You can't be full. My treat." Ezra winked when my stomach growled. I held a hand to it, blood rushing to my cheeks as I wondered if he could see right through me. "You've told me where you're going to work and what your brother loves, but what about you? I like baseball and teaching and reading, but Neviah likes...? I don't know what Neviah likes, because you haven't told me."

"You're not what I was expecting, you know that?" I asked, conveniently avoiding the question. He walked ahead of me, the residual hints of leather from his jacket effusing as he moved. The scent was intoxicating and masculine, drawing me to it, begging me to follow. He smirked, turning to walk backwards as he looked at me.

"Is that a good or a bad thing?" he asked.

"Good, I think..."

"Still lots of time for me to disappoint." Another flashy smile that sent heat to my belly as we neared our cars. I wondered if he noticed I'd been staring at him; he had an uncanny way of making me feel like he was looking straight through me, without looking past me.

"Funny." I chuckled, shaking my head and turning away.

My phone vibrated in my pocket.

"You need to take it?" Ezra asked.

"Nah," I said, looking at the screen and silencing it, occupied by a mental battle between chocolate chip cookie dough, cotton candy, and heavenly hash. "It's just my brother. We meeting there, or did you want to just take one car?"

Rather than answer, he cracked open the passenger door of his truck, motioning for me to get in. When I got near the door, rather than open it fully, he lingered so that I was between him and the truck, his hand still resting on the handle. I couldn't tell if the warmth I felt was his body heat reaching out to me, or if it welled up from somewhere deep within; regardless, the space between us seemed to vibrate, filled with energy and warmth.

"I'm not really good at this," he said, not conceding an inch as I sank back against the truck. "I spent a lot of time focused on school, then shiftwork. This job with the schoolboard is the first chance I've had to take some time for myself and, you know...I haven't been on a date in awhile, and I guess I don't quite know the etiquette anymore..."

"Me neither. I, um...yeah, I don't know. For a long time now, I just..." I tripped over my words, unable to focus on anything but how close he was to me—too close, yet not close enough. "Things are different, with me. And with Jaak. And, I mean, our home situation..."

"You don't have to explain if you don't want to."

"Three dates is standard," I choked out.

"For?"

"Kissing. I mean, no, not really—not anymore. But traditionally, three dates is how long one would wait before finding an acceptable moment to attempt a first kiss."

"Three dates it is," he said, stepping away so I could catch my breath. He pulled the door open for me, and I slid across the worn leather seat, moving aside papers and work binders.

I raised one to read the label on the spine: "You teach religion then? I guess I had you pegged for math, hard sciences, maybe," I said, trying not to sound too disappointed as I set the binder aside like a bomb that might detonate spontaneously. "You seem so—What?" I looked up after tossing my bag in the backseat only to find him staring at me, a foolish grin plastered on his face.

"Welcome to date number two," he said. The instant furrow of my brow only made his smile widen, stretching across his face until it reached his eyes. "Dinner was date number one," he insisted, turning the key in the ignition, engine purring. "Ice cream is date number two."

I looked out the window to hide my smile as he announced:

"Two thirds of the way to that kiss."

Chapter Three

One hand ran along the multitude of book spines lining the shelves throughout his living room; the other hand gripped a cold glass, filled with ice, cherry Coke, and whiskey. Sweat from the glass rolled over my fingers as the room filled with the sound of *Dark Water* pouring from the speaker system—a slower album, full of acoustic instruments and inspired lyricism.

"I always loved this album," Ezra commented, sipping his drink. "All of their albums, really. They got me through some hard times. Their second album was a God send after my parents died." He picked up the old vinyl case sitting on one of the shelves while I wondered how literally he meant it when he called it a 'God send'. The shelves were lined with any number of books: classics, thrillers, education, but also an abundance of theology books.

My smile was slow to fade after our previous date, sticking around long after he'd dropped me off at my car after ice cream. I was giddy as I drove back to my apartment, too elevated to notice that I'd left my bag heaped in the backseat of his truck. I waited for three days, unable to prepare for my interview without the contents of the bag but unwilling to ruin the night by calling him too soon afterward. Three days passed before he finally called me over to his house.

The moment I arrived, he poured us drinks.

"Why's that?" I asked, wondering at the band's role in his life.

"I just felt like I could sit with my anger when I heard it echoed back to me in their music. Their singer had a rough life, and his music is so...raw. Vulnerable, even." Ezra walked up behind me, close enough that I could smell the subtle scent of shaving cream hovering around his body. He reached out as though he was going to touch me, but his hand continued past me to straighten one of the books. I took a deep breath and tried to relax, his scent trapped in my lungs.

"I still can't believe we were at that concert together." He shook his head, sipping from his glass. "It's weird how much you don't know until you know, you know? We could have been back-to-back and not known it, and here we are," he said, clinking his glass against mine.

"It's for the best." I swallowed hard, taking another drink.

"Why's that?"

"You'd have hated me back then." I shrugged. "I was in the throes of what *I* would call regular, teenage rebellion—tail end of it, at least, though my mom would tell you it was far from regular and point to my brother as a shining example of good conduct." I took a step back from the books, swirling the ice in my glass and staring into it as I debated how much to explain to him.

"Mom and I had a falling out when I started middle school. Started before then, but...when I was a kid, she always used to do these really nice braids for me, then after her accident she stopped—still expected me to braid my own hair because she hated when it was in my face at dinner, but she never bothered to teach me, so..." I made snipping motions with my fingers and clicked my tongue. "I left the braid on her pillow before school the morning I started sixth grade."

I pulled a book off the shelf for further inspection, smiling at the back cover. "She'd hate this. Both my parents would. You believe this stuff?" The back cover boasted lofty ideas about the inevitability that all people find salvation. An author stood posed on the back cover, arms over her chest against a backdrop of full books. "That everyone can be redeemed?"

"Sure. Why not?" He took the book and looked it over like he'd forgotten it was on his shelves as he clarified, "I mean, more accurately, I think everyone is already redeemed. I think redemption is a gift, not necessarily something you have to work for. She talks about the idea that we can all be saved," he said, referencing the author. "That we don't understand the extent of our actions enough to be held accountable for the consequences indefinitely."

Ezra paused to take my empty glass to the kitchen, refreshing our drinks. "I mean, if God is supposed to perfect, complete knowledge, which I believe is true, then he, she, whatever, must know our knowledge is always going to be lacking, imperfect by comparison, and if that's the case...how can we be held infinitely responsible when we can never understand the full consequences of our actions?

"Like, sustainable energy, right? We try to do our part to take care of the planet, but then there's plenty of studies that show that some of our solutions actually end up doing more damage to the environment in the long run. Intention must count for something though, right?"

I took a seat on the opposite end of the couch from him, my brows still drawn together in thought as I said, "When I was nine years old, I broke my arm sledding. My dad didn't even wait 'till I'd finished crying to let me know it was stupid of me to go sledding down that particular hill, and how I'd have known that if I'd bothered to ask around first or looked around at how steep and uneven the hill was. As far as he was concerned, I earned the broken arm."

Ezra made a face. "Sheesh—"

"In the Ross household, there are right answers, and there are wrong answers. No such thing as middle ground when it comes to doing the right thing. If I ever came up with an answer that was somewhere in the middle, it was wrong. Automatically." I crossed my legs under myself on the couch, repositioning to accommodate the weight that settled across my shoulders as I spoke. "I promised myself that if I have kids, I won't do that to them. It sucked."

"Is that something you want? Kids, I mean? Or is it too soon to—"

"It's fine." I smiled at my feet. "Eventually, I would. Jaak and I have seen some stuff together that makes me a little be leery about it, but I think my desire outweighs my fears. He and I both get...night terrors, I guess, is the best way to describe it." Though, that description didn't do the scope of the Koels' presence justice. "Don't worry," I assured Ezra when he frowned. "Not, like, the screamy kind. Just really bad, vivid dreams that take awhile to go away."

"I'm sorry."

"Why? It's not like you control the dreams," I mumbled, my eyes darting to the rows of religious texts on the shelves. I shook my head and dismissed them. "Mom seemed to think I could, though," I said, the ball in my throat rising once more. I drank deeply to flush it down, realizing that I couldn't explain much further without giving away all of my secrets. "She thought that my behaviors must have been inviting the bad dreams, that I got the ideas from somewhere."

"How long have you had the dreams?"

"I was around eight, I think. Jaak's started when he was about the same age. It was nice to be able to help him through it, since I'd already gone through it. We'd stay up at night reading stories Mom gave us, usually stories from scripture, until the dreams went away. That stopped working for me, though—started to make it worse, a lot of the time—so we'd read other stories, then when we got older, we started making up our own. He'd write them, I'd draw pictures."

"I didn't know you were into that kind of thing." He nodded approvingly.

"Drawing, painting. I like watercolor pencils—best of both worlds. I like to look at things in different ways, ways that other people don't. I don't really have a choice," I murmured. "Everyone needs a way of decompressing. Art's mine, I guess—or at least, it is when Jaak has something for me to work on. Otherwise, who has the time?"

"Keeps the demons at bay?"

"You could say that," I agreed, eying him cautiously. "I almost went to art school, you know?" Though, of course he didn't. It was something I realized I hadn't thought about in years only after the words were out. "I told my mom I didn't want to apply at the last minute after we toured the campus," I said, thinking he might ask more about it, though he didn't.

We sat in silence for awhile, with him listening to the music, me lingering on memories of the drawings hanging on the college walls. Hundreds of self-portraits by the other students; the seamless flow of lines, the masterful blending of shades of grey to create stunning depth. I could see the curvature of a hundred retinas staring back at me from the two-dimensional canvases, glints of light that didn't exist giving volume and shape to the eyes as they bore into me.

A cold draft brushed past us, though Ezra didn't seem to notice. I took a slow sip, wondering at Ezra's intense gaze. It seemed to suggest he knew something about me that I didn't. We stayed like that for some time, until I started to take a drink and found my glass empty again. Ezra was across the couch in one smooth, quick motion, taking the glass from me.

Rather than stand to fill it, he set it on the table and slid forward.

Close enough to touch.

"I'm scared," I admitted, wincing as soon as the words were out. He understood that it wasn't a 'no' and scooted closer so that our knees were touching. Ezra placed his hand on the curve of my hip, then paused again. The heat in his palm greeted me, and the heat in my body rose to meet it. The thin fabric of my shirt was the only thing keeping me from sinking under into God knows what—seeing something that I might not want to see.

"I'm weird about touch," I said as vaguely as I could, expecting a Koel to materialize. My eyes must have widened as they darted to the window, locking onto a shadow that was only a shadow. I breathed out as Ezra turned to look. He stared down at his hand on my hip.

"Is this not okay?" He frowned, touch becoming lighter.

"It's fine."

Ezra moved forward again so that his knee rested on top of mine, his hand sliding around to my back as he leaned in closer. He paused there for a third time. "If it makes you feel any better, I don't do this—not ever. It's been a long time since I've been on a first date, longer than that since I've been on a third. I can't even remember the last time I kissed someone."

"I mean, I still don't know if this is technically date three..." I pulled away from him, regretting it when he wilted. "I should probably go." I blushed and stood up, tripping over my feet as I did. "I only came by for my bag, is all I meant. Not really a date. I only—my interview is in a few days and my bag has all of my notes, so I just..."

Needed to stop getting so distracted.

"It's okay. It's in the truck still. Should be unlocked," he said, looking up at me below heavy lids. "You can grab it on the way out. But, uh, date three, then. Did you want to—"

"This weekend," I filled in promptly. Ezra smiled cautiously; the expression penetrated by disappointment. We lingered by the doorway for a few seconds longer before I finally turned away. I slipped outside the screen door, expecting to hear it thump shut behind me, but instead—

Ezra's lips were on mine the moment I turned, crushing into me as I stepped back against the side of the house. Color, sound, light, shape, texture, all melted together with a dizzying impact, every pore in my body its own utopia. I lingered there for a moment, on the edge of oblivion. He was gentle in everything but the way he kissed. It was piercing, penetrating, and still, I held myself back, using everything in me to stay just shy of drowning, fighting every sensation crashing into me and threatening to pull me under; to see him or to show.

"I'm sorry," he said, drawing away. "I didn't...I shouldn't have..."

I pulled him back to me, pressing against him, drinking in the taste of whiskey on his lips and revelling in his heat. My heart thudded with unprecedented terror, afraid to know him.

Afraid to be known.

Chapter Four

"Miss Ross?" A man in a suit stood up from the booth in the corner, straightening the cornflower blue tie hanging from his neck like a lazy noose. I smiled and reached out to shake the hand that was offered to me, then straightened my hair behind my ear. A pearl earring glinted from each lobe, the most expensive jewelry I owned; a flimsy pillar upholding my nerves, an outward token of 'faking it' until I made it.

"Call me, Neviah, please."

"It's good to meet you in person, finally. Shall we sit?" He let go of my hand and motioned to a table in the corner where his laptop and briefcase were already opened, turning the café into a personal office. He slid past a group of teenagers sharing the bench seat that lined the entirety of the wall, smoothing out the lapels of his suit jacket as he sank behind the laptop.

"So, Neviah, tell me a little about yourself," he started, already typing notes, though I hadn't said anything. I was distracted by the muffled chatter of the teenagers at the next table. Two girls leaned in toward one another, shoulders hunched over the cellphone screen they both stared at, occasionally shaking their heads, creasing their foreheads, and muttering, 'It's so sad' and 'What a tragedy.'

"Sorry, umm—" I shook my head, trying to focus my attention back on the interviewer. He glanced at the teenagers and nodded sympathetically.

"Sorry about the location." He frowned.

"It's okay—"

"Scheduling conflict with the board room," he clarified, smoothing out his tie again. "I didn't even ask you if you wanted something to drink. How rude of me," he noticed, grinning as a waitress came to our table. "What would you like? It'll be my treat for dragging you out here."

"Give me the job and we'll call it even." I laughed, momentarily mortified by my own brashness, relaxing when he snorted a laugh in response. "Just a coffee," I said, turning my attention to the barista. "Black will be fine."

The interviewer nodded. "Make it two. Thank you," he said, sliding a tip across the table to her. As she walked away, he shook his head. "Did you know that once upon a time, tips were a way to control the dining experience?" He continued when I shook my head, "Literally means, 'to insure prompt service'. Tips. It's an acronym."

"I didn't know that." I smiled with feigned interest.

"You'd be surprised how much quicker your—oh, thank you." He grinned as the waitress set our drinks in front of us, waggling his eyebrows as though to say, 'see, I told you'. "There's a lot more in life we can control than people think."

"Yeah, if you have money." I choked on my coffee, hoping the remark didn't sound half as snide out loud as it did in my head.

"Which is where we come in. We get to be the voice of reason in peoples' lives—we help them save, help them invest, then we make sure they have the insurance policies to cover their investments if disaster happens. Full package service. And then..." He winked, looking at the barista now busily wiping down tables and looking none the happier for it. "People who invest wisely have extra money and do nice things like tip pretty waitresses. Everybody wins."

"Sure, which is why—"

"Did anyone see it happen?" The voice of one of the girls next to us seeped into our conversation. I blinked and took a deep breath, clearing my head and returning to the matter at hand. Out of the corner of my eye, the girl shook her head, brows lifted. Her friend said something, nodding, and the word 'tragedy' drifted across to my table.

"So, I'm dying to know more about you," the interviewer prompted, steering my attention away from the girls. "You were highly recommended by the facilitators of the business-to-business nights. You've been attending those, correct?"

"Yes, after I graduated I started—"

"Excellent." He nodded, sliding aside some papers on his keyboard to reveal my resume. "Now, tell me, how does someone graduate from Sterling with marks like yours and end up back someplace like this? And perfect scores on your licensing exams, nonetheless. Not that we're not grateful to have you, but there are certainly bigger towns, bigger ponds for someone—"

"Yes, well...I have a passion for this community. I grew up here, and my family lives in the area." A small lie padded by a truth he would be able to interpret whichever way best suited him. "I got a psych degree because the program was fascinating to me—"

"Why not go for a master's or a PhD?"

"Took too long," I admitted. "I wanted to help people—" *Help Jaak get as far away as possible.* "And applying my degree to sales seemed like the easiest way of doing that while earning a solid income right out of the gate. My family ran into some financial trouble when I was younger, and I figured I might as well help other kids not have to go through the same as..."

I trailed off again, blinking as two young men joined the girls beside us, their boyfriends, most likely, judging by the way they intertwined their feet beneath the table. One of the girls planted their lips on the boy nearest to her, then said, "We were just talking about that kid that killed himself." One of the boys interrupted, insisting it was an adult, but the girl shook her head and held her phone up for him. "No, I saw online it said it was a kid. Do you think we know him from—"

The other girl cut in, "He wasn't old, but he wasn't like, *our* age. College maybe? I bet it was drugs. Mom said everyone that lives over there is either high or pregnant. Do you remember when I was dating Remy and his dad lived over there after his divorce? My dad—"

"Oh God! Yes! He practically kicked in the door—"

"Embarrassing, but I totally get it now."

"You dodged a bullet."

"No shit—"

"So, what drew you to our company?" The interviewer tilted his head, driving my attention back to him. My mouth snapped shut, having lolled open as I listened to the teenagers talk. I swallowed and picked nervously at the hem of the pencil skirt pressed against my thighs.

"Well, I...I want to help people to control what they can, and your company's mission statement was really focused on the idea of—"

"I can't even imagine jumping like that. See? You were wrong, it wasn't an old lady that found him. This one says it was one of the cops out patrolling. Oh my God, do you think it was...I mean, that's a long way to fall, would it...?" The girl trailed off, twisting her face.

"It would be messy," a male voice answered.

"Ew!"

"I wonder how he did it," the other young man said. "If he went feet first, he'd probably blow out his kneecaps. Shatter his legs, but die slowly. But if he went headfirst then he definitely—"

"Geeze, Jason, shut up! That's—"

"If he went headfirst..."

"Jason, enough!"

"I'm just saying..." Jason paused to slurp the last drops of his girlfriend's smoothie. The sound was grating and terrible, but better than the things he was saying. My heart thundered in my chest, and I had to tilt my chin down to hide the throbbing vein in my neck from the interviewer as Jason continued, "His head would have exploded on impact. *Sploosh.*" He splayed his fingers in the air.

"I want to help people be okay when the unexpected happens," I said, heel clicking against the floor, my foot hammering uneasily.

"Look up 'guy jumping from seven story building—"

"I see it as a kind of duty," I added.

"And what would you say your three biggest strengths are when it comes to sales?" the interviewer asked, jotting notes from my previous answer without looking up from his legal pad. The teenagers jostled playfully in the booth and rocked their table so that it slid into ours.

"I'm good at finding things that fit with beliefs clients already have about their lives so I can build our products into their narratives. I'm very good at reading other people, and...I'm really good at putting aside everything else to focus on the end goal, I guess."

"Ew, don't look that up!"

"Jason!"

"I'm sorry," I finally gave in, shaking my head apologetically at the interviewer so I could turn to the teens. "What are you guys talking about? What happened?"

Almost everyone at the table looked offended that I had been eavesdropping, if you could call it that, or were already indignant, anticipating, based on experience, no doubt, that someone older than them was going to tell them to shut up. One of the girls still seemed too preoccupied and sad as she looked up from her phone to notice the general atmosphere. A migraine was knotting behind my eyes.

"It's awful," she said, wilting.

"What is?" I paled at the sight of a Koel outside the café window behind her. I jolted as its hand slapped against the window with a quiet *thump*, my mind racing with unthinkable possibilities. I didn't wait for her to speak, but added, "Was it Fifth Street?"

"Drug addicts and pregnant girls," the other girl said, flipping her hair over her shoulder. The interviewer watched curiously, shaking his head in a dad-like gesture of disapproval at her words. The girl noticed, turning away to invest her attention back to her phone.

"Did they release a name?" I asked, hands growing cold.

"No. No pictures, either," the first girl said, surprisingly intuitive compared to the herd around her. "The only thing they said was it was a seven-story drop, and he was found about three this morning by an officer. They thought he was homeless, at first, because he was really scruffy looking, I guess, but the building manager identified him."

"Was anyone notified?"

The girl shrugged, shaking her head to indicate there was nothing more she could tell me. I frowned and pulled out my phone, stumbling toward the door, pausing halfway to turn back to the interviewer. He stood behind the table, looking more curious than annoyed.

"I'm sorry," I stammered, bumping into a table as I moved backwards.

"It's—"

"I need to make a call," I mumbled, the sound of my voice muffled as I pushed out onto the patio. The warmth hit me instantly, tiny prickles of sweat already forming on my skin, begging me to return to the air-conditioned café. My body was numb as I fumbled my phone.

Jaak was the first name when I opened my messages; the conversation was littered with read but unacknowledged messages sent to him since I'd seen him last, save for last night's texts, which were all unread. A ball formed in my throat as I dialed, greeted only by voicemail.

"You've reached Jaak. Don't care what you do with the beep."

I hung up and dialed again.

Beep.

"Hi, you've reached the Ross'." The extended absence greeting was on when I dialed my parents' line. "Sorry we can't make it to the phone. We'll be out of town, returning on the 28th, so please leave your name, number, and we'll get back to you when we can," Mom concluded, pacified enough by their security system to announce their absence to the world without hesitation.

Tears formed as I listened to my parents' voicemail greeting, shivering violently as I looked to the Koels gathering inside the café. I squeezed my eyes as though it might undo what I was suddenly certain of. I tried Jaak's line again, this time hanging up before the beep.

"Is she okay?" someone asked when I re-entered the café.

"Miss?"

I looked up through the writhing army of Koels and, for only a moment, I was certain I saw Jaak standing in the midst of them. When I blinked, Jaak and the Koels were gone, and I found myself staring into the wide eyes of a pregnant woman in line at the counter, hand on her belly protectively, looking at me with disgust as I sobbed openly in the middle of the café. I blinked again to clear away the tears, and from the corner of my eye, saw Jaak outside the window in a red and yellow button-up; his head concaved on one side of his skull.

Half of his expression was missing.

Tick, tock.

Chapter Five

When I was seventeen, my cat died. Hit by a car. Jaak was the first to find him. I was busy with something, schoolwork, probably, or maybe I was in the middle of illustrating one of his stories; whatever it was, it was getting under my skin, so when I saw him staring listlessly at the grass, I had a million reasons why I didn't need to check on him—he was thinking about his garden plans, he'd spaced out from smoking weed again, he was being overly sensitive and it would pass if left alone.

Then the backdoor opened.

And he was *sobbing*.

Wailing? Crying? There aren't actually words for the sound he was making as he told me what happened. I looked up every synonym I could: weeping, bawling, snivelling, lamenting. Nothing came close. You don't know what death sounds like until you've heard it possess the mouth of someone you love.

I ran outside in my pajamas and saw the cat face-down in the grass, so I could only imagine what his face looked like where he'd kissed traffic. I dropped on my knees in the mud, crying with Jaak. Not because the cat was dead. Cats die. It happens, and it's sad, but it's life. I cried because Jaak didn't deserve for the most innocent thing in his life to be taken from him.

"Today we're here to celebrate the life of..."

We stared at the cat for what felt like eternity, my mind running through a long list of denials. Sure, it was close to our cat, but the fur was too long. And I was sure our cat didn't have that much white in his fur, just the tips of his paws. And he looked too big. And were we sure it was even a *him*?

Jaak seemed sure, promised me he'd done his due diligence, so I held him, rocked him as he cried, made plans for the burial. And damned if I didn't find our cat sleeping in the garage when I finally let Jaak go long enough to retrieve the shovel—very much alive, purring, sunning in the window, unaware he had just died.

That was the second time in my life death lied to me.

I wanted it to lie to me just once more.

"We're here to celebrate the life of Jaak Ross."

The weeks after Jaak's death vanished in a blur of condolences until I suddenly found myself at the front of a funeral parlor, feedback humming through the speakers. My fingers curled around the edges of the podium, its lacquered finish peeling so my fingers pulled away stickier than before. I glanced over the edge; a patch of gooey rectangular adhesive clung to the wood, perhaps the remnant of where a cord or script had hung covertly during another gathering.

Someone coughed up ahead of me. Ezra stared up patiently at me from the back row. I didn't feel like I was attached to my body.

My heart felt leaden in my chest, and for a moment, I was standing in a parking lot, staring up at a handsome stranger, silencing Jaak's phone call while thinking about which ice cream flavor I was going to get. I felt nauseous—never wanted ice cream again. My feet itched with the overwhelming urge to run away as far as I could, or perhaps shove

Ezra from the room, because if I hadn't been on that date, if I'd have answered my phone, if I'd have listened...

"I was saying..."

My mother stared up at me from the audience, her eyes hollow and ringed with dark circles, the rest of the skin around them blotchy with red spots as proof of hours spent crying. I frowned, wondering how someone could simultaneously look so forlorn and impatient as my mother did, glaring up at me from the sea of mourners that surrounded her.

I glanced beside me to the memorial table that dozens of eyes were focused on. There was a reason there was no casket. They incinerated Jaak the moment the autopsy was complete, insisting there could be no open casket in his state—evidently, the boy in the cafe had been right about certain aspects of Jaak's death. They handed him back to us in a tiny grey urn that made me wonder how a human life, seemingly so substantial, could amount to less than a shoebox.

That's what everyone was staring at, unbeknownst to them. It was just a cardboard box on the table below a cheap, satin cloth to make it look more significant than it was. The photo of Jaak perched on top was so old I could hardly be sure that it was him we were holding a memorial service for. None but the three of us—Mom, Dad, and myself—knew that the box was as empty inside as we all felt, everything that was left of him too insubstantial to display.

"Intuitive," the interviewer said to me the morning after the interview. "You knew your brother was in trouble. That's the kind of intuition we want on our team," he said it enthusiastically, as though my brother hadn't just jumped off a seven-story balcony. The next day.

He'd called the *next day* to be sure I received the flowers the office sent and offer me the job, but I wasn't home, I wasn't anywhere. Physically, I was in bed, the ghost of a human, pale skin with dark, sunken eyes and red, blotchy cheeks; but my mind was far, far away.

I hadn't known he was in trouble; I'd known he was dead.

There was a big difference.

"Jaak was..."

My fault.

I scanned the audience, thankful for their patience as I returned my attention to the sticky podium. Pulpit? I didn't know the difference. Did I have a right to be behind a pulpit? I started to take a step back, remembered the microphone was fixed to the stand, stepped forward again. Feedback hummed from the speakers.

I scanned the faces of the Koels interspersing in the empty seats between mourners. I hardly recognized anyone in the crowd.

"The thing about Jaak..."

Some of the audience could be identified easily as other tenants from Jaak's apartment, evidenced by their sloppy demeanor, glossy eyes, and wardrobe that made Jaak look like he was a no-nonsense, upper-city executive, by comparison. But whether they were friends of his or bored rubberneckers was still undecided. I frowned.

"Jaak didn't like a lot of fuss."

When the numbness subsided in the days following his death, there was intense energy. Bursts of cleaning everything I could get my hands on, making casseroles to stash in my mom's freezer even though she didn't deserve them. Dad called me a few times once I went back to my apartment, but never Mom. She stayed in her room; on a good day I could hear her crying, flipping through her phone to look at photos of Jaak; on bad days, she wailed so viciously that it sounded like she was being disembowelled, which, in a way, she was.

The Koels never left her bedside.

Or mine, for that matter.

"When we were younger," I said, tapping together the pages of my eulogy, straightening them on the stand, "Jaak always moved a lot slower than I did, it seemed. I remember one time when we were kids, calling him an old man trapped in a young man's body."

I scanned the unfamiliar faces, hoping one of the strangers might confirm it with a subtle nod or shake of the head. They all just stared back emptily, eyes glassy with tears as they waited expectantly for me to fulfil my speaking role and send them over the edge. People came to funerals wanting to cry, wanting the release of it so they could move on with life.

"It wasn't just because he tended to take things on slower—take time to stop and smell the roses, so to speak. Jaak was full of wisdom. He saw so much beauty in the world, in the garden he created and the plants he put there, in the natural world at large. I always felt like he was tapped into some hidden stream of wisdom that no one else was pure enough to touch."

I thought again of the cat, of the innocent dead thing that wasn't really dead. I waited for the back door of the parlor to swing open and Jaak to walk in. My grandparents died long before I met them. No peers had passed away unexpectedly in my school. Death to me was what the Koels were to other people; always there, always pursuing me, but always just far enough out of reach that when I turned to confront my stalker, there was nothing there.

"I remember one time, when we were kids, being out in the garden with him hunting for treasure. I had it in my head we were going to find something amazing—buried treasure, a fossil, something—always moving on to the next thing as soon as I was sure what we'd found wasn't good enough. I just wanted to show him something amazing," I said, my voice wavering.

"But Jaak didn't care that we never found treasure. I remember he found a ladybug once and sat there, letting it crawl up his arm, moving it to the other one when it got too high, fascinated for what felt like hours even after he realized lady bugs bite." I blinked, staring at my mom when she whimpered in the audience, losing track of my notes again as I focused on her. My heart pumped faster.

"You know, when I was nine, we sold my first horse." I steered hard into the tangential wave, letting it crush me. I inhaled deeply and pinched the bridge of my nose, trying to ease the tension behind my eyes. "The pain was excruciating, like someone ripped my heart out of my chest and every once in awhile just..." I held up my hand, clenching my fist to demonstrate crushing something. "And then for awhile I'd feel nothing, like it had dried out, like there was nothing left to squeeze...but the feelings always came back."

Mom shot me a warning glare from the crowd.

"It was just a stupid horse, but I remember sitting at school and having to get up and leave the room because all of a sudden I would start crying and I couldn't stop it, or I'd get angry just because I could—because I had to. And then I got older, and the pain changed. I realized I could get another horse one day, that maybe I could even buy back my old horse..."

My fingers clung to the podium adhesive. "But I can't bring Jaak back no matter what I do," I managed audibly, though I'd pressed the back of my hand to my mouth, shoulders shaking with fresh tears. "It's like learning what it's like to feel pain all over again...but this time..."

Through a veil of tears, I saw Ezra straighten in his seat, ready to rescue me, if needed. I heard a few choked cries and burbles echoing back from my audience, evidently moved by the uncensored display of pain. I tried hard to pull back, compose myself, but my breath wavered. "He's gone because—"

The tears ended abruptly, soldered by guilt so white-hot that it shut off everything else, sobering me, reminding me where I was and that a group of strangers was watching. Ezra stood.

"And you didn't even—" I was cut off by another choked back sob, refusing to let it best me. "Jaak didn't even bother to tell us why," I conceded, on the verge of throwing up.

Not that there was anything in my stomach *to* throw up.

"Which is so like him to just fade into the background, watching people, learning people; he was always kind of like a shadow, giving depth to everything and everyone around him. The world feels bloated with that shadow now, though—like you've wedged yourself into every idea, every memory, every crevice—because you didn't say goodbye." My eyes darted to the door again. I stared, and stared, and stared, but it didn't open. No one burst in to make it go away.

For the first time in my life, death had not lied.

Death had made a promise.

I kept staring at the door and then steeled myself, tears receding like the change of a tide when I looked out into the ocean of faces;

their pity was too much, threatening to swamp whatever raft was holding me afloat. My fingers gripped the podium one more time, as though holding on tight enough might keep me from falling through the well that opened up within me, threatening to pull me into its depths.

The words on the paper became my sole focus, my lifeline:

"Jaak was..."

Chapter Six

Water circled the drain grate, swirling at the center of the fountain as I stared blankly into the flow of water without drinking. The service was done, refreshments were served, and all that remained was waiting for the mourners to retreat back to their regularly scheduled programming. I let go of the button on the side of fountain when a familiar set of heels clicked up behind me, having already guzzled down enough water to drown myself but not knowing what else to do.

"What a day." My mom shook her head, arms crossed on her chest.

"Definitely been better ones," I said, watching the water drain a moment longer before stepping back to make room for her. As she leaned down to drink, I imagined the water that dripped past her lips making its way into the drain, twisting into some unknown labyrinth of pipes down below, never to be seen again. "How are you holding up? And Dad—where is he?"

"In the office, settling up payments I think."

"Why didn't he leave it until—"

"You know your father," she said, shifting side-to-side, staring at the hallway floor. She sniffed and looked up at me, giving a weak smile. "Jaak would have hated all of this." My shoulders relaxed, comforted by the first honest thing she'd said about Jaak in weeks.

My mother stared down the empty hall to the last room before the glaring, fluorescent 'exit' sign; inside, mourners helped themselves to a banquet table of refreshments. Some of them shared stories with one another of Jaak, crying enthusiastically despite never having been close enough to him to warrant an introduction to his family. Others lingered quietly in corners, shoving profiteroles and cookies into their pockets when they thought no one looked.

"Had to get away for a second," I mumbled, wondering if the punch bowl was full enough to satisfy the mourners, wishing I'd gone with my gut and brought a flask. Everything in me ached for it in the absence of something productive I could do to help the day along.

"Me too," Mom said, angling away from the reception hall. She crossed her arms over her chest, her skin paler than usual against the simple, black dress. Her arms stayed crossed there, her shoulders hunched as though a strong draft had suddenly kicked up from somewhere and stolen her warmth. We lingered in silence for a moment, unaccustomed to entertaining each others' company for so long.

"Your speech was nice," she finally offered.

"You can say it." I rolled my eyes. "It was a disaster."

"At least it was honest." She shrugged, another tired smile turning up the corner of her lips. I laughed a little—more of a sharp exhale than a laugh—to let out some of the tension I held.

"I'm sorry you had to do it...it should have been someone else that spoke. Me or your dad should have said a few words, at least, but—"

"I'm sure everyone will know you were too choked up to say anything," I offered, unfolding my arms so they hung limply at my sides, palms turned up with an awkward openness I could hardly remember expressing towards my mom. "People aren't themselves in times like this. Feelings change people—for better or worse."

"I hope that's true." Her gaze bore into the top of my head as I looked away, avoiding the prolonged eye contact with her that felt as foreign as inhaling water. "I feel awful. I should have been there when it happened. You shouldn't have been the one that had to go—"

"It's fine," I lied, realizing that at some point, the tears had stopped, drying on my cheeks so that the skin felt stretched and taut.

"It's not," she insisted, stepping towards me with a frantic sort of plea in her expression. Her brows drew upward, gaze softening as it fell across my face, as though she was pained by the trace evidence of tears and sleeplessness stamped on my features like a fresh branding mark. "It should have been us that spoke with the police. I don't understand how I could have planned to be away so long when he was clearly—"

"Hindsight's 20/20, right?"

Her frown deepened. "I suppose..."

She seemed unsatisfied, so I sighed, stepping closer to her. "It's fine, really. I mean, fine as any of this can be, right? It's not your fault."

Her arms wrapped around me, and I crouched to keep myself from dwarfing her tiny figure. As I sank lower, I felt myself enveloped in her arms and smelled a hint of the lemon hand lotion she loved. Warmth flooded the hall as she held me, gently rocking.

"It's been so hard," she said, tears choking her voice in a way that primed me to cry all over again. Nestled into the warmth of her, I started to let myself go; a few quiet tears hovered readily on the rim of my eyes, ready to come to fruition, but then—

"I'm glad there's still hope for you, Nev. I'm glad I can still have hope that you won't go down this road. It's such a waste of a life."

I froze, sensing something unpleasant behind the words. She stroked my back reassuringly, seeming unaware that every muscle in my body was suddenly taut. If I was an animal, every inch of hair along my spine would have stood on alert, sensing a threat lingering somewhere just out of sight. "I'm not sure what you're getting at."

She pulled away to look at me, still holding me by the shoulders. It felt like a vice grip, a surgical belt meant to hold down a patient while they had their insides opened and rearranged. My mom squeezed me against her again, sensing the change now, not wanting to submit to it.

"He jumped, Neviah. He gave up the gift he was given, took away from the world whatever he was meant to do for it. It's a selfish thing. And look at what it did to us. How could he do that to us? To me?"

I shuffled back.

"I don't understand why you're getting mad at me." She stepped forward, face twisted in an unheeded expression of hurt. She reached out to touch me again, hand lingering mid-air before dropping defeatedly to her side. "This isn't about me. Your brother—"

"People don't just jump off buildings! Do you know how many things in his life could have pushed him to that? If you'd take your head out of your—"

"I lost my *son*, Neviah!"

"You lost him when you kicked me out! You think he felt like he could be himself after he saw how you treated me?" I paused, bile rising in my throat as we stared at each other, neither conceding. My insides felt like a pressure cooker, and whatever had been cooking there for years was ready to be let out. "How welcome do you think he felt after that?"

"Oh, get off your high horse," she spat, face turning red. New tears threatened to form, the familiar burn of them lingering behind my eyes as she said, "God forbid we have one nice moment that doesn't become about Neviah and what Neviah wants. The Neviah show, everyone, tickets on sale now." She dramatically swung her arms out to welcome the imaginary spectators, not knowing several Koels had gathered to witness her theatrics.

"What I *want* is for Jaak to be alive," I hissed.

"Well, maybe you should have considered that before—"

"Before what?" I dared her.

"Before you encouraged him, Neviah...you know...got him involved in your...thing. You know, your *thing*..." she said, watching my eyes dart back and forth between her and the Koels each time one of them moved, though she wasn't able to see them anymore than the next person. "Maybe if you hadn't filled his head with all of this, he would have actually had a chance, made connections, gone to church, found some peace in his life instead of—*this*."

She'd glimpsed the Koels once, when I was a teenager, after dragging me to my bedroom by the arm when I was caught sneaking back in one night. I was scared, angry about something she'd said that day—which could have been anything, really. I don't remember the words anymore, only the feelings. She touched me and for one, brief moment, she saw what I saw. Mom saw her own Koel and denied it more fervently than if she'd received a terminal diagnosis.

"Wow," I breathed. "That's rich coming from—"

"Did you not see some of the stories you were encouraging him to write? Some of those shadow things you two always talked about—or whatever," she snapped, waving her hand dismissively, afraid to give too much credence to the idea. "Do you know how unhealthy that was? And that *last* story he wrote, my God, Neviah, do you understand—"

"You act like we could have—"

"They're *toxic*, Neviah. It's a toxic thing you're involved in, and like it or not," she added, turning her palms up to ward off a fight, "it rubbed off on your brother and now he's paying for it. Forgive me,"—she rolled her eyes—"if I didn't want that in my house anymore. When you make certain choices, you invite things into your life," she explained, patronizing me again, "and I did not have to submit myself to the kinds of things you were—"

"So, it's my fault."

We stood, eyes locked onto each other in a quiet standoff of disbelief and hurt, until the door opened next to the exit and deposited Ezra into the hallway. He crossed the hall to us cautiously, appraising the possible damage of inserting a third person into the tense fray.

"He came to our house every week, you know," Mom said.

"What?"

"Your brother? The one you claim was so put out by us? He came to dinner every week for months. Try figuring that one out, why don't you?" I started to protest, but she looked at the ceiling and began to laugh. "Seriously, Neviah? Why is it so hard for you to believe that everyone might not hate me quite as much as you always have?"

"I don't *hate* you." My eyes rotated.

"Oh, bullshit." Mom's unexpected curse riled me.

"Yeah, well, Jaak doesn't remember the accident. Oh, right, I forgot. We don't talk about that. We *never* talk about that."

"Watch your mouth," she snapped, crossing her arms only to unfold them again a moment later as she added, "And I *have* tried to talk with you about it. Multiple times. You haven't exactly been eager to have that conversation yourself or maybe we wouldn't be..."

Mom stopped, noticing Ezra shifting uncomfortably beside us, waiting for a chance to cut in. She conceded, looking away before I could continue. A Koel chittered noisily in my ear, nearly drowning out Ezra's voice: "Hey, people are leaving..."

"Good." I took a breath.

Mom shook her head, a thick veil of showmanship shrouding any genuine emotion she might have felt even moments before. She rubbed her face in her hands, making sure that a smile was pressed on when she raised her head to face Ezra. The perfect, mourning mother.

"Mrs. Ross." He nodded.

She reached out to shake his hand, patting the back of it in a gesture that could be interpreted as either maternal or dismissive, depending on how well you knew her. "I'm sorry to be meeting you under such...difficult circumstances." The sidelong glance she gave me was cutting. "Please, call me Lori. It's wonderful to meet you."

"It's okay, I—"

"If you'll excuse me," she interrupted, patting his hand again and drifting past him as though someone was beckoning her from the other room.

Ezra breathed out when she was gone, scratching the back of his head before turning to me and asking, "How you holding up? Didn't look like you two were doing much consoling." I shrugged, both of us staring at the door where mom disappeared. "Why don't I give you a ride home? Or we can go back to my place and—"

My eyes widened. "What?"

"A ride home?" His brows drew together as he cocked his head to look at me. "I know you've still got some stuff to take care of here, but I figured I'll stick around and help out, and then tomorrow we can come back, and you can get your car. Or we can get it later today, if you want. You just look like you could use some sleep. If you want to stay at my place until—"

"Really?" Anger washed over me. I pressed the bottom edges of my palms into my eyes, then stared at the ceiling and shook my head. "My brother's dead and you're trying to get me back to your house? I think maybe you need to just go now," I insisted, starting to walk away.

"You know it's not like that." He straightened. "Neviah—"

I pushed past him, shoving my shoulder against him as I moved to the exit. I paused halfway, turning back momentarily, an apology lingering, then shook my head and kept going. I thought of Mom's lemon lotion, could smell the lingering citrus in the air—it wasn't real, just a figment of my imagination, a memory of a different time that I couldn't return to.

Ezra's footsteps followed behind me, so I hastened toward the door, glancing back worriedly as he called out to me. I shuffled faster, not quite running, not quite walking, loping awkwardly somewhere in between as I retreated, kicking off my heels as I went.

"Just go away!" I yelped, unable to pull my hand away fast enough when he reached for it. In a single moment, recognition and then horror befell him as he touched me. I felt myself slip, whirled around and ripped my hand away just in time to see his gaze lift above my head, staring at the apparition over my shoulder.

The Koel hovered, the talons at the end of each long finger dragging against the floor even as the crown of its head peaked two feet above us.

"Are you happy now?" I cried out.

Heads poked out from the reception area as I retreated from Ezra. He looked to the floor, denying what he couldn't understand, then jerked his head up again just as quickly to confront what was no longer visible to him. My lip trembled and a ball formed in my throat so thick and wide I thought I would choke on it as I stumbled outside; the Koel followed, a gorged mosquito that had sucked the mourners dry but still wanted more, more, *more*.

Always more.

Chapter Seven

"Your mom is gone now." Minutes had passed or maybe hours before Ezra showed up beside me. I tried to curl deeper into myself as we sat in silence on the parking divider, my arms crossed over my shins, each hand cupping the opposite elbow. "Are we gonna talk about what happened in there, or...?" He sighed when I didn't feign to look up.

Birds sang noisily in the trees hedging the parking lot as the sun warmed the earth, but the smell of garbage from the disposal I didn't realize I'd collapsed next to permeated the air and turned the beautiful day rancid with decay. I thought of all the food scraps wasting away inside the bin, thought of Jaak in his box.

"I think I left a sweater at your house."

"What?" Ezra frowned.

"My sweater," I repeated numbly. I turned so he could see my face, hear what I was saying, witness my humiliation front row center. I felt like a flower whose petals had been peeling back one by one, revealing the rotten pistil at the center. "I'll come get it tomorrow, and then I'll be out of your hair."

Ezra slid closer, wrapping an arm around my shoulder so that I was forced to lean into his chest—though he hesitated to let his arm drop. It was a brief hesitation, so quick it was hardly a hesitation at all, but it was enough to make my body seize up as I fell against him, propped into his side like a tent pole. For a moment, he'd second-guessed touching me, and that was enough for me to know it was over.

The breeze seemed cold despite the heat.

"Did I ever tell you about the cat that got under my porch when I was a kid?" Ezra stared forward as I shook my head against his side. "When I was little there was this cat under my porch. Every night when I came home from baseball practice—mind you, that was only twice a week, but still—I heard this cat making noise under the porch. I was so excited about having a cat, I tried to get my parents to go under for it, but they always waited until it was earlier in the day to look and then there was never anything there, so they didn't believe me.

"I thought I was losing my mind," he said, scratching his chin. I noticed now that it was coated in stubble, that his eyes were shadowed, like something had been keeping him awake lately, as well. "But no, I knew there was a cat under there. I'd heard it. I'd seen eyes glowing under the porch one night. It was real, and I was hell bent on making sure my parents knew it."

"Did they ever see it?"

"My dad heard it once, but he had a million excuses—it was the wind, it was the bush hitting up against the house." He shook his head, rubbing his fingers against my arm, not letting me pull away, though I tried. "We were on a schedule on game nights. There wasn't time to stop and take a closer look without messing up my bedtime and..."

Ezra's nostrils flared, his eyes red and glossy. He stared at the ground like he was somewhere else, like he was no longer at Jaak's funeral but his parents'. My lips parted, eyes rimmed with tears again, though this time they weren't for me. I stared at his hand for awhile before taking a chance and intertwining my fingers with his.

He looked up, smiling slightly.

"It turns out it wasn't a cat," he continued, wiping his cheek and sniffing when a rogue tear fell loose. "We had a racoon living under the porch. So, I mean, I was right—there was something there. It wasn't what I thought it was, mind you, but there was something there, and my parents, I swear to God, were about to bring me to a doctor because they thought I was losing my mind."

He glanced at me. "I guess it's a little different. A lot different," he revised, paling slightly. "And I'd be hard-pressed to explain what the hell happened in there, but I know what it's like to have people not believe something that's right there for them to see, you know?"

When I said nothing, he filled the silence: "I think that's part of why I wanted to be a teacher—to encourage people to entertain the things they don't know, or don't know they don't know. I wanted to teach kids to ask the right kinds of questions early on, but it's limited, right? I guess I recognized that some things we just can't know, and to me, that's what God is—perfect, complete knowledge."

I raised a brow, clarifying that I understood what he was saying: "The only one who knows if the cat under the porch is a cat?"

"Exactly." He grinned. "And, knowing that we can't always know, it's beautiful because it pushes us closer to that source of knowledge—or, at least, it can. Does that make sense? I don't think that's the whole picture, but it's part of it. It's nice to feel like someone out there knows what the hell is going on, 'cause I'll be the first to admit that I sure as hell don't. Not when..."

He glanced at the funeral parlor, shaking his head.

"So, I should just pray it away." I looked aside with a dramatic eye roll. "I should just pray away every bad thing that's ever happened to me and confess to my evil ways and sing kumbaya with my mom and we'll be a big, happy family with a dead brother, or son, or whatever, and on Sundays we'll just—"

"Not what I said."

"Maybe my mom's right about me, maybe—" My doubts were cut short by an unexpected sob. It came out as a muffled wail. Ezra coaxed me back against his side, letting my arm wrap around his stomach, urging me to melt against him as I continued, "I mean, I saw Jaak like...has it really been six weeks? No. Geeze. That can't be right...but the test, and then the interview, and, oh God..."

A migraine twisted the sensitive nerves behind my eyes.

"You're allowed to have a life," Ezra insisted, face drawn in anger. "You know that, right?" He let out a deep sigh and rose, reaching out a hand to hoist me from the divider. I didn't realize how long I'd been sitting, except that my joints were stiff when I stood. "C'mon...let's get you back to...what's wrong?"

"I'm sorry, I can't. I need to go in and take care of—"

"Everything's taken care of already." He opened the door of his truck and motioned me in. "I'll drop you back off at your place if—" I grabbed his hand and squeezed, eyes widening at the thought of being alone. "Never mind." He shook his head, ushering me inside the truck. "You can take the bed at my place, and I'll take the couch."

"I'm embarrassed you saw me like this."

He touched a hand to my cheek.

"Like what?"

"Like this," I repeated, this time swooping my hand in a circle around my face, as though my unkemptness was explanation enough. "I don't want anyone to see me like this, ever, and all the stuff with my mom, and having to deal with me through everything with my brother—it's too much. We hardly even know each other. And then for you to see...to have to explain—"

"You don't get to control if I see you, Nev."

And see me he did.

He saw me that night at his house when I had too many drinks and insisted on burning all of the notes from my insurance exams, screaming into the wind that there was no longer a reason for me to waste time on boring pant suits and business-to-business meetings.

He saw me breakdown on the bathroom floor crying, keeping close company with the toilet bowl. He saw me lose my temper when he brought up art school, suggesting that if I was done with insurance, perhaps it was time I do something for myself, instead of Jaak.

And he saw me apologize for it repeatedly.

What he didn't see, couldn't see, was the color seeping out of the world around us with every minute, every hour, every day that passed without Jaak. Or the drinks I sipped when no one watched after promising I wouldn't. Or the days spent holed up in my apartment with nothing but take-out containers and shadows for company.

There wasn't a lot of in-between for me; if I was going to be exposed, I might as well be exposed like a floodlight. If I was going to close myself off, it was behind walls so thick I might as well have been separated from the world by Guantanamo Bay.

I didn't bother explaining to Ezra that the Koels became a sort of comfort to me in the weeks after the funeral. They were my only true companions in mourning; the only ones who knew Jaak as I knew him; broken, messy, horrible, and wonderful pieces in all.

They didn't complain when I kept the blinds closed or stayed in my pajamas until dinnertime. They didn't turn away when I woke up on the floor after the sun had already risen, unsure how I got there.

Sleep was sleep, in my opinion, no matter how many times the doctor would reiterate in the coming months that passing out was not the same as sleep. Even if that was true, it was as close to sleep as I could get, so I welcomed it the way a war prisoner welcomes whatever meager rations the enemy allocates to them. And I hid my lack of sleep and my affection for the Koels from Ezra with the skill of an Oscar-winning actress. I was sad, but not desolate in his company.

Until, of course, hiding it became impossible.

Until, in the late hours, eager for something full of carbohydrates to comfort me and fill the chasm opening inside of me, I made a pot of macaroni and cheese; and, when it was done, when the pot was removed and the glowing, electric coils of the stove top were the only light in my apartment, drawing me to them like a bullseye on a target, I set my hand against the red rings, just to see if I would feel it.

And God, did I ever.

Enough to make me revaluate my circumstances. Enough to make me certain that I needed something better to do with my time than sit around in solitude, blowing through the little savings I had. Emotion was hard to come by still, but the welt forming on my hand signalled that I had gone too far, that the ruse was only good so long as I could convince those around me that I was fine, that I was healing.

Because if I couldn't convince them, how could I convince myself?

Chapter Eight

The social service agency scheduled my interview for noon, but I was ready to go by 11:15. I'd spent several days contacting classifieds for jobs, forcing myself to get up earlier and earlier each day and thus sleep earlier and earlier each night. My eyes were still ringed with dark circles, but I pushed myself through the motions of being a functioning, adult human and covered them over with makeup. My actions were automated, but at least the machine was moving.

The nights still smelled like whiskey.

But healing was a process.

I'd cleaned the apartment fervently as though I was hired to clean up a crime. The unit looked ransacked; throw blankets were piled haphazardly on the cheap futon in the living room, books were stacked in random piles everywhere, and there was a mountain of dishes in the sink I'd been avoiding like so many other things in my life.

Still, it was an easy mess to confront.

Next, was the job search. I considered calling back the insurance company, quickly kiboshing the idea when I thought of the pitying looks that would no doubt confront me at the office; everyone would know my story, and everyone would talk about it behind closed doors.

I ran through a long and impractical list of careers ranging from circus performer to private investigator before finally landing on an ad for an entry-level social service position: *Degrees in sociology, social work, or psychology preferred. Make a living helping others.*

With almost an hour to kill before the interview, I took my time searching through my closet for the messenger bag containing my list of references. I sorted clothes into a pile for storing and a pile for donating; most of what remained in the closet were remnants of the life I had just abandoned: pencil skirts, high heel shoes, a makeup bag and hair products I hardly used anymore.

I shifted aside worn shirts and dress pants discarded on the floor without elegance, until the satchel I was looking for revealed itself; the oiled, black leather stood out like a beacon at the bottom of the closet. My fingers groped at the strap of the bag, pulling it into the light where I could see its contents clearly. My hand plunged in, searching for the folder of references only to brush against the heap of pages.

The stack screamed to me; my fingers felt frostbitten, burning and yet filled with ice as they brushed against the thick clip containing the pages. Binding the manuscript. Holding the story together.

Jaak's story.

My face turned white as I lifted the pages from the bag, feeling as though they might form a will of their own and leap out towards me at any moment. Tears burned my eyes, my throat swelling as though I was allergic to the ink. I tried to hold the pages away from me as I dropped onto my bottom and scuttled backwards, but my hand refused to release its grip on them. Maybe it was the alcohol talking, but I felt as though Jaak was sitting on the bed watching me.

I pinched my nose, eyes welling with tears.

I sobbed at the sight of his handwriting. Had I even thought about his pages since the day at the bar? For a moment, I recalled Mom's words at the funeral, her fleeting indication of how dark his last story was. I'd thought about it then, hadn't I? Yet it seemed that at the first chance I got I'd buried the memory of it away, and I wondered if it was because I'd already known in some way what the pages would hold. *Intuitive.* The interviewer's voice popped into my head again.

I opened to the first page.

Dear sister,

Please water the plants at Mom's and, if you ever find time, take a moment to sit by the pond and wonder at what you see there. I write this with the upmost love and respect one could possibly conjure for another human being. I'm expecting you won't read this until after, given how busy you've been (if not, please disregard), but when you do read it later, I hope it serves as an adequate explanation of the things I've done.

I'm so sorry, sister, and I hope that one day you can forgive me.

All my love,
Jaak

Sir Ivanguard

J. Ross

The knight, Sir Ivanguard, carried with him a terrible and lonely secret; though he appeared hardly old enough to wield a sword, his soul was nearly 102 years old, reincarnated into the body of a young knight, barely older than his youngest son had been at the time of his passing.

Though people once fought to hear Sir Ivanguard speak, no one listened to him as a young man the way they had as an elder. Confined to the body of a child, Sir Ivanguard, stayed mute, a choice that awarded him special privileges in a kingdom cleaved in two for as long as he could remember.

You see, in those times, the kingdom was divided into two pillars; the first, to the west, was governed by pious efforts to appease the white dragon that granted them protection from his twin—a black, scaled beast that pillaged their fields and livestock from the sky, left their homes in disarray, and separated husbands from wives and mothers from their children.

Sacrifices of prime cattle and buckets of milk were left out as burnt offerings for the white dragon so that he would continue to offer protection. When offerings were forgotten or insubstantial, the black dragon would appear and take twice as much until they appeased their protector.

The second pillar, to the east, was not subject to the terrors of the black dragon but instead, the wrath of the white dragon. Rather than attack them, the black dragon protected them from the white dragon, but was uninterested in sacrifices of cattle, instead preferring silver and gold. The east allocated their resources toward economic development, strengthening their commerce, bringing business to the city, and using the funds to leave offerings for their protector.

Each pillar believed, in their own way, that it was the other who was responsible for the presence of their dragon:

"Why does the black dragon plague you, but not us?" one would say. "Surely, it's because we have done something right in his eyes."

The other would respond, "One could ask why does the black dragon plague us, but not you? Could it be that you have sent the dragon to destroy us?"

And so, the conflict continued on and on.

By way of his silence and considered by both sides of the kingdom to have nothing worth saying of his own, Sir Ivanguard was appointed a special commission: He was to act as the municipal liaison, communicating back and forth between each pillar of the kingdom.

He was given a special plot of land in the uncultivated expanse that held each community at bay from one another; the only other habitant of the neutral zone a lonely, old hermit.

Sir Ivanguard spent most of his time there reading, exploring the woods surrounding his home, tending to the plants there and pondering the follies of the world beside the lake nestled within the heart of his secret garden.

One day, summoned forth by the magistrate of the second pillar, he arrived to find that she was more irritable than usual, pacing along the grand table where important meetings were held. Her face lit up when Sir Ivanguard entered her chambers and bowed at the waist.

"Your Majesty."

"Sir Ivanguard, it has come to our attention that we cannot continue to ignore the threats of the first pillar. Just yesterday, the white dragon was seen in the fields just past the millwright's farm, plucking up livestock and burning crops. Surely, he is angered by their mock piety, their paltry offerings, and is choosing to take it out on us.

"'Look how pure and white his scales are,' they say. 'Impossibly white, just as snow that has never been tamped down'—how can they say such things when he continues to provoke us with such destruction?"

"What is the message I shall bring them?"

"This time the message is for you, Sir Ivanguard. You have served us adequately through the years, and we have enjoyed your loyalty to the kingdom more than can be expressed; for that reason, we have been withholding a fund that will allow you to live among us permanently in the east, no longer divided or vulnerable living between the pillars."

"But Your Majesty, my loyalty is to the kingdom."

"Even to those fools?"

"They have done much to advance the quality of life among the people, Your Majesty. Why, just last week they were able to join together the community to repair the old bridge that was laid to ruin during the last siege by the black dragon; why does he attack them, Your Majesty, and not us? And why does the white dragon attack us, but not them? And why—"

"Oh, you poor child; you do not have a mind fit for such questions, yet I pity you and would like to explain it as best as I can. A serpent's nature is to bite, is it not? And we must not tempt it with our hopes that it might instead be something other than what it is. Just because it does not always bite does not mean that it will not bite again. Do you understand? Now, go away to your home and think about the offer that has been granted to you."

But when Sir Ivanguard returned home, wanting to go to his secret place to think, he received a summon from the first pillar and was forced to set out again immediately; when he arrived, the magistrates to the west had prepared a feast for him.

"It has come to our attention as of late how loyal you have been to the realm; we hope to celebrate you with this meal and advise you that we have learned, through our little birds, of the offer that has been prepared for you by the second pillar. We urge you not to be tempted by their tricks, Sir Ivanguard, for sooner or later, their community will fall. A single magistrate cannot prevent their ruin, and it is only through our sacrifices to the white dragon that we continue to thrive. We hoped she might learn this and return, but alas, in lieu of it we can see no hopes of reconciling our realms."

"What message shall I bring them?"

"Oh, you poor fool. There will be no message, except the one we have for you: An invitation, the same as that offered to you by the east, has been arranged with the small council of the first pillar; it is requested that you no longer subject yourself to the dangers posed by the second pillar. Come live with us and we will offer you protection against the black dragon, its origins undoubtedly chained to the heretics in the east."

"I will think on it, Your Majesties."

Sir Ivanguard returned home, hoping again for a moment of peace beside the lake to ponder the two offers, but instead he was met at his doorstep by the old hermit. His hands shook from too many years holding a bottle as he implored of Sir Ivanguard: "I wonder if you too have seen the way the dragons plunder both of the cities, being out here, as I am? It has seemed to me, as of late, that each half of the kingdom has faced no more and no less damage than the other."

"You think I haven't noticed this?"

"I only ask. Surely, I would have thought that in noticing, you might have done something about it by now, given the position that you hold. Does that sword not have power? Does it not allow you to speak between the realms?"

"What would you have me do?"

"Approach the counsels, noble knight; beg them to join forces and defeat the monsters once and for all! Only then can we be free of the true monster that has divided our lands."

"You old fool, you old fool! If only it were that simple, do you think I would not have tried my hand at this already? The first and the second will not tempt the other dragon to set its sights on them by disobeying; better to face only one dragon than risk two."

"You have heard them say this?"

"I have not; but I am no fool, and I know it in my heart and in my mind to be the truth, for I have been among either one of them more than you yourself have been among people at all. Don't you know I am the only one the dragons do not touch? Away with you, you old fool!"

"As you wish." The stranger bowed. "But if you follow the road to the bricklebush and turn towards the tree that winks, you'll find a creek that leads beyond the bend to the old millhouse. Past that, you will walk east toward the brightest star, and when you have reached the place where two become one, you will know you have found it."

"Found what? I tire of your riddles!"

"There exists a third pillar."

"Nonsense."

"The third pillar lies beyond the dragons and their keeps; only the brave dare to go. What is a pillar except that which holds all else aloft? Go and seek the dragons. Only then will you keep the first and the second pillar from buckling in on themselves. Only then will you change their fates, and thus, your own. Be warned, be warned; all is not as it seems."

Despite Sir Ivanguard's attempts to the discredit the hermit, he realized quickly as he journeyed away from his home that he had nowhere to go; to go west would show one allegiance, to go east showed another. He found himself standing on the road facing the bricklebush, following it until he found a tree with two holes that looked like eyes, one of them thinner than the other so that it appeared to wink.

He followed the rest of the directions, walking for two days until he finally came to a place where two roads veered together into one trail, leading directly into the mouth of a cave. Heat radiated from the entrance as he approached and the inside walls shook, the smell of sulphur lingering in the air. Even his shadow trembled at the sight of the cave.

Sir Ivanguard stepped into the mouth of the rocks, hugging his body close to the walls to avoid the smattering of bones that littered the cave floor.

He placed his hand on the hilt of his sword as a voice cried out in the darkness: "Who dares to enter?" Just then the earth began to quake around him; a dragon stepped out from the shadows as the knight froze in awe.

"I have come in search of the third pillar!" Sir Ivanguard boasted.

"Who dared to speak of it?"

"A wise man has come to me and shown me the way. I have spent many years wandering between the two pillars; still, I have not found what my soul seeks."

"And what is it you seek?"

"To no longer be cast between the mighty shadows of two cities," Sir Ivanguard requested as though it were a djinn and not a dragon he had stumbled upon.

The dragon lapsed into waves of laughter that made the ground shake below their feet.

The creature stepped forward with his mighty claws so that Sir Ivanguard felt damp each time the dragon's breath washed over him; however, the cave was still too dark to see which of the dragons he had discovered.

"You are a clever man for giving form to the old man's riddles, Sir Ivanguard, so I will tell you what you want to know, but I shall say it in a way that is my own; to understand will prove you clever beyond doubt. The thing I will tell you is this:

"The villagers to the west leave sacrifices outside their houses each night to be sure the white dragon comes to protect them, and though the white dragon has taken many a cow just for the pleasure of it, they continue to leave their offerings and praises rise from the masses as they celebrate the success of their ploy. Tell me, has their arrow found its mark?"

"What a foolish question!" Sir Ivanguard hardly had to ponder the dragon's query. "Not only does the white dragon eat their livestock, but they have invited him to live among them by leaving out their buckets of milk! No, the mark is missed."

"You have proven clever, Sir Ivanguard; perhaps you can handle another. When those to the east fortify their walls and leave sacrifices of silver and gold in the streets, do they not also offer invitation to the black dragon? Do you think that if he wanted, he could not break through any barrier they fortified around their city and take great pleasure from it?"

"Indeed, he could," Sir Ivanguard pondered. "But the black dragon gains more from their continued sacrifices than he does by laying them to ruin in one fell swoop."

"Look on my flesh, tell me what you see."

The peculiar creature took three steps forward and began to blow short puffs of flames from his nostrils. Torches Sir Ivanguard hadn't noticed were suddenly ablaze, washing the cave in light. In the center of the cave stood a dragon unlike any the realm had ever seen.

One side of it was covered in scales as black as coal, yet the other side of him was coated in scales shining like ice crystals laid atop freshly fallen snow.

"You are a curious creature!" Sir Ivanguard yelped.

"But what have you learned?"

Sir Ivanguard considered the monster. "I suppose you appear as though you might be two creatures. One might walk into your cave and see you face the east, saying, 'Look at this mighty creature with scales as dark as a sky stripped of its stars!'. Then another comes in on the very same day when you have turned west, saying to himself, 'Look at this mighty creature with scales as pure and white as a doe's tail!'"

"Clever indeed," commended the dragon.

"Will you correct me if I'm wrong?"

"I will," the dragon promised.

"Very well. When the first pillar sees you coming for their livestock, you come facing the east so they see only your darkest half. When you accept their sacrifices and pass over their cattle, you come from the west, so they see only your white half and think to themselves, 'He has spared us!'"

"Indeed, this is true."

"Very well, then it is the same with the second pillar; however, to them, you approach facing west when you are taking their cattle and facing east when you are taking their offerings. Have I been right in this, as well?"

"Indeed."

"When the people of each pillar encounter one another, one might say to the other, 'It is the black dragon who is evil!' while the other says, 'It is the white dragon who will destroy us!'. If one of these people said to themselves, 'Let us kill the dragon who steals our cattle and takes away from our livelihood!" the other might say, 'We will fight against these evil people that would seek to harm our protector.'"

"What will you do with this knowledge?" the dragon tested him.

"If I say to the people of the first pillar that their oppressor is here in this cave, they might come to you and you would only need to turn to the west and they will say, 'This is not the one who harms us!' and call me a fool. They might even erect a temple nearby. And If I say to the people of the second pillar that their oppressor is here within this cave, they might come while you face the east and say also, 'This knight is a fool!'"

The dragon applauded Sir Ivanguard for his intelligence and invited him to stay in the cave with him: "You can enjoy my spoils," he promised, "for you are as clever as I."

Late that night, however, when the dragon slept, Sir Ivanguard crept away and journeyed back home, calling a meeting between both magistrates so that they might see reason. Unwilling to come together in a neutral place, he met with each alone to tell them of all that he had uncovered.

"This is why you must come together at once! If one of you from each pillar were to come, you might both lay eyes on him so that neither could say, 'This is the white dragon!' or 'This is the black dragon!'. You would concede that there has only ever been one and, in doing so, come together, joining your finances and your armies to remove him!"

But neither pillar would concede.

"Sir Ivanguard is a fool," each said.

So, unable to convince either of the pillars that they might come together and form a third, he returned home only long enough to visit his secret place one last time. He stood staring at his reflection in the water for some time, then held his sword high in the air and dropped it into the lake so that it sliced through his reflection, distorting the surface with ripples.

"You have seen something it has taken me too long to see." Sir Ivanguard returned to the dragon. "I wish to accept your offer and live here with you; these people have not listened to me because I am but a young man, and it is their loss."

"You will gain in my spoils?"

"No such thing; I do not want the boon of either kingdom, for it is poisoned and rotted from the inside though it looks sweet to the tongue on its surface. You may keep it to yourself, and I will hide here, consuming only what is needed to sustain my life."

The dragon agreed at once and prepared a feast for the two of them; he cooked an entire deer, using his talon as a spit while roasting it with his breath, then removed all of the animal's bones, setting them into a fat cauldron filled with water. The dragon lit a fire below the pot with his breath until a broth had formed; he gave Sir Ivanguard the broth, then ate the remaining bones himself along with the roasted meat.

It went on like this for many days, until Sir Ivanguard was happy in his new life, albeit, always saddened when the foolishness of the magistrates sneaked into his mind.

Each day he ate and drank from bottles of mead offered as sacrifice to a dragon who had no use for such things. He ate, and drank, and was merry until one day, his vision started to fail him, and his stomach churned unhappily with disquiet.

"Drink this and you will feel better."

Sir Ivanguard thanked the dragon and drank a deep bowl of the broth, thinking his taste buds had been affected by his ailment; the broth did not taste savory as it often did, but had a bitterness that could not be washed away by the bottle of wine the dragon offered soon after. Sir Ivanguard went to bed that evening dizzy and ill while the dragon watched over him.

In the morning, he had gone blind.

"What trick have you played on me, dragon? Where has the room gone? Where have you concealed your scales and banished your flames?" The dragon snickered in the darkness, taking pleasure watching the young knight stumble blindly in a cave awash with light; the torches still burned strong around him, but their aura was just out of Sir Ivanguard's grasp now.

"You are a clever boy, Sir Ivanguard, but not clever enough; for you looked on my scales and you discovered my secrets, and you thought that you could use this place for your own gain and live out your days here, but you did not ask my name; for my name is *Discord* and it is my nature to deceive. You have consumed readily each day, not wondering if perhaps the thing that gave you life was poisoned. Now the poison has done its work, and it is too late for you."

"What will you do with me now?" The knight trembled.

"Tomorrow, I will eat you."

And so that night, with the dragon fast asleep, the young knight felt his way to the front of the cave, relieved to feel fresh air against his face for the first time in a long while. His vision was blurry, and he could not be sure for how long he walked or in which direction; he made it to the fork in the road but could no longer remember whether he ought to go to the left or the right.

Certain the dragon was following behind him, knowing he would never be able to get away far enough or fast enough, no longer able to rely on his sight, he did the only thing he could:

He felt his way forward to the edge of the cliff.

And he plunged.

Chapter Nine

I kicked off my shoes in a hurry inside my parents' foyer—more an old habit than a sign of respect. The cold marble floor slapped against the soles of my feet as I crossed with bullish intent. Dad stepped out of his office holding a tumbler of bourbon, judging by the smell and color of it, despite it being hardly an hour past lunch. My desire for it made me pause for only a moment before continuing past him through to the living room, peeking in doors as I went.

"Where's Mom?" I demanded.

His mouth opened but didn't have time to form a response before I caught sight of her sitting at the island in the kitchen, the countertops a perfect match to the floor. She sat with her glasses perched on the tip of her nose, gardening magazines and seed subscription mailers scattered around the table. Looming shadows hovered around her, perched over her shoulder like they too had an interest in landscaping.

She scribbled something onto graph paper where she'd sketched garden boxes, all positioned within the perfectly scaled parameters of the yard. Every year she started preparing for the next season so far in advance that I wondered if she thought careful planning could negate the violence of nature—as though enough forethought could stop the damage of a drought or the pestilence of aphids on her crops.

"How could you?" I asked, dropping Jaak's story on the table, ignoring the insufferable cacophony of the Koels cackling around her in a dissonant halo of sound. My breaths were shallow and fast, fingers clenched into fists at my side. I tried to breathe through the tension, but each exhale only made me more impatient, as though there wasn't time to breathe.

"How could I *what?*" she said slowly, staring at the pages as though his name wasn't glaring at her from the cover. Mom took her time before saying anything else; she folded her glasses first, then used the corner of them to push the papers off of her schematics as though she couldn't bring herself to touch Jaak's final offering to us.

"You *knew*, Mom."

"How could I?" She sniffed, feigning innocence.

"You told me at the funeral how dark his last story was and blamed me for what he did even after you saw this? How could you? How could you do that to me, to *him?*" I noticed that Dad, up until now lingering in the doorway, retreated slowly, shaking his head as he went. The stairs creaked as he climbed them, no doubt sighing as he shied away from the familiar collision of the two women in his life. "Did you read it before he died, or after?" A long pause, and then: "*Answer!*"

"Before we left."

"Before you left..." I felt lifted from my body momentarily, watching us lock eyes across the island from a distance. The sound of the Koels felt as encompassing as white noise, a dull static in my head that silenced everything else, like a gunshot fired directly next to my ear. The house smelled like lemons—not her lotion, but a synthetic lemon scent, like mom recently scrubbed down the countertops. And a pot roast was cooking in a crock pot on the counter.

I was surprised my eyes were dry as I watched the scene unfolding from afar; my anger was so hot that it singed away any chance of tears, dried me out entirely. I felt barren and parched, raw with the sting of hatred that burned through my center and sent blood to my cheeks.

The nothingness I'd felt for days subsided; like a defibrillator, the pain of her betrayal shocked life back into my being.

Understanding crashed into me like a shotput tossed into a cabinet of precious china; everything fragile inside me that I'd so diligently guarded shattered, sharp edges exploding and stabbing and piercing, alighting me with a plethora of feelings that popped out in a disorganized stream like a confetti popper, leaving a mess.

My head swung in disbelief as I paced in front of the counter. I slammed my palms against the island, the jolt of it leaving my hands red and vibrating as I edged the pages closer to her, waiting until she looked at it to say, "You went on a fucking vacation after you read this?" The welt on my hand responded to the countertop assault with a steady hum of pain; I clenched my fist to conceal the bandage.

"How was I supposed to know?" she yelped, face red.

"You're really that *blind?*"

I snatched the manuscript off the table and flipped through, rendering various points of the story into something she might properly digest. Jaak as the wise middleman in an enduring fight between the two sides of our household. Each competing kingdom so caught up in their own grievances they couldn't see how much they hurt Sir Ivanguard by making him the messenger. A lonely garden where he could reflect and see the world for what it really was?

"I'm not saying I didn't have a role," I added as I slammed the pages down in front of her again. She stared blankly at it as though it wasn't there. "But *I* didn't read it until it was too late to do anything. *You* could have stopped it. *You* could have done something about it, and instead you were on a fucking road trip, of all fucking things, travelling around like you—"

"Language, Neviah."

"What are you going to do about it?" I shrugged, pursing my lips, arms crossing against my chest. Blood rushed from my veins, replaced by a chill so cold that it burned. "I'm willing to fess up to my role in things. But what about you? What are you going to do about it? Keep in mind, won't you, that you're my mother too, so if I fucked up, that's a little bit your fault too."

"What do you mean 'what am I going to *do*' about it?"

"You were his mom!"

"I *am* his mom. And what, you think that gives me superpowers? You think I can turn back time and make him change what he did? He made his choices, Neviah!" She stood from the table abruptly as though she was going somewhere, remembered that all her papers were set out on the table and that it was her house, then sank back onto the stool resolutely and motioned at the door.

"You and Jaak are grownups who make your own decisions, Neviah. The rest is between you and God. I did my part."

"And what part is that?"

My heart went from beating out of my ribcage to suddenly being stuck in my chest, like the exertion of my anger was too much and had caused it to seize up inside of me. My fingers and toes felt cold, as though the ice inside me had circulated to my extremities. My tongue swelled as adrenaline took over, my heart jolting back to life when she continued to say nothing.

"Don't tell me that your part was being our parent." My finger jabbed in her direction, my words spoken through clenched teeth. "I've heard that before, and it's bullshit. You hated me and you babied him—as though Jaak wasn't fully capable of getting into his own trouble without me. You didn't see it because you didn't want to."

"Your brother's dead," she spat, pausing for a moment, leaving just enough time for me to feel like she was rubbing it in my face, accusing me. She took a breath and shook her head, ending the quiet staring contest by adding, "And you're going to point fingers at him? My God, Neviah, I've always known you were selfish, but this is above and beyond what I'd expect, even from you."

"I'm not making it his fault! I'm saying you were a shitty parent! You played sides! You made me feel like garbage. I'm saying that you hurt him just as much as I did and he *knew* that, but you still won't fess up to it. How can you keep acting like you haven't fucked this up? You're responsible for creating two, utterly fucked up kids. So, stop acting like—"

"I've given you the answers, Neviah," she said, her voice so calm in the face of my accusations that I froze, realizing only once I froze that I was pacing again. I stared at her from the other side of the island. She tented her fingers under her chin, elbows resting on the table, leaning in as though she was schooling an indignant or incompetent child holding up the class.

"The right answers," I echoed, disbelief ripe in my voice. She started to tidy her gardening papers into a neat stack; I glanced at the garden templates from across the island, noted that she wanted to tear out Jaak's greenhouse to make room for a porch swing by the water, and despite already being at my capacity for anger, I somehow made room for more.

My hands were immediately on her plans, tearing them into thin strips that I let twist and fall to the floor, no better than a pile of newspaper clippings used to mulch a flower bed. The side of my foot slid against them, shovelling them aside in a tiny heap. She was speechless for a moment, and then she stood and wiped her hands against her thighs, straightening her blouse.

"Touch his garden and I'm done," I scolded.

She sneered. "I wish you would be."

"I mean with *you*, Mom. I'll care for it, do whatever needs to be done every year to keep his greenhouse going, but it was his spot. It was the one thing that gave him peace in the middle of the hell you brought us both, and if you can't find a way to be better for what you did to him, at least let me keep this much of him alive."

"Fine. But I did everything I could to make him see the truth, Neviah." She sighed, this time exhaling through her mouth so that the sound came out as a loud whoosh. "He knew better and chose to do this to us anyway. It was a selfish thing he did, and that is not and will never be my fault. I suggest you go now, since I know how much it pains you to be here and all."

"You seriously think I'll just—"

"Goodbye, Neviah."

Chapter Ten

"And then she had the nerve to tell me to get out of her house as though I didn't have a foot out the door already." I spoke over a mouthful of food, legs draped over Ezra's lap as he flipped through movie options for the evening. I helped myself to a second portion from the takeout containers strewn across the table, plucking out a potsticker and biting into it with a groan. I hadn't told him about Jaak's story or why I'd gone to Mom's, only that I'd visited and been challenged by her usual, confrontational self.

"She said she'd keep his garden, though. For now, at least." I shrugged and reached for another dumpling, watching Ezra cast me a side eye as I drowned my feelings in takeout. My face twisted in a curt sneer as I plopped the dumpling into my mouth, moaning theatrically, murmuring 'mmm' and 'so good' as I chewed.

He rolled his eyes and squeezed my knee, earning a pained yelp from me, though it didn't hurt. I said, "Okay, okay, I know...I'm avoiding your question. No...the interview didn't go great."

"How come?"

I would tell Ezra about the note and the story eventually, but for the time being, I shook my head, muttering excuses about it not being my primary field, about being out of practice with interviews outside of the financial sector. "*But,*" I added, pointing a dumpling at him, "it's good because it made me realize how much I really want this."

"Oh, yeah?" He raised a brow.

"Yeah, I think it'll be good for me. Helping other people, getting out of my own head. You know?" *Helping someone the way I couldn't be bothered to help my own brother.* I licked the tips of my fingers and wiped my hands on my pants, finally finished with the makeshift buffet. "I think botching the interview lit a fire under my ass. In the morning I'm gonna start scouring the listings again and maybe—"

"I have a connection I can hook you up with," Ezra said as I gathered the takeout boxes to put into the fridge. Ezra's hand pressed firmly on my knee when I tried to stand, his face drooping grimly as he urged me to sit back down, studying me in a way that made me shrink. "I just worry you're gonna rush things, that's all."

"It's been months," I protested.

"But I mean...have you done anything to...I know things get easier with time, but it just seems like maybe there're some things you ought to look into first, especially in light of...you know?" Ezra shrugged and looked away, fingers crossing in his lap. "The woman I'm thinking of is the counselor I talked to after my parents died...she really helped me. If I give you her number, I think you should just talk to her first."

"Talk to her? I'm fine."

He hesitated. "I know, but—"

"And she won't hire me if I'm a client. I'm *fine*," I repeated, standing before he could anticipate it and urge me to stay seated again. The pile of containers teetering in my hands required only a single trip to the kitchen. They tumbled on the counter, and I picked them up separately, nesting each into the fridge as I called over my shoulder to Ezra: "I've got energy again. I'm wearing something other than sweatpants. I'm the spitting image of wellness," I boasted.

"You're just so angry at your mom and I don't think—"

"Really? You're defending her?"

"I'm not saying she hasn't done some shitty stuff..."

"Then why are you defending her? She's the parent," I said, sipping a can of soda on the coffee table, contemplating reaching for the whiskey. "It's her job to make sure we turned out okay, not the other way around. If I can't blame her, then I can only blame my—"

"Maybe it's not about blaming someone."

"It's someone's fault."

"Pointed fingers aren't obligated to land on the truth."

"Wow, you get that out of a fortune cookie?" I rolled my eyes, though I grinned to lighten the mood. "Are you gonna give me her card or not? This isn't about my mom, anyway. Sorry I even brought her up. I need to figure out my next steps. Wouldn't I need to go back to school or something to work with an actual counselor?"

"Probably..."

"That's a lot more work than the job I applied for with social services," I added when he continued to look uncertain, rocking on the balls of his feet. "So, I don't even know if I want to do it. Maybe she'll let me job shadow for awhile to get a feel for it and see if it's something I even want to pursue. What's rushed about that?"

"Okay, fine. Fine." Ezra handed the card to me, pulling it back before I could grab it. He held it just out of reach, scrutinizing every detail of my face before finally relinquishing it. I smiled despite the flash of annoyance his inspection invoked, stashing it before he could change his mind. He looked like he wanted to as he warned, "Just don't rush it, okay? Focus on taking care of yourself first."

I smiled, squeezing his hand. "Of course. No rush."

Chapter Eleven

"This is Neviah, the student I was telling you about on the phone." Mrs. Park, the counselor, introduced me to a family as they entered the portable building housing her office; a few bookshelves lined the walls, degrees hung prominently alongside them so they would be visible from the armchairs where clients sat; minimalist art hung from the walls in soothing shades of green and grey, giving depth to the plain, white walls of the office. "She's been shadowing with me for several months now while working on her Master's—in family treatment. I'll have you sign the consent form in just a minute. In the meantime, come in, please. Make yourselves comfortable."

Mrs. Park smiled, unaware the first Koel of the session entered as she ushered them inside. The first person through the door was a burly middle-aged man who looked around distractedly, impressed by the setup of the office but not wanting to admit it. He identified himself as, "Dan, and you spoke with my wife, Joyce, on the phone."

"Yes, welcome." Mrs. Park took the man's hand before reaching for the woman's. She accepted the handshake, though her shoulders tensed at the touch. Mrs. Park's eyes darted to their hands, feeling the change in the woman's posture. She smiled, giving a short nod.

"So, how do we do this?" Dan's voice was gruff, his shoulders squared as though he'd just entered a fighting pit.

His wife looked like she matched him in height, but her shoulders pulled forward as though a great weight was on her back. She stepped in behind him, hands clasped together in front of her chest like she was in prayer. She glanced at her husband repeatedly, little worried looks as though she was afraid that he was about the say something that would embarrass both of them.

It was the look of a first-time mother about to brave a busy, weekend supermarket with a colicky toddler who was bound to cause a scene and force them home ahead of schedule and empty-handed.

"Grab a seat in one of the comfy chairs." Mrs. Park ushered them to the armchairs in the corner of the room, then paused before shutting the door. I craned my neck to look out at whatever had given her reason to pause. Mrs. Park frowned. "Is someone else joining us?"

"Our daughter, Martha," the man said. "She's being a little—"

"Being difficult," his wife censored.

"Well, hello," Mrs. Park greeted the young girl, her voice taking on an uncomfortable sing-songiness as she moved aside to let her in; the contrived pleasantry of her tone made it clear that Mrs. Park was neither accustomed to nor comfortable working with youth.

There was a long pause, then the quiet tap of sneakers against the concrete steps outside the door as Martha made her way inside. The hood of her sweater was drawn up over her head, the strings pulled tightly so that only her eyes showed through the opening.

A growling bear emblem dominated the front of the hoodie.

"Pull up a seat," Mrs. Park encouraged Martha, launching into questions for her parents as soon as the girl's bottom hit the chair: What brings you in? *We just don't know how much longer we can do this.* This? *Our marriage has been falling apart for awhile now, and* *we've tried everything but...*How long have you been having these problems? *He lost his job last year and things haven't been the same since.* Who else is in the house? *Just our daughter.* And how old are you, sweetheart? *Silence.* I get it, it can be uncomfortable the first time.

Tick, tock. The clock chimed on the wall as we waited.

Martha crossed her arms.

"She's fifteen," her mother finally answered, poking her daughter with an elbow, urging her to correct her posture. The girl let out a short huff and wiggled marginally straighter, reaching into the pocket of her hoodie, and pulling out a phone. I looked away quickly when she glanced up at me, unnerved by the intensity of her gaze, thankful when she turned her attention to the phone screen.

I snuck a glimpse of myself in the reflection of a photo frame on the table, able to see myself only well enough to tamp down a few rebellious hairs, feeling dishevelled and weighed down by the pressure of balancing school and office hours. In a few weeks there would be enough Adderall to facilitate a few intensive study sessions before final exams, followed by a long and luxurious term break.

"She's why we're here," Dan huffed. Joyce started to say something to him but shrank under his glare. His words felt like a bull let loose in the office. "Oh, just cut the shit, okay? You're always defending her and I'm sick of it—dragging me into meetings like I have anything to do with it. Maybe if you'd take that damn phone away from her..."

"I thought—" Mrs. Park was cut off.

"I mean, we *are* having marital problems that we need to address," Joyce tried to recover, glancing at her husband with the wounded gaze of someone watching a promise being broken. "And you said you would be open to this," she addressed him directly. "Namely, there's a lot of...how would you put it, honey? Discord? In the way we think it's best to handle the problems we've been noticing at home and school with Martha. Do you want to tell Mrs. Park about some of the things that have been going on, sweetie? Martha, we're here for you."

My heart jolted. The girl didn't want to talk. I felt adrenaline seeping through my limbs, compelling me to say something on her behalf. It might as well have been my own mother sitting in the chair across from Mrs. Park; not listening, not wanting to, giving me permission to speak only when she was trying to paint me into a corner.

Joyce started to speak for her daughter:

"I caught her...she was..."

"Yes?" Mrs. Park encouraged. "Take your time."

"I tried to tell her that she's beautiful just the way she is and that she didn't need to be so restrictive about her diet, but she still...she was throwing up after dinner one night. I wasn't *snooping*," she defended prematurely. "I just happened to hear her and was worried that maybe she was coming down with something, that's all, but then I got worried and so I found out that she'd been hiding bits of her dinner under the bed and so we took away her door because obviously we couldn't..."

Martha worked through an itinerary of annoying behaviors. She tapped her foot, one leg crossed over the other as she slouched in her chair, knocking the tip of her sneaker against the edge of the table. When that failed to rile anyone, she stared at her chest, pulling the string of her hoodie so that it snapped against her covered chin, then fidgeted in her seat. She fished in the mint bowl on the table, loosening her hood just enough to pop a spearmint candy in her mouth, then another, then another before finally shoving a handful of the candies in her pocket.

"Would you sit up straight?" her mom pleaded.

"Sit up," her dad demanded.

"Dan—" Joyce's voice was desperate. Her husband turned to look at her, making her sink back in her seat, angling her body away from him ever so slightly. I watched with fascination, listening to a Koel click and chitter behind me as it moved closer. Joyce seemed smaller suddenly, curled up in her seat, and Dan's presence seemed to grow.

Martha faded into the background of their quiet standoff.

"You know, for marriage issues, I suggest that children are left out of it, at least until you've had time to make sense of the situation for yourselves, locate the heart of the problem, get the process started," Mrs. Park finally suggested. "It sounds like you've got some things you'd like to talk about that maybe wouldn't be best in front of—"

"She should hear this," her dad insisted.

"Dan, stop it," Joyce barked.

Dan leaned down to whisper in his wife's ear. Her face turned milky white, and she pulled back, mouth dangling open like there was something more she wanted to say. Joyce made eye contact with him then snapped it shut again, lips pinched together.

My heart clopped like a racehorse, rising higher in my throat with every beat; I wished I could excuse myself to fish around in my purse for one of the tiny, blue pills the doctor had given me after Jaak died. They were meant for moments like this when my heart wouldn't stop racing no matter how many deep breaths I took. I could pop it into my mouth as casually as if it were an ibuprofen tablet. My fingers itched, twitching as I resisted the urge to reach for one.

Mrs. Park started nervously tapping the end up her pen against her notepad. "I mean, eventually, our goal is absolutely to have the whole family involved, but a third person can complicate things when everyone isn't on the same page about what we're—"

"Why don't you ask *her* why we're here." Dan nodded to Martha.

"It doesn't seem like—"

"It's her fault," he repeated, cutting Mrs. Park off again. Dan frowned as though everyone in the room was wasting his time by not coming to terms with the fact of it already. A second and third Koel weren't far behind, joining in with the elation of the early bird. I watched the shadows swim dizzying, excitable circles around the room.

After the warning in Jaak's story, it was clear that I could no longer treat the creatures as friends; however, it was unclear whether they ought to be ignored in their entirety; it seemed, though veiled in Jaak's message, that perhaps ignoring them carried its own dangers.

"Why do you think it's Martha's fault?" Mrs. Park pressed.

My initial query to her conveniently omitted any mention of Jaak. If I told her, I'd have risked her looking at me with the same awful, pitying look I'd gotten so many times when others found out, and then she'd have sent me home to 'rest' or 'get well'. The sentiments always made me wonder how many other Jaaks would jump while I was 'resting'; conjured the taste of chocolate ice cream from my date, made me imagine my phone vibrating in my pocket when it wasn't.

Right after he died, I'd strongly considered killing myself, if Jaak hadn't already done it first. It's not that I wanted to die, only that I wasn't quite sure how I was supposed to keep living after I left the police station, having confirmed what I already knew had happened. They'd uttered their apologies and well-wishes, asked if there was anyone I could call and, when the answer was no, let me wander out of the precinct and into the nearest bar without a crutch to lean on.

I'd spent the night getting acquainted with the floor of my apartment, unsure how I managed to get home. With the alcohol besting my senses, I was happy to indulge myself when I imagined Jaak appearing in the corner of the room, half of his expression missing where part of his skull was crushed from the fall. I slurred drunken profanities at him, choking on saliva, face wet with snot and tears and burbled spit as I begged him to wake me; to tell me it was all a dream; that we were children again camping in the backyard below the stars.

Yes, I'd have earnestly considered doing anything it took to end the pain I felt, even such a permanent solution as death, if anyone would have cared. But because Jaak did it first, I would always be remembered in his shadow. My tragedy would be absorbed into his, making his death more devasting in its ability to suck other lives along with it. And my parents would forever remember me as the selfish one; I would be responsible for, not only the pain my death would cause, but the pain caused by Jaak's death, as well. I would be the one who was selfish enough to put them through the death of a child a second time despite knowing firsthand the pain it would cause them.

The tense silence in the office had loomed too long.

"I can take her outside," I said suddenly and without thinking, compelled to stand by a force that seemed outside of myself. Everyone's eyes were suddenly on me, as though aware for the first time that there was a fifth body in the office. I laced my hands together, brow beaded with sweat, trying not to pick at the skin around my fingernails as nervous energy shocked through me.

"Yes," Mrs. Park said abruptly, standing next to me. I smoothed down my blouse and straightened my shoulders the way someone only does when they feel small. I lifted my hand in a curt wave, letting it drop when the man turned his glare from his daughter to me.

The girl stood and headed wordlessly for the door.

We all held our breath.

Yes, I'd have hurt myself if Jaak hadn't done it first, and in the days and weeks and months following the revelation of his death, it was difficult to find reasons not to. But suddenly, I was being given an easy answer by the universe, by Jaak: *Help the girl.* After all, it was easy to be strong for someone else, hard to be strong for yourself.

"See? This is what I mean." Her dad crossed his arms against his chest, shoulders pinned back so that he loomed in the leather tub seat. He raised an arm only long enough to point at his daughter's back as she disappeared outside. "No respect for other people. No manners. Always on that damn phone doing God knows what with—"

"I hardly think—" Joyce started.

"You know she's been talking to that kid again!" Dan glowered. "Do you know how fucking hard it's been for me since you—" He abruptly turned away from Joyce to stare at Mrs. Park and I, the words stopping as though a failsafe activated. "Joyce needs a lot of rest," he said weakly, sinking back into his chair. I realized suddenly that his chin was marked with stubble and his eyes were glazed over as though he hadn't slept in a long time. Dan sighed tiredly, rubbing his eyes.

"Excuse us." Mrs. Park guided me outside by the elbow after flashing a reassuring smile at the couple. We followed Martha to the yard and watched her take a seat on a bench several feet away from the door, just out of earshot. Mrs. Park leaned in close, speaking low, hand still cupped over my elbow in a way that made me wonder at her unspoken opinion regarding the lack of restraint I'd shown. I started to apologize but she shook her head, cutting me off before I started.

"Too late now," she said, confronting doubts I hadn't voiced.

"We could go back in, and I could tell them—"

"Babysitting."

"What?"

"Try to get to know her, get her talking, use some of those development courses you said you're taking. We'll talk about things after if there's anything you think it might be good for me to know about her parents or home life, or if any concerns come up with Martha you think we ought to address. You're doing me a favor, really, by keeping an eye on her." She scanned my face as though she was a robot calculating the probability of error in her decision to leave me unattended, then gave a short nod. "You don't have to do any more than you're comfortable with, okay? Just watch her and make sure she's safe. Poke your head in if she tries to take off or something."

"You're sure you don't want me to try—"

"I know you want to be a counselor." Mrs. Park squeezed my arm reassuringly, a maternal gesture. "But this isn't the kind of situation I'd like to see you starting from—hence, babysitting. This was supposed to be an easy intake, so really, today is *just* about getting information." She cocked a brow as she assessed me, waiting until I nodded to continue. "You don't need to be a hero right now. Just keep an eye on her until we're done and make sure she stays out of trouble."

"Don't worry." I looked at the teenager as she pulled blades of grass apart, saw the frustration keeping the muscles in her forehead permanently furled. A ladybug crawled up the side of her shorts and I watched her let it crawl into her hands, just like Jaak might have done if he wasn't charred in a box on my parents' mantle.

"I'll take care of her. I promise."

Mrs. Park gave a short nod.

Tick, tock.

Chapter Twelve

"That your high school?" I nodded at the bear printed on the front of her sweater. She was small for a high schooler, even for a freshman, her arms and legs collectively no bigger than one of my thighs. She crossed her arms over the emblem; bone-thin rails that hardly covered the image. She appraised me quietly, making quick calculations of my age when I told her that her high school was my alma mater, as well.

"Twenty-five," I said, saving her the guess work.

Martha nodded, retreating into silence as she molded a pile of slush in her bare hands. In our region, spring and winter never failed in their tumultuous courtship—every year they brushed up against each other, clinging to one another long after their doomed affair ran its course. The sun was hot, promising an early spring, and bugs and early blooming daffodils were already making an appearance; still, piles of snow lingered in shaded corners that the sun never touched.

After some time, the silence wore on her; her fidgeting became more apparent. She pulled down her hood to reveal silky black hair hanging straight down past her shoulders, running her fingers through it like a comb and twisting the ends as she huffed: "You don't know my family, okay? I already told Mom I'm not gonna talk to anyone."

"Sure." I shrugged, faking disinterest.

"I'm not talking to anyone about our business," she repeated, turning away again. Her hands moved restlessly; she cracked her knuckles one by one, then threw her head back with an embellished sigh. After awhile, she glanced at the door of the office and scoffed.

"You know, my mom always used to tell me female bears are the baddest creatures alive," I said, deciding to fill the silence with something she would deem non-threatening. I nodded at the bear on Martha's sweater when she looked confused. She twisted her face, puzzled.

"How do you know it's a *she*?"

"Just something Mom used to tell us." I shrugged, plucking a dead blade of grass to fidget with. "She said, 'There's no force on earth stronger than a mama bear who thinks her cubs might be in danger.' They'd kill without mercy, attack unprovoked just to be sure they struck first. But it was just a story she liked to tell," I admitted, flicking the blade of grass away. "Truth is, I looked it up and realized most cubs die from disease, starvation, predators, male bears. Turns out there *is* something out there more vicious than a mama bear."

"Sure, but God as a school mascot would be a little intense, so..." Martha glanced up and smiled. "But I'm still not talking," she added quickly with a scowl, not wanting me to mistake the quip for an indication of how the rest of our conversation would go. I shrugged again as though I didn't care one way or another.

"Besides, I know what you'll say," she added. A Koel leaned out from beside the portable office building. "That boys are bad and I ought to wait until I'm older and married and whatever," Martha said, sinking lower against the bench, arms against her chest. "I tried to talk to Mom about it, but..." She drooped, then shook her head. "But like,

I'm allowed to talk to people. I'm fifteen. It's not like I'm ten or whatever. I know not to talk to strangers or whatever they're so afraid of. He goes to the other high school, and we've met a couple times in person so—"

"Who's this now?" I quirked a brow, trying to keep up.

"It doesn't matter," she sighed, realizing for the first time that maybe I wasn't as filled in on her parents' concerns as she thought I was. She chewed her bottom lip, deciding how much to share with me. "Dad thinks I'm gonna end up pregnant or something but we're not even having sex. He just gets me, you know?"

"Your boyfriend?"

She shrugged. "Like, what person doesn't want to feel like someone loves them and cares about them? Dad thinks I'm like, boy crazy or something stupid, though, and Mom doesn't do jack shit when Dad says something about it. She's always in bed lately," she complained, rubbing a leaf between her fingers until it was ruined. "Can't blame her, though."

"Why's that?"

"Because my dad's an asshole," she scoffed, doubling down when I frowned. "No, seriously, he's a dick. He's a dick to my mom. He's always at work and then when he gets home, he's tired and bitchy—and he wonders why I'd rather be on my phone. I just wish my mom would work up the balls to tell him she's had enough of his shit by leaving already," she huffed, saying a surprising amount for someone committed to saying nothing at all.

"Do you feel unsafe?"

"Nah, nothing like that." Martha rolled her eyes and crossed her arms against her chest again, though her foot began tapping nervously as one leg crossed over the other. She noticed my quiet appraisal and rolled her eyes, uncrossing herself to gesture with her hands. "Seriously, it's nothing."

"My parents were assholes too," I said, vulnerability rewarded when Martha perked up. She wrinkled her face, not entirely convinced, so I nodded. "It's true. I mean, my mom's always been a real gas lighter—she'll back you into a corner so you say or do something she can use to convince you she's the victim and you're the worst person to have walked the earth. I wouldn't wish it on anyone..." I trailed off, letting Martha decide what to do with the information.

"You still talk to her?" she finally asked.

"Rarely," I admitted, but unsure of what answer she was looking for, I added, "I could see her more, if I wanted. It's just a choice I've made for myself. Boundaries are important in relationships, especially when they're toxic. A little hard for you, though, since you can't exactly control how much you have to see your parents right now."

She scowled. "Yeah."

"But it gets better as you get older and can stretch your legs a little. And in the meantime, that's why I'm here. I didn't have anyone when I was your age." *Except for Jaak.* Poor, dead Jaak. "I don't want other kids going through that like I did. Parents don't know everything—in fact, I suspect there's a mountain of things they don't know."

I pulled out my phone and nodded for Martha to pull out hers. I few seconds later, her phone pinged as I wirelessly transferred my contact information to her.

A Koel moved in closer behind us.

"My phone number," I said, shivering as I thought about what little good that had done for Jaak when I didn't pick up. "I know you said it's nothing, but if you ever feel unsafe or need anything, you can give me a call or shoot me a text. I might not be able to pick up right away, but I promise I'll do my best to be there if you're in a crisis. Mind you, if you ever feel *really* in danger, just call the cops. Don't wait up for me to answer if you're in danger or think you're going to..." *Hurt yourself.*

Martha picked at her fingernails. "What if it's not me that—"

The door creaked open, drawing our attention to the three voices previously contained in the office. They laughed as they came out, a stark contrast to the mood when they'd entered.

"Good news," Mrs. Park said to Martha, boasting the confidence of an underdog presented with a gold medal. "Mom and Dad agreed it's best if you don't come until they sort some stuff out. I've given them lots to think about, and in the meantime, you just hang tight and try not to get into too much trouble, alright? What's wrong?" Mrs. Park sagged when Martha didn't immediately look thrilled by her victory. Martha glanced at me, then at Mrs. Park.

"What if I want to come back?" Martha asked, looking back at me as though it was my decision to make. I shook my head at Mrs. Park, unsure what to say. A Koel tucked into the doorway behind them tilted its head as though it was curious what my response would be.

Mrs. Park crossed her arms, staring at us for several, lingering moments before answering: "I would still supervise, of course, until Neviah gets her license. But I don't see why not. Neviah?"

Adrenaline poured through me as I nodded.

Chapter Thirteen

Only three other students remained in the auditorium when the proctor announced the final ten minutes of our exam, which worked just fine for me; it turned out Koels liked exam rooms just as much as counseling offices. The shadows positioned themselves throughout the empty seats of colosseum-style lecture hall, while more yet leered in through the ground-level windows at the top of the room.

169. **What distorted thinking patterns are best represented by this statement: "I didn't get 100% on my exam, therefore, I am a bad student."**

(a) Labeling, mind reading

(b) Overgeneralizing, discounting the positives

(c) All or nothing thinking, labeling

(d) Emotional reasoning, fortune telling

Your Answer: _C_

My eyes were dark and swollen underneath from the late nights I'd spent studying and juggling appointments. I'd only seen Martha once since their first session; her mother called an emergency meeting the following week but failed to show up. Martha's father left in a rage when his wife didn't meet him at the office as expected, but Martha, much to his surprise, asked to stay and talk to me.

Martha didn't say much during the session, but the fact that she was there at all must have impressed Mrs. Park, who immediately made me responsible for four other, low-risk clients.

It came with a price.

My hair was dry and tangled, barely long enough to gather into a stumpy ponytail that might hide the evidence of my neglect while cramming for exam week and spreading myself thinner than the walls of a soap bubble. The words started blurring together on the paper, but I continued to mark answers as the clock ticked aggressively on the wall above words on the whiteboard welcoming students to their *Counseling Psychology 1200* final exam.

Tick, tock.

170. **All or nothing thinking (aka Black and White thinking) is** *best* **characterized as (the):**

(a) Belief that if you will fail you shouldn't try

(b) Belief racial inequality is no longer an issue

(c) Belief life is a never-ending pattern of defeat

(d) Thinking in absolutes (i.e. there is no such thing as doing a task moderately well; you either succeeded completely, or else you failed entirely)

Your Answer: _D_

My mind wandered despite the tension in the room as everyone rushed to finish the final questions. It was the last midterm before the long weekend, and Ezra had special plans for us. There'd be a nice dinner Friday in the city, followed by live music and a fancy hotel room with a jacuzzi tub and view of the city so high up that the Koels hardly mattered. I took the tiny sparks of excitement I felt thinking about it as a sign that the worst of my mourning was behind me.

171. **What is a cognitive distortion?**

(a) when head trauma impairs vision

(b) an exaggerated or irrational pattern of thinking

(c) the reversal of sensory data from the retina

Your Answer: _B_

I tapped my pencil faster, glancing up as the proctor updated the time on the whiteboard, letting us know that only five minutes remained. The long nights caught up to me as I neared the end, rapidly circling answers, eager to get home and sink into a hot bath, surrounded by soapy bubbles that smelled of vanilla and coconut.

172. **It is the duty of the counselor to invest in the care of their client while also doing what?**

(a) Responding to 'emergency' calls at all hours

(b) Maintaining clear professional boundaries

(c) Not indulging in vacations that make them unavailable to clients for extended periods

(d) Taking time to practice appropriate self-care

(e) Answers 'b' and 'd'

Your Answer: _E_

173. Under what condition(s) is a counselor required to fulfill their 'duty-to-report'?

(a) When someone is at immediate risk of harm.

(b) Suspected abuse of a minor or senior

(c) When they feel like they should

(d) When asked by a family member for updates

(e) Answers 'a' and 'b' only

Your Answer: _E_

The pencil eraser thumped erratically against the desk, my foot tapping the floor in an off-kilter rhythm. I glanced at the clock, its hands booming through the auditorium like shots fired with each movement. In just a few short hours I would be clean and curled up under a blanket with a fresh cup of tea, maybe delve into the pile of books I'd neglected, possibly with a clay face mask absolving my skin of the impurities brought on by stress and too many therapy-carbs.

174. When should the counselor refuse care?

(a) They don't like the counselee

(b) They are outside of their competencies

(c) They develop feelings for their counselee

(d) They disagree with the counselee's beliefs

(e) Answers 'b' and 'c' only

(f) All of the above

Your Answer: __E__

"Pencils down!"

175. The ability of the counselor to affect change is limited only by:

(a) Strength of their desire and willingness to help

(b) External factors in the counselee's life (e.g. support networks, income, transportation, etc.)

(c) The counselee's willingness to enact change

(d) Answers 'a' and 'c' only

(e) None of the above

Your Answer: ___

I checked to be sure my name was at the top of the booklet, no time left to complete the final question. My pencil clattered as it dropped on the desk, and even without taking time to question my responses, I was certain I'd done better than most of my peers.

After all, when an answer comes to you so easily—when the right choice feels as natural and self-evident as taking your next step or drawing you next breath—how could it be wrong?

Chapter Fourteen

The knock on the door came in the same moment that I turned off the faucet, bathtub adequately filled and brimming with bubbles. My lips curled up in a semi-formed smile, though my brows drew together in confusion, certain that Ezra was staying home to get some work done before our weekend outing. He'd been very forthcoming about the pile of projects he had to grade before we left the following evening, but I wondered if perhaps it had been a ruse to surprise me.

I threw on the fluffy, orange robe hanging on the bathroom door—a Christmas gift I hadn't taken the time to indulge in yet. The soft fabric caressed my bare skin and my smile widened, thinking perhaps my bubble bath had enough room for two. I got ahead of myself, wondering if he'd brought something delicious for dinner in honor of me finishing my exams; dumplings, Chinese food, pad thai, or maybe just burgers from that place I liked downtown...

I threw open the door to a teary-eyed Martha.

"Martha?" I gaped, hand immediately darting to the folds of my robe. I was covered but felt as though I was stark naked. Seeing a client in a bathrobe outside of work felt no less foreign that the idea of seeing a client *in* the office wearing a bathrobe.

"Neviah?" she choked, stifling back a sob. "I had nowhere else to go," she explained, cheeks puffy and eyes brimming with tears. "Can we talk? Please?"

"Come in before anyone sees you." I nudged her elbow, ushering her inside. I forced myself to breath normally, body straining not to hyperventilate as I thought of what emergency might have brought her to me, worsened by thoughts of what would happen if I crossed a line professionally. I glanced at her, smiling comfortingly as if nothing was wrong with her crying in my living room while I stood half-clothed.

"Why don't you have a seat?"

I pointed at the futon, then made my way to the kitchenette to grab her a glass of water. While there, I shoved dishes off the counter and into the sink, creating a small mountain as a testament to my neglect while studying. "Sorry about the mess," I said, hand trembling as I held the glass of water toward her. I left her long enough to throw on sweatpants and a hoodie, though the attire still felt too far from professionalism for comfort. I did my best to feign confidence as I said, "You'll understand my surprise at you being here. How did—"

"I'm sorry." Martha put the water on the table, untouched. "For showing up like this, I mean. You said that if I ever needed anything I could call, but you weren't answering," she continued as I realized I hadn't bothered to check my phone since the exam. I hit the lock button and was flashed with a dead battery indicator. "I didn't really think about it, I just had to get out of there. I, uh...when you dropped me your contact information, your address was saved in your phone."

"Why were you in such a hurry?" I strained to keep the words casual, wondering what the penalties were for having an underage client alone in your apartment at seven o'clock at night.

"I just need a place to stay for the night," Martha insisted, eyes wide, brows drawn up in the middle as she pleaded with me. She leaned forward, lip trembling like she might cry again. I scanned her body, looking for indications that she'd been hurt; whether by herself or by someone else was irrelevant, but images of her dad's heavy-handed demeanour in the office flooded my mind.

"Martha, you know I can't—"

"Please. You were the only one I trusted, you know?" She smiled, head nodding as though it might subconsciously change my mind. I shook my head and looked away, suddenly wishing I'd poured a glass of water for myself so I would have something to do with my hands. I mourned the bath that was growing cold a room over.

"I get that, but it's wrong, Martha."

"I just need some place to stay until tomorrow morning," she said. "Just until my friends have a chance to ask their parents if I can stay at any of their places without them snitching to my mom, or until I can come up with another plan or whatever. I'll take the couch. I don't even care. I just can't go back home for awhile, okay?"

"I'd need to tell your mom," I insisted.

"But *why?*"

"Due diligence." I shrugged. "I'll explain it to her, make sure she understands that you're somewhere safe, that I'm handling the situation. I'll suggest we meet for mediation if you're—"

"This is bullshit!" Martha shot to her feet, voice rising.

"Martha, why can't your mom know you're here?"

"She just can't, okay? She can't handle it right now, she's...got a lot going on. You don't need to know my family's business, alright? I'm not asking you to hide a fucking body, I'm just asking for a couch. You wanna know why I came here?" Martha took her seat again, realizing she had no idea where she would go if she left. "Because I thought you understood."

"I can lose my license." A license I didn't even have yet. The thought of being pegged for malpractice before even graduating had a golf ball-sized lump working its way up my throat. I twisted to plug my phone in beside the couch, knowing I couldn't do anything until it was charged, at least. "I have to call your mom, Martha."

"My mom would be upset if she finds out I'm here."

"That's why she needs to know."

"I'm doing this *for* her," Martha insisted, looking worriedly at the wall. "She just...she's got a lot on her plate, you know? So, the less on her plate, the better. I'm just gonna stay with my boyfriend for a while until her and dad work things out, then I'll go home," she promised, raven-feather hair swinging against her back as she paced; no doubt weighing her options, trying to figure out if other options even existed. I doubted it, since she'd shown up at my apartment in the first place.

Buying herself time, she wandered to the bookshelf and lifted a picture of Jaak. My fingers curled, resisting the urge to snatch it from her hands. She raised a brow curiously. "This your husband?"

"Brother," I clarified.

"Hm." Martha nodded and set it back down. "He's cute. Real lumberjack, folk song, indie artist vibe going on that I'm into." She waggled her eyebrows as though she was talking about a relative of a close friend, not her counselor. I saw him, though. For a second, in the lamplight, I saw his image in the photo juxtaposed next to her; there were obvious differences. His hair was a much lighter shade of brown, almost blond; her eyes were so dark they looked like they were missing irises while his were green like dark, earthy moss.

But I saw the resemblance, nonetheless; maybe in the way they both needed me—Jaak past tense, Martha present tense. A Koel peeked in from the balcony window. The clock ticked while she waited me out, letting the silence wear on me.

"I'll get you some blankets," I finally said, certain I'd be pouring myself something stronger than wine once she fell asleep.

I squeezed the bridge of my nose and stared past her as she wiggled in a presumable happy dance; she sang my praises and promised I wouldn't regret it, which was impossible to be sure of.

She stayed up later than expected, giving me plenty of time to wonder if I'd made the right choice by letting her stay. Each time I crept out to check if she was asleep, she was another episode deeper into the reality series she was watching, the volume from the TV too loud for the time of night. I snuck past, drowning out the drama unfolding on the screen—a woman talking to a friend about 'baby-trapping' a peer—and poured myself a drink before retreating back into my room; it was nearly morning before I was able to tip-toe past her fragile, sleeping body into the hallway to enlist backup.

Mrs. Park answered on the second ring: "Neviah?"

"Hi. I wasn't sure if you'd answer this late—or this early, I guess, depending on how you look at it. I'm in a bit of a situation and I need some...mentorship, I guess? Martha's here."

The line was silent for a beat.

"You're not at the office this late, are you?" Mrs. Park finally asked, grogginess fading from her voice. I could hear objects shifting in the background and the sound of a door opening as she snuck away somewhere more private to keep talking.

"She's at my apartment."

"Oh, dear..."

"I know. It looks bad, that's why I called—it was the first chance I got to step away. She was begging for a place to spend the night and was really upset. It sounds like home has been rough for her lately and I kind of just, panicked, you know? I told her I had to tell her mom and she looked like she'd just as soon dive out the window. I figured at least this way she's here; she's safe until someone can come and deal with this, right?"

"You've gotta let her mom know."

"I know, I know. I just..."

"You can't have clients sleeping on your couch. What if her mom finds out before you can tell her, and she decides to sue you? You know they've been having money problems, right? You might not have money yet, but you've got a liability policy that could make them pretty rich if they ever felt the need to sue for damages. This is why the rules are in place—to protect the client, yes, but also to protect you. Do you have her phone number?"

"Yeah, I think so."

"Good," she said, then lingered on the line for a few seconds before adding, "do you want me to call for you? One of us needs to call; if you don't, I have to. I know parents can be a bit tricky sometimes. I don't mind making the call if you need me to."

"No." I sighed, leaning a hand against the wall for stability.

"You're sure? I really don't—"

"Yeah, it should be me."

Her assurances that I was doing the right thing worked only minimally to stop the iron fist that gripped my insides. We lingered in silence for a few beats while I worked up the nerve to ask, "Is there something going on with her mom that I should know about? Martha seems pretty spooked about something going on at home."

"You don't need to worry about it."

"But I keep thinking—"

"I've got it under control. I can't tell you what my conversations have been with her parents, but I think Martha is trying to manipulate the situation a bit. Her dad had concerns about her and a boyfriend, right? And between you and me, there've been some indications that Martha hasn't been very honest about it with her parents, who have their own stuff going on right now. Try to take everything she says with a grain of salt, alright?"

She told me to call her with an update in the morning and we said our goodbyes. I searched through my recent contacts to a few weeks earlier when Martha's mom was running late to the appointment she never showed up for. The thought of it made the ball in my stomach tighten, but I clicked her number anyways, dialing twice before she answered.

Twenty minutes later, it was her dad who pounded on my door.

"I'm sorry, Marth—"

I stopped short at the glare she cut to me across the room as she jolted upright, her dad pulling her up by the elbow before she could get her feet under her. Her dad was yelling, though it sounded like a sea of static between me and Martha as I tried to mutter my apologies. I was certain that the neighbors on either side were being roused in their beds, hands groping for their phones, ready to call the police with a noise complaint at any moment. Martha smacked the glass of water she'd left on the table so that it shattered, water soaking my carpet.

She didn't speak as she was pulled out, but her eyes stayed on me until they couldn't anymore, face furled with betrayal. The sound of her father's voice echoed down the hallway as he continued to yell at her; that he'd deal with her in the morning, and how her mom was in bed sick again because of her, and why couldn't she ever just listen?

When they were gone, I slept uneasily.

"You did the right thing." Mrs. Park applauded me the morning after, calling to ensure Martha's parents were notified and I hadn't lost my nerve. I told her about Martha's dad, the way he'd yelled, but Mrs. Park seemed to only shrug on the other end of the line, insisting, "He's really just a big ol' teddy bear once you get to know him."

"So, they're good? Everything's good with them?"

"They're not your concern anymore," she said instead of answering the question, which made the room feel like it was dancing around me, spinning and swaying. "You've got a nice vacation coming up this weekend, don't you? Focus on recouping. Take some time."

I hung up, later pretending it was an accident.

The whole evening with Martha played over in my head a million different ways, wondering where or if it had gone wrong. Was it letting her come upstairs? Was it trying to get her to talk instead of just being there for her? Was it going by the book and notifying Mrs. Park, who clearly didn't have a shred of concern for what might be happening at home? Should I have told Mrs. Park, but waited until morning after Martha and I had talked more?

If only, if only, if only...

All of my imagined worst-case-scenarios paled in comparison to the scene unfolding outside Martha's house less than twenty-four hours later, when Ezra and I drove past on our way to the highway. We weren't even supposed to drive down her street—would have never been there if a water line hadn't happened to break on the main road earlier that day, routing us through a detour, or if Ezra had finished grading his papers on time and we weren't leaving town late.

Police cars lingered in Martha's driveway. Neighbors gawked as they passed by or otherwise leered out from behind their curtains for a better look at the unexpected interruption to their quaint, suburban lives. My heels clopped against the pavement as I approached the officers huddled in her driveway, and time shifted. I was in my nice interview clothes again, and my makeup was done up prettily as I approached the police station. One of the officers in Martha's driveway asked if I was okay, and I blinked hard to reorient myself.

"Where's Martha?" More of a demand than question.

"Are you related to the family?" They frowned.

I wasn't sure if I could say I was their counselor without breaking confidence, so my mouth snapped shut. The officer sighed while Ezra hovered beside us in his best dress shirt. Cool air snaked around the bare legs below my dress; it rippled my skin with tiny goosebumps.

"I work with them." A half-truth.

"I'm gonna have to ask you to get back into your car then," the officer insisted. Another whispered in his ear when I refused to move. He nodded once then pulled out his notepad, heaving out a sigh as he offered to take down my information in case they needed anything from me later. "In the meantime, it's best if you went home. Or to wherever it is you're heading," he said, issuing a second nod at our attire. My fingers curled tighter into my palms with each incline of his head, his assurances falling short. I started to protest, but Ezra stepped in to interrupt me.

"C'mon." He pulled me away, but my shoulders slumped forward, escaping his loose grip; my eyes locked onto a thin figure swaddled in an emergency blanket two houses over. Her raven hair fell messily around her face, skin pale and smooth like porcelain as she sat on the neighbor's steps, clutching a scratchy swath of fabric around her shoulders. An older woman spoke to her, jotting onto a legal pad, a child services badge dangling from her blouse.

"That's her," I muttered to Ezra. "That's Martha."

Martha raised her head, doing a double take when she saw me standing in her parents' driveway. I lifted my hand to wave, letting it hang motionlessly in the air when she only wrinkled her brow. Her brown eyes looked black from far away, and even in the low light, I could see that they were dark and puffy underneath. Her gaze dropped to her hands as if I wasn't there.

I glanced down at the hand that was suddenly on my arm as Ezra pulled me toward the truck. The officers were stiff, standing close, ready to escort me if Ezra failed. He looked at them nervously, pushing me back to the truck, but I kept my gaze over my shoulder.

I waited for Martha to look up and wave, but she never did.

"I have to help her, Ez..."

Ezra didn't start driving once we were back inside the truck, instead merely sat with his hands gripping the steering wheel, trying to make sense of the chaos happening around us. Martha didn't look up from her hands until the front door of her house opened, spitting two paramedics into the driveway. They each carried one end of a stretcher down the steps; the bag on top of the gurney was zipped tight.

Martha screamed.

She tried to rush toward it, but the social worker's grip was strong. Martha's face contorted as she wept, mouth forming around the same word over and over again. I couldn't hear her from inside the vehicle, but I could see that she was screaming for her mother. Her bottom lip stuck out as she sank to the ground, collapsing against the cobbled driveway.

It wasn't until Ezra shifted the truck into gear that I realized I was tugging at the door handle, trying to get out and go to her; he'd locked the door from the inside so that I couldn't open it from the passenger seat, but it didn't stop me from thumping the window as though I could break through it. I was screaming, unable stop myself any more than Martha could as she watched the officials slide the stretcher into the back of a truck and take it away from her.

In the coming weeks, the local news would be obsessed with the story of a 42-year-old mother who was found dead in her bathtub from self-inflicted wounds; of her mourning husband and sweet, innocent child who were holed up in a local hotel, their house too haunted by bittersweet memories to return to; of their sudden disappearance from town, pushed to their limits by the constant scrutiny of the press when rumors began to circulate of the abusive climate in their household.

The court would subpoena Mrs. Park's session notes and she would keep me at the edge of things, scaling back my involvement until it was as though I'd never met them, as though Martha hadn't trusted me to make things better. As though I hadn't promised Martha I would listen, only to ignore her muted implications that her mother was unwell. I'd missed the warning signs not once, but twice.

A group of Koels trailed behind the ambulance-turned-hearse, the sound of them echoing with the garishness of an approaching train or a tornado waiting to touch down. And in the midst of the noise and chaos scarring the evening, a flash of red and yellow appeared between the houses; Jaak stood in the shadows, shaking what little was left of his head as he watched my failure play out around us like a soap opera.

A cold draft snaked across the floormats; my body trembled discretely as every muscle clenched in shame. I looked behind me, head moving slowly and then all at once. A massive shadow occupied the back seat, its smile stretched with heartless fascination as I cried.

I envisioned Jaak stumbling through a stark and unyielding darkness he didn't deserve; watched Martha beat the ground until her hands were bloody, growing smaller in the rear-view mirror.

Tick. Tock.

PART III
Chapter One

Our house was overloaded with an assortment of decorations for Gabriel's birthday party: red, yellow, and orange streamers twisted across the ceiling to form a canopy above the table. I busied myself setting down rolls of napkins filled with cutlery while Ezra worked across from me with his back turned. He looped lengths of duct tape together and placed them on the backs of painted cardboard—the 'walls' of the castle he was constructing, turning our living room into something out of a fairy-tale. He pushed a panel up beside the window and stood back, nodding his approval before moving along to the next.

I sighed, relieved with how well the party was coming together, a happy distraction from daily life. I wanted to go to Ezra, place a hand on his back, praise his handiwork, but didn't. I was reminded for a moment of an old folk tale; an ice witch formed a wall of ice between two lovers. They watched each other parish through the glassy surface, an illusion cast in the ice by her magic, then went their separate ways, discouraged entirely by her trick, thinking the other was forever lost.

If there was a happy ending, I couldn't remember it.

Upstairs, our costumes waited on the bed; I would shimmy into a pair of leather pants with a sequined black shirt and a dragon mask reminiscent of Maleficent, while Ezra would be Prince Charming from head to toe, equipped with a fake metal sword and leather hilt. The clash of attire was a testament to our growing asynchrony, but soon, the evidence of our poor coordination would be swept away in a sea of children sporting costumes of their own.

Koels hovered noisily in the corner. There was no rhyme or reason to their presence anymore; they lingered readily at all hours, taking over for the natural shadows in the room. Every so often, I would catch sight of one wedged in behind a bookshelf or flattened below a dresser, or a shadow would pass by on the other side of the shower door, sweeping through the steam floating in the room.

A banner hung across the wall above the fireplace and television, proclaiming 'Happy Birthday' to Gabriel. I placed favor bags next to each child's place setting; the rest of the children living at the farm had grown fond of Gabriel during his stay, and almost everyone would be in attendance. The cake was the last piece to be hoisted off the kitchen counter and put in place, a leering, sugary castle that would sit at the center of the table, seven candles glowing boldly in the dark.

Knock, knock, knock.

I jolted at the intrusion from the kitchen, pressing a hand against my chest to quell its sudden throbbing. Ezra and I looked up and made eye contact for the first time in hours, though words had yet to enter the dialogue. He simply shrugged and nodded for me to answer it. I took a quick glance at my to do list, mentally checking off completed items until I felt confident that every detail of the evening was taken care of before rushing along to open the door.

Julie beamed at me from the porch.

"Hi, Nev. Okay, so—" She let herself in as soon as the door opened, counting the candles in her hands before setting them on the kitchen table. Jack-o-lanterns leered in from the porch rails. "I couldn't remember how old Gabriel was turning, so I grabbed six, then I was thinking, no, that's not right, is it? Because Riley's twice his age or so. Anyway—long story short, I only grabbed six and now I'll have to go grab one more. Do you need anything else while I'm at it?"

Julie finally took a breath, looking at me expectantly.

"No, I think we're good. Ezra's finishing up the decorations then we were gonna get changed. Why don't I come with you, though?" I offered, already slipping into my boots. I peeked back at Ezra as I shrugged on my coat. "I could use a ride. Just give me a second to tack up and I'll catch up with you. Go on, I won't be long. Promise."

I made quick work of saddling Nidhya and joined Julie on the road, smiling as I loped up beside her, countering her renewed protests: "It saves you the ride back and you've got two of you to get ready for tonight, so really, I don't mind. It's nice out today, anyways," I reiterated, trying too hard to hide how desperately I needed to get away from Ezra's silence. "How's Riley doing? He's been getting along well with his schoolwork?"

Julie lit up. "Yes, very."

"Glad to hear."

"I think the boys are off playing right now, actually," she said, looking through the trees as though she might catch a glimpse of them running through the woods, silhouettes darting through the dull reds, browns, yellows, and oranges of mid-autumn. Tiny, swaying ghosts hung sporadically throughout the trees; decorations made by the children as an art project leading up to Halloween. "I think they're at that fort they built on the other side of the creek. Have you seen it yet?"

"Nope," I said, struck by a pang of jealousy and unwilling to admit that it was the first time I was hearing about their fortress.

"It's nothing special," she briefed, waving a hand. "And, well...I wasn't really invited to see it, per say, I just followed the boys out one afternoon because I wanted to know where they were...you know? Anyway, it's a silly fort, but they're obsessed."

Oh, to be a child again.

"You know, Neviah, really...I can't thank you enough for the work you've done with us. I don't know if it's because he's coming into his own naturally, or if we're just addressing his needs in the right way now and it's snowballing into other areas of his life, but I don't think I'd have expected him to make a friend so easily, before everything here."

"Gabriel's a sweet kid. I'm glad they found each other."

"Do you think they'll stay?"

"Friends?" I frowned, stroking Nidhya's neck.

"No, no. Just...I imagine Martha will take Gabriel back soon. She's been doing good, it seems—her and I have been getting together for coffee on Thursdays when Riley's at school for the full day and with the tutor—and so I guess I haven't worked up the nerve to ask her if she'll be staying here with him after, or moving back to town."

"I'm not sure, to be honest."

The thought of them leaving made me nauseous.

"I hate the idea of Riley finally making a friend and then losing him that fast. But I guess that's how it goes," Julie said, back rippling as though she'd been struck by a sudden chill. She smiled and touched my arm. "I'm not sure what would have happened without us coming here. I know I said it already, but I just really can't thank you enough."

"I'm sure you guys would've been fine," I overstated.

"Too modest. You know, not to overstep, but...have you and Ezra thought about kids of your own?" She didn't seem to notice me pale. "I mean, I know it's probably rude to ask, but I just imagine you and Ezra would make such great parents." Julie beamed as though the idea was ingenious and entirely her own. "I imagine you raising them here, and Ezra teaching down at the school full-time so that—"

"Sorry, Julie, could you excuse me for a second?" Martha caught my eye through the window as we neared her cabin, sparing me the need to conjure a response for Julie's unsolicited musings. Martha threw something at the mirror, disappeared, paced in front of the upper window again. Retreated. "I just want to stop and see how Martha's doing. If you want to go ahead, I'll catch up in a few minutes."

I motioned at the row of cottages that came into view. "If you have the candles ready, I'll meet you at the house to grab them when I'm done here. I'll be awhile," I added when Julie insisted that she didn't mind waiting for me. "Maybe leave them in the mailbox and I'll grab them before I head back so that you can start getting ready, yeah?"

I waited until she was gone to knock.

Tick, tock.

Chapter Two

When no answer came, I knocked once more and then entered. Martha's cabin was immaculate, looking the same as when she'd moved in, save for the layer of dust that no longer coated the tops of vacant shelves and tables throughout the living room. I moved past the couch, up the stairs leading to a bathroom on the upper level. Martha was on the floor when I entered, her back arched over the toilet, lifting visibly with each labored breath, gaze cast into the bowl.

She held her hair back with a headband, her slipshod bleach job one of the first things she abandoned upon arrival, chopping it off with a pair of shears to start fresh. It was a short, dark pixie cut now, growing back slowly along with the rest of her. She'd put on weight over the last six months, but still, she was a small thing, never having reached her father's stature, though there was something to be said for his temper; I didn't blame her for any moodiness though, given the circumstances.

It was enough that she was alive and safe.

I swallowed hard.

Her head jerked up when she heard me exhale. She scowled for a moment, the look so fleeting I wasn't sure it had even happened. Looking up at me from the toilet bowl, her eyes went dark, face muscles drawn together with the same displeasure one might have when biting into something unexpectedly spoiled. She looked away and down at the spattered inner bowl again, her eyes drawn together as she caught her breath, neither of us daring to speak.

I searched the counter and then the floor, stepping forward when I saw the empty, yellow pill bottle beside the shower. A prescription taken out under my name—sleeping pills with an inscription on the side warning of the potential for nausea and vomiting when taken in excess of the recommended dosage. She mumbled something unintelligible as I analyzed the pills, turning the bottle over in my hand.

"Martha...where did you find these?"

Nidhya rattled the short rail installed outside the cabin for visitors to tie their horses, urging me to look up from the prescription label. Martha continued to mutter unintelligibly as she flushed the toilet, and I could tell by the way her lips moved that she was stuck in the familiar spiral that had threatened to bury her since the first night of her stay.

He's coming for me. Repeated often, after waking, before meals, after meals, before bed when she had lived with Ezra and I during the first few weeks of her stay, too fragile to be left unsupervised.

I frowned, face softening as I shut the door behind myself and slid my back down it, pulling my knees to my chest, trying to remember that she was still fragile. She remained where she was on the floor, giving no indication of moving away from the toilet bowl. I studied the pill bottle, then tucked it in my pocket.

"I'm sorry," Martha mumbled, doe-eyed when she looked up.

"Don't be. But..."

She pulled the sleeve of her shirt down so that it covered her palm and sniffled, dabbing away the tears on her cheeks. I frowned, certain her face was dry only a moment before, then shook my head as she stammered about eating something bad for dinner or a twenty-four-hour flu. "I feel better now, though," she insisted, still not rising.

"Martha—"

"Really, I feel better now."

"What's holding you back?" I wanted to reach out and touch her, put a hand to her cheek and find out for myself. For a moment, my face flushed as I thought of the day I'd brought her to the *Sanctuary*, wondered why I hadn't taken her under right then, gotten it out of the way so that I could guide her treatment more effectively.

A missed opportunity; a new 'what-if?'.

"What do—"

"I can't keep covering for you. Not every time. Not like this," I said, dropping my head into my hands and raking my fingers through my hair. Finally, I laced them behind my head and leaned back against the door. "We're supposed to be sending Gabriel with you tonight, remember? And before that it was two weeks ago, and before that it was a month ago, and every time you just keep saying the same thing. Why do you still think he's coming for you? It's been months now."

"I don't know..." Martha sighed, shoulders sagging.

My heart fluttered as I sympathized with the stress the transition had caused her, adrenaline seeping through me like an IV bag had switched open. "It's stressful, to be responsible for someone like you are for Gabriel, and...I mean...if you're not ready, it's natural for...I mean, it's natural to..." I searched for an alternate word for 'self-sabotage' but couldn't find one, so I let myself trail off. "If you're not ready, Gabriel can stay with us awhile longer. You know that, right?"

"I'm sure he could." Her eyes were dark, impenetrable.

"Really, it's no trouble. He's a good kid." I smiled distantly at the ceiling panels, noticing the stain of a watermark. "Obviously, we want you two back together as soon as possible, but—did he ever make you play that stupid game? The one with the knights and the castles and whatever? *Throne Astray?* He and Ezra have been having a hell of a time playing. They always crush me, but it's been fun having him there. And he's so helpful around the ranch and with..."

My smile wilted as I wondered at the empty nights to come.

"I can help, Martha. I just need you to be honest though, tell me what's going on in your head. It puts us both in a really weird spot if you're lying to yourself about your readiness to be a mom to—"

"I *am* his mom," she hissed, then clamped her eyes shut and exhaled. When they opened again, she softened her features and slid away from the toilet, pushing back with her heels until she was leaned against the cabinet below the sink. She mirrored me by dropping her head back against the cupboard, staring up at the blotchy spot on the ceiling panel. Martha's head shook as she apologized, eyes two dark circles amid the milky white ocean of her skin.

"It's just been hard, coming here."

"Have you been purging again?" I gestured to the toilet and her head lolled to the side so she could look at me as she rolled her eyes. She opened her mouth then snapped it shut, turning her attention back to the ceiling. There was nothing but silence for several minutes, save for the drip of the faucet, as each of us waited for the other to speak, to end the stand off.

I broke first.

"All I'm saying is that recovery is a difficult process. It's normal to be scared about going back to daily life, and maybe if we unpacked some of it...I mean, it's been almost six months and you still haven't told me much I didn't already know." I raised my hands then dropped them when she stayed quiet. "Why don't you get ready for the party? I know this isn't a great development, but I'm confident we'll get you back on track. Tonight, let's hold off on the big announcement though, okay? For Gabriel's sake, I think we should wait a bit longer."

Martha looked up at me as I stood, analyzing.

"You really don't mind?" she asked.

"Of course not." My shoulders melted, abandoning the tension I hadn't noticed building between them. I clung to the crumbs of Gabriel's presence, staving off the pitiful silence that would come in the days and months after the remnants of a child's presence once again departed our home. "Everything's okay now," I insisted, extending a hand to Martha. "Everything's going to be okay now...I'll make sure no one ever finds you here. I can promise you that much."

Martha glared at my hand and didn't take it.

She stood on her own, brushing past me to the hall and onward to the bedroom where an elaborate Snow White costume waited on the bed. It was my suggestion, her hair black as ebony, her skin white like the fairy tale namesake.

I grazed the pill bottle in my pocket as I followed, wondering for a moment if she'd really put on weight or if I'd only imagined it. Her steps hardly made a sound on the creaky floors as she disappeared into the bedroom. A cluster of Koels huddled at the end of the hall, bodies bent in unnatural poses, grinning, clicking.

One of the shadows plunged lazily over the upper banister, letting gravity tip it across the rail so that it fell, beating me to the ground level; I held my breath as I passed, doing everything to disregard that it had taken Jaak's form at the bottom of the steps, body splayed out and bent on the living room floor. It felt like a warning, an omen.

Though of what, I couldn't be sure.

Tick, tock.

Chapter Three

I held my soda to my chest, sipping as I watched Martha sit cross-legged in the armchair in the corner, keeping to herself as children flurried around her. She was hardly recognizable as the girl perched in front of the toilet only hours before; her hair was tousled and silky against the cream of her skin, lips popping red and drawing the attention of anyone with eyes to see. Her dress was as a vibrant blue and white velvet that hung in just the right way to give the illusion of curves clinging to her skeletal frame; the pang of jealousy it roused made me contemplate what was wrong with me to be jealous of a child.

I curled my fingers around the can to keep them from shaking.

The house clamored with activity, the shouts and whoops of twelve boys and girls talking over one another permeating every conversation. Some of the parents loitered in corners of the house, drinking strong wine and laughing just as rambunctiously as their children. Other staff from around the property, teachers, tutors, and residential supervisors, chatted about work, seeming to take it with them everywhere they went. There were elaborate zombies, colorful demons, a pair of vampires—one sparkly, one covered in fake blood.

"No one else dressed up as knights. I told them to," Gabriel pouted, crossing his arms next to me and scowling at his guests. His body was adorned with a suit of armor I'd crafted from cardboard coated in thick aluminum foil; his sword was a miniature version of Ezra's made from wood and painted with metallic spray paint. "You told them on the invitations, didn't you?"

"Don't worry about it," I said, ruffling his hair. "It's Halloween. I bet some of your friends have been planning their costumes all year. We can't just make them do what we want them to. Besides," I added when he sighed, "it just means that you win the prize for best knight."

Gabriel lit up and ran off, delighted by the thought.

"I think I'm gonna take Riley home soon." Julie touched my arm, jolting me. She frowned apologetically and pointed to Riley beside the table. His fingers flapped up and down as he glanced nervously from side-to-side; he winced as the other children ran past him again.

I nodded to Julie. "We'll save him a piece of cake."

"Cake?" Gabriel chimed in, eyes gleaming.

"Yupp." I nodded at him, prompting him to impatiently tug me to the kitchen by the hem of my shirt. He shoved a stack of dessert plates and serving utensils in my hands, shouting for Ezra to bring out the cake. Ezra smiled at me, a brief ceasefire brought on by the gravity of Gabriel's delight as candles were lit and the melody of 'Happy Birthday' echoed through the room. When we reached the final crescendo of the song, Gabriel blew his candles out with gusto.

For a moment, with Ezra on one side of Gabriel and myself on the other, time hovered like a hummingbird suspended above a flower—in constant motion, yet seemingly motionless. A shutter in my mind winked shut, sealing the perfection of the moment into a mental photograph to tuck away forever.

Gabriel reached for the serving knife. Ezra laughed from somewhere deep in his belly, urging Gabriel to slow down before he knocked the entire thing over. Martha stared at me from the corner.

"Quite the party," she said when I joined her.

I took a long pull from my drink, wishing it was something stronger, inundated with thoughts of strong rum punch: ice-cold, sweet, and citrusy. Martha set down her cup and propped her elbows against the arm rests, tenting her fingers below her chin.

"Why don't you go help them serve the cake?" I urged.

"Is that an order?" She cocked her head, chuckling when I protested. "I'm only kidding." Martha smiled; a toothy grin that made me think of an animal sinking its teeth into prey. She stood, smoothing her dress, and moved closer to me, voice dropping to a near whisper. "So perfect, isn't it? Like something out of a photo album. I wonder how long it can last for. These moments tend to fall apart, don't they?"

Not a sentiment to be said with a smile, yet she beamed.

Martha eyed my costume in a way that made me tug nervously at the bottom of my shirt, smoothing out the black sequins. The dragon mask sat neglected on the kitchen table, leaving me feeling bare and unpolished under the weight of her gaze. It was a good costume, just out of place, the villain to Ezra's prince charming. Martha's costume, on the other hand, was a perfect match for his. She looked like the kind of person he was destined leap in and save.

As she made her way to Gabriel at the table and handed out plates laden with cake to the guests, I froze, arms hugged against myself. Martha moved effortlessly through the group, touching an arm here, complimenting someone's earrings there—I wondered where she'd learned to socialize so effortlessly, a skill that still felt second nature to me even after so many years of making a living connecting with others.

Martha's hand fell against Ezra's arm as she spoke to him, drawing away just as quickly like toes dipping in to test cold water. His face lit up as she said something inaudible from across the room, arms crossed over his chest, eyebrow perked attentively.

As she made her rounds, it was my turn to disappear into the armchair in the corner. I watched her leave her cake on the mantle as she spoke animatedly with her hands, distracting everyone around her as she drew them into whatever tale she was weaving. She ruffled Gabriel's hair as he whizzed past to the pile of gifts under the window.

It was an easy disposal; she never returned to her plate.

I glanced around at the other unfinished plates strewn about the room—many of them with half-eaten slices of pizza from children who had begged their parents for one more slice, their eyes bigger than their stomachs—wondering if any of them belonged to Martha.

Wondering if she'd eaten anything at all.

Chapter Four

"I'm telling you, Ezra. She's not getting better. She keeps saying she was getting treatment at the group home, but it's been almost ten years and I don't see any indications that she's better than she was when I first met her. She's sick. Beyond even what I'd expect for a relapse."

"You're unbelievable," he muttered, turning up the volume on the television. A newscaster began outlining the stories to come. Ezra grabbed his reading glasses and turned his attention to a book in his hands when it went to commercial, continuing to ignore me. He took a pen off the table to underline a passage in what I realized was my father's book: *Posterior Analytics and Moral Antecedents.* The title leered at me from the cover like a cypher.

"You really don't think something is off?" I asked, picking up discarded streamers and wrapping paper. I nursed a rum drink I'd concocted with leftover punch, admittedly a little too strong considering I'd already snuck some into my drink while the guests lingered. I suspected some of his frustration came from the smell of it on my breath, so I did my best to speak intelligibly, to act sober.

I wasn't sure if I was succeeding.

"Neviah." He rubbed the bridge of his nose between his fingers and put the book down, words becoming more pointed with each of my interruptions. My name was laced with venom, spilling over with it so that I stepped back, afraid that to touch the poison would be to succumb to it. He looked at me as though he'd just finished building something only to see it fall apart the moment he turned his back.

Finally, he shook his head and sat back, turning the television up only to talk over it a few seconds later as though he needed the last word. "You brought her here, said that she needed help, that you could help her—and you have been, more than any other client you've ever had. So I have to believe she's getting better and is ready to move on. *I'm* ready to move on." He corrected himself when I paled, "*We* need to move on. You got exactly what you wanted."

"You don't—"

"He needs his mom. His *mom*. You don't get to have your cake and eat it too," he snapped, diverging into a conversation I had yet to catch up with. Ezra glanced at me when I said nothing and shook his head again. "Geezus, you really don't see it, do you?"

"See what?" I groaned, tossing my hands up.

"If you wanted kids, we should have—"

"Are we really doing this again?" I huffed, temper matching his. I marched to the table and snatched the remote, lowering the volume only to have it grabbed out of my hand and turned even louder than before. "We're not doing this again. This has nothing to do with us."

"The fact you think it doesn't says it all." Ezra gave up, tossing the remote on the couch and standing. He shook his head all the way to the coat rack, pulling on his outdoor apparel and grabbing his keys off the hook. I followed him, standing in the doorway, cold wind licking the soles of my bare feet as I teetered on the threshold of the house.

"She isn't the person she was back then," I warned him.

Ezra started to laugh. It was a slow rumble at first, the back of his shoulders shaking up and down in a way that made me think he was crying. But then the quiet rumble erupted into full bellied laughter, rocking him so deeply that he had to prop a hand against the truck for support. His other hand clutched his stomach as though the laughter was hurting him, trying to tear through him.

"The fact you thought she would be says everything, Nev."

"I need you on my side…" I pleaded as he got in the truck, engine echoing through the trees beyond the house. "Where are you going?"

"If you must know," he said through the window, "Martha called about an hour ago and said Julie and her kids came down with something. She brought them over some soup and medicine from her place, but I need to run to town and get more in case we end up with a bug that spreads through the whole damn farm," he retorted sharply, slamming the door shut. The tires spit up gravel as he pulled away, giving more urgency to the errand than was necessary.

A stomach bug. It *was* that time of year. I thought of Martha leaning over the toilet, claiming to have eaten something rotten; wondered at the mysterious virus supposedly making its rounds through the *Sanctuary*, unable to accept that it could really be that simple, that perhaps she'd been telling the truth after all.

A lump formed in my throat, clogging itself there until swallowing took so much effort that I wondered if I was coming down with something too. My hand grazed the empty pill bottle still in my pocket, turning it over in my hand as I calculated the chances that I was finding faults where there were none; not liking what it said about me if I was.

Chapter Five

It wasn't that I wanted Martha to fail, only that the stakes were too high to be wrong when it was Gabriel's well-being on the line. I didn't bother informing Ezra of my plans as I met Martha at the trailhead; it would have been like stopping to explain the importance of vehicle safety to a child already on the verge of stepping in front of traffic.

Sometimes, it was better to act first, explain later.

Martha followed me uphill through the woods for several miles, trekking through bush and crossing the river at one of the bridge points. A four-hour hike in total, from beginning to end, picnic lunch packed for the journey. It was a long way from home; nowhere to discard her lunch or sneak aside to let loose her stomach afterwards, no chance of not being hungry after the hike. If she harbored any lingering doubts about eating and retaining her meal, it would show.

"I heard that Julie was sick the other day," she said, as though my suspicions leapt forth and manifested visibly around me; a thick web ensnaring my entire being. My pulse jumped, hammering in my neck from more than just the physical exertion of the session. It was a hike I'd taken a hundred other times with a hundred other clients, but never carrying so much weight or meaning attached to it.

"Yeah, her and the kids," I confirmed, trying not to pant. "It seems like you two have been spending a lot of time together, as of late...not that it's any of my business, of course, unless it starts to interfere with either of your treatment programs, at which point—"

"Sounds like there could be something going around." Martha's eyes flittered across my face, analyzing my reaction.

I shook my head and pressed forward, reminding myself that it was my responsibility to test Martha's progress before advancing her—for Gabriel's sake, for her sake, for my own peace of mind.

"It's possible," I admitted, voice breaking.

"Maybe," Martha continued, sweat clinging to her brow. "Maybe that's what I had last week? You know? I thought it was only food poisoning, but ever since Julie and Riley, I couldn't help but thinking...Oh, man, hope that wasn't it, though. I'd hate for Gabriel to get sick. Have you noticed anything? Has he seemed off at all?"

"He's been fine. Upbeat, as ever," I confirmed.

I slowed until she took the lead, following the little red arrows marking the trail; needing to observe her without feeling observed in return. Martha seemed so different from the girl hunched over the toilet; she looked earthy and healthy, like she belonged on the trail with the breeze licking at the sweat beaded on her forehead; and so different from the girl at the party; she seemed at peace with the world.

"Gabriel's taking me to see their new fort later, actually," I said, realizing only after it passed my lips that I was bragging. "The one that him and Riley built? He calls it the *Castle*. Took the panels we made for the birthday party to decorate the outside of it."

She nodded thoughtfully. "Where at?"

"On this side of the creek. It's about halfway between the house and the first bridge," I disclosed, hesitating to tell her, enjoying that Gabriel had trusted me enough to share his special place.

We veered off-trail, delving deeper into the woods to a spot where the trees thinned. Just past them, an old field grown over with weeds and wildflowers stretched ahead of us, cut off by a row of trees dotting the horizon. Somewhere further out, roads and highways led back to civilization, but at the edge of the field where we smoothed out the grass and laid blankets, we might have been separated from the outside world by a thousand miles, by an entire dimension, even.

She dug into our feast the moment it was presented.

I blinked as she bit into her sandwich.

"You gonna eat?" she asked when I didn't immediately fill my plate. I shook my head to clear away the cobwebs of my doubt; my suspicions seemed so flimsy and insubstantial as she shovelled pasta salad in her mouth, washing it down with a mouthful of passion tea. She held the drink in her mouth for a moment, staring at the thermos as though momentarily captured by her thoughts, then swallowed.

I fixed my plate, heaped with potato salad, macaroni, cut veggie sticks with ranch, and a thick, turkey club sandwich. We ate in silence for a time, each of us fixated on our plate. I set mine aside once the shaking of my hands became noticeable, a rush of adrenaline racing through me as I watched her. My throat was raw, heart palpitating.

"What's up? You okay?" Martha looked up at me from below thick lashes, and I wondered if she knew she'd made her eyes just a little bigger as she did it, washing her in a look of innocence that was hard to ignore. She continued to eat, lacking any of the signs of distress I had hoped for...not *hoped* for, I corrected myself. *Watched* for.

No, to hope for a setback would have been...

"What are you thinking?" she interrupted.

"Just...enjoying the food," I lied.

"'Cause I was wondering..." Martha chewed quickly, having talked over a generous mouthful of macaroni salad as though to draw attention to it. Each chomp felt like it was me her teeth were pressing into. "How long before we talk about me taking Gabriel again? I know there've been a few setbacks, but really, I do think I'm ready for him."

I blinked and forced myself to swallow, then wiped my lips. The day grew cold as sweat from the hike dried, carried away by the breeze drifting through the clearing. I stared at the ground between us, though really, I was watching her polish off the last of her sandwich, sucking at each finger afterward like she could have eaten more, if she wanted.

I felt like someone inflated a balloon in my belly; the pressure was unbearable, pushing outwards as though something in me was begging to be noticed before it ruptured.

"You know, I admit, I do feel like I've let you down," I said, responding before I could reconsider my words. Even as I longed to reel back the first admission, another burbled over, guilt compelling it up and outward like steam from a geyser. I cleared my throat and continued, "I think maybe you've been doing better than I've given you credit for, and maybe I've been...maybe I've been a bit harsh about some of the setbacks. But it's more than that..."

A Koel perched in the trees above us, watching.

Martha stared at her empty plate.

I paled. "I feel like this has been a long time coming. When your mom died, I tried to find you, but you have to understand I didn't have many resources back then. And I get that you don't want to talk about it, but surely you can understand the questions I have about—"

"If it's all the same to you, I'd rather we just dropped it," she interrupted. "None of it matters now anyway," she mumbled, tugging down the sleeves of her sweater so that they covered her palms.

"I'm sorry you went through what you did with your mom. Not long before I met you, my brother...he took his life too," I shared, opting for vulnerability with the hope she'd reward it by sharing details of her own life like on the day we met. "I wouldn't wish it on anyone."

"Yes, let's talk about *you*," she said tartly. "Married, graduated. No kids, though? That's interesting...Seems odd you'd have all this—" Martha gestured at the nature preserve as though I owned every inch of it and not just a few dozen acres of farm on the outskirts. "And take care of so many families without having your own. What...Ezra have weak swimmers?" She grinned as she took a second helping of macaroni salad, leaving me blinking at the vulgarity of her words.

"Look, I know it's not something you want to talk about," I empathized, reminding myself that when people were hurting, they hurt other people. "But the last I heard, you were doing well at the group home you got moved to, and then when I tried to see you, you were just...gone. They said you'd ran away."

Crickets chirped in the grass.

Martha ripped a shred of skin from the side of her thumbnail.

"And before that...what happened with your dad? My understandings is you were with him for awhile? Did he hurt you? Did he..." The questions I'd been polite enough not to force on her spewed over ineloquently, my patience worn thin from months of playing the good doctor, of acclimating her to the process slowly. "I know it must have been hard to leave Gabriel like you did, and I'm trying to understand what led you to making that decision so that we can—"

"And if I don't want tell you?" She crossed her arms.

"Well, that would be your choice," I said evenly, though my heart felt heavier than it ought to. A Koel leaned out from behind a birch tree, seeming to enjoy Martha's protests. "But talking about things is what helps us make sense of it, you know? If you told me a little about what happened after your mom died, maybe we could…"

I reached out to hold her hand; a maternal and instinctual gesture that made her recoil before I could touch it. I snapped my hand against my chest, wincing as she jolted up, scurrying away from me like a child playing strange with a distant relative that was intent on a hug.

"I'm so sorry, I wasn't—"

"Julie told me about your…your *thing*," Martha spat, eyes wide. "I don't want anything to do with it. Are we done?" She didn't wait for an answer before gathering the Tupperware from our lunch, pressing lids on with aggressive snaps that sounded like gunshots in the clearing.

"I wasn't planning to take you under, Martha, I just…"

"You need to mind your own damn business," she snarled, back on the trail before I could protest or offer more apologies. I rushed to gather up the blanket and the rest of my things, darting onto the trail behind her only to freeze as a garter snake slithered across our path.

Suddenly, I was the one at risk of losing her lunch.

Tick, tock.

Chapter Six

"This is the guillotine," Gabriel explained, noting with childish gravity that all castles had a spot to deal with traitors and enemies of the kingdom. It was little more than a cardboard box with a hole cut into it for a head to stick through and a child's chalky handwriting underneath spelling *GEE-O-TEEN*. Gabriel then pointed at a stack of cardboard boxes—the castle tower. Two slabs of flat cardboard leaned against one another to make a tiny roof above it, shingles colored with marker. "And this is the moat."

I stood back to watch Gabriel run in a wide circle around the fort where the boys dug a small waterway surrounding their castle. I squatted next to it, knees creaking in ways they hadn't even a year ago—premature aging as a result of stress, and more coffee than water over the years—unable to help the smile that peeled across my face as I examined the tiny, toy alligators occupying the trench.

"Pretty impressive," I said, poking a tiny paper boat so that it swam across the surface. The water was thick and muddy, stopping the boat as it collided with a few thin twigs floating along the top. "How'd you get water to fill it?"

"The creek! We carried it in buckets. And Riley did this part, over here," he said, gesturing to the 'draw bridge'—a wooden skid Ezra helped them drag over from the barn. Beside it, one of the boards was broken off and staked into the dirt with Riley's messy handwriting painted in chunky letters: DO NOT CROSS OUR BRIDGE.

"That's so intruders stay out," Gabriel said, nodding proudly. "'Cause we don't really want any of the other boys over here, 'cause sometimes they break stuff.'"

"It'll be our secret then."

"Come inside!"

We squatted to enter the ramshackle wooden structure at the heart of the castle, where Gabriel showed me 'chairs' sculpted out of dirt, along with various sticks and woodland things that might have been a sword or a wand or a slingshot depending on the boys' preferences that day. I raised a brow at the stack of books hidden in the corner behind a chunk of stripped tree bark. Gabriel blushed and gathered the books, anticipating punishment as I knelt beside him.

"I took them from the house," he acknowledged.

"I can see that." I raised my eyebrow.

Some of the covers were muddy, while others had wet pages. I breathed a quick sigh of relief when I tugged the leather binding in the center of the pile and found Jaak's book was still bone dry, shielded by the other casualties. Gabriel prattled nervously, fingers twisting around themselves like they were too slippery to hold onto one another.

"I was gonna ask, but you were working, so I thought that I would just borrow them for a little bit. I'm sorry—want them back? I had to show Riley the story about Sir Ivanguard," he added, pointing to the book in my hands. "He likes knights too, and he thought it was really cool. We played Sir Ivanguard after by the creek 'cause we didn't have a lake like he does in the story. We couldn't read all the words, so we just made up our own stories to go with the pictures."

I stared at the book, not saying anything—probably for too long. My mind was fixated on the images, reflecting on the uncanny ability of the mind to create stories around fragments of reality like Gabriel and Riley had done. I wedged the book under my armpit.

"Are you mad?" Gabriel asked.

"No."

The conversation fell silent, replaced by the sounds of Gabriel making half-hearted sound effects while swinging a stick weakly in front of himself like a sword. He puckered his lips at it and put it down again just as quickly, losing interest. Nidhya fussed outside where she was tied. The muscles between my shoulders tightened; my clenched jaw sent tiny sparks of pain shooting up the sides of my neck behind my ears, a headache waiting to manifest.

I inhaled sharply at the cackle that erupted outside the castle. I pinched my eyes shut, taking a few long breaths to quell the sudden fear surging through me. It was happening like that more frequently—it didn't matter that the Koels were suddenly everywhere, more abundant and present than ever, they were still catching me off guard: while I worked, while I drove, forcing my foot to slam the brakes only to have the shadows disappear from the street a moment later, while I prepared dinner, jolting me so that the kitchen knife slipped dangerously close to my fingertips.

The fear they conjured left no room or energy to dissect the sudden change, only to dread the sight and sound of them.

When I opened my eyes, Gabriel stared at me.

"Are you sad?" he asked astutely.

"A little bit," I admitted, mustering the nerve to tell him. "Ezra and I have been talking." Hardly. "And we think it's time for you to start living with your mom again." *Because there's no room for Gabriel and our problems in the same house anymore, Neviah.* "She's been doing a really good job getting better and she misses you so, so, so much that we were thinking that you could move in with her again next week."

"Next week?" His face wrinkled, but I couldn't tell if it was because a week felt too far away to a seven-year-old, or too soon. I wanted to believe it was the latter.

"I know. It's soon." I ran my fingers through his shaggy black curls, pulling my hand away slowly as though it had touched something sacred and forbidden. The horses continued to stir outside—the ride to Gabriel's castle had conjured old fantasies I'd had of riding through the fields with my own children, watching them grow and progress and bond with their horses as Gabriel had over the summer months.

I took the fantasy out of a deep closet and set it on a pedestal where I could watch it but not touch it, a precious gem of a lost life that I would never possess, and for the first time in a long while I questioned whose fault that was. Gabriel interrupted my ruminating.

"Will we stay here?" he asked, staring at his hands.

"I don't know, Gabriel. Your mom—"

"I don't want to go!" His bottom lip trembled, and I had to sit on my hands to keep myself from reaching out to soothe him as he continued, "I don't want to leave Riley and my other friends and the castle and the horses. Can't you tell her we have to stay?"

"I tried, kiddo, for as long as I could. But kids are supposed to be with their moms. Maybe she'll bring you out to visit, though, if you do go. Don't you think that'd be fun? If you guys did have to move, you could still come back here, and she could take you riding, and maybe we could all have supper together sometimes, and you can see your old friends." I pressed on the best smile I could, unsure whose benefit I was painting the picture for as I insisted, "This is good news."

"I guess..."

Something in me stirred, fluttering violently. "I mean, unless there's something you're not telling me, you know. Like, if your mom has maybe said something or done something that makes you feel like it's not a good idea...like you're not safe...or maybe she hasn't done anything, but you just don't think that it's the right time, I could—"

Gabriel shook his head. "No."

"Then why so quiet?"

"Just sad."

"That's okay." I gave in to the desire to pat his knee, did my best to smile and pretend that the thought of him leaving didn't rip all kinds of holes through me. "C'mon, what can we do that will cheer you up? Maybe we can play knights, or we can head back with the horses and you can do some more jumps, or we could ask Ezra if he wants to—"

He shook his head again. "I just want to go home."

I wondered what 'home' meant to him.

"Really? We can—"

Gabriel launched at me; arms spread wide to clamp me in a hug. He leaned his head on my shoulder and let loose a sigh from deep in the recesses of his tiny lungs. He took a few more breaths and sat back, leaving me frozen and bewildered.

I blinked, asking, "What was that for?" His only response was a small, secretive smile. "You're sure you don't want to do something?"

"No." Gabriel stood up, brushing the dirt off his pants as he bent down to waddle back out into the sunlight.

I crawled out behind him, stretching as I stood on the other side. I followed him to the horses, untying them as he stood beside the saddle, concentrating on it. He jumped when I came to help him mount, as though his thoughts were somewhere else entirely.

"What are you thinking about?" I touched a hand to his hair.

"I think...I think sometimes it's okay just to be sad. When I was really little, Mom got me a pet fish 'cause I remember I really wanted a pet, really badly. And I didn't really know how to take care of a fish, so he got sick, and mom said he had to go to stay with a vet forever so they could take care of him better than I could. It was really sad, and I cried, and Mom's boyfriend got really mad and said that it was just a stupid fish and so I never cried in front of him about it ever again."

"I'm sorry to hear that." I frowned as we set off.

"So then I read lots of books about fish 'cause I wanted to get another one even though I didn't cry anymore," he continued, story not yet finished. "And Mom just kept saying 'later, later, later' and I learned all about cleaning a fish tank and how much food to give them, and she finally got me my new fish, and his name was *Orangesicle* 'cause he was an orange goldfish, and you know what?"

The corner of my lip twitched into a perplexed half-smile.

"What, kiddo?"

"I was still sad my old fish had to go to the vet." Gabriel suddenly thumped his heels against the pony, picking up our pace.

I squeezed my heels in and clicked for Nidhya to keep up, still processing his words. He seemed buoyant as he steadied himself on the horse's back, sun piercing through the treetops to illuminate him.

He smiled as though remembering the story had made everything better again, deftly steering the small horse around a low-hanging branch as he added, "Sometimes it's okay just to be sad—you said so. Does my mom know? Can we go tell her right now ?"

The thought of finalizing the arrangements stopped my breath, holding it hostage in my lungs so that I had to work extra hard to release it. Nidhya jolted when the wind picked up, rustling the treetops, and sending their shadows dancing across the trail.

"Tonight," I decided, closing my eyes and taking a breath, trying to quell the dread that came with the deadline. I tried to focus on Gabriel just ahead of me, bright-eyed and smiling, as Nidhya fussed below me; instead, I saw only the ticking hands of a clock, an ambiguous timer carrying the threat of the day he would be gone, and all would return to how it was. "You can start packing, and I'm gonna head over to her place to tell her the good news after dinner."

Tick, tock.

Chapter Seven

Outside Martha's door, I felt as giddy as I did when I planned to surprise Ezra with a thoughtful and unexpected gift. It was as though I'd spent months picking out the perfect present and was finally going to witness the moment the gift wrap was torn off to reveal not just what was within the package, but also the joy harbored within the receiver. Martha's entire being would alight with it. Her son was going home with her and, finally, all would be right in our little worlds.

If I was feeling butterflies, it was only excitement. I had to believe that, or else I might have turned around and marched straight home to tell Ezra that I couldn't go through with it. I bobbed outside her door, hopping lightly on my feet as though I was a boxer getting amped up for my next match, though really, I was staving off the cold autumn air and my doubts. I practiced smiling a few times, as though if I went through the motions of it, I would suddenly feel it in earnest.

"Martha?" I knocked, calling her name from outside. My neck stretched up like a hydraulic lift, staring into the upper window to get a glimpse inside when she didn't answer. Perhaps she was in the shower or taking a nap upstairs and hadn't heard.

I knocked louder, hearing something faint inside.

"Martha?" Again, a noise.

I'd brought Martha out of her old life, nursed her relentlessly, but that was no longer enough. The goal, all along, had been to reunite her with Gabriel, after all; and maybe restored motherhood was exactly the challenge Martha needed to finish hoisting her from her own darkness. The responsibility of being a mom would be a goal to strive for rather than a weight that would drown her.

For a moment, I felt a hurried pluck of grief as I thought of motherhood; brushed away its gruff hand like I had so many times over the years. Jaak momentarily came to mind too, and the ever-present ticking clock in my head that hadn't stopped once he'd died continued its steady toll. I coughed to clear my throat, opening my airways for a deep, steadying breath before entering.

"Martha?" I opened the door, slower than usual.

The room was quiet and ordinary, save for a glass vase shattered across the entrance rug, its sharp edges pointed out at dangerous angles. I stared down at it for too long, trying to make sense of what I was seeing. A mug laid in pieces on the area rug in the living room.

A trail of broken things led to her. She was visible through the arching doorway at the back of the living room, seated at the dining room table, whimpering every so often. She nestled a mug snuggly between both palms at the table, staring blankly into its depths.

"He isn't coming back," Martha said blankly, hardly looking up as I walked in. *He isn't coming back.* The words resounded through my interior like a gong signalling the end of a long war, the liberation of the people, a triumphant end to a prolonged battle. I let out a heavy sigh of relief, sliding into a chair beside her, my smile effervescent.

"Yes, that's right," I encouraged.

"He's gone."

"Absolutely." My smile widened. I adjusted myself so I could lean forward, closer to her, trying to pull her gaze toward me. The ball inside of me loosened its grip, the pathways of the frayed strings becoming clearer—this was the final step, this was the breakthrough, this was what I had spent so much of my time working towards. "Gary isn't coming back for you."

Martha's brow drew down as she considered something.

"You're safe," I voiced, putting words to what she was surely just discovering. The relief of knowing he wasn't coming back for her seemed to overwhelm her. In much the same way, her epiphany overwhelmed *me*. It was like all the stars had lined up to bring us to that moment; her realization, the serendipitous release of Gabriel back into her care. "This is such good timing, Martha. I was coming over to tell you some really good news, and now I think—"

"He's gone," she repeated blankly.

"Yes..." I pushed my brows together. "That's what I've been—"

"He's *gone*." Martha sipped the stale coffee, continuing to clasp her hands around it as though there might still be warmth hiding somewhere within it that she could draw into herself, though no steam rose from the mug. I glanced around, distractedly looking for the thermostat, while Martha stared ahead like I wasn't there, talking to the wall as she repeated, "He's gone. Because of you."

"This was all you, Martha," I beamed.

"You *stu*pid bitch."

Silence hung in the room; an aggressive hum of static; white noise intensifying with every millisecond it lingered. She looked up at me slowly and finally took her hands off her cup, leaning back in her chair and crossing her arms over her chest. The eyes that looked up at me were no longer distant but alert, scanning me with the same predatory precision I'd almost convinced myself I'd only imagined at Gabriel's birthday party.

"Pardon? I don't—"

"You really are dense, aren't you?" she asked, as though saying it out loud only confirmed what she'd already been convinced was true. Her face twisted as though I'd suddenly transformed; as though a hideous monster ripped forth from my skin, harmless, but so distorted and disfigured that there were few options but to leer at it in horror.

My words felt slow and disoriented, like a drunk:

"I don't...understand? Martha..."

"You want to know?"

Martha looked around as though trying to figure out where to start, gaze occasionally passing over me, her disgust renewing with a short huff or shake of her head. She was tightly wound, a cobra ready to strike, and I dared not move or blink or breathe, lest it provoke her.

Finally, I started to rise, slowly like I was backing away from a bear, hoping it hadn't quite noticed me yet. The air disappeared from the room as she spat out a single syllable: "Sit."

"I don't think—"

"*Sit*, damnit!" Martha snarled, voice cracking against the last word. Her fingers trembled as she held them to her lips, brows drawn together as though to berate herself for the sudden error, the uncontrolled presentation of herself. She was just a girl, I promised myself, starting to reach out to rest a hand on her arm. She was upset. So many changes. So many...

"Martha, it's okay."

"Don't fucking *touch* me!" Her fingers wrapped around my wrist to stop my hand. It felt like a gun shot ripped through my arm. A scream filled the room, my own, echoing off the walls, deafening as it reverberated through my skull, shook me, rattled me, the pain a coursing fire that snaked through my entire being, toppling me to the floor. The pain was made worse only by my confusion.

I tried to talk but couldn't.

Martha stared down at her hands like she was staring at a murder weapon, shocked by the realization that she was capable of such violence, not quite understanding the mechanism behind it. I stared down at my wrist where she grabbed it, groping at it, and wishing desperately that it would just detach itself from me to end the pain.

"What was that?" Martha bent down beside me.

"I...I don't know...Martha, please..."

She straightened and sipped her coffee, grimacing at the sudden realization that it was cold. I was left writhing, tears streaking my face as she set the cup in the microwave, standing by as the timer counted down, warming her drink. She pulled it out and took a testing sip, nodding as she returned to her seat, too close for me to catch my breath.

Behind her, a young Martha skipped in circles around the island at the center of the kitchen, hardly more than Gabriel's age. She danced as though she was circling a maypole, tossing red and yellow begonia petals around like she was in a bridal procession.

"Martha, please..."

Jaak looked in on us from the window. My first instinct was to assume it was pity I saw in his eyes, but it was only an illusion; there was no emotion to be seen. The side of his head was gashed in so deeply that any emotion contained within the portion that remained was twisted beyond recognition, distorted by the self-imposed injury.

Koels swam at the edges of my vision. They called to me, chattering, reaching for my hands, my legs. Blood trickled from the spots they touched, deeper than cat scratches but hardly as bad as they could be if I let myself slip all the way under.

"You want to know, then?" Martha repeated, staring down at me and arching her brow. I hardly processed the words, fighting with any ounce of energy that wasn't focused on resisting the pain to keep myself from slipping into the *Other Side*. Martha had pushed me half-way, to the in-between; any further than that, the Koels would be on me as prominently as blood on snow.

Martha took a long, slow sip as she said, "This isn't right, is it?"

"Martha—"

She took another long drink as she stood, taking a few gulps before she set it down, trying to get her fill of it before kneeling next to me. She stroked back the hair from my temple where it was slick against my skin with sweat and tears; the skim of her fingers against my bare skin was like burning coals dragged along the edge of my face.

I couldn't tell if it was Martha's pain that was buckling through me or my own. Or whether, perhaps, they had become indistinguishable from one another. She laid down on the floor next to me, shoving the leg of my chair away from us and making herself comfortable. The pain consumed my faculties, demanding the full force of each of my senses like an attention hungry prima donna starved for the spotlight.

"Martha, please don't," I begged. I'd wanted answers for so long, but suddenly, I was begging her not to give them to me.

"Why not? You wanted answers." Martha gripped my forearm and somehow, in the all-encompassing darkness of the pain her touch induced, I saw the world change around us. Up became down, down became up, right became wrong, and wrong became...what exactly?

"So, I'm going to show you," she chided.

The world spun around me, circling me down, down, down until I was tucked deeply inside its hidden places. She clicked her tongue, a sound not unlike the Koels, as she dragged me into the darkness.

"Where to begin?"

Chapter Eight

"When I was fifteen, I saw a counselor." Martha narrated as the memory solidified around us; a familiar scene of a girl and young woman seated outside a portable office, one with clipped auburn hair, the other with a black train of midnight falling between her shoulders. I inhaled sharply as she pulled me forward. The pain of her touch was dull compared to what it had been on our side of reality, and I was grateful that, for a moment at least, the Koels had yet to catch up.

Martha led me through a door in the middle of the yard and into the living room of my old apartment where I watched her father drag her out, relived the forlorn look in her eyes as she disappeared into the hall. Another door appeared ahead of us, and we stepped through, ascending a set of stairs waiting on the other side.

Several times I tried to stop, suspecting what was waiting for us at the top, yet several times her gravity pulled me behind her anyways. I was tethered, unable to choose my own direction—or perhaps I'd already chosen, somewhere outside this space and a long time ago.

The whole house seemed to groan, protesting our presence.

"Martha, we don't have to look."

"We do, though." Martha nodded, opening the door to her parents' bedroom. "You do because I do. I have to relive walking in on her like this over and over in my head, because it's how I found her. She had one of her migraines when I got home that night after your place, but I was so fucking amped up...I told her that I was unhappy, told her about Dad being an asshole to us both, about the things he said about her behind her back, that she needed to do something instead of just letting him ruin our lives.

"And, until things got better, I wasn't going to get better the way she wanted me to. I'd keep not eating, I'd keep tossing out the food from the fake family dinners that meant nothing. I told her that just because she cooks and cleans and plays the part doesn't make it true that we're happy. It didn't matter how hard they tried to hide it; I knew deep down we were fucked. The next night I went for a walk to stave off the hunger, and when I came back, this is how I found her."

"I'm sorry, Martha..." I trailed off; shards of a broken heart lodged in my throat. We walked past a bed, slipping through another doorway into the master bathroom where her mom waited for us, stared at us.

Her head was lolled to the side, eyes open, unblinking, and half-submerged under the water. One eye was ringed in a dark purple and blue circle, swollen partially shut. She seemed, from certain angles, to be staring at her own reflection in the water; though the water was too muddied with red to see anything clearly in its surface.

Streaks of blood dripped down the white porcelain edges where the water had sloshed over as her mother sank further into its depths. Several empty pill bottles were scattered on the vanity; for migraines, anxiety, insomnia, and others for ailments I didn't recognize. But a razor blade on the floor, dropped on the tiles below her mother's hand where her arm dangled over the side of the tub, was the true culprit.

The blood streaking it was undiluted, potent, and crimson.

"I remember," I whispered.

Martha glanced at me as though she forgot for a moment that I was there. She nodded at me, and the bathroom window shot open. Wind howled into the room from outside; the branches of a tree scratching against the upper pane of the window as though gesturing for us to follow them out. Martha moved forward and climbed through. As she moved from in front of the mirror, I caught a glimpse of my reflection. I was pale and swaying dizzily on my feet, dark circles around my eyes. Jaak was behind me for a moment, unblinking.

But when I turned, he was gone.

I followed Martha down the tree as she continued, "Dad was home. I heard the front door and didn't know what to do, didn't know what *he* would do. I didn't have time to grab my stuff or think about it, I just knew that if I went downstairs and was the one to tell him about—if it was me that he always thought about when he thought of *her*—I didn't know if we'd ever recover from that. She might have..." Martha coughed, choking on the nature of her mother's departure, leaving it unspoken. "The black eye, though. That couldn't have been her. That had to be Dad. They must have been fighting again."

"Anyways, it wasn't Dad at the door." Martha shook her head. "Mom called 911 before she did it. I think she figured that I was going to be out late with my boyfriend, but I hadn't told her that we already broke up. That's why I had to come to your house that night..." she explained, glancing sideways at me. "I was planning to stay with him, but at the last minute, he bailed and told me it was over...in a text.

"I'm sure the paramedics had good intentions," Martha said vacantly, watching two of them branching around the side of the house to check the back door as we lowered ourselves from the final branch. "They caught me climbing out the window and called child services, who found me less than a block over and brought me back, as though I'd wanna be anywhere near that fucking place or my dad when he found out. They took me into custody until they got a hold of him.

"There was an investigation and a custody trial, but no one really mentioned much about Mom's eye. The fact that she did what she did said it all to them, and I didn't have any other family so..."

Martha snorted out a laugh, ushering me through a new door into a postage stamp apartment that hardly had room for a couch in the living room. The appliances in the kitchen looked archaic, yet everything in the house was spotless, with not a single layer of dust.

"Where are we?"

"Dad's apartment after we left town. As far as child services was concerned, they didn't have any foster families who would wanna take someone older like me, and there wasn't room in any group homes. So, I stayed on the couch at one of the homes for like three weeks while Dad did some anger management bullshit, and that was it."

"Did he hit you...?"

Martha glared, annoyed with the questions, wanting to tell the story at her own pace. I submitted and stepped back, eyes forever scanning each new turn for Koels. The pain in my wrist had gentled, but pressure swelled behind my temples as we walked around the apartment. Her dad was in his bedroom, passed out with a bottle of scotch and an unlabelled pill bottle beside him. Martha closed the door as though respectfully shrouding a corpse.

"He was fine after that—to me, I mean. We couldn't afford the house, and Dad was surprisingly messed up after Mom died. He wouldn't even get out of bed once the moving was done. I think he was excited, at first, because it gave us an excuse to get out of that place, get away from all the bills, and he just got to tell people we were leaving because of what my mom did. People're always finding bullshit excuses for the shit they're doing, you know?"

She raised a brow at me as though she was certain I did.

"But honestly, I think he really did love her," she said, sitting down on the couch and lighting a cigarette. It wouldn't do anything on the *Other Side*, but for her, the memory was enough. Martha ashed into the small tray beside the couch. "I don't think I'd ever seen him like he was once we moved to the new apartment. He just...shut down. Except for one day when I came home from school and he was drinking again. The hydro was off, and there wasn't any food."

"Martha..." Anything I wanted to say sounded too much like pity.

I trailed off, salvaging her dignity through my silence.

"There wasn't any food, and I was so pissed off at him for everything. I remember saying that it was God punishing him for being a shitty husband and dad. I wanna say that I didn't mean it, that I was just angry, but I *did* mean it. I still feel like he deserves everything that happened. There still should have been food in the house even if I wasn't going to touch it, you know? It was the principle of it."

Martha progressed into the hallway and pushed open the neighbor's door without knocking. "I was friends with my neighbor, though. Him and his little brother lived here with their mom, who was about as available as Dad was, only she was *actually* gone, out on the streets, drinking, pills, whatever. Not in, like, a lady of the night way—she just always had new boyfriends taking her out all the time. Sometimes she'd be gone for weeks, so they were on their own too.

"Anyways, he was really nice. Like, the nicest guy I'd ever met." She smiled sweetly. "We hung out in his apartment so I could get away from my dad—and yeah, Dad smacked me after I said the thing about him being punished for Mom, but that was it. After that, he just kinda...went inside himself someplace he never came out of."

"What was the neighbor's name...?"

I had already guessed it, but wanted to be sure.

"I thought you'd have figured that out." She grinned, staring down at her toes as I whispered Gabriel's name. "Me and Gabe saw each other every day, and I would do the cooking and cleaning for him and his little brother. I just kind of moved over permanently. Gabe and I had a pretty good life for awhile, taking care of each other."

Martha smiled wistfully again, lost for a moment in the happy memories. She watched a younger version of herself curl under the neighbor's shoulder on the couch. He stroked her chin with boyish hands. I thought of Ezra as I vocalized, "You were in love."

"We were, until one day someone came knocking like the building was on fire. We had a neighbor move in a couple weeks before and they got an idea in their head what was going on at our place. I think there was an incident one night when Gabe's mom came home drunk. I don't know if the neighbor called protective services because she actually cared about us, or because she was pissed at his mom, but they came, and they took all of us that same day. No warnings."

Another door formed in the middle of the hall.

We walked through into the group home.

"Did you ever see Gabe again?"

"Nope," she said succinctly, as though it didn't bother her.

The group home was unimpressive; an old house, split into three levels, with enough bedrooms that the hosts could fit six girls, if they shared rooms. One extra room waited at the end of the hall for residents who proved to be either extraordinarily good and deserving of their privacy, or else extraordinarily bad and ill-suited to company.

It was almost always the latter.

"Last I heard, there was no place that would take them both, so him and his brother split up. They didn't have any other family around, so I think Gabe got sent to a group home upstate and his brother got adopted by a family somewhere close by. I tried calling his place once, but the lady working said the boys weren't allowed to take calls from people who weren't family or on the approved call list. Said she'd tell him I called, but I doubt she did.

"Then the doctor's told me the news."

We walked into the single bedroom at the end of the hall where a young Martha was seated on the bed. A doctor kneeled in front of her, and suddenly Martha was inconsolable. She struck him across the face and bleated against the other staff as they reached to contain her. Martha looked possessed as the staff descended on each of her limbs, pinning her to the bed so that her spine arched up, the only thing that could move as she resisted their grip.

Someone slid a needle into her arm.

She went limp.

"Apparently, I was pregnant," Martha mumbled, sounding dazed. "Gabe's baby. I couldn't believe it. When they told me, I had flashes in my head about how they'd have to let me and Gabe live together now because they'd want what was best for the baby, right? But not even two seconds after I think I'm getting the best news of my life..."

We moved to the edge of the bed as the scene reversed. Martha became erratic on the bed again, nurses moved away from her instead of toward her, her hand stretched out to slap the doctor in reverse, until everything was quiet again, back at the beginning.

Everything started again.

"Now, the good news is," the doctor insisted, smiling and patting Martha's knee, "it looks like you had a miscarriage already. By the looks of it, it was fairly recent, so we'll set up an appointment to have things checked out, make sure all is good, but otherwise—"

Martha slapped him, sending him stumbling back as he said, "Based on the results of your physical, your body fat is too low. Sometimes, when we don't get enough food, our body fat drops enough that it stops us from reproducing." He made eye contact, stooping to her level, but was met by a feeble attempt by Martha to spit in his eye. "Do you understand, Martha? Your body couldn't support the baby. Our bodies resist children when we lack certain resources."

"I think in the beginning they thought it was malnourishment from living in a shitty situation." Martha sighed, watching the staff restrain her younger self. They slipped the needle in her arm again until the world melted into a thick putty that she was resigned to sink into.

"I think they were trying to say it *wasn't* my fault, but it took them awhile to realize I was the reason I was too skinny. I was pretty crafty about where I'd hide my food, how I'd get away with stashing it, but when they saw that I wasn't gaining anymore weight after a couple weeks they finally made me talk to a shrink—brought in a special doctor from outside the home and everything who specialized in treating eating disorders in teenagers."

"I tried to see you," I said numbly, lips hardly moving.

"I know. I told them I didn't want to talk to you," Martha said, and I fell silent again. I blinked at her, my stomach rolling over itself. "I heard them saying you probably made things worse, that you and Mrs. Park weren't qualified to handle families like mine and what I needed was a real psychiatrist. A doctor with a PHD, not just a cheap PsyD."

"Martha..." My face furled with anger, shoulders snapping back like I'd been hit in the chest with a bullet. I wanted to protest, but my own doubts screamed from within, silencing me.

"Anyway, it all worked out. I really liked my doctor, and he really liked me. We'd get talking when he was visiting and go over our time, but he never made me feel like anything I was saying wasn't right, not like the staff did. I was really upset about Gabe and the baby for a long time. I told him if bodily stress caused the miscarriage, it was the stress *they* caused by bringing me there in the first place, because that was more stressful than anything I'd ever done to myself."

Martha tilted her head at a new door forming.

"C'mon." She opened the door, dumping us into a dark room. The smell of sweat and musk saturated the air and, as my eyes adjusted to the light, I saw two bodies moving on the bed. The doctor's folio laid propped against Martha's bedside table, next to a pair of leather shoes toppled haphazardly against each another; his suit jacket hung neatly on the handle of the closed bedroom door to thwart wrinkling.

"He was excellent in bed." Martha grinned wickedly. Moans erupted. The room spun. "This was probably the last good moment before it all went to shit again," she said, preceding a deep sigh.

The walls of the room picked up and traded places around us as though a cosmic card deck was being shuffled; the couple on the bed was plucked up as though they were tethered on invisible cables; clothes rose from the floor to dress them before they were rearranged on the bed like dolls in a toy house. Young Martha looked serene, sitting on the mattress with her legs crossed, lips tightened into a thin smile as she watched the doctor rise and begin pacing.

"Someone found out?" I asked, frowning.

"Oh, much worse. Much worse for *him*," Martha corrected. "They told me I couldn't get pregnant, that I was too skinny. Even after he started coming around, I didn't really start eating again. He kept buying me time—buying *us* time. When the staff commented I wasn't gaining much weight or didn't seem particularly interested in a meal, he would shrug it off and tell them some bullshit about how it was a process and took time and blah, blah, *blah*."

"It *is* a process."

"But I didn't *want* to change." Martha glared at me again. "He kept saying over and over again that I needed to *want* to change, and if he had any kind of brain, he must've figured out pretty quickly that I didn't want to and wouldn't want to. Starvation was a constant for me."

"But you got pregnant anyway?"

"Yeah." She watched the scene closely, moving to sit next to herself. "He was furious, and I couldn't understand it, but I also knew I couldn't show it because whatever we'd been doing was done. There was this desperate look in his eyes after he found out—I remembered seeing that same look from my dad when him and Mom would fight about his job. I did everything I could not to show my cards, so much so that I think I convinced myself things were fine and that I wasn't even a tiny bit scared of the plan I was coming up with in the moment."

I gave her a confused look. "The plan?"

Martha stroked the cheek of her younger self, looked at her sadly. "It's funny, isn't it? They told me it was my fault that I couldn't get pregnant because I wasn't eating enough, so, by their own logic, I didn't need to be taking the birth control they gave all of us every morning with our vitamins, right? Why did I need to prevent pregnancy if I was already doing that every time I threw up?

"That's what I said to him. I said it was their own stupid logic that got us into the mess, and I was fuming because it just proved that I'd been right all along, that *they* were the only reason Gabe and I weren't together and our baby had died. The doctor called me the worst names after that, though." She frowned, staring up at him as he yelled, lips forming around vile words. "He said he'd been making them supplement my food—extra proteins and what not in my drinks every morning so that I was eating more than I thought I was."

Young Martha stood and slapped the doctor.

Her hand recoiled under his glare.

"I told him he needed to calm down—that if anyone found out about us, he was going to lose his license, and he couldn't very well take care of things right there and then without other people finding out what had happened. He wasn't a medical doctor; even if he killed me right there and then, the doctor doing an autopsy would know I was pregnant and check the DNA."

The thought of murder and DNA tests was such a drastic and sudden leap in logic; I felt like the soap opera she had convinced herself she was living in could collapse at any moment, crushing and burying us both, leaving us trapped in the delusions of the *Other Side*.

"There was a time that I thought he was going to be happy when he found out. To be honest, it was more wishful thinking than anything. I loved him, and I trusted him, and so, it hadn't really crossed my mind that maybe he was pulling one over on me. I was thinking he was gonna take me off somewhere in a couple weeks when I turned eighteen, maybe set me up in a nice apartment to hide me and the baby until I was a little older and we were happy and no one would think to sue him, considering that we'd have built such a nice life.

"The plan happened when I realized that wasn't going to be the case," she said, with only the mildest hint of disappointment. She voiced over the movements of young Martha's lips as she confronted the doctor: "The only option you have is to help me sneak out of here. Give me enough cash and a head start, and you'll never hear from me again. I'll disappear for a few weeks until I turn eighteen, and then no one in their right minds will come looking for me; I'm not a criminal, just one more kid that's going to get released and disappear."

A final door appeared ahead of us.

Martha didn't hesitate.

We stepped through onto a familiar green carpet covered in dahlias. The smell of smoke and unchanged kitty litter lingered in the air; Jaak was at the far end of the hallway, hovering in the corner like a spiderweb. Martha pulled a key from her pocket and opened the apartment door beside us, dragging me in behind her without touching me as she said, "And that brings us pretty much up to here."

She slipped into the kitchen to pour a drink. Her fingers shook violently against the glass tumbler as she held it to her lips, evidently spent by the effort she'd exerted in bringing me through each of the doors. She went to the couch and curled up against the furthest arm of the sofa; the far end of the couch was occupied by her limp body, exactly as I'd found her the day I'd brought her back to the *Sanctuary*.

"I'll admit I looked rather awful, at this point," she said.

"You were going to die, Martha."

"No," she denied, shaking her head and glancing over at herself. Her sidelong glance was the kind someone might give to a peddler on the side of the street; her curiosity compelled her to look, but not so directly that she might have felt she owed her old self something.

"How long since you'd eaten?"

"Awhile," she confirmed.

"And Gabriel?"

"He always got what he needed. I couldn't breastfeed—another failsafe of my body protesting kids." Martha shrugged. "But I took care of him. I started shacking up with my first boyfriend after the doctor's money ran out. It wasn't ideal, but it was a solid transaction."

I touched my cheek, unaware I'd started crying.

She shook her head.

"I got an allowance from him every week as long as I kept the house organized, which I was good at doing, most of the time. It was enough to get Gabriel diapers and formula, and there was some help at the women's shelter for those things too. But then there was an issue with the teachers in Gabriel's kindergarten class after I showed up late a couple of times, and they started asking a lot of questions about home, and my boyfriend was getting a little rough with us anyway, so it felt like it was a good time to split and find a new place to live."

I frowned, thinking back to my first ride with Gabriel. "I asked Gabriel where he went to school when he got here, and he didn't..." I stopped when Martha smiled knowingly.

"Mount *Olivet*. He always just called it *Mount Olive*, though."

"Why did you come back here though? You could have moved somewhere else within the city," I continued, though inside I was screaming over the fact that one letter could have made such a drastic difference in my search. Sometimes the little things didn't need to add up to have an affect; sometimes the little things were enough.

"Where else could we have afforded to move?" she sneered. "Anyway, Gary's construction crew was doing an extension on the shelter I stayed in when we got back to town. Lot of shit-out-of-luck moms—building was practically busting with them. Gary must've known I didn't belong there though because he asked if I wanted to go for a drink after work one day. Didn't mind that I had to bring Gabriel, as long as he stayed quiet, which he usually did...he was a good kid."

"Still is," I reminded, a gentle prompt that we ought to return to him. We were lingering too long; I felt like a rabbit following its same familiar path in the woods, leaving a trail of scent with every step; the Koels only had to follow long enough and they would find me.

"Anyway, Gary ended up being a dud, too," she said.

"We need to leave," I begged.

"It didn't matter, though. The exchange didn't change just because he turned out to be a loser, just meant he was a little rougher some nights. In a lot of ways, I kind of liked it. It was the same feeling as when I didn't eat—a dull ache that felt like something rather than nothing, and that was all I could ask for. I was in control of our lives."

"You call that control?" I asked, muscles tensing.

"Then I met Gary's brother, Andy, and everything changed again. He was really sweet." Martha lit another cigarette and stared straight ahead at the television set, not noticing that a black cloud was forming outside the balcony window. Dark figures swam in tight circles around one another, the spaces between them hardly discernable.

"We need to get going, Martha."

I expected her to lash out at me again for interrupting, but she had retreated somewhere so deep inside herself that even her magnetism couldn't take me the full way there with her. She continued to stare blankly at the screen. I saw her face mirrored in the glass below the actors and actresses, wondered what it was she saw reflected there.

"Andy reminded me of Gabe—old Gabe—in a lot of ways. Sometimes, when Gary was out of town long hours on projects, Andy came over and stayed with us, always bringing Gabriel new toys or movies or take out. For a while, it felt just like it did when it was me and Gabe taking care of his brother again. We'd get high, make love.

"But Gary got suspicious, towards the end," she mumbled, not looking up at me. "He came home early one day, and it was a bit of a surprise to find out he wasn't as dumb as he looked. He told Andy not to come around anymore and started taking it out on Gabriel and I just because he could." Martha looked up, eyes growing dark.

"For a minute, he had control—of my life, my money, *Gabriel.* He took hold of everything and choked it out with his fat, greasy hands," she spat, "and I had to leave as soon as I could. There was no other way. Andy was making plans for us; he'd lined up a job in the city and was planning for an apartment big enough for the three of us. He'd never had a problem with Gabriel. I think he liked him, really, even though I'd never say he, like, *loved* him or anything."

"If things were so good, why did you leave him with me?"

Martha tensed her fingers, flexing them in and out as she spoke. "The city is a bit of a mess for housing and whatever he was making in town was worth half as much there, so we couldn't afford much more than a dinky one-bedroom. He said that with Gabriel it was gonna be way too small and there weren't parks or anything nearby for him."

I watched the mass at the window darken.

"And that's when you come in, more or less." Martha grabbed another cigarette and smoked it as far down as she could in one, drawn-out inhale before extinguishing it in an ashtray. "You always seemed like such a sucker for kids...I figured you owed me."

"Martha—" It was hard to hear her past the roar in my ears as I watched the Koels gathering outside. There was too much to be said, not enough time to say it.

"You know, I even planned to take some classes once we settled in," she said, moving to the balcony window, staring past her reflection and past the storm raging just beyond. "Maybe nursing school or something. I thought it's something I would have liked...taking care of people. It's why I was so jazzed when I found out I was pregnant."

"But you can't just quit being a mom when—"

"Why not? Mine did." She cocked her head, that same composed, predatory look returning that was present before taking me to the *Other Side.* "Yours did too, if I remember correctly. I figured he'd be better off with you, but I realize now how stupid that was."

Martha pulled us out of the memory, and when I came to in the kitchen, she was laying beside me, breathing long and deep as though she was still on the *Other Side.* I reached over to shake her out of her trance, but she reached up without looking to stop me. The hand that snapped around my wrist brought with it all the same pain I'd just escaped from.

"Martha, you can't keep this—"

"Shut up."

Her voice was curt and unemotional. She stroked the side of my face; a comforting maternal gesture that brought with it all the pain of shattering bones. Spit bubbled at the corner of my lip as I cried, unable to do more than whimper and moan as the world grew dizzy and dark. She frowned and poked gently at my arm, leaning in to check my cheek where she had touched. Then Martha smiled in a way that brought me more terror than it did comfort.

"No marks," she said.

"What?"

"It didn't leave any marks," she repeated meanly, as though the repetition was enough to drive her to violence. "Which means that I have you now. I have your life in my hands. I can destroy your entire world, and no one would see it happening; not even Ezra would believe you—what? You don't think I've seen the way you two fight? Please. I'm a lot of things, Neviah, but I'm not an idiot. You'd have to be blind not to notice the way he glares at you."

"We're fine," I insisted, straightening.

"Lie to yourself a little more. Doesn't matter to me." She shrugged. "But this is what's going to happen..." Martha crouched next to me, considering a list of demands. "Gabriel gets released to me. Tonight. Not tomorrow, not next week. Tonight. Tell Ezra it's because of this great heart to heart we had—just leave out some of the gorier details."

She winked at me, her eyes darkening with pleasure.

"You can tell him that I told you all about what happened and finally opened up, just like you needed me to. You can tell him that I humbly requested client-patient confidentiality be maintained, so you can't disclose many of the details, only that I went through some terribly tragic events and am remarkable despite them. You can get creative on how you explain that you're never allowed to see Gabriel again." She reached out a hand when I started to protest, sending me crawling back against the wall, away from her touch.

"You don't have to do this," I insisted, words staggered between tears and quick pulls of breath that didn't seem to make it all the way into my lungs. I paused, waiting for her to reach out and start the pain all over again, but she stood and went back to the table, back to sip the remainder of her coffee, though it was cold again.

"The real kicker is that Andy knew exactly where this place was and never bothered to come looking when I was suddenly gone. This morning his profile was full of pictures of him and some bitch—I stole your tablet to check, by the way. Hope you don't mind," Martha announced sourly, face twisting as though she'd forgotten what had led us to this moment in the first place. "Just like I took the last of your pills. Oh, and yeah," she confessed, tapping her temple with exaggerated remembrance, "the laxatives I slipped Julie and her kids to make them sick."

I tried to tell her I could still help her.

"The only thing I want from you," Martha said dispassionately, resuming the tableau she'd been enacting when I arrived, clutching her mug between both hands, "is for you to leave. I would recommend you do it quickly. Tick, tock, Neviah..."

Tick, tock.

Chapter Nine

Ezra swung at a ball tied from the base of a tree up to one of its lowest branches. His bat arced as he pivoted toward the ball, sending a loud 'thwack' echoing around our yard as ball and bat connected. The ball itself had been damaged and replaced several times through the years as it took the brunt of his feelings after budget cuts or schedule changes or the rare occasion he and I weren't in agreement.

Lately, it was almost always the latter.

"When's the last time you asked me how my day was? How the job is? Have you even noticed I've been home more?" He exhaled sharply after I told him what had happened while visiting Martha's cabin that evening. "I wanted this job because it would make you happy and meant we'd have more time together—or at least I thought we would. I never would have taken it if I knew that this is how things were gonna turn out. Hindsight's 20/20, right?"

He swung a little harder the next time.

"Why would I lie?" I threw my hands up, bending at the knees. I shook my head, arms crossing against my chest as I began to pace behind him. For the first time in our marriage, I fought the urge to curl my hands into fists and thump them against his chest—or give a nice, open-palmed swipe across his face—as though a physical jolt might disengage him from Martha's trance long enough to listen.

"I honestly don't know anymore, Neviah. To be honest, I don't think it's me you're lying to—I mean, you are, but it's like a secondary effect of the original lie," he corrected, not bothering to explain when I drew my brows together. "You could just as easily ask why Martha would want Gabriel back now if she didn't want him in the first place."

"I don't *know*. To get back at me for before?"

"*And*, added to that, how can you say she's manipulating you? That she can hurt you like that? I get that it makes about as much sense as you being able to do what you do in the first place, but it seriously makes me call into question where the hell it comes from in the first place. She shouldn't have this power over you, Neviah, and I wish I would have seen that sooner—I think I *did* see it sooner," he said, mumbling to himself. "I told you not to move too fast with things..."

"What the hell are you talking about?"

"You're too close to this, Neviah!"

"Of course, I'm close! I care about—"

"Bullshit, bullshit, *bullshit*," Ezra cried out, taking his feelings out on the ball again. "This has never been about her. When her mom died, you blamed yourself, and you're never gonna let this go until you feel like you've fixed it. Same with Jaak—"

My mouth fell open in astonishment. "That's not true!"

"Why can't you just be happy that you brought the kid back together with his mom and leave it alone? Oh, right." Ezra paused to tap his fingers against his forehead in mock realization; his words dripped with sarcasm. "Because that's not what it's about. It's about you trying to fix something you can't fix instead of fixing the things you might actually be able to *do* something about."

"What are you even talking about?"

"You *gave* this to her! A long time ago." Ezra groaned and looked up at the sky, dragging his bat behind him as he walked away, only to turn around again and point it at me as he marched forward. His presence felt like the walls of a booby-trapped chamber as he moved closer, as though he would trap and pierce me clean through if he got any nearer, so I took a step away. "And what about the other stuff? Huh? She told me she's considering the seminary."

"Saint Martha." I shook my head. "She's playing you, Ezra."

"More like Saint Neviah. She's got all the free childcare she needs here to turn her life around and you want to find a way to get rid of her because it's 'in everyone's best interest'?" Ezra shook his head sadly. "She's been talking to me about the seminary. The *sem-in-ary*," he repeated as if I was dense. "And I'm sure we could find her some kind of bursary or grant to—"

"This isn't about what's logical or makes sense or goes together neatly, Ezra. She's been through trauma and that makes it less important how the world actually is and way more important how she *thinks* it is. She sees me as the bad guy; I stood in the way of her having some picture-perfect life, not once, but *twice* now, and no amount of reasoning is gonna change that. She's out for blood."

" *You've* been through trauma, Neviah!" He pinched the bridge of his nose; I blinked. "When are we gonna talk about that, huh? When are we gonna address that elephant?"

"You're an asshole."

Ezra tossed his bat at the base of the tree and marched to the house, swinging the backdoor open with enough force that the screen clanged against the side of the house. I followed at his heels, stopping momentarily to check the door for damage, asking, "What the hell is wrong with you? You're gonna walk away in the middle of this to—"

"I'm getting ready to head to *Martha's*, if you must know," he said through his teeth. "She came by asking to learn more about meditation. As it happens, she said we're the inspiration for her wanting to pursue a deeper faith-life, which means, yeah, *you're* kind of the one being the asshole."

He tousled a hand through his hair and went into the bathroom, lathering his face with shaving cream and giving it a quick once over with a razor to erase the day's stubble. He grabbed his satchel from behind the bedroom door, shoving in an assortment of books; one I recognized as a history of Buddhism and meditation, another a book of mindfulness practices in nature that I often used with clients. The last item he threw in was a spare set of Rosary beads.

"You have to work in the morning," I floundered, looking for any reason to keep him from going to her cabin. The spritz of cologne he'd donned and the care he'd taken in his appearance made me sick as I remembered the way she'd touched his arm at the birthday party.

Ezra stopped to glare at me, then said, "You know, I used to be fun, Nev? Once upon a time, I made plans last minute and stayed out past my bedtime once in a while and could just go with my gut now and again. I used to be able to do stuff like that. There was a certain balance in my life before you started—"

He clipped his words, shaking his head.

"Before I what?" My jaw tightened.

Ezra heaved out a sigh and rubbed his face as he moved into the kitchen. Before leaving, he cocked his head at me as though I was the most curious and peculiar creature he'd ever seen. He tossed up his hands as he turned to walk out, mumbling indiscernibly until a select few words were muttered loudly enough to reach me:

"Deal with your shit, for once."

Chapter Ten

"I'd like to make a toast." Ezra clinked his glass at the head of the table, decorated for the Thanksgiving feast Martha insisted on preparing for the residents. Several families gathered at the table, overflowing onto chairs pulled in from other rooms and placed wherever they would fit. A few stragglers stood in the doorway of the kitchen; some of the children had already been dismissed to go out in the yard and play while the adults had coffee and wine. I considered the empty glass in my hand and dragged the wine bottle closer from across the table.

It scraped loudly against the wooden tabletop.

"First of all, I'd like to thank our host, Martha. The house looks gorgeous." Ezra nodded to her as he gestured around the room. Squash and tiny pumpkins were ornately arranged on the center of the dining room table, others decorated shelves and side tables throughout the house. The smell of burnt cinnamon and cloves filled the air creating the perfect ambience for what Ezra seemed to think was the perfect gathering. I dabbed a dribble of red wine from my mouth.

It stained the white linen like a split lip.

"You've done a spectacular job making a home out of this place over the last few months, and we're happy to have you with us—and Gabriel." Ezra winked at him then raised his glass and took a sip to complete the toast. The adults in the room followed suit, some of the children who lingered inside taking long gulps from their goblets of sparkling juice, following the example set by their parents.

"I would like to make a toast, as well."

Martha stood, smiling invitingly at her guests; her gaze lingered a second longer on me. I slouched in my chair and hugged my glass to my lips. My eyes dropped to the floor where the hem of her long, bohemian dress hung low against the hardwood, skimming over the spot where she had taken me under. A cascade of dark bangles graced her wrist, clinking as she talked with her hands. I wrapped my fingers around my wrist, remembering the pain when she'd touched me. My breaths came quicker as fear turned to anger, rebellion following close behind.

"Here, here!" I raised my glass, sloshing wine over the rim.

Martha's attention turned slowly to me. I focused on the large, black hoops swinging from her ears below the cropped, black silk of her hair, not meeting her gaze. She shook her head and smiled sweetly, intentionally. "I think it's me who should be thankful. It took a lot of guts for Neviah to track me down after all those years..."

She let the words linger until I looked at her directly to make sure the meaning of her words was not lost on me.

"I can only imagine what my life might have looked like if she hadn't stepped in. Thank you," Martha repeated, raising her glass towards me, "for bringing me someplace I can have a fresh start." She took a drink, then paused, adding, "And for giving me a new family."

Her gaze slid to Ezra.

Everyone around the table took dainty sips from their glasses then set them down, returning to their conversations. I gulped the rest of my drink and reached for the wine bottle again, only to have my hand intercepted before it made contact. Ezra grabbed my hand, wrapping his fingers around mine with enough tenderness to be mistaken for an endearing gesture by anyone watching; he pressed it against the table.

"Don't you think you've had enough?"

"Hardly," I whispered back, ripping my hand out from under his. It shot out toward the wine bottle, nearly toppling it over when he didn't try to stop me again like I had expected. It tilted on its edge for a moment before my fingers wrapped around its neck, steadying it.

I glared beside me at Martha's dinner plate. Her food was chopped and pushed around but hardly eaten; I wondered how Ezra couldn't see it. Instead, he leaned in and whispered to me through his teeth, "I think you should excuse yourself and get some air."

"Fine." I stood too quickly, shaking the table as I pushed back from it, the chair grinding horribly against the hardwood floor. "Have a nice night, everyone. Long day. I think I'll turn in," I said, taking the wine and glass with me, even as I sipped straight from the bottle.

I wasn't more than halfway to the road when Gabriel caught up, and I wondered momentarily if he'd been running to keep up or if I'd been stumbling and staggering in a slow zig zag along the driveway for what already felt like hours. Gabriel waved his hand, flagging me down.

"Nev! Neviah! Wait!"

"What?"

"Wait for me."

"Your mom will wonder where you went. Go back inside or go and play with the other kids out back." I slurred my words as I twisted open the lid on the bottle, remembered there wasn't one, and tilted it back against my lips. I wiped my mouth with the back of my wrist, a tiny burp escaping against it. "It's past your bedtime, anyway."

"You never come around anymore." He pouted.

"Uh huh."

"Why?"

"Because I'm busy, kiddo. Got a job to do." I started walking again, remembered he was following me, and stopped to stare back at the house. I saw the curtain fall closed without seeing who was behind it. Fear bubbled up from the deepest, darkest places inside me. I was suddenly aware of how cold the air had become as the seasons traded places and hugged myself.

"That's how it works," I stammered, wishing he would go away but wanting desperately for him to stay and understand. "I help families get better and then they go their own way and I go mine and help the next family that comes around and so on."

"I thought you were my friend."

"Not how it works."

I denied it, the words wrapped in the candid, misguided anger of a drunk, remembering who I was talking to only after it was too late to undo. He stared up at me, eyes pleading below the mop of hair Martha hadn't bothered to trim. It hung over his eyes, and I fought against the urge to tuck it away from his face. Gabriel's lip trembled for a moment before his face hardened.

"Fine."

"Gabe—"

"Mom was right," he spat, turning to march back to the house. I reached him in a few strides and took his arm, stopping him. Gabriel turned back to me, tears no longer contained as I let go of his arm and staggered back a step. "She said you would get tired of me."

"That's not—"

"She said that you'd get bored of us once we didn't have anymore problems for you to fix and that you'd move on to somebody else because that's what you do and she knows 'cause you did it to her, only you gave up 'cause it was too hard! You stopped looking for her!"

"Gabe, that's not..."

We stared at one another for several moments, each quietly begging the other to say something, anything, that would make the nightmare disappear. The curtains rustled again in the house; this time Martha's face was there plainly, framed by the window as she stared, waiting for my next move. My mouth opened to speak, but there wasn't anything left to be said; at least, not while Martha still supervised us.

"Gabe, it's complicated—"

"I don't care."

"Adults can be tricky, sometimes." I forced a half-smile. He continued to stare at me, tears shaking precariously on his lower lashes. These tears, unlike the sad tears I'd seen him shed for his mother, were a spillover of frustration, harbored long enough to have evolved into a shallow sort of hatred. The look he gave me—half need, half hate—burned into my mind like a branding iron, leaving a dirty, swollen scar I'd be forced to live with long after he was gone.

"I haven't had a choice in not seeing you, Gabe."

"I. Don't. Care." He emphasized each word. "You're an *adult*," he spat out. "Adults always have choices. You know who doesn't get to choose anything? *Me!*" His lip trembled seismically. "I didn't get to choose to live with Gary, and I didn't get to choose to live with you, and now I don't get to choose whether we stay or leave, and I didn't get to choose whether Mom ever left in the first place!"

"Adults can't control everything either—"

"You can control *some* things!"

"Gabriel—"

"Screw *you!*" he yelped, spit bubbling from his lips. He wiped slobber and tears on the arm of his sweater as he ran to the house, leaving me in the dark, but not alone; the night was full of dark shadows, a cloud of pestilent gnats, clicking and cackling in the cold.

I headed home, polishing off the wine on the stable floor.

Tick, tock.

Chapter Eleven

I was grateful for the moonlight lighting my way as I crossed the pasture later that night; my feet ached, but I couldn't stand the thought of crawling into bed next to Ezra after falling asleep on the barn floor. It was late—probably too late to linger outside of Martha's cabin—but the pull was extraordinary. I didn't bother with the horses, just started to walk, unsure where I was going until I got there.

I crossed my arms against my chest, the long-sleeve t-shirt and puffy vest I'd thrown over it in my office hardly enough to keep out the cold; I'd deny the change of seasons a little bit longer, unwilling to submit to the truth of autumn's inevitable departure. The winter nights were too long and dark to contemplate, and the melancholy winter would bring with it too foreboding to consider without despair. I savored the false warmth of summer's memory, staring at Gabriel's window until the Big Dipper had travelled halfway across the night sky.

I ruminated on everything that had happened since Martha's arrival, certain that if I could just place the events in the right sequence, rearrange them perfectly in my mind, everything would align, and the right path would reveal itself like a map made of puzzle pieces. The more I dissected and rearranged, however, the more fragmented the path between events became until the last fifteen years of my life were one, indistinct mass, full of writhing forms and blurred lines.

A creaking porch swing interrupted my thoughts.

"Julie?" I frowned, glancing at my feet like they had betrayed me. I didn't realize I'd started walking again. When I looked up, everything around me had changed. I'd wandered further along the path to the rest of the guest cabins, had to check my watch, lost in both time and space as I considered that surely Julie wouldn't be sitting on her porch so late at night. When I looked up, the constellations had shifted yet again.

"Oh, hi, Neviah." She was bundled in blankets on her front stoop as I greeted her, evidently lost in her own thoughts judging by the way she jolted at my voice. Julie tucked her hair behind her ear, stiffening when she realized it was me. "What brings you out tonight?"

"Couldn't sleep," I said cautiously.

"Ah, yeah...me neither."

"You seem restless," I noted, taking a few steps closer, watching Julie's back straighten against the swing. I paused, doing my best to smile. "Actually, it's good I ran into you. Things have been so busy; I keep forgetting I've been wanting to book you and Riley to come in for a follow-up, do a kind of formal, post-treatment interview and figure out what the next steps will be for—"

"That's okay, really. We've been doing well."

"Yeah, no, I'm glad to hear it, I just—"

"We haven't needed anymore help with teeth-brushing," she said quickly, as though anticipating the questions I would ask. "Not right now, at least. He's up to a minute in the morning and at night. And he's made a good friend in Gabriel, so I'm less concerned about that. It's a relief, really, just to know he can make friends and be out doing things like they've been. Eating and sleeping still need a little work, but

I'm starting to feel like I can handle it on my own—and Martha's been a big help with things, so really. Better." She shrugged.

"Better," I repeated.

"Yes."

"You—"

"In fact," Julie added, straightening again though her spine couldn't possibly have gotten any more upright. "I don't think we need to keep seeing you. We're truly grateful for what you've done, but...well, I can't help but feel...it's come to my attention, I guess..."

"What is it, Julie?"

"I guess I don't know that we agree with how you run things around here." She glanced nervously at the toes peeking out from below her blanket, taking a moment to fuss with it until her feet were covered again. I tried to guess what she was talking about but had to ask.

"While I'm grateful for everything that's happened as a result of you..." Julie elaborated. "Martha explained how it works, with the drugs, you know? How you lace the tea you bring to the meetings, and it causes all kinds of...I mean, I wouldn't take it back now, but I didn't exactly consent to that, did I? Or at least, I wouldn't have, if I'd known."

"What *drugs*?" I gaped.

"Oh, you know. Martha told me about that special tea you use, that makes people...kind of like a spirit journey, I guess...? Like a sweat lodge or...what is it they take out in the dessert so they can go find themselves? Ayahuasca. That's it. Something like that in with the tea so that clients have to confront their inner demons, so to speak."

The night suddenly felt too cold to be out walking.

"It really is clever, how you set the mood, plant thoughts of the Koels so we know what the things we're confronting are going to look like. I just wish you'd have been honest with me, let me decide for myself if that's what I wanted—you shouldn't have made that choice."

Shock turned abruptly into anger.

"Do you realize how illegal that is? Drugging without consent? You really think I would do that? You think I would drug you even *with* consent?" I asked a little too meanly. It was a bad time to encounter a challenge. My brain swam with drowsiness and my body overcompensated by flooding my veins with adrenaline. My muscles tightened. Oxygen oversaturated my lungs as I panted in the cold.

"Actually, we were thinking we'd look into checking out soon, going back to the city. I imagine out here is probably the best place for us, for the time being, but I didn't want there to be any confusion about our intentions while we're making our arrangements."

"And Riley? Making new friends?"

"He'll be fine." Julie brushed the question aside, then sighed when I stayed silent, knowing she was holding back. Her shoulders jostled as she admitted with uncharacteristic brusqueness, "Martha mentioned getting a place together. The boys already get along so well, and Martha and I are both single moms, so it makes sense..."

"You sure this doesn't have anything to do with ..?" I didn't have to say the name of a college sweetheart she'd revealed during one of our sessions to make her blush, though the rouge on her cheeks could just as easily have been anger piquing her skin.

Julie straightened, but the way her brow drooped was enough for me to know the guess was accurate; attraction could make you believe anything, as long as anything included the possibility of being together with the person you were enamored by.

"She doesn't care about you, Julie. Not like that, not at all."

My body felt like it could melt into the ground, disappearing as Julie made an excuse to retreat inside, flustered by my observation. Martha wasn't stupid; she needed a backup plan if I found a way to get around her threats; she'd primed Julie with platitudes and meaningless bonds forged from their shitty parenting scenarios in case I won; but I couldn't win, I realized, not if she still had Gabriel.

I didn't like feeling left with only one option.

But without any other choice, I made the call.

The social worker's number was still scribbled on the calendar from early in the spring when Gabriel first arrived. I dialed the numbers quickly while Ezra still slept the next morning, frustrated to connect to her voicemail when the matter felt so urgent. I glanced back at the bedroom door, thought of Ezra tucked away inside, promised myself he'd thank me eventually, and left a message:

"Hi, Inaya. It's Nev. I'm hoping you can help me with something. I've got a client and his mom living here with me, and I'm concerned about her fitness to resume care. I'm looking for a second opinion since she's started making some serious allegations against me. Hoping to avoid a liability suit here, so if you could get back to me, I'd love to have a third party come in as soon as possible to investigate and advise on best practices for moving forward. Thank you. Talk soon."

Ezra stood in the doorway when I turned, bare chested and wearing only the boxer shorts he'd slept in; he shook his head tiredly, making me wonder how many cracks it took before a marriage shattered, and how much shrapnel it created when it finally did.

He walked out without putting on shoes.

Chapter Twelve

Ezra crossed his arms against his chest as we watched a sedan pull into our driveway. A woman stepped out, head covered in a dark orange hijab that was worked into a long side braid. It hung across her shoulder, over her chest. I touched a finger to my own messy braid as Ezra shook her hand and said it was nice to meet her, though it wasn't.

"I'm used to entering people's lives during less-than-ideal moments, so I understand that this might be awkward," she said, recognizing when her presence wasn't welcomed. "I promise though, I'll do what I can to make this as quick and painless as possible. Obviously, if we find anything, we may take longer to make sure the results are in everyone's best interest, but otherwise..."

"Quick and painless," I parroted, smiling.

"Exactly." She grinned, shoulders rising as she took a deep breath, dropping as she exhaled. "Well, why don't I get started?" She followed my finger as I pointed to the main road, giving directions to the cabins.

"If you need anything, there's cell service, but it's spotty," Ezra said, glancing at the house as though he'd left something on the stove and was anxious to get back to it. "Once you get to the cabins, the staff usually communicate with walkies, so let them know if you need us."

"Sounds good. I expect I'll be back around lunch to say my goodbyes, but it'll all depend on what comes out, really, and how long your guests would like to talk. Sometimes it's hard to get them to shut it down—well, you would know." She winked at me, at the inside knowledge between two professionals. The casual good-naturedness of the gesture made me frown as I wondered how to pass the time.

I started the wait by organizing the bedroom closet, feeling like the sound of the clock stalked me from the kitchen. The house seemed perfectly settled around me; no boards creaked, and the furnace was little more than a purr in the background. No voices; no child in the bedroom; Ezra disappeared down the road the moment Inaya pulled away, leaving me alone to wonder where he'd gone and who he'd gone with. I pulled the batteries out of the clock, silencing it.

Still, the sound followed me.

After an hour organizing the closet, stowing away clothes that had been haphazardly stored on the chair in the corner, I made my way to the kitchen. Another three quarters of an hour was spent peeling potatoes and chopping them into quarters, boiling them, mixing gravy and browning beef for a shepherd's pie, Ezra's favorite, stored in a ready-to-bake casserole dish for when everything was over.

The third hour drained away even slower, and I began pacing. I wandered to the living room and sat on the couch, only to stand and go back into the kitchen when the remote wasn't immediately in reach; wandered back to the bedroom to open the closet and examine my handiwork once again, having taken time to gain perspective on it.

Everything was exactly where it should be.

Not a thing out of place.

An alternate universe.

I rummaged the bedside drawer for something to occupy myself with when the walls began silently screaming their doubts. Had I made it clear to Inaya that I didn't drug my clients? Oh, God. Had I denied it *so* fervently that I actually made myself look *more* guilty? How many others would Martha have gotten to testify, aside from Julie?

Was Ezra talking to Inaya privately?

That thought was new to me.

I plucked out my father's book, *Posterior Analytics and Moral Antecedents*, needing to absorb myself until the awful stasis of waiting had passed. Ezra, evidently, had been enjoying the book—the pages were marked cover-to-cover in notations and underlined passages:

> *And thus, we will argue herein that, <u>to hold oneself accountable, one must possess without variance a certain level of agency</u>, without which, one would find themselves remiss to expound further on the notion of culpability. Ignorance confounding even the best of intentions—a certain level of variability factoring into each equation—it would be naïve to think that the calculations might be so straightforward as to place them completely within our grasp; However, we will assess in depth the consideration of <u>motive and intention</u>, peeling back the layers of each so that we might see clearly the parts which we must hold ourselves in account of, <u>recognizing that neglecting to understand those things which are reasonably within our control is truly the highest, and perhaps only moral offense</u>*

we can commit against those to whom we have a
duty of care.

A knock on the door stopped me from reading further, though what I'd read was enough to have a headache forming. My fingers felt cold and numb, trembling as they rushed to open the kitchen door; rushed to welcome whatever chapter of my life would be heralded by the social worker's evaluation; rushed toward the part where I was right and Ezra and I could begin to heal what Martha had broken.

Koels gathered outside for the verdict.

Chapter Thirteen

She stood back from the door so I wouldn't ask her in. I did anyway, moving to clear a path inside, arm raised in invitation. Her brows drooped together as though she was pained by the offer, or perhaps by having to decline it. I fumbled with my boots when it was clear she wasn't coming inside. Inaya considered her watch, then gestured to a bench beside the barn as I stepped out into the cold with her, struck by the calamity of Nidhya braying in the barn, beating at the stall door.

"Let's sit for a minute," the social worker prompted, settling in for a late lunch break that I was certain she'd rather spend at her office. "I guess, counselor-to-counselor, I want to give you a heads up, so you aren't blindsided. Without evidence to substantiate some of the things you said, there's no way for us to say Martha is a threat to Gabriel. I can see some of the warning signs you talked about, and I sense there's something to what you're saying, is what I'm getting at, though."

"Sense it?" I perked up, glancing at the shadows.

The social worker shrugged and proceeded to pull a sandwich from her briefcase; she sat with it in her hands for a moment and I wondered if she wasn't saying a silent blessing over the meal. After the moment of silence passed, however, she relaxed into the conversation as though we were simply two coworkers at the water cooler.

"Books can teach you a lot about people; you need a certain level of intuition to do this job, but I remember when I first started out, reading every book I could find on body language and non-verbal communication. A lot of the time that's all the job is—body language."

"It's a gift," I said, speaking for us both. "Reading others."

"No...I mean, I didn't come by it naturally, if that's what you mean. I had to learn, which, in some ways I think is better. I'm sure you've heard of the studies connecting high levels of empathy with neglect or trauma during childhood." She smiled with more confidence than was warranted, given my ignorance of the subject. I nodded anyway.

"Of course," I lied.

"They say when people are 'intuitive' about these kinds of things, it's often tied to unpredictable environments that force them to learn to read people early on in life, to watch for signs of trouble..." She said it casually like it was a simple throw-away comment, though the way she watched me said it was anything but. "I guess I'm glad I learned the easy way, instead."

"Ah, yeah," I said, masking my disappointment.

"Anyway, we try to keep parents and children together as long as we can, recognizing that it's never going to be one hundred percent in every situation. It's not good for kids to be separated from their parents either, so, depending on the circumstance, better for them to be in a kind of shitty home than in the system. Pardon my language," she said, blushing as she swallowed a mouthful of her sandwich.

"The main thing I wanted to give you a heads up about, though, is that some of the concerns you raised about consent, involvement, that sort of thing—there have been a few allegations. Nothing too serious, nothing you don't already know about. But unfortunately, it's likely your word won't stand up in court in the face of those allegations, if you know what I mean? They don't have much of a case against you either, so there's nothing to worry about, it's just that the court is still going to consider it as a factor, and it could still hurt your credibility."

"So, I can't do anything?"

Inaya shrugged and flicked crumbs away from her fingers when the sandwich was gone. "I mean, you could suit up with lawyers and go to court still, if you wanted, but in the meantime, Gabriel would stay in his mom's custody and the whole thing would get drawn out and messy. Martha also had some interesting things to say about the nature of her coming here..."

I wilted, feeling the weight of the atmosphere closing in on me. The breeze kicked up, sending a cold burst of air under my unbuttoned jacket. I wrapped it tightly against my chest and crossed my arms against the folds, but still, the cold permeated.

"Anyway, you can make them a referral elsewhere—that's always within your right, if you feel you're no longer the best fit—but if they refuse to leave, you basically have to evict them. We're talking full legal eviction since they have no address on file, cops involved."

"But Gabriel will stay with her through that?"

"Exactly."

We sat in silence, staring at the side of the house. Her gaze wandered the longer we sat; her eyes scanned the driveway toward the edge of the road, then assessed the stable from top to bottom.

"You know, really is a nice place here. Reminds me of a camp I went to as a kid," she began, crossing her legs and getting comfortable. "My parents sent me because my older sister got sick. She came through, but they wanted me to talk with counselors and other kids who were going through similar things, just in case."

I tilted my head, brow raised as I mumbled empty apologies.

"Thanks." She shook her head and looked down. "It was a grief camp—for kids who lost someone or were in the process of losing someone. I don't think many of us would have talked to someone if they hadn't called it a camp and had so many fun things on their website. Some of my closest friends are from that camp."

I fussed with the buttons of my coat.

Nidhya squealed in the barn.

"My sister fought hard and won the first time around. I was glad for the camp because when she went into remission like the doctor said she would, I felt a little more prepared to ride the wave of it. The cancer finally got her about six years ago now, I think."

"That's why you're a counselor now?"

"No. I mean, maybe it's part of it, but there were so many factors that came together for it to work out like this. I didn't want to be far from my family when I went off to college because mom was dealing with some health issues of her own and her English wasn't great, which limited schools, which limited program options. It was this or a jewelry making course," she remembered, snorting a short laugh. "I figured the jewelry wasn't going to pay the bills."

"Family can definitely hold you back," I said, frowning when she raised her brow as though she didn't understand the sentiment. "You know how it is, right?" I pushed, certain she must. "It's hard to balance everything, your clients, your loved ones, your job, your home..."

"What about taking care of yourself?" Inaya's smile slowly dissolved into a half-frown. "I mean, in a basic way, the reason we connect with others is because we share the experience of being human." Inaya toyed with the end of the braided fabric covering her hair. "Might look a little different, person to person, but we're all more or less trying to meet the same needs."

I stayed quiet, unsure what to say.

"So, the act of helping is really a process of learning to meet our own needs, then sharing what we've learned with our clients, our families, our friends...we don't see other peoples' demons so much as we recognize our own reflected in others, so to speak."

"But how do you—"

"Some of the best advice I ever got was at that camp: 'Take care of yourself first.' It sounded so decadent, so indulgent when my family was going through so much. But the way they explained it—they said that every person was kind of like a horse and a rider."

"I haven't heard that one before."

"Well, you've got the horse, which is your emotions, and you sit on top of it, as the rider—that's your mind. Then the reins are your will," she said, holding her hands in front of her as though she was guiding a horse. "As the rider, you interpret signals from your horse, then use your will to guide you both. But it's a symbiotic relationship—everything has to work in balance to make the ride smooth. Too much rein and..."

"Miserable horse."

"And miserable rider." She smiled. "Taking care of myself was the only thing that made sure the ride was smooth. There were definitely times I let the horse lead too much or was too quick on the reins without considering what my horse was trying to tell me, but still...I couldn't have gotten through if I didn't keep finding the time to check in with myself and find balance.

"Hell, I even speak with a counselor myself, now and again." Inaya threw the words out casually, glancing sideways to gauge my reaction. "Talk through my own baggage—some might say we have more than the average person because of what we do, not less. Doctors need doctors. Teachers need teachers. Helpers need helpers...you should consider it sometime. Even your husband talks to someone, by the sounds of it."

The news that Ezra was speaking with a counselor was pushed aside; I was too busy contemplating the fact that he had, in fact, spoken to Inaya in private, wondering what he'd said and how much of what Inaya and I had talked about was guided by things that were said about me in private. The thought made my stomach churn.

"When will we hear an official ruling on things?" I resisted the urge to swat a Koel who began pestering me; its tendrils kept lifting to my cheeks as though it was trying to pluck the corners of my lips into a smile, growing frustrated when it couldn't quite touch me.

"A week or so. But Neviah..." Inaya unlocked her car and slid in, rolling down the window. "If I were you, I'd go ahead and proceed based on what I already told you; Martha and Gabriel aren't going anywhere without a fight. You can ask her to leave, provide her with some options, but..."

"I can't control what she does."

Wind howled through the trees like a restless phantom; a wailing banshee professing my defeat as I went inside. I turned on the television as loud as it could go to drown out the noise humming in my ears, stuck dinner in the oven, and prepared for Ezra to return from wherever he had wandered to.

He came home to find me staring at the oven, tears streaking my face. Smoke poured from the burning casserole dish, though I only stared at it, as frozen as the hands on the clock, less its batteries. Minutes had passed, or maybe hours, or maybe a lifetime.

I didn't know anymore.

Chapter Fourteen

"Take one in the morning and one at night," the pharmacist advised, handing my prescription refill to Ezra. He kept one arm wrapped around my shoulder, the other reaching out to take the yellow bottle rattling with pills. "Make sure you take it with food and book a follow up in about two weeks with your doctor," the pharmacist cautioned as I stared catatonically at the register. "And limit your caffeine intake."

"Thank you." Ezra dropped the bottle in his pocket.

When we got out to the car, each of us slid in wordlessly. I stared at the seatbelt for a moment, disconnected from my ability to use it until I heard Ezra's belt click into place. The task happened for me in slow motion, but finally, I was buckled in. Ezra turned the key and sent the engine roaring to life. He reached out to turn the radio off as soon as it started to play, letting the silence linger.

"You're quiet," he finally said; his hands flexed against the steering wheel, foot hovering on the gas pedal, though he didn't start the car moving. He froze in the ready position as the silence in the car clamored around us, fighting for our attention. His shoulders slumped when he finally took his hands from the wheel and turned in his seat to face me. I stared at the hand placed on my knee.

His warmth seeped through my jeans.

"I ruined our dinner," I whispered. My heart thundered uncontrollably again the moment I spoke, my lungs expanding and contracting unnaturally as I tried to remember how to breathe.

"That's—"

"I *ruined* it," I repeated louder, looking at him through a glossy veil of tears. I cursed that they were waiting to overflow the moment my lips moved, lingering like racehorses barred at the starting gate, ready to spring into action at a moment's notice. Suddenly, I was sobbing again, pulled into Ezra's chest as I burbled out hardly intelligible apologies through the cascade of tears and slobber.

"It's okay," he cooed tenderly, stroking my back.

"It's not."

"Nev, I can't pretend like I know what's been going on with you lately, but whatever it is, we're gonna get through it." He took a breath. "I mean, I don't know if I didn't want to see it, or if I genuinely didn't see it, but this is more than I was—"

"I just wanted to make you dinner."

"I know."

"I wanted things to be normal." A bubble of spit formed from my mouth. I laughed at it sardonically for a moment before my lips twisted into an ugly, tear-soaked frown. "I just thought that after today everything would be fixed and—" I sucked in a breath of air. "I can't stand the silence anymore, Ezra. I can't stand it. Where did you go? I needed you with me today."

"I know, I know," he said, resting his cheek on the top of my head. Ezra rubbed it back and forth against my hair, settling in deeper against me; still, his gaze was cast distantly out the window at nothing in particular as he added, "I hate it too."

We stayed pressed to one another for a few more minutes, until a woman walked past the window toward the clinic, reminding me that we weren't alone. I sat up abruptly and wiped my eyes, rubbing them aggressively until the tears withdrew. When it was over, I dropped my head back against the chair and let it roll over to look at him.

"I'm sorry," I said weakly.

"I know."

My lip was still trembling a little, enough to warn me that another round of tears was inevitable. Ezra continued to stare at me as though the apology might not be real, as though I might not be real. His eyes were circled with dark, puffy bags that made me aware for the first time that he hadn't been sleeping as well as the silence in our bed would have me think.

"It just feels like I've been in this maze," I choked out. "And every choice seemed so obvious, but all of the sudden, I find myself in this cul-de-sac, and for the first time, I actually have to look behind me at where I came from because there's no way forward."

The tears welled up fresh. I swore a muffled curse and tilted my head back, eyes cast up toward the roof of the truck so that gravity might help keep the tears at bay. My stomach twisted at the thought that surely, after so much crying, a person might become permanently empty. I continued to gaze up at the ceiling until the tears were controlled, staring longer when I noticed the dark brown stain in the fabric above me. I reached up to touch it with my fingertips.

Ezra looked up, his gaze following my fingers. I dropped my hand to my lap, head still rolled back, smiling up at the blotch. "Do you remember this?" I turned my head to look at him. "When we went to the drive-in? And I dropped that stupid can of pop during a scare and then forgot about it and opened it during the second movie. It exploded everywhere." I touched the tip of my braid.

"Oh yeah..." A smile bloomed across his face as he stared with me. "Your hair was soaked. Do you remember how sticky it was by the time we got home? I think that was the day you had to cut a chunk out of it because the sugar had like, congealed in it."

I winced, smirking. "Don't remind me."

"*Nightmare on Elm Street.*"

"Yeah, that was it."

"We had a lot of good dates in this truck."

"Yeah, we did." I frowned at my feet, chest tightening. My breaths were coming more organically than before, but a lump in my throat still prevented easy passage. The tears were ready to return as I confessed, "I don't remember when our last date was."

Ezra didn't seem to remember, either. He thought about it for a long time and then sighed, turning away and staring out the opposite window. I'd seen the face before, when he wasn't necessarily ready to get into something with me, but fighting was inevitable. Sooner or later, we would have to talk, and the weight on my chest demanded that it be now, lest the anticipation of it crush me.

"You talk," I urged. "I'll listen."

He sighed.

"I don't really know where to start, Neviah, and you've already had such a long day—*we've* had a long day. It's just been a long day." He leaned his head against the steering wheel as he gripped it, looking weary as he sat straight again. I didn't say anything, just stayed quiet, nodding for him to continue anyway. He sighed again and looked out the driver side window.

"I feel like I've been by myself these last few months. No matter how many good nights we had with Gabriel, no matter how many ways I tried to be there for you even after you pissed me off with the way you handled it, it was like I was following you through the maze you're talking about, only, you just left me somewhere in the middle because you were moving so fast.

"The new job was a struggle," he added, the grievances coming easier now that he had started, one snowballing into the next. "I could have handled not liking the new position, but it'd have been nice to talk to someone about it. You've always been my sounding board for things and it's like you weren't even there, you were just...I don't know where you were..."

"I really am sorry—"

"And Gabriel."

It was Ezra's turn now to cry. His eyes were red and glassy as he turned to look at me, his hands still clinging to the steering wheel as though it was the only thing holding him up. My eyes watered again as I slid toward him, into his arms; we held each other like that for awhile.

"I love that fucking kid." He sniffed.

"I know." I kept my face pressed to his shirt, the smell of laundry and body wash overriding my other senses, followed by the wonderful awareness of his body heat and form pressed against mine. I squeezed him tighter, clinging to his sweater. "Me too. I don't know what I can do to make things better now. He's going to be gone because..."

Because of me.

"I just don't know what to do next anymore," I confessed, staring out the passenger window, pressing my hand to the cold glass, relishing the feeling of it. My body was warm from crying, warmer yet from the heater that had been cranked since turning the car on.

"It feels like a game of cat's cradle I've just lost," I mumbled, numbness settling around me like a cozy blanket, begging me to sink into it deeper, trap myself within it. "Pluck here, pull there, and the design can keep going; one wrong pull or pluck though and..." I dropped my hands into my lap, watching the imaginary strings fall. "Whole thing falls apart in your hands."

"You really still don't get it."

"What do you mean?"

"You've spent so long trying to..." He shook his head, searching for the right words. I offered 'to help people' but he quickly rejected it with another adamant shake of his head. "No. I mean, yeah, but...it's more than that. It's like, you're trying to make the right decisions so that nothing bad ever happens to the people you love—like you're still selling insurance, almost, but instead of policies, you're selling yourself by making promises to them that you can't keep."

"I've never promised anything," I lied.

"Maybe not out loud." He shrugged, letting the words linger. "All I'm saying is that there's lots you can still do. You have an infinite number of choices available if you focus on the things you actually have control over. Or, who knows?" He backpedalled. "Whatever. I mean, you could just keep doing the same thing you've always done. That would be a choice too."

"Not really..."

"A bad one, but a choice," he insisted.

Ezra turned on the radio. I tried to process what he was saying but was overwhelmed, so much so that my mind felt almost entirely blank, incapable of drawing even the most basic conclusions. Ezra smirked and nodded at the radio, making me frown. I stared at him, blinking, my head swimming dizzily. *Dark Water* poured through the speakers, a familiar favourite. The singer's voice filled the car with a haunting ballad professing his gratitude for the safety of his family in the midst of so much calamity in the world, thankful for their time together.

I choked back a sob and squeeze his hand.

"Let's grab dinner on the way home." He backed out, pulling the truck onto the main road. Ezra looked at me when we hit a red light. "I get that this is a lot; just think about what I said, and we'll talk again later, when you've had some time for it to sink in. I feel like I need some time to sort out my thoughts about all this too. And you need to get back on a schedule with your meds. In the meantime, we eat."

Right on cue, my stomach growled.

Chapter Fifteen

The room was silent as we readied ourselves for bed later that night, stomachs filled with savory butter chicken. I stood by the dresser, pulling out my braid, though it had already mostly unravelled throughout the day. Ezra moved behind me, reaching to touch the small of my back as he passed; the most touch we'd had before bed in months. He pulled away when I reached for his hand, head swaying with his objection when the other hand slipped under his t-shirt.

"Oh..." My hand dropped away limply, feet shuffling back a step.

"Not tonight." Ezra sighed and sank onto the edge of the bed, patting the spot next to him. I sat beside him so that our knees touched as he explained, "It's not never...I'm just not ready for that yet. I mean, it's been a long few months, and I just...there's still so much that's unresolved, you know? I want to believe you about Martha, I really do, but..." My shoulders fell slack as he trailed off.

"You don't trust me."

"I don't know. Yeah, I mean, a little bit." Ezra slipped under the covers and motioned for me to follow. "It isn't for nothing. Today, I mean," he promised as I settled against him. "I appreciate your apology and know you meant it. I just...right now, I need you to focus on getting better." He traced the tip of his finger against the front of my hand, then the back. "I was praying. When Inaya was talking to everyone," he said after a period of silence, answering a question I'd all but forgotten. "I went to one of the trail heads further out, walked, prayed. I didn't tell you because...honestly, I didn't think you'd understand. You've never exactly been open to that part of my life."

I paused, curbing any judgements. "Did it help...?"

Ezra peeked one eye open, then closed it again, no doubt wondering if I was baiting him, if he'd missed the sarcasm that was uncharacteristically absent. "Yeah. I like to think it did."

I hesitated, feeling foolish for asking, adamant I didn't actually care, yet the question came anyways: "What did you pray about?"

"It was an old prayer my mother taught me when I was little. If I'm too mad or scared to know what to pray, I pray it because I know it the best, and it almost always applies, and it makes me think of my mom," he said, a tear dropping against my hair.

"*God, grant me the serenity to accept the things I cannot change, courage to change the things I can, and wisdom to know the difference.*" I recited in tandem with him, having heard it a hundred times before from my own mom.

"Ezra?" I whispered, turning my head on the pillow to face him. He turned his head at the same time and opened his eyes, saying nothing. I looked away, my next few breaths shaking as I tried to take hold of words that escaped each time I tried to speak them.

"I think we need a vacation."

He smiled, so I added, "A week away somewhere."

"I mean, I like the sounds of it, but...I guess I'm just not sure how we'll swing it. We haven't been away for a week in what? Five years? I don't even think we've gone on a weekend trip since..." He blew out a breath, no doubt thinking of the day Gabriel arrived. "Since before."

"Then we're overdue for a long trip." I rolled onto my back to stare at the ceiling, deciding, "Maybe a few weeks. A month, even—or we could just never come back. I'm exhausted, Ez."

"Then go to bed." He laughed and kissed my hand, but I shook my head before he could roll away. I sat up so that I was looking down at him for a moment before he shimmied up, mirroring my position so that we were on equal ground. My breaths were shaky and labored.

"I mean, I'm *tired*, Ezra. I don't feel like I did when I started." I sucked in a breath as he placed a hand on my bicep, giving me an encouraging squeeze. "How can I help people after everything that's happened? Who's going to want to come here once they hear about this?" I grabbed my ears at the sound of Koels clattering around us, though I couldn't see them any more than I could see my own breath.

"Nev?" He furrowed a brow and held a hand to my back. "I just don't see why it has to be all one or the other." His voice was angrier than I was expecting, so I straightened as he continued, whimpering quietly as I prayed for the Koels to quiet themselves. "Why can't you have helped some people and not others? Or even, helped the same people in some ways, and then not helped them in other ways. You think Gabriel didn't gain something from being here?"

"I don't know."

Ezra sank onto his pillow and rolled so he was on his back. He sighed and turned his head to consider me, then reached out to squeeze my hand. "You can still help some people even if you can't help everyone. Just like you can take responsibility for some things without taking responsibility for all the things. And we can make mistakes sometimes without everything being a mistake—without *being* a mistake. You're good at what you do, Nev."

"I don't know if I believe that anymore. I'm not saying that I'm sure about any of this, I just think maybe I've been off my game and should take a break until...when...if..." My hands twisted in my lap and Ezra reached out to still them. He tugged until I laid down beside him.

"Just don't make any decisions until you get some rest." He smiled and brushed the hair away from my face as I yawned into his chest. "Why don't you sleep in tomorrow morning?" he suggested as I started to doze, nestled into his shoulder. "I'll make sure your appointments are moved before I start work and maybe when you're up we can do something for lunch. Don't make any decisions right away."

Don't rush this.

Sleep-drunk, I murmured my consent. As I faded into sleep, Ezra's prayer echo through my mind. Each time the prayer repeated, my inner voice seemed a little louder, a little surer in its recitation, disbelief suspended a little further so that I might enjoy the words and find comfort in them like an old, familiar bedtime story.

In my dreams, however, the peace never lasted.

Ezra woke me more than once in the following weeks as autumn abdicated its throne and gave way to winter. I called out for Gabriel in my sleep, twisting in bed, tangled in sheets that were soaked with sweat and tears, warding off shadows that grew darker and more restless every night. Martha's voice echoed, repeating in maddening loops until it was clear that only one option remained:

"Tick, tock, Neviah."

Tick, tock.

Chapter Sixteen

Christmas had come and gone by the time I finally called the residents and staff into a meeting, gathered into the indoor arena where riding lessons were held during inclement weather. Snow fell in fat flakes outside the barn, and each of us was disguised in layers of winter gear, bundled under puffy coats and scarves that covered the bottoms of our faces. Whispered questions hovered indiscreetly between attendees as they contemplated the reason for the meeting.

Only a few days had passed since everyone last gathered there, toting stacked plates of turkey, ham, stuffing, mashed potatoes, and desserts sweet enough to induce a sugar coma. One of the dads dressed as Santa and handed out gifts to the children while adults sipped generous glasses of spiked eggnog and cider. Silver strands of tinsel still stuck out from the dirt.

"The thing is, I wanted everyone to hear the news together," I said after opening the meeting. "Chances are, if one of you has questions, someone else in the group will have the same ones. The truth is that as we move into the new year next week, Ezra and I have decided the business will be changing a little." Ezra glanced at me; he squeezed my hand encouragingly, though his eyes suggested that there was still time to change my mind. I sighed, realizing it did no good to sugar coat it.

"Changing a lot, actually," I corrected.

"Changing how?" one of the residents asked.

With the ghosts of Christmas still lingering in the decorations that had been taken down but not yet stored away, everyone would soon be gathered again to tack up New Years banners. Party hats and noisy blowers would be passed around while the adults drank fancy, sparkling wine and the children drank sparkling grape juice and stayed up too late.

"We've decided to sell the farm," I said, ripping off the Band-Aid, expecting the crowd to gasp or protest or react to the revelation. Instead, silence. The thrum of my blood pumping echoed in my ears. I felt as though I was in a nightmare, standing in front of a crowd, realizing a moment too late that I'd forgotten to put on pants.

Martha's gaze tore into me from the crowd.

Heat rose to my cheeks as I prattled: "I know this is going to be a bit of a shock to everyone, but we need you to know that it's been the time of our lives taking care of all the families that have been through our gates over the last ten years. I can't express how thankful we are for the support you've all shown us." My gaze darted to Martha again.

"That being said, it's a hard field to be in. We've been blessed with more success than we could have imagined when we first opened our doors, but it's taken a toll. We don't regret an ounce of the efforts we've poured into our community; however, we need to pour into ourselves again for a little while until we decide how to proceed."

People began speaking over each other: *Where will we go? Where will you go? Are you going to open again? How do we*—I wrung my hands together. I'd prepared for their questions but suddenly worried that my answers were too loose, too vulnerable. But then, perhaps they weren't vulnerable *enough*. Perhaps I was too measured in the way I'd just voiced a mass eviction notice—and in the middle of the holidays, no less. I opened my mouth, but no words came out.

"We've spent a lot of time this last month figuring out how we can best go through with this and not have it take too much of a toll on all of you," Ezra spoke for me when I was silent. I stared at all the familiar faces, the reality of the decision sinking in only once it was said out loud. "Those families that are near discharge, I'll be speaking with directly about some housing and job options we've looked into for you. We won't leave until everyone is taken care of."

"When?" someone asked.

"We've had buyers that are interested in looking at the property before we put it on the market. If they like it, they want to move sometime early in the spring. If it goes on the market, we're not sure. We plan on having the property assessed sometime in the first week or so after the holidays, so we expect that things will move fairly quickly after that. Like we said though, we plan to make sure everyone is taken care of before we officially move forward with this."

Martha watched me, wondering at the game I was playing, too calculating to realize that the closure wasn't a move; I was conceding. It took the entirety of my will to break away from her gaze.

"We need time," I said, picking up where Ezra left off. "I have high hopes I'll come back to things after some time away, but we can't start to guess at what that will look like. I just know I'm not going to get the perspective I need in the thick of it. After the holidays, we'll send out formal letters advising on what's happening, but I wanted you to hear it from me first, since we're not sure when the couple will be coming to tour the farm. I didn't want this to sneak up on people anymore than was necessary. It's been quite the surprise for us too."

"We'll be around if anyone has questions," Ezra concluded.

People glanced at one another or stared at their feet, hovering in silence as the reality of the announcement struck their senses like a tranquilizer dart. They finally started to stand, some clumsily bumping into the seat ahead of them as they staggered to the exit.

"Neviah?" Ezra and I straightened as a resident couple made their way to us through the group that still lingered in conversation. The woman took my hand in both of hers, an older woman with mottled, grey hairs. "I'm so sorry that you're selling the farm; I can't imagine switching careers after everything you've done here, but I understand needing a break from it all. It really is exhausting, isn't it?"

"Thank you," I said numbly.

"You know, my oldest daughter is a paramedic up in Woodslee, and she just has such a God-awful time with it some days. I can't tell you how many times she used to call us when she first started because this or that had happened, and she was thinking of quitting. I imagine you've probably seen a lot of things you'd rather not in your years doing this too. It's just awful, and I'm glad you're taking some time—I wish my daughter would, but you know..."

She shrugged, resigned to her daughter's choices.

"If you need anything over these next couple months," she said, perking up again at the thought of lending a hand, "you just let us know, alright? You've done wonders for our family, and we're happy we'll get the chance to help pay you back for some of that. We'll be just fine; don't you worry about any of that. Okay?"

I felt something loosen inside of me as they left, but it tightened again when Martha approached, clicking her tongue. "Wow..." She shook her head and addressed Ezra, ignoring me for a moment.

Martha reached out to touch his arm. "I'm sorry to hear you're leaving. I can't imagine how much stress it's going to be moving—"

"We'll make do," Ezra promised her, patting the hand on his arm and stepping away from it.

"What about the horses and the—"

"Nidhya and Atalante will come with us. The rest of them we'll sell," I answered, stepping closer to remind her I was there. "We want to focus on our horses for awhile, so we need to scale back the herd."

A reptilian flicker crossed her eyes; they seemed to change shades when she looked at me. Gone were the soft, dark doe eyes that fluttered beneath thick lashes every time she glanced at Ezra. Hers were the eyes of a predator as she reached out to pat my shoulder.

I jerked away before she could touch me.

"Well..." Martha smiled, tilting her head as I held my wrist against myself like I was shielding a broken paw, remembering the pain her touch could bring. She turned back to Ezra and tucked her hair behind her ear, happy that I was no longer standing between them. "I will say... it's a bit of an inconvenience for us. Gabriel's been stressed since...the investigation was hard on him and I'm afraid he hasn't fully recovered from that. I can't imagine who would have reported such a—"

"I'm sure he'll be fine," Ezra interrupted.

"Maybe...with everything that's happened, being uprooted from his home, seeing me in the state I was in, then answering accusations against me even after I've been at my absolute best behavior..." Her eyes were red like she was about to cry, but no tears came.

"I'm sure he'll forgive you for uprooting him." Ezra smiled, earning the kind of glare from Martha that was usually reserved for me. "We'll set you up with some good resources; obviously, we don't want Gabriel to struggle more than he needs to with the adjustment."

She adjusted her expression, giving a slight nod as Ezra reached out to shake the hand she offered as a farewell. Rather than a quick tug and release, Martha gripped his hand firmly and pulled him in at the last moment for a hug. She rocked back and forth, nearly taking him off his feet, turning him so she could glare at me over his shoulder.

She reached out to touch his arm again, but he sidestepped, looking down at her outstretched hand as though a stranger had tried to take his hand in a crowded room. Ezra wrapped his arm over my shoulder and tugged me against him so that our bodies melded into one, puffy mass of winter coats. Martha's cheeks flushed.

"This decision," Ezra said diplomatically, "was made as much by myself as Neviah, and I would appreciate that you didn't confuse my feelings about the change. While we're both incredibly sad about the decision," he continued in an unbridled display of togetherness that made me ache for the time we lost fighting, "we're optimistic it's in the best interest of all parties involved, including Gabriel and yourself."

"Of course." Martha nodded and stepped back. Ezra kissed my head and turned to address another mother who waited behind Martha to ask questions, evidently convinced he'd put any further altercations with Martha to rest. I, however, knew better.

Martha backed away slowly, waiting for me to make eye contact with her through the crowd of people and shadows. For a moment, it was only the two of us in the room, and it felt like she was consuming all of the air, leaving none for me, watching me asphyxiate.

She smiled wickedly, giving a quick wink before turning, a quiet promise that she wouldn't allow me to have the final word; that conceding was not the option I'd hoped it would be.

It wasn't enough for her to win.

She needed me to suffer.

Chapter Seventeen

Later that night, the kitchen door shook with tiny knocks, the sound like birds flying at the window. Ezra glanced at me, raising a brow as though asking if we were expecting company. I shook my head and answered, surprised to find Gabriel swaying outside the door; his face was red and blotchy with tears like it was on the day of his arrival.

I thought again of *Slaughterhouse-5*, of Vonnegut's Billy Pilgrim shifting through time and space, past and present, memory and moment—and of the aliens observing Billy's life unfold, a recollection prompted by that half-dozen Koels that swarmed in the driveway.

"Gabriel, what—" I stopped when he thumped his fists against my thigh, tiny hammer blows that did little to harm me but didn't fail to set my blood flowing in response. I frowned, allowing him to continue a moment longer as I made sense of it, then stepped out of reach.

"It's all your fault!" Gabriel screamed.

Ezra joined us when he heard the commotion, extending an arm to urge Gabriel inside, offering hot chocolate and cookies so that the three of us could sit and discuss what was bothering him. Gabriel faltered for a moment as he considered it, then became resolute again as he stabbed a finger at my thigh, yelping, "Mom told me everything!"

"Told you what?" I frowned, wincing when he pulled away.

"That it's your fault we're getting kicked out and that I'm never gonna see Riley again!" Gabriel stared directly at me as he spoke, ignoring Ezra. "That it's your fault that Ezra hardly comes over anymore and that it's *your* fault we have no place to go, and that you're going to sell my horse and I won't even be able to come and visit like you promised I would! I hate you."

"Gabe, that's not—"

"I *hate* you!"

"Geezeus," Ezra breathed, running his fingers through his hair. He looked at me, entirely bewildered. "Why would she tell him all of this?" He mumbled the question, already knowing the answer. I sighed, eyes soft as I reached out and squeezed his arm, not proud of the 'I-told-you-so' burbling just behind the gesture.

"I *hate* you!" Gabriel shrieked again, his tiny hand reaching out to strike me across the face as I kneeled to his level. It was a gentle hit, but the shock of it reverberated through every inch of me and left me standing like a struck gong, forced to endure the thousand cascading vibrations of the initial impact. Ezra's fingers wrapped around my wrist and pulled me to him, holding me securely as Gabriel bolted down the driveway, disappearing into the dark.

"We have to go explain..."

"Neviah—"

"We have to!" I tried to break free of Ezra's grip and follow.

"Neviah." Ezra waited for me to look at him, my vision blurry with tears. Keeping his hold on me with one arm, he used his other hand to smooth the hair away from my face, tucking it behind my ear. The back of his fingers brushed the side of my face, his cheeks damp. I tilted my head, begging for a solution he couldn't provide. We stared into the empty shadows, doing all we could to hold one another up.

The furnace kicked on as the cold seeped inside.

Chapter Eighteen

A fresh breeze rolled in, billowing the curtains draped across the open bedroom window. The smell of early bloomers wafted in through the window, along with the scent of damp earth produced by the torrents of rain we'd had since the beginning of March. Ezra's gaze lingered on the property outside, his voice trembling a bit as he reassured himself that we had made the right decision, that the couple buying the property seemed nice enough, that the timing had been ideal.

I waited until he started packing again to glance out the window, noting the storm brewing behind the trees, watching the sheer white curtains lift and twist as a cold front moved through the room. "You know, maybe now that we're downsizing, we'll have some money to do a real wedding. Could see this place as having held onto our money over the years, plus interest. We could do it right like we should've a long time ago, before we sank everything we had into this place."

"If we're doing it, we're doing it big," he joked.

"A poofy, white dress?"

"And a tuxedo," he said with a nod, stroking my arm. We fell silent as he wrapped his arms around me from behind; we stared at the empty closet, at the boxes duct taped shut and stacked against the wall. "But honestly, right now, I'd be happy just to rewind back a year or so. Go back, find a *Dark Water* cover band somewhere in town, eat sushi and pot stickers, get a hotel room. Or, hell, why not the real deal? Go out East to see the band like we'd planned to before we got the farm?"

His gaze wandered to the bedroom door, across the hall to where Gabriel's room sat empty, containing only the old ghosts of children. "Do you ever question the sacrifices we made?" I wondered in response, though I could already feel the weight of what he'd lost over the years. Thunder boomed outside the window as the rain began.

As a response to my question, Ezra quick stepped across the room, taking me with him as he swayed. Music echoed in his head as I gripped his hand, and I felt familiar sparks of electricity as I tried to keep my balance. The room alighted with the soundtrack playing from his memories. He sang the words to the love ballad, however poorly, as we danced to the music echoing from our own invisible frequency.

Ezra started to kiss me, peeling away sharply.

Knock, knock, knock.

"Were we expecting someone?" Ezra mouthed. He stepped away to peek out the open window, edging up against it so he wouldn't be seen by the visitor. My heart hammered, quick to dredge up the hidden hope that even after months of silence, Gabriel might still come to our door again, that something would send him back to us, even if only one last time before Martha took him away. Ezra frowned and straightened. "Julie's here. I'll see what she wants."

"Do you want me to—"

"No, um..." Ezra searched distractedly for socks and a sweater to throw on. He opened the bedroom door and gave a quick smile. "Hang tight. Let me try to get rid of her and we'll pick up where we left off." Ezra winked, tapping the doorframe on his way out.

I reclined lazily on the bed, letting the outside air wash over me. I considered joining Ezra to move Julie along; perhaps grabbing a bottle of wine from the kitchen on the way back and a couple of glasses, indulging in the box of chocolates we'd been given the month before on Valentines Day, but Ezra was suddenly back, breathless as he tugged on a rain jacket. My body straightened in response to his.

"Get your coat," he demanded, out the door before I could ask questions. I leaned down and rolled socks over my feet, nothing but worst-case-scenarios and eager shadows to keep me company as I dressed. I'd only seen the look on Ezra's face once before, in a memory tucked away in the deepest place I could find for it

I held a hand to my belly.

"Would you slow down? Ezra!" I hastily fastened my jacket, readjusting buttons to the correct holes as he led me into the barn. I repeated his name for what felt like the dozenth time before he acknowledged me. Ezra took my shoulders, studying me with such intensity that he seemed to second guess involving me in whatever was happening, before resigning himself to my help. "What's going on?"

"Gabriel's missing," he briefed, grabbing a saddle.

Lightning cracked, revealing dark shadows hiding amidst the trees, the woods blanketed by a moonless night so dark it felt like drowning in ink. The Koels stood at attention amid the white-barked birches, the forest alternating between them—black Koel, white birch, black Koel, white birch—illuminated each time lightning struck.

And a little boy, lost somewhere among them.

Tick, tock.

Chapter Nineteen

"Julie says Riley's with him, that they took a horse." Ezra jerked a second saddle from its hook. I shook my head, trying to clear away the immediate impulse to panic with him. He spoke quickly, clamoring around me as I stood dumbly in the door of the barn. My heartbeat echoed off the walls, filling my ears, riddling my mind with static. "Riley hasn't had his meds. Some of the other staff are already out looking, but we need to go."

Ezra pushed a saddle into my hands, forcing me back a step as it pressed against me. I stared at it in confusion, unsure what I was meant to do with it. Ezra swept back his hair in a rough, impatient movement, nudging me with his hip toward Nidhya, urging me to saddle her.

"Julie is running to tell Martha, then they're going to meet us," he explained, already cinching the saddle around Atalante's belly. "They tried calling for help, but the storm is interfering with the signals. We'll sweep the woods, try to figure out where they went. Julie is worried that they tried to hide until after the move is over—Neviah?"

I stared down at the saddle. "I can't—"

"You have to."

"I *can't.*"

"Neviah, listen to me." Ezra gripped my shoulders and leaned down until I was forced to make eye contact. I was too exhausted by the constant tears to fight them anymore. They welled up, burning behind my eyes like hellfire. Nidhya waited in her stall, pawing the ground with her hoof at the tension filling the stable. She tossed her head back, alert, fussing irritably when Ezra nudged me closer to her.

"I can't. I can't. Please—"

"Gabriel needs—"

"No!" I yelped, raising the back of my wrist to my mouth as a burble of saliva passed my lips, nearly dropping the heavy saddle. I sniffed as tears overwhelmed me. "I'm sorry, okay? I won't do it. Every time I get involved, he's worse off. I'm not going to..."

He took the saddle from me and set it down.

I felt like I might float away without its weight as an anchor.

"I get it. I get it, okay?" Ezra pulled me against his chest, though I could sense that he was staring past me out into the night where two boys were hiding somewhere in the woods. I thought I heard a coyote somewhere far away and shook my head to tame my imagination.

"I get it," Ezra repeated a third time, stroking my arms.

"You don't—"

"I *do*. And I need you to trust me right now. Riley needs his meds, and it's not good for the two of them to be out there alone. I'm just asking you to come with me, Neviah, to saddle up your horse, and come. We'll work together to find them—you, me, *everyone*."

"Let me take Ata," I said, needing to draw on her calm.

"Fine, but hurry." Ezra changed course, reaching for a harness and clipping reins onto Ata so that I could take his horse instead. "I'll get Nidhya ready. Do you have any idea where the two of them might be?

Think about it while I get her tacked," he insisted, interrupting my desire to protest before giving the question due consideration.

He stroked and cooed at Nidhya, calming her while I took several deep breaths. I grounded myself again in what I could see and hear and feel; rain pattering against the tin roof, Ata whinnying, Ezra's whispered assurances to Nidhya. The answer broke free from the static that might have otherwise clouded my judgement.

The castle.

I blinked, shaking my head as the thought took hold of me; glanced up at the rain that poured down, engorging the river that stood in the way of it. Suddenly, my feet were moving below me, stepping into the stirrups and hoisting myself onto Ata's back.

Ezra moved faster, saddling Nidhya with a few quick movements, shaking his head as I reminded him about their fort. "They haven't been there since things started to thaw," he protested. "There's no way they'd be able to cross the river right now. It would be..."

I angled my head, bottom lip trembling open.

"Gabriel will think he can cross it."

"It's too early—"

"It doesn't *matter*," I growled, urging Ata forward beneath me. She seemed to know the way, moving with little prompting from me. The night was blanketed in darkness so thick—lacking any trace of the moon—that I didn't think I'd be able to see where I was going anyway. I called back over my shoulder as Ezra cantered to catch up. "Last year we crossed to find one of the horses. I don't think he'd know the difference between a safe cross and a bad one..."

"Why?"

I tried to answer him, could hardly speak past the monument that had taken residence in my throat, the ball of guilt finally reaching its fullest form as it choked its way out into the light.

"Because I crossed with him when I shouldn't have."

"Nev, you can't possibly—"

"It's my fault."

I knew with sudden, paralyzing certainty the sky was dark from more than just the storm. The rain assaulted me from every angle as I tapped my heels against Ata's sides, forcing her to move faster though the field. The sky up ahead was filled with dark, swirling forms, gathered in frenzied masses across the sky, silhouettes alighting with every strike of lightning. The silhouettes of barren tree branches reached up in veiny black cords toward the Koels.

Tick, tock.

The river was overflowing with rainwater and thawing ice when we arrived. The horses pulled back, braying uneasily at the edge of the gorged bank, lifting their front hooves as though the river was a wolf coming for their throats. Ezra and I backed up until the horses calmed then scanned the opposite shore for signs of life. There was nothing, save for the roar of water rushing past. Chunks of ice floated in unbroken sheets atop their melted counterparts toward the lake.

"They couldn't have crossed this way," Ezra said.

"You're right, they couldn't—"

Nidhya's ears flicked forward, head snapping up. I leaned to stroke her neck, cooing as I considered other places the boys could have wandered. Ata shifted uneasily below me. I turned her in circles trying to calm her, then paused. Nidhya's ears flicked forward again, head turning to something I couldn't see. My grip tightened on the reins for a moment, then released; I closed my eyes and breathed deeply, listening, attuning myself to whatever the horses had sensed before us.

The horses were as still as concrete pillars.

"Ezra, listen..."

The sound was muffled, barely audible beneath the sound of the runoff current. I leaned forward, head lowering closer to the horse's neck as though the nearness might somehow amplify my own senses. Leaves rustled distractingly; chunks of ice bashed the shore.

"Help!" a tiny voice cut through the noises.

My head shot up and I turned to Ezra, who hadn't heard anything. I paused again, closing my eyes once more to block out everything else, attuned only to the sound beneath the current.

"Help!"

Ezra heard it. His head perked up. The horses both turned their attention to the sound, shifting restlessly, anticipating our urgency. The cloud of Koels waited to let loose from the sky, writhing around one another, blanketing the *Sanctuary* with darkness so thick I felt like I could breathe it in and drown in it. I gripped the horse's reins to keep her focused as we galloped. If something happened to the boys...

There wouldn't be a drink or a pill strong enough to forget.

Chapter Twenty

Ice and debris clogged the stream where it bent to the east, straining to meet the mouth of a faraway lake. Chunks of ice pressed together, locked against one another where a log had fallen across the bend, jammed against yet more ice. It created a small island of debris that blocked the nearest side of the water. The current rushed towards the blockage, passing below it through any crevice it could find, while any detritus lingering on the surface of the water was caught up against the tree trunk or swept below it where it would inevitably drown.

"Ezra, look!" My finger shot out ahead of us.

Gabriel and Riley were pinned against the log, clinging desperately to the wet bark to keep their heads above water. By the time we arrived, they already looked as though much of their energy had been spent from the effort of holding on, and soon, they would have none left.

The horse Gabriel had taken from the barn was across the river, bleating the ground with so much force that I worried the vibrations might shake the dam loose; if it broke, the boys would be swept downstream with the current; if it stayed blocked, the boys would continue to be trapped, each moment creeping closer to hypothermia.

Gabriel's screams were frantic as he screamed our names.

"Gabriel, I'm coming. Hold on!"

"Be smart about this," Ezra cautioned, both of us jumping to the ground, fastening our horses to whatever stump or branch might hold them. Ezra removed the heavy boots he was wearing, as well as his coat; both would weight him down too much if the current took him.

"It's too cold," I warned. "You'll freeze, and then what?"

"Across the log." He pointed, scanning the shore for other options, but finding none. "The strainer caught them. The ice palates are shifting." I listened as they cracked against one another, occasionally dislodging. "But the log looks pretty sturdy, and they've got a good grip on it without rolling it. I'm gonna try to reach them across the log and move the—"

Gabriel cried out, wincing as another piece of ice slammed into his back. I took one last look around and saw no other way. "Do we have any rope?" I asked, squeezing his hand. "To harness you?"

"Just the reins, and they're not going to reach."

"What do you need me to do?"

"Be ready for us."

Gabriel yelled again, panic overcoming him as he tried once more to claw himself onto the log. His face was the same color as the cloudy ice blocks, lips trembling and blue. Riley was beside him, hitting his forehead against the log, repeating some mantra we couldn't hear over Gabriel's screams. Ezra yelled, "Hold tight guys! I'm coming! Whatever you do, don't let go."

He crept onto the log while I stood paralyzed, not sure what I was meant to be ready for, nothing to do but stand there, available to them. The lack of action gave my mind time to wander; it quickly pivoted from fear for Gabriel to fear for Ezra as he tiptoed along the precarious beam—if something happened to him, would that be my fault too?

All because of a choice that seemed so inconsequential.

So much distance between then and now.

The log shifted, rolled ever so slightly.

"Ezra!"

Ezra yelled across his shoulder that he was fine, bending into a catlike crouch to steady himself. His legs shook almost imperceptibly as he continued the slow crawl forward. I couldn't hear what he said as he reached the boys. They were too far away, and the river was too loud, and the Koels above us squabbled even louder above it all.

I couldn't look away.

Ezra found his balance and shoved a chunk of ice that held Riley trapped below it. The boy clamored out of the water, Ezra giving a quick tug to help him up. Gabriel stayed pinned, and somehow, his sobs drowned out even the noise from the Koels.

Tick, tock.

"Neviah!" Ezra called when Riley charged forward along the slippery log. He thrashed out trying to gain balance, he and Ezra both nearly toppling across the sheets of ice. Every so often one of the sheets near the edge was pushed so that it broke away from the blockage and continued downstream; if Ezra's weight fell against the ice, they'd likely dislodge and he would go under in their place, never to surface.

A childish whimper escaped me.

TICK, tock.

"Nev, I'm gonna bring him to you," Ezra instructed, struggling to restrain Riley as he made his way back to the edge of the water where I waited for them. I held my breath as they crossed, making the passage feel as though it took an eternity, their lives held in the balance.

"What about Gabriel?" I cried out.

"I'll go back," Ezra promised.

Riley beat his limbs against Ezra as he flipped the boy over his shoulder. Riley was tall but rail thin and easy enough for Ezra to maneuver on a good day; this, however, was not a good day. The journey to the shore was perilous. Riley's every movement threatened Ezra's footing. Twice, his foot slipped against the log, and he went down hard on his knees without letting go of the boy.

Riley's flailing only worsened when Ezra reached the shore. Ezra worked frantically to restrain him, to return for Gabriel. Adrenaline pumped through Riley's muscles so that his movements were erratic, hostile, and super-charged. Blood dripped from Riley's brow where he had been thumping his head against the log, and it was impossible to know what he'd do if Ezra let go.

I started moving down the log.

"Neviah!" I paused to look back when Ezra called my name, expecting him to protest. His Adam's apple made an exaggerated bob as he swallowed, his mouth hanging open, poised to tell me there was another way, that I should come back to shore, that I was being reckless. Our eyes met. Tears rimmed my eyes as I took a shallow breath through my mouth, shaking my head to indicate there wasn't.

Ezra nodded only once, as though in the time it took for a second or a third tilt of the head, he might change his mind. I lingered hardly a moment longer, consuming the image of him there on the shore, nestling it someplace deep and safe in my mind as I turned to Gabriel.

"Hold on," I called out. "I'm coming for you."

"I'm so sorry, Neviah. I didn't—"

"Hush," I ordered, noticing his voice shaking. There was no more screaming; it was replaced by a sleepy sort of protest; his words slurred as water continued to beat against him from behind. His fingers were blue and wet but no longer trembling as I approached. "You focus all your energy on getting out of here, okay? I need you to climb."

"I can't—"

"You can," I insisted, distractedly testing my grip on the ice for the best way to push it, finding my footing on the wet log. Gabriel nodded half-heartedly. "C'mon, buddy, on three. One, two..."

"Gabriel!" Martha's voice echoed behind us.

"Three!" I urged, pushing the ice and hoisting Gabriel into my arms. He clung like a wet monkey against my chest, arms around my neck so my own were free to keep us balanced. We started back across the log as Ezra screamed from the shore, warning me to watch out.

Martha charged across the log.

The dam shook from her frantic movements; twice she fell, twice she rose. I tightened my grip on Gabriel as she screamed for me to stay away from him. Her hair stuck to her forehead where water sprayed her during a fall, but she hardly noticed. She surged forward, her body shaking miserably with cold despite the heat rising into her cheeks as she screamed, "I told you never to touch him—"

She lunged at me to grab him.

Her foot slipped.

"Ezra!" I cried blindly, risking a step onto a large chunk of ice to dodge her. It bobbled uneasily but held long enough for me to spring from it and back onto the log, nearly slipping as my foot hit the wet trunk. Martha's hands flew out wildly, looking for something to take hold of as she fell; her body slid down between the loose sheets of ice when she found nothing to grip; she cried as they slammed her back.

"I'm here," Ezra called, halfway between us and the shore, motioning us forward like he was guiding us into a parking space. Martha was held against the tree just as the boys had been; the color drained quickly from her face as she tried to claw her way back up.

I deposited Gabriel into Ezra's waiting arms and turned back.

"Martha, just hold on!"

"Careful!" Ezra protested as I inched my way closer to her, the journey more difficult than before as my limbs simultaneously shook and seized from the cold. My jaw chattered erratically, adding a slight stutter to my words as I called to her. She grappled with the log, eyes wide and panicked like a cornered animal, unaware that she was taking in water each time she opened her mouth.

Unaware when she gripped my jacket and pulled me down.

I laid prostrate on the log, grip tenuous.

"Martha!" I reached into the water to grab hold of her as she lost her grip, fingers grasping her forearm below the surface to hoist her up. Rather than work with me, she resisted the effort, clawing her way up my arm, pulling me further down in the process so that I had to turn my head to the side to keep my face from entering the water.

Her touch burned even in the cold.

"Neviah!"

I didn't realize I was screaming from the pain of her hand in mine until Ezra called my name. He was trying to make his way to us down the log again, a rope Julie and the others had brought now fastened around his waist, but the ice started to shift from Martha's efforts. I tried to call out to him but felt mute as I stared into the black water; thousands of Koels swam beneath the surface like the dead in the river Styx, or hungry fish waiting for their next meal.

Martha grabbed my hair and pulled.

My entire body finally slipped into the water then surfaced, fingers scratching at the tree limbs for something to hold. I gasped for a breath, water dripping from my hair and lashes, only to be pulled under again as she continued to climb up my back. Martha's touch seared into my skin as I divided my attention between keeping our heads above water and keeping my mind away from the *Other Side* where the Koels waited for us.

I tried to soothe Martha, taking her to the in-between place, but any happy memories she held paled in comparison to her terror. Ezra inched along too slowly. I couldn't speak, couldn't breathe. Between gasps, I couldn't even hear myself apologizing to her repeatedly before finally closing my mouth, focused on taking in air and not water. I clung desperately to the log, fingers digging into a small groove in the wood. The water roared like static in my ears.

"I'm almost there!" Ezra shouted. "Hold on!"

Martha struggled to hold me, to scale up my back, and found nothing but fistfuls of hair to grip, pulling us both further from salvation as the Koels reached for our ankles, waiting for a slip of the mind to pull us under completely. I shook to loosen Martha's grip on me, dislodging both of our holds in the process. Her fingers loosened from my hair; my fingers fell from the log.

Together, we sank.

Chapter Twenty-One

My eyes shot open. Everything was peaceful and beautiful and nothing hurt anymore. I saw my mother's pond first, glistening at my feet, then turned to a sound beside me. Martha stared down at the water next to me, her hair long and dry, face young and unblemished by time as she wiped her tears on the back of her sleeve. We rested beside the pond—Jaak's hidden lake—for several moments before speaking, the only noise thus far the gentle sound of her whimpering and sniffing.

"My memory, or yours?" she asked, looking up.

"Not a memory. Made of bits and pieces from each of us, but not a memory," I decided, looking around. A high rise stood to the left of the pond full of enlarged dahlias teeming out the windows, a church steeple towered to the right. A field of black and white begonias stretched out as far as the eye could see to the north and south. A knight walked through the flowers, looking lost.

"What then?" She frowned.

I opened my mouth, then snapped it shut. My head shook sleepily from side to side, the answer evading me. "I...I don't know that I've ever really stopped to ask..." I nodded toward the water as she stuck her hands in her pockets. "What do you see when you look?"

Martha peered down, then shrugged the way only a teenager could.

"It's black," she said.

"That's what I thought," I mumbled, watching the Koels swimming below the surface. "When I look, I see myself. Part of myself, at least. But the reflection is so rippled and distorted by everything moving underneath that I can hardly recognize myself." I surprised us both by reaching out a hand to cup Martha's cheek. I held it there, blinking at the solid warmth of her skin against my palm. "It's incredible, isn't it?" I whispered, forehead wrinkling as I considered her.

"What's wrong?" She grimaced.

Her cheek was rosy in the cold that settled over us. My breath clouded in front of me like the echo of a dragon's breath as I murmured, "You've always felt so real to me. It's all always felt so real. Do you feel that?" I frowned and stared at my feet where icy water began rushing past my heels. When I looked up again, we were in her parents' room and the water was rising all around us.

The bedroom door wouldn't open.

I blinked several times to clear my head, looking for another exit when the water made it past my ankles. Leaves, ice, and debris floated around us, brushing against my legs as I waded to the window, neither of us wanting to go into the bathroom where we feared her mother would be waiting for us, drowned in the bathtub. A loud thump on the window knocked me back a step, closer to the bathroom door. The thump was followed by another.

And another.

"What was that?" Martha paled. I swallowed the lump in my throat and crept to the glass panel of the window, wincing each time the noise repeated. Outside, thousands of Koels lined up, each taking a turn throwing itself at the window like birds hitting freshly cleaned glass.

The wall shook with each impact, the speed of their procession increasing with each failed attempt, their efforts becoming desperate.

"Martha, the bathroom!"

"But...I..."

"Now!" Water poured from below the bathroom door, the source of the flood waiting somewhere just beyond it. Martha stepped back from it, afraid to turn the handle, so I shoved her aside and darted in. Water rushed out once the door was opened, then settled again, a few inches deeper than before. I was relieved to find the bathtub vacant, slipping and landing on my knees next to it as I twisted the knob controlling the water, though the water continued to flow from the tap, overflowing onto the floor, spilling from one room into the next.

Another thump, closer now than the bedroom.

The bathroom window.

"Martha, stop!" I pleaded, slowed by the water as I moved toward her. She fumbled with the latch holding the window shut, hands shaking too much to do the job. I grabbed her arm and tried to pull her away from the window where a thousand new Koels had convened.

"Martha, please—you open that window, we're dead."

"Let me out!" she screamed; her voice was shrill as she pleaded for help. She stared at the water around our feet, sobbing as she beat the window, fingers fumbling for the lock again when assaulting the glass failed. Tears dripped from her cheeks and joined into the pool below us. She couldn't see the Koels blanketing the window; didn't know the only escape she could see was the thing that would ruin her.

"Martha, I need you to see," I cried to deaf ears.

More frantic yelps and attempts to flip the lock.

Then, a gentle 'click' as it unlatched.

"Martha!" I reached out with my hand raised as though she were a child about to cross in front of traffic. She smiled manically, overcome by laughter as she started to tug the window open. There was no screen in it, just as there hadn't been the day she'd climbed out of it after her mother died; the day that the Martha I knew had gone away and never returned—not the way she'd been, at least.

Desperate, I grabbed the heavy, steel toilet paper rack.

"Martha, please..."

"C'mon," she urged me to follow her.

I raised the rack, caught a flash of my reflection in the curved, metal surface of it, watched it disappear just as quickly when I brought the rack down against the back of Martha's head. She stopped propping open the window, letting it fall back into its place before the Koels could pass; when she touched the back of her head, a tiny spot of blood rouged her fingertips.

"What did you..."

Martha staggered back a step and dropped.

I raised her so that her chest laid across the toilet seat, face clear of the water though her hands dangled limply over the edges into it. Tiny breaths puffed around her face, her chest rising and falling, albeit, weaker every moment. I dropped, scrambling backwards away from her, huddling into the corner of the room as the water kept rising.

I stared at her, everything moving slowly.

Ezra's voice echoed from far away:

"Just hold on!"

But the glass was breaking. And the water was rising. Koels, one after the other, hurled themselves against the glass. Cracks were forming as it neared its breaking point, every hit bringing the creatures closer to getting inside. I crawled to glance out the door at the bedroom window where a crack had already formed and the Koels were all fighting, clawing at the small opening, trying to make a hole big enough for them to break through. Martha mumbled incomprehensibly.

My breath caught in my lungs.

Tendrils slipped through a fresh opening in the glass. I drew my knees to my chest and shook my face against them, sobbing into the soaked fabric. The water was high, almost to my chin when I hunched, but I couldn't feel it anymore. Tears burned against my cheeks as I continued to shake my head, sobbing, begging for another answer and finding none.

Grabbing Martha under her arms, I dragged her to the tub.

She looked peaceful as I laid her inside.

"I'm—s-sorry." My teeth chattered. I stroked her hair away from her face, a raven against the snow, petting it back a few more times until it was slicked down cleanly. My bottom lip protruded, chest heaving with every shallow breath, sobs wracking my entire body.

"I'm s-sorry," I repeated, clasping my mouth as I whimpered. "I'm s-sorry I couldn't find you sooner," I added, hoping that Martha, wherever she was, might hear me; that my platitudes and apologies might ripple throughout the void and bring her peace.

Because the girl in the tub was not Martha.

Had never been Martha.

The girl in the tub was the idea of a girl that I'd hardly known. The girl I'd dragged back to the farm had not been Martha either, except in her flesh and bones. The Martha I'd been trying to save was little more than a distorted memory, a depthless phantasm that could hold no weight against reality; yet I had clung to it like a deflated life preserver tossed from a ship, drowning all the while. Martha had been swept into the river with me, but I sensed with unprecedented certainty that I was alone now, as something deep inside me threatened to burst.

"You asked why I never had kids," I said.

"Neviah..."

"I know it wasn't fair what happened with your parents," I sobbed, hardly able to speak as the dark water pooled around my legs, dripped from my eyes, overflowed from the faucet. "They were supposed to protect you. They were supposed to take care of you. But how can you take responsibility for another person when you can't even control what happens to them? I couldn't do that to someone else," I wept.

Martha's face was suddenly Jaak's.

I pressed on his shoulder, holding him in the water.

"How was I going to have kids?" I cried. "Mom was a good person. She was a good mom, and a good wife, and then the accident happened, and she was never the same. She was scared, she was weak. And I couldn't forgive her for that. If I couldn't forgive her, if something like that could happen without any kind of precedent and ruin her...how was I supposed to be sure I wouldn't ruin a child's life the same way that she ruined mine? Or that God, the universe—whatever, you want to call it—wasn't waiting to ruin me the same way it did her?"

The figure in the tub tried to sit up again.

The face was once again Martha's.

"But I gave you bad advice," I said, reaching down to hold her head under, staring straight ahead at the wall of the bathtub as her body twisted, fighting for air. My shoulder ached as I continued to hold her under the water, until finally, her movements stopped. I pulled my hand away from her face slowly. "At some point, you have to take responsibility for yourself, for the present moment, whether it was your fault or not. I'm sorry I didn't tell you all that back then."

A bubble floated up, then the water was still.

"I did everything I was supposed to, you know?" I said vacantly. "When Ezra and I got pregnant, I was eating right, doing my exercises. I was even slowing down at work to make sure the best of me was going to the baby. And then one morning, it was all over. Just like that. The doctor said it was just one of those things—that I was healthy, that we could try again right away. But I couldn't. I couldn't bring someone into the world knowing I couldn't protect them...Ezra wanted to try," I sniffed, glancing down at Martha, "but I couldn't go through that again."

Martha was sinking. It was as though the bathtub had no bottom as she slid down, face pale and pure and white; black hair swimming around her face; eyes closed as though she were simply a mermaid sleeping at the bottom of a lake. The water was still now, tap having shut itself off, and in its surface, I could see myself. My reflection was layered over top of her face, bits and pieces of me melded together with bits and pieces of her so that the two were one and the same.

And when she was gone, I saw more of myself than I wanted to.

"Neviah, come on," my mom's voice called out.

"Mom?" I blinked as she rushed past me from behind, startling me from the moment. All at once I was aware of the room again, my fingers, numb with cold, my jaw chattering, the Koels still fighting to get to me through the window; they hadn't stopped despite my revelation, and I whimpered, overwhelmed by their pursuit. Fatigue drained my resolve. Mom's dress flowed down, dragging against the surface of the water, collecting debris as it skimmed across it.

The bedroom door yielded under her touch.

I stepped through.

The breath I heaved out when the door shut behind us and crumbled into nothingness was exceptional; the Koels were sealed safely away somewhere else, at least for the moment, and I looked around, realizing I'd entered yet another bathroom, this one scattered with a little girl's toiletries: unicorn toothpaste, a pink electric toothbrush that sang to tell you how long to brush. Everything looked exactly like it had when I was a child, hardly seven-years-old.

My mom had vanished, leaving only me and my reflection; a young girl struggling to work through the knots in her dark red curls, grimacing in the mirror every time the bristles snagged. It was such a seemingly inconsequential moment, but I recalled my frustration easily. My tiny fingers worked ineloquently to separate the hair into three strands, weaving them around one another into a braid that looked nothing like my mother's handiwork.

Finally, thinking my braid was passable after several failed attempts, I made my way downstairs into the kitchen, not wanting to miss dinner. Mom spent so much time sleeping in the year following the accident that dinner was a treat, one of the rare times she seemed to consistently leave her room. She asked about my day, fussed with the baby in the highchair, but I noticed now what I hadn't noticed then; her affect was flat, her eyes puffy like she'd been crying.

My braid started to slowly unravel.

Hair fell from the elastic holding the little girl's curls in place, our shadows intertwining on the floor. In all the years since that moment,

I'd remembered being yelled at as it happened, with Mom criticizing my hair for being in my face at the table. As I watched it unfold, however, she hardly looked up from feeding Jaak, preening over him incessantly just like she had every day after the accident that almost stole them both from me.

Borrowed time.

That was the *first* time death lied to me.

I didn't like to think about it: Dad pulling over. Me with my earbuds in not understanding what was happening, still reeling from the sleepover I'd insisted on going to. Horses screaming in the overturned trailer. Dad shouting Mom's name, prying on the door of the truck to pull her out. My shoes crunching on the gravel at the side of the road. Shattered glass, shards covering the driver's seat as Mom leaned over the steering wheel, screaming for her baby, powerless to stop what might be happening to the life inside her.

And red. Bright, bright red.

All other color fading to black and white static.

They'd pulled through, but something inside her unraveled after that. The news talked about it for weeks before moving on, and each time I watched, nameless fear nestled me in its arms the same way my mother held Jaak to her breast. For a year after, I watched her coddle and preen over him as though at any moment death might come back to claim him. I listened to her scream at night, watched my father tend to her, sneaking out once she'd settled to find comfort in his office.

Chittering filled the spaces between us at the kitchen table.

The little girl's curls fell loose.

Little baby Jaak cried.

A Koel waited for the little girl around the corner when she stormed from the room; it was smiling that God-awful smile I'd come to know so well but wasn't yet accustomed to. The apparition advanced toward the little girl as she ripped out her elastic band, mind packed with the blame and fear and regret she didn't understand but that was about to become her reality, nonetheless. She fell backwards at the sight of the creature, screaming unintelligibly, though no one listened.

"I've spent so long fighting you," I whispered, stepping between the creature and the girl as water seeped through the floorboards, leaked through the ceiling, burst from pipes in the walls so that a fresh pool formed around my calves. My reflection stared back from the dark water. My mirrored self moved of her own accord, gaze turning in the direction of the Koel before mine did. Hundreds of them now stood where there had been only one; a lifetime's worth of demons coming out to play.

Their dark tendrils skimmed the surface like water snakes.

The girl whimpered, clinging to my legs.

"I see you now," I declared, screaming over the deafening sound of rushing water as time slowed to an unbearable crawl. As I screamed, the Koels melded so that they became one looming shadow, a destructive wraith called forth by a little girl too frustrated and scared for her family to fasten her own braid. I turned away to comfort her, stroking the curls away from her face as I whispered against her ear, "I'm sorry it took me so long to come for you."

An intolerable rush of cold air slammed into my bones as the mammoth Koel moved through me, leaving me untouched as darkness flooded the hall; the little girl disappeared into it. The floor opened up below me and drew me down, water entering my eyes, my lungs, my ears, my nose, my mouth. Wherever there was empty space in me, there was suddenly water, and I felt every ounce of it as though it was no different than a familiar limb, or a breath.

Then, there was light.

Chapter Twenty-Two

I broke to the surface of the creek, gasping for air and choking out water from my lungs. Ezra's arm wrapped around me, propping me against his shoulder as he swam toward shore, holding me upright, dragging me behind him as someone secured his rope on the other side. I tried to talk, but it was too difficult, so I muttered his name.

"You're okay," Ezra promised, pulling me onto the shore, and I wondered if he was saying it for my benefit or for his. We hobbled weakly to a spot upstream where Julie had started a fire for the boys. Another resident was hoisting Riley onto one of the horses, Gabriel already situated neatly at the front of it, cocooned in blankets. Riley's pill bottle rattled in Julie's shaking hands as she approached us and handed me another blanket brought from the cabins.

"We called an ambulance," Julie addressed Ezra.

"Good. Gabriel's fingers?" he asked.

"Frostbite, we think."

They continued to talk in hushed voices as I dropped beside the fire, hands poised above the flames. I considered that the outsides of my fingers might blacken and char before the warmth reached my bones where it was needed most, but I didn't care. Any warmth was welcomed with abandon as I shivered in the cold, no longer doubting the illustrious scent of fresh blooms that hovered in the midnight air. Ezra sat next to me, his mouth hinging open, then closing again.

"Martha?" I finally asked, certain I already knew.

Ezra shook his head.

"Come here," he urged, pulling me to his side so that we shared the blanket. I huddled against him, staring at the fire for a long time before he added, "It wasn't our fault. I've thought about it a million different ways, and it isn't. They sign off on liability for property use, they know their kids are their responsibility, right?" His voice sounded desperate, weak. I squeezed his hand, cinching off his doubts.

"We did everything we could," I promised, angling toward him, draping my legs over his lap as I leaned forward to kiss him. His hand wrapped greedily around my back and pulled me closer until the world vanished, except for us. I deepened the kiss, acknowledging for the first time since reaching the shore that it was a miracle to be with him at all; that our last kiss had almost been our last kiss.

Shadows observed us from the opposite bank.

But now, they were silent.

Chapter Twenty-Three

Inaya waited in our living room, chatting with Ezra while Gabriel finished packing the last of his things. He'd spent most of the week in bed recovering from a bout of pneumonia after what most of us had already begun referring to as the 'incident'. It was the first time Gabriel was back in his mother's cabin since then, and he packed hastily, glancing around as though her ghost was in every corner, haunting him.

"How's packing coming along?" I asked, hovering at the door.

"Fine," he mumbled.

My hair was in a passable French braid after watching a few tutorials; some of the strands were loose enough for me to suspect they'd fall out soon, but I took a deep breath and tried my best not to fuss with it. Gabriel didn't look up when I knocked, but I stepped in anyway. Item after item was shovelled into his bag without care or precision, wanting to flee as soon as possible.

The pain felt like ice lodged in my throat, but I didn't try to fight it, didn't try to swallow it or cough it out; I sat with it, knowing that eventually, it would melt on its own and I would be able to breathe again. I caught a glimpse of myself in the mirror above his dresser and denied myself the impulse of turning away from the reflection.

"I have something for you."

I stepped in, handing Gabriel the copy of *Sir Ivanguard* I'd meticulously revised for him, hoping he might not notice the changes; however, he immediately noted, "The pictures are all different."

"Yeah." I sat on the edge of the bed despite the glare that indicated I wasn't welcome to sit there. I scanned the room, realizing that soon I wasn't going to be welcomed into the rooms or halls of the *Sanctuary* at all, wondered if it had been too idealistic to have believed in the idea of a true sanctuary at all. Gabriel continued to frown at the pages until I explained, "My brother wasn't without his demons, kiddo. Jaak wrote the ending he thought he had to, but that doesn't mean he was right."

Gabriel looked like he had questions but stayed quiet.

I swallowed past the lump in my throat.

"His thinking was too distorted to see another way, but I wanted a different ending for you. An ending where Sir Ivanguard learns to make peace with the things he can't change; where Sir Ivanguard makes changes within himself instead of trying to change others; an ending where he takes the power away from the dragon by seeing it for what it is and realizing he's no more immune to the dragon's tricks than anyone else—that he has to stay vigilant."

Gabriel didn't say anything, so I stood.

He wasn't allowed to stay with us.

Didn't want to if he could.

"A lot has happened over the past year for you...a lot of changes. But if there's anything I hope you remember, it's that you get to choose how the story ends from here on out. You get to choose how you want to frame everything that's happened and how you're going to let it change you, because it will change you. I hope one day I see you again, kiddo, I really do. And I hope one day you'll forgive me and that when you think of me you won't just remember the bad things, but that we love you so, so, so much, and will always be thinking about you..."

Gabriel sniffed but didn't say goodbye.

"Goodbye, Gabriel."

I left before I could change my mind, trembling when I saw Ezra waiting downstairs. He took me into his arms and squeezed. I clung to for a moment then stepped back, gripping my hips and arching my spine, looking skyward as I tried to hold back the tears just a little longer, explaining, "I'm afraid that if I start now, I'm gonna go back in there and try to make him say goodbye, or worse, try to convince him to come with us."

"You planted a seed, Nev. Now you've gotta walk away." He kissed my forehead and ushered me outside when we heard Gabriel and the social worker in the hallway, needing to get out before we saw him again, lest we crumble. As we left the cabin, Ezra added, "It takes a lot of faith to walk away and trust he'll have the resources and support to make it grow."

"I just don't get it." I sniffed as we approached the truck, pausing in the driveway so that Ezra was forced to stop and turn to me. "Working on the story, on the new drawings—it helped, like you thought it would. But why didn't it help Jaak? He did stuff like that more than me, better than me..."

Ezra thought about it.

"Rumination and reflection look very similar. Did you ever finish reading that book your dad gave me?" He continued when I shook my head, "The writer establishes that when it comes to culpability for our actions, it's hard to be responsible for most things, since we often can't predict the outcomes of our actions in full. We might act with the best intentions, but that doesn't necessarily guarantee best outcomes because there's often too much that's outside our purview.

"However, the author also argues that it's not enough to simply fall back on 'our heart being in the right place'. It's far too easy to conceal our motives from ourselves, since we usually try to paint ourselves in the best light and avoid suffering, where possible. So, it becomes critical that we know how to properly reflect on our motives and intentions, since self-reflection is one of the few things we *can* control."

"Easier said than done," I pouted, sliding into the truck.

"Yeah...they suggested that by understanding the needs we're trying to meet with our actions, we can act more effectively to meet those needs, both for ourselves and for others. And since self-reflective habits are so important to the theory, the writer give a number of suggestions for how we can create good reflective practices: art, music, sports—and prayer, when it's used effectively."

I was stricken. "But how do you know the difference? Between using it effectively and using it ineffectively? There's a very fine line between the way you use prayer in your life and the way my mom does. Obviously, just as fine a line between the kind of art that heals and the kind of art that drives people to cut off their own ear or take their own life. How do you know?"

Ezra shrugged. "Maybe you should consider taking some art therapy classes when you start your booster courses in the fall—learn the difference from someone who uses art for exactly what we've been talking about."

The Koels were still there, chattering as the occasional thought popped into my mind assigning blame, thinking I had failed Ezra, Gabriel and Martha, thinking that I should have done more or done less, that I'd done nothing but hurt the people I cared about. Now, however, I simply acknowledged the their presence as they arrived and let them pass like cars on the freeway, always coming and going.

I didn't try to repress the thoughts with denial or fight them with platitudes and flimsy assurances to myself. I simply let them pass, watching curiously until they moved far enough away to seem small; neither sitting in the middle of the road where they could run me down nor running blindly in the opposite direction. I found a comfortable median on which to sit and observe the thoughts as they came and went, trusting they would not hurt me if I didn't let them.

Trusting that existing didn't make them real.

As the engine roared to life and the tires kicked up gravel beneath us, my thoughts reflexively reached for the comfort of the words that had increasingly overtaken the Koels' presence in my thoughts: *God, grant me the serenity to accept the things I cannot change; the courage to change the things I can; and the wisdom to know the difference.*

Epilogue

Ezra steers onto the exit ramp and drives for a few more miles, signs popping up along the street for coffee shops and restaurants. Side streets appear off the main road, leading into the complicated veins of the suburbs. Ezra takes a few turns into the maze—in the opposite direction of our new home—pulling the trailer to the curb and turning on the blinkers to show that we've stopped. The lights 'tick' and 'tock' as they blink red against the wet pavement.

I lean over to kiss his cheek, then slide out of the truck. I've thought about the events that led us to this moment enough to be certain I have to talk to her, just like one knows instinctively to start with the edge pieces of an elaborate puzzle. I suspect it will take much more time before I fully understand the final image, but I've started the process of putting the pieces together again.

Mom lurks in the window of the house when we arrive, curtain pulled aside to watch me coming. She pauses at the door, arms raised as though she's going to hug me before short-circuiting, unsure what to do about the packages of red, yellow, and orange begonia seeds I hand her. She stares at them as she asks:

"How have you been coping?"

"One day at a time," I admit.

Mom guides me to the sitting room off the foyer where my eyes start to water. She sits down on the stiff loveseat and pats the spot next to her. I wipe frantically at my eyes and take a seat, not yet ready to move into her arms when she raises them again. But I can smell her lemon lotion as she reaches out, toying with the end of my braid.

"I can't stay long." I suck in a breath. "But I was thinking maybe I'll help with the gardens again this year. Maybe we can make something new together for Jaak, us. A memorial, or something. I'm not saying everything is resolved now," I choke out before she can look too pleased with herself, then force myself to take a breath instead of being angry at her for a response she hasn't made yet. "But I don't want to keep feeling like this, Mom. It wasn't your fault; it wasn't mine. But it doesn't mean we can't both do better."

The truck idles when I return to it, horses calm as they wait in our trailer. Ezra waves at my mom as we pull onto the street, waiting until we're moving before looking at me. I clutch the registration form for the church retreat in one hand, the card for the fertility clinic mom has pushed on us for years now clutched willingly in the other. We haven't decided if we'll use it—if it will make any difference after waiting so long—but a dialogue has begun between Ezra and myself.

"How'd it go?" he finally asks, glancing sideways.

I think about it for a moment as we drive through the neighborhood, watching the pretty houses of the suburbs pass behind us in the side mirror. I catch a glimpse of myself, notice some of the stray hairs from my braid as the wind musses it, and smile. Ezra makes a few turns toward the highway, the truck and trailer sliding easily between the two pillars walling off the community as we head home.

"Who knows?" I eventually shrug. "But I left her the seeds."

And she'll decide how to use them.

BONUS: Playlist to Accompany the Book

'Body in a Box' (City and Colour)

'Before I Sleep' (Joy Williams)

'Truth' (Alex Ebert)

'Stars' (Grace Potter & the Nocturnals)

'Oh That I Had' (Mt. Eden)

'One Day I Will' (Joy Williams)

'Darkness Visible' (Mumford & Sons)

'Picture You' (Mumford & Sons)

The songs listed all have lyrics that were important to me through the process of writing this book. For an explanation of why these songs made the list, as well as bonus tracks that didn't make the cut, you can visit my website at www.kodievandusen.com.

Acknowledgements

My husband, Mike, for being the most supportive spouse a writer could ask for. You challenged me to become a better storyteller, read countless drafts (on my timeline, no less), and never doubted that this story should be told. I love you more than there are words to express and can't wait to share our love of stories with our daughter.

My grandpa, Marvin, for telling the best bedtime stories. If you hadn't indulged me every time I insisted you be the one to tell me a story (and you really did tell the best ones), I might have done something sensible like become an accountant.

My fourth-grade teacher, Madame Pereira, for the elementary school writing award that made me confident enough to continue writing. I could win a Pulitzer one day, and it wouldn't mean half as much to me as that vote of confidence did.

My mom, for filling my childhood with creativity.

My editor, Ashley Olivier, for making my story shine. You ensured that every line popped and made me seriously doubt my vocabulary, something I will be eternally grateful for.

My beta and alpha readers, with a special nod to Alexis Alexander. You all helped beat this story (and my ego) into its final form. Your contributions were paramount.

And to Jordan, for everything.

About the Author

Kodie Van Dusen resides in Southern Ontario with her husband, daughter, and three fur babies. She began winning awards and being published in poetry anthologies from a young age. Her manuscripts have since been shortlisted for multiple awards. Kodie holds a degree in psychology and spent several years incorporating storytelling into her private practice counseling business, helping clients overcome personal problems through the power of narrative. **For news, promotions, and the chance to beta read Kodie's upcoming works, subscribe by visiting www.kodievandusen.com.**

Join the Big Cheese Community

"An emerging community of independent authors and readers promoting empowerment, quality, and accessibility in independent publishing." **Visit www.bigcheesebooks.com to sign up for access to bonus content, interviews, discounts, and promotions sponsored by our authors, as well as indie book recommendations vetted by our team.**

Mental Health Resources

Canadian

Canadian Mental Health Association: https://cmha.ca/ Offers national and province-specific health resources.

BounceBack: https://bouncebackontario.ca/
No-charge self-help (aged 15 and up) for mild-to-moderate anxiety or depression, stress, and emotional regulation concerns.

Talk Suicide: 1-833-456-4566 or talksuicide.ca 24/7 phone support or text 45645 between 4 p.m. and midnight ET.

Good2Talk Helpline: 1-866-925-5454 or text GOOD2TALKON to 686868. Support for postsecondary students.

Kids Help Phone: 1-800-668-6868 or text CONNECT to 686868. 24/7 support for children and teenagers.

Hope for Wellness Help Line: 1-855-242-3310
Counseling and crisis intervention for Indigenous peoples available in English, French, Cree, Ojibway and Inuktitut.

Talk4healing (for Indigenous women): 1-855-554-4325

International

HelpGuide: https://www.helpguide.org/find-help.htm Lists various phone/online support options by region (United States, UK, Ireland, Canada, Australia, New Zealand, India, Philippines, South Africa)

IMPORTANT: Some or all resources listed may become inactive over time. If these resources are not available, please contact your local emergency department for direction to the appropriate supports if you feel you or someone you love is at risk of harming themselves or others.

www.ingramcontent.com/pod-product-compliance
Lightning Source LLC
Chambersburg PA
CBHW021754190726
48290CB00005B/1269